THE WOLF WHO LOVED ME

LYDIA DARE

WITHDRAWN

Published by Sourcebooks Casablanca, an imprint of
Sourcebooks, Inc.
P.O. Box 4410, Naperville, Illinois 60567-4410
(630) 961-3900
FAX: (630) 961-2168
www.sourcebooks.com

Printed and bound in Canada.
WC 10 9 8 7 6 5 4 3 2 1

*For the ladies at Clarkston who have been
my beta readers since day one:
Michelle (who is quite attached to
Lady Madeline's surname)
DeShelia
Lesley
Melissa
Tyler
Susan
I love you all—Jodie*

Prologue

LADY MADELINE HAYBURN WAS MORE THAN READY for the Season to be over. Ball after ball. Soirees and garden parties after more soirees and even more garden parties. There was no point to it all. Oh, she knew her father was hopeful Maddie would somehow stumble upon her destined husband at one of these inane events. But if it hadn't happened during her three seasons on the marriage mart, Maddie wasn't terribly optimistic it would happen tonight.

"Madeline," whispered her grandmother, the Duchess of Hythe, as she nudged Maddie's arm. "Do you see Blackmoor over there?"

Maddie glanced across the sea of people littering the ballroom until her eyes fell on the intimidating duke. "Yes, of course," she whispered back. What on earth did her grandmother care about the Duke of Blackmoor? He and both of his brothers were married and hardly prospects as far as Maddie was concerned.

"The man was a degenerate," Grandmamma informed her. "One of the worst rogues London has ever seen."

Just idle gossip then? Maddie smiled at her grandmother. "So I've heard."

"His wife should be commended for bringing him to heel." Grandmamma gestured toward the pretty duchess who was still greeting her newly arrived guests at the entrance. "Let that be a lesson to you. The right woman can take charge of even the most imposing man."

Not idle gossip, but another lesson on the management of men. Maddie nearly sighed, but doing so would only earn her another lesson of a different sort. "I can manage Papa," she said instead.

Her grandmother agreed with a nod of her head. "Of course you can. You're my granddaughter."

Maddie giggled.

"And you can manage any other man you set your mind to, as well."

"Thank you for your confidence."

Grandmamma continued as though Maddie hadn't spoken. "I just wish you weren't so finicky about this whole marriage endeavor, my dear. I would like to actually meet my great-grandchildren, you know."

Maddie couldn't help the laugh that escaped her. "In that case, you should probably have this conversation with your grandsons." Who knew how many great-grandchildren her grandmother might already have.

Grandmamma scowled, but before she could begin a lecture, Lieutenant Hawthorne bowed before them in greeting. "Your Grace, Lady Madeline."

"Lieutenant." Maddie smiled with relief. Thank heavens he'd saved her. "I hope you are well this evening."

"I will be better if I can urge you to stand up with me."

And whisk her away from her grandmother? Maddie could have kissed him, if only she liked him a little bit. Alas, she didn't. Besides as the fourth son of a baronet, Lieutenant Hawthorne needed to find a wealthy wife. His interest in Maddie began and ended with her dowry. Still, he was her salvation, if only for a moment. "Thank you, sir. I would be honored."

He offered her his arm and then led her to the middle of the ballroom where sets were being formed for the minuet. As they circled each other, Maddie couldn't help but glance across the crowded room and her breath caught slightly in her throat.

Heavens. What was Weston Hadley doing here? Maddie stumbled and would have fallen if Lieutenant Hawthorne hadn't caught her arm.

"Are you all right?"

Maddie shook her head and tried to regain her composure. "Just clumsy," she muttered. Though her eyes still fell on Mr. Hadley, as if she just couldn't help it. The Duchess of Blackmoor's ball was the last place on earth she would have expected to see a man of his ilk.

Oh, he was born of nobility like everyone else in attendance. And he filled out a coat better than most, even if the coat tended to be a bit on the shabby side. But there was something dark and mysterious about him. And then there was the scar he sported across his cheek.

Lieutenant Hawthorne must have followed her gaze

because an expression of amusement settled on his face. "Weston Hadley?"

Maddie straightened her back and stared at her companion as though he was an imbecile. "Hardly." When they turned the opposite direction, she cocked her head to one side. "Are you well acquainted with Mr. Hadley?"

The lieutenant shrugged. "We've met." He glanced over her shoulder and smirked. "Seems he can't keep his eyes off you, either."

And it had been that way ever since she'd met Weston Hadley. She wasn't quite certain what to make of him. She never had been. And whenever their paths crossed, his gaze followed her. "My dowry has that effect on most men."

Lieutenant Hawthorne chuckled. "You do know how to wound a man, Lady Madeline."

She hadn't meant to insult him. "That wasn't my intent at all," she hastened to explain.

"I'm certain it wasn't," he agreed good-naturedly. "But I can understand your concern about him. He's hardly the sort I would imagine has any honorable intentions."

That was an understatement. He was a Hadley, after all. The most degenerate set of brothers of Maddie's acquaintance.

"Do you know how Hadley came by that scar of his?"

"No." But Madeline had wondered about that very thing every time she saw Weston Hadley. "Do you?"

The lieutenant shook his head. "Sadly, no, but there is a bet on the books at White's about it. I would love to know."

"Has he never said?" she asked, even though she shouldn't think about Weston Hadley or his scar. After all, he was one of those penniless Hadley brothers. Even worse, he was a friend of her brothers. That alliance on its own was hardly one to recommend him.

"Never breathed a word about it, as far as I know," the lieutenant muttered just as the music came to an end. He smiled and then bowed. "Ah, here comes your admirer now."

Maddie glanced over her shoulder to see Weston Hadley headed straight for her. His dark eyes raked across her form, sending shivers skittering down her spine. Something about his gaze always left her the tiniest bit breathless.

"Lady Madeline," Mr. Hadley drawled. "What a pleasant surprise."

Before she could think better of her actions, Maddie offered her hand to the rogue. And when he touched his lips to her gloved knuckles, her knees threatened to buckle beneath her weight. Maddie snatched her hand back and stood her tallest, hoping she appeared more poised than she felt.

"Do have a good evening, sir," she said before turning on her heel and heading for a small group of ladies at the very edge of the room.

His eyes were still on her; Maddie could feel them. But she refused to turn around, to acknowledge him any further than she had already done. No, everything would be better if she just kept her distance from Weston Hadley with his penetrating dark eyes and his even darker scar.

One

Castle Hythe, Kent
Four months later...

MADDIE HAD ALWAYS SUSPECTED THAT MEN WERE THE most perfidious of creatures. Now she was certain of the fact. It didn't seem to matter whether the man in question was one's own derelict brother, a detestable fortune hunter, a disreputable gambler, or even the King of England. Not one bit. Men *were* perfidious creatures. All of them. Well, at least all of them that Maddie knew.

She leaned across the expanse of her bed and squeezed her dear friend Lady Sophia Cole's hand. Poor Sophie was the last person Maddie would have ever imagined as a victim of men's perfidious natures. Yet it had happened nevertheless, and there wasn't a blasted thing either of them could do about it. Perfidious men, after all, ruled the world. However, one particularly powerful lady might be up to the challenge of that ambitious endeavor, if anyone was.

"I'm certain we'll think of something, Soph," she said soothingly.

Sophie shook her head as though she knew Maddie had no real hope of solving her dilemma. "Something? Shall we dress as highwaymen and rob Lord Radbourne with pistols as he returns to Kent from that farce of a trial?"

Well, that wouldn't be the *first* plan to pop into Maddie's mind on how to reclaim Sophie's pilfered fortune. Still, the idea made her smile. "And don trousers? Grandmamma would be scandalized."

Despite her new status as an impoverished gentlewoman, Sophie giggled. "Heaven forbid we scandalize the Duchess of Hythe."

Maddie rolled her eyes. Sophie had never been a particular favorite of Maddie's grandmother, but if ever there was a time to try and appease the duchess it was now. "Do *try* to stay on Grandmamma's good side."

"Does she have one?"

"Indeed she does," Maddie declared. "And Lady Eynsford happens to live on it. So if we play our cards right—"

"What a terrible thing to say." Sophie groaned and flopped backward across Maddie's feather mattress and stared at the canopy above them.

Considering that Sophie's recently deceased father had played his cards *wrong*, Maddie could see her friend's point. "Poor turn of phrase on my part. I apologize. But you're not listening, Soph. Lady Eynsford is the key to getting your fortune returned. Or as much of it as possible, whatever that blackguard hasn't spent."

Sophie pushed up on her elbows, her grey eyes intent enough to make Maddie wince inwardly. "I'm listening now."

Maddie took a deep breath, and words just poured from her mouth. "I don't know why, but Lord Radbourne and those brutish brothers of his follow Lord Eynsford around like a pack of puppy dogs."

"Puppy dogs?"

"Like he's their master or something. It is very strange. But what is more important is that I've never seen a man so besotted with his wife as Lord Eynsford is."

"You're right. That is strange."

"Do be serious." Maddie folded her arms across her chest. "If we are able to whisper the circumstances of your predicament to the marchioness, she could have her husband order Radbourne to return his ill-gotten gains."

Sophie dropped back onto the bed and laughed which, considering the fact that Maddie had just suggested the best plan for restoring her friend's place in society, was the tiniest bit irritating.

"I hardly find it amusing."

Sophie brought her mirth under control and sighed dramatically. "Maddie, you've never had to live without. But Radbourne has most of his unfortunate life. I don't care how devoted Lord Eynsford is to his wife or how obedient Lord Radbourne is to the marquess, the blackguard would never return my fortune simply because someone asked it of him. All I truly want is Bindweed Cottage. Papa had no right to gamble it away. It belonged to Mama. It was *my* dowry. The rest would belong to Cousin Freddie now, anyway."

No, Maddie had never had to live without the most expensive and lavish of luxuries, but that didn't mean her plan was silly. "You'll have to trust me, Soph. I've seen Lord Eynsford order Lord Radbourne about, and you haven't."

Sophie narrowed her eyes on Maddie as though she were a simpleton. "You're not making any sense. Why would Lord Radbourne pay one whit of attention to anything Lord Eynsford has to say?"

"Because they're brothers." Maddie covered her mouth so quickly she nearly fell backward. Heavens! She couldn't believe she had uttered such a horrible thing aloud.

"I beg your pardon?" Sophie sat back up, giving Maddie her full attention.

Maddie shook her head, refusing to repeat any more vile rumors and still mortified she'd said the last one.

"Madeline Hayburn! Are you suggesting that Lord Radbourne was born on the wrong side of the blanket? That he is the late Lord Eynsford's by-blow?"

Maddie shrugged.

"Tell me!" her friend ordered.

Maddie dropped the hand from her mouth and sighed. Once Sophie made her mind up to know something, there wouldn't be any peace until she learned it. "I don't know anything for certain."

"But you suspect?"

"They look so much alike, is all. Almost like twins. In fact, they look more similar than Radbourne's ill-mannered twin brothers, the Misters Hadley. Of course, *those* twins did look the same until one of them acquired a most unflattering scar across his cheek." She couldn't help the shiver that raced down her spine. There was something wild about Mr. Weston Hadley, and the way he always stared at her was the tiniest bit terrifying. Besides, that scar was most unappealing.

"So do you believe Eynsford is blackmailing Radbourne with this information? That he can depend upon the man doing his bidding in order to keep his secret?"

Maddie shook her head. "No. You'd have to see them together. Blackmail would never cross my mind with regard to their relationship. It's more like brotherly devotion. In fact, all of the Hadley men look to Eynsford in the same way. So if we can gain Lady Eynsford as an ally, I am certain she will see your entire fortune, including Bindweed Cottage, returned to your hands and not the new Lord Postwick's."

"Wouldn't Cousin Freddie be furious if I ended up with my fortune after all is said and done?" For the first time since Sophie arrived at Castle Hythe, Maddie saw a glimmer of hope in her friend's eyes. "Do you truly believe this is a possibility?"

Maddie grinned. "And Grandmamma asked Lady Eynsford for tea this afternoon, mainly to gossip about that travesty occurring in the House of Lords. But regardless of the reason, Lady Eynsford will be *here* without any of her husband's sycophants in tow. We'll have her all to ourselves."

"Tea, huh?"

"Indeed. Should we go in search of Grandmamma?"

Sophie winced. "If we must."

"We must."

"No ideas that *don't* include the duchess?" her friend asked hopefully.

"Sorry." Maddie giggled. "But as Grandmamma is the reason Lady Eynsford is paying a call, I suggest you try to get along with her."

Sophie swung her legs over the side of the bed. "Very well then. Let's go face the old dragon, shall we?"

Another giggle escaped Maddie. "If she heard you say that..."

"She wouldn't be surprised in the least."

Silently Maddie agreed. Nothing much ever surprised her grandmother, who both knew and relished her reputation as a terrifying matron of the *ton*. Maddie linked her arm with Sophie's and started for Grandmamma's favorite parlor. With a little bit of luck, she could see her friend's fortune returned to her in less than a fortnight.

"You said Lady Eynsford lives on the duchess' right side?" Sophie asked as they descended a circular set of stone steps.

"Grandmamma adores her."

"And the lady controls her husband *and* the brothers Hadley?"

Maddie nodded.

Sophie laughed. "Heavens, I can hardly wait to meet this paragon. She must be nothing short of magical."

What a ridiculous idea. "I think it has more to do with the fact that men find her beautiful and Grandmamma finds her cunning."

"A dangerous combination," Sophie agreed.

As they rounded one corner, Maddie could hear her grandmother's laugh filter into the hallway. Lady Eynsford must already be here. Very few people had the capability to make her grandmother laugh. She pulled her friend to a halt and whispered, "Now let me do all the talking."

"I'm perfectly capable of telling my own tale."

"Yes, but your talking usually annoys Grandmamma." Sophie rolled her eyes and sighed dramatically.

Maddie tugged her friend over the threshold of Castle Hythe's white salon. Her grandmother and Lady Eynsford were seated together on a brocade settee. They turned their heads at once at the intrusion.

"Madeline." Her grandmother gestured toward a pair of high-back chairs close to her. "You and Lady Sophia should join us. We were just discussing hypocrisy at its highest."

"You're discussing the trial then?" Sophie asked, blatantly ignoring Maddie's advice to remain quiet and sitting in one of the appointed chairs.

"Indeed," Lady Eynsford agreed as her gaze settled on Sophie, as though she were assessing her.

Maddie stepped forward. "Lady Eynsford, allow me to introduce my friend Lady Sophia Cole who is staying here at the castle for a time. Sophie, this is the Marchioness of Eynsford, our nearest neighbor."

"A pleasure." Sophie flashed her most winning smile.

Grandmamma and Lady Eynsford exchanged a glance that Maddie suspected meant Grandmamma had already told the marchioness all about Sophie. Blast. She had hoped to get to spin the tale her own way first. No matter how many times one heard a tale, the first telling always held the most influence. And Grandmamma had no love for Sophie. "A pleasure indeed," the lady replied with a gentle smile.

"You're Scottish?" Sophie's grin widened. "Lady Madeline didn't mention as much."

"Aye, I'm from Edinburgh. Have ye been north?"

"Oh, I've been all over," Sophie replied. "I had a very adventurous mother, my lady. We once traveled as far north as the Orkneys when I was much younger."

"Sophie just returned from a stay in Venice," Maddie supplied, getting back to the matter at hand as she took her own seat. After all, Sophie would still be in Italy if she hadn't gotten word of her father's death and if all her funds hadn't dried up.

Grandmamma narrowed her icy eyes in Sophie's direction. "As you were most recently in their country, what do you make of these Italian witnesses?"

The marchioness frowned. "I doona think this is an appropriate conversation, Eugenia."

Grandmamma dismissed the suggestion with a wave of her bejeweled hand. "Posh. They're both literate, Caitrin. All that rubbish is printed in *The Times* anyway."

"I feel terribly for Queen Caroline," Maddie offered softly.

"Don't we all," Grandmamma agreed. "The poor woman has been ignored and maligned for the length of her marriage. Instead of trying to dissolve their union, the King should be apologizing for his treatment of Her Majesty on bended knee."

"Speaking of ill-treatment—" Maddie began.

"But to parade those foreigners," her grandmother

spoke over her, "into the Lords and have them tell such lies for all the country to hear…"

"Do you think they're lies?" Sophie asked, sliding forward in her chair.

"You tell me, Lady Sophia," Grandmamma replied. "You are more familiar with Italians than I am, but I do not trust witnesses who have been paid for their testimony. If one is telling the truth, there is no reason for payment."

"There is no quality finer than one's impeccable honor," Maddie agreed. "And speaking of honor—"

"You should repeat that to the throng of young lords your father is bringing home with him this evening."

Maddie's mouth dropped open. A throng of young lords? "I beg your pardon?" Though she had a fairly good idea what her grandmother meant, and her stomach twisted at the thought.

"He sent word last night that he had invited a number of unmarried peers to the castle for the break."

Blood drained from Maddie's face and she felt a little weak. "Pray tell me he didn't accept an offer on my behalf."

"If he *had*, I'm sure he'd only be bringing *one* unmarried peer with him instead of a number. But if you would only set your cap for one, he wouldn't have to resort to such tactics."

Maddie scoffed. "After the conversation we were just having, how can you even ask that of me? The King himself only married Caroline of Brunswick so Parliament would increase his income. He was no different than the fortune hunters pursing me, only on a larger scale. Please forgive my reservations about wanting to leap into such an unfortunate arrangement for myself."

"Not all men are fortune hunters, Maddie," her grandmother grumbled.

"Oh, only the ones I've met then?"

At that moment Lady Eynsford gasped. Her hand flew to her chest and she bolted from her seat. "*Havers!*"

"What is the matter, Caitrin?"

The marchioness started for the door. "I am terribly sorry, Eugenia. I just had the worst feelin' that somethin' awful is about ta happen at Eynsford Park. Do forgive me." And with that, the lady rushed into the corridor.

Sophie turned her bewildered expression to Maddie, who could only shrug an answer. More unsettling than Lady Eynsford's sudden dash for home was that Maddie hadn't been able to even mention Lord Radbourne's fleecing of Sophie's late father, though not for a lack of trying.

Two

WESTON HADLEY WOULD LIKE NOTHING MORE THAN to pound his twin brother's face into the rug at their feet. After a quarter of a century together, he'd had all that he could take of Grayson's boastful demeanor. "You most certainly are *not* a better curricle driver than I am."

Gray's eyes lit with humor as the two of them bounded past the Eynsford nursemaid and into their niece and nephew's nursery. "Would you care to wager on that, little brother?"

Wager? Wes would be much happier knocking the jackass' head from his shoulders. "We are the same bloody age," he growled. Then he softened his voice when tiny Lady Aurelia Thorpe winced from her spot at her miniscule table and chairs. "There's my little angel," he cooed to Lia, one of the few females who didn't flee in fear of him or his scar.

"You always say we're the same age," Gray goaded.

"But I beat you into this world. And I can beat you at anything else."

Wes sank to his haunches beside his adorable niece who'd captured his heart the first moment he'd laid eyes on her. "What do you say, Lia? Do you want to go down and see Uncle Weston's new high-perch phaeton?" He shot his brother a sly look. "It's ever so much more grand and faster than your Uncle Grayson's old pile of rubbish."

"It's a miracle you even made it from London in the thing."

"Hate to admit that I'm a better driver than you?"

"Hardly." Gray reached out his hand to Lucien Thorpe, the two-year-old Earl of Brimsworth and Aurelia's male counterpart. "It appears the *ladies* would like to venture outside, pup." The child toddled over to Gray, who held out his finger for the little boy to grasp with his pudgy hand. "If we don't go and take a look at the contraption, Uncle Weston will never let us have any peace," he added in a conspirator's tone.

Ladies, indeed. Gray was perilously close to sporting two blackened eyes. Pity the bruises would only last a few minutes. Wes rose to his feet and scooped Lia up in his arms. "Word of advice—always ignore Uncle Grayson, love. He never says anything of importance. Let's go for a ride, shall we?"

Lia smiled up at him, her blue eyes round with adoration. No question about it, Lia was his most favorite female.

Somewhere behind him, Gray scoffed.

Wes couldn't help looking back over his shoulder at his twin. "Are you coming or not?"

"And miss you strutting around like a peacock? Oh, it's my favorite pastime." Gray lifted Lucien onto one of his shoulders as they all headed for the door.

However, the children's nursemaid blocked their exit, her arms folded beneath her breasts. "Are you quite certain her ladyship would be all right with you taking them? You know what happened the last time…" Her voice trailed off in an anxious quiver.

Of course Weston remembered what had happened the last time. Though it wasn't his or Gray's fault, the stables had gone up in a blaze. *Archer* was the one who'd tossed the lit cheroot to the ground. Besides, the children had never been in any real danger. Lia and Lucien were always safe with their uncles. Still, the blistering that Eynsford had given the three of them had rung in his ears for days. Their oldest half brother acted as though the children were breakable. Good lord, if his own mother had felt that way, he, Gray, and Archer would never have had any fun as young lads. And fun was just what his niece and nephew deserved.

"Lady Eynsford is at Castle Hythe," Wes informed the fretful nurse as he sailed past her with Lia in his arms. "She won't be back for hours."

"We'll only be outdoors," Gray added in a much more placating tone.

The nurse flushed when his brother winked at her.

"You are such a letch," Weston murmured as Gray and Lucien followed him down the hallway.

"Because I know how to get what I want?"

"Because you're not above flirting with the servants to smooth your path."

Gray's mouth flew open in mock dismay. Then he pressed Lucien's head against his chest and covered the lad's ears. "You dare to speak of *my* flirting? I vaguely remember that you took a member of the household staff to your bed just weeks ago." He grumbled beneath his breath. "And you dare to cast censure on me because I *flirted* with the nurse."

Wes felt a grin tug at the corners of his mouth. "She was quite well satisfied with the entire situation."

"Until Cait sacked her," Gray shot back.

"I was a little regretful about that," Weston said as they walked past Eynsford's startled butler. "But it's not my fault she was caught absconding with the family silver." Wes stepped out into the sunshine and clutched Lia tightly to him when she jumped in his arms at the sight of his shiny, new high-perch phaeton, so sleek and glistening in the sun. "Beautiful, isn't it?"

"It's all right," his brother said drolly, as he appraised the vehicle with a critical eye. "A bit light, isn't it?"

"All the better to make it faster," Wes said proudly.

"All the better to make it flip," Gray retorted.

"All the better to win races." Wes recognized immediately that his tone was abrasive. But he didn't care. He was tired of being the ugly twin. Ever since he'd received the scar that slashed across his cheek, he'd been considered to be beneath his brother. Not by the family, of course, but by the *ton*. None of the Hadleys had ever been sought out by society, but they'd managed to fit in on rare occasions. Now he didn't fit in anywhere.

"My curricle is still faster," Gray taunted.

"I highly doubt that," Wes tossed back.

"Would you care to make a wager on it?"

"How much?" Wes had spent a good deal of money on the new vehicle, and his pockets were nearly to let. But he didn't want his brother to know that.

"How much do you have?"

"How much do *you* have?" Wes shot back.

"Fifty quid."

Wes didn't have nearly that much, not now anyway. But it didn't matter, he'd win. There was no way Gray's curricle could touch Wes' new phaeton. Then he'd take his brother's blunt and walk away as the winner. He couldn't ask for a better day. "Deal," he said before Gray could change his mind. "The road to Hythe, then?" It was the smoothest path in the vicinity. One could truly pick up some speed going that direction.

"Hythe!" Gray tipped back his head and laughed. "Do you think you'll beat me, burst through the castle doors as victor, and swing Lady Madeline into your arms?"

Wes would have growled in response, but he refused to give his brother such satisfaction. Lady Madeline, indeed. The chit tried her hardest to never meet Wes' eye on the rare occasions they were in the same room. "On the contrary," Wes replied evenly as he placed Lia on the phaeton's bench, "I thought to boast of my accomplishment to Rob, as he was quite impressed with my purchase." Then he climbed up beside his niece and settled Lia on his lap.

"Oh!" Gray chortled. "*Robert* Hayburn, is it?" He gestured for the groom to bring his curricle around. "We are twins, Weston, or have you forgotten? And I know exactly which Hayburn you want to *boast* to."

Wes unhooked the reins from the seat irons and clutched them tightly in his hand. When he looked over at Gray, his brother was tucking his arm around Lucien's middle.

"Don't worry, love. It won't even be a contest," he whispered to his niece who giggled.

Gray met Wes' eyes. "I'll go first, shall I?"

"Might as well. It'll be the only time you lead this afternoon."

Gray scoffed as his curricle pulled out of the drive. Wes followed until they were out of sight of the manor. Heaven forbid anyone from Eynsford Hall should see what they were about to do. Gray finally stopped at the widest part of the road.

Lia danced with excitement in Wes' lap. "That's right, love," he cooed to her as he lined his phaeton up beside his brother's smaller and bulkier curricle. "We're going to take Uncle Grayson for all he's worth."

His niece looked back and patted the side of Wes' face, and he kissed her tiny palm.

"To the crossroad?"

One road leading to Castle Hythe, one leading toward Folkestone. A good long run from their current position. Wes nodded in agreement. "Very well."

"Are you ready?" Gray called.

"Just try to keep up, brother," Wes goaded. "I'd hate for you to be thoroughly embarrassed."

Gray ignored the remark and began to count down. "Three… Two… One… Go."

With a flick of his wrist, Wes sent his bay bolting forward past Gray's curricle. Honestly, this wouldn't even be a contest. His phaeton was much lighter and faster than his brother's clunky conveyance, but since the race had been Gray's suggestion, Wes couldn't even feel guilty about his predestined win.

The late summer wind rustled Wes' hair, and on his lap, Lia clapped and laughed as they sped down the lane. Wes couldn't help his smile as he yelled over his shoulder. "You are falling behind, Grayson!"

"The race isn't over, you arrogant arse!" Gray called back.

Though it might as well be. Wes laughed as he and Lia pulled farther and farther ahead of his brother's curricle. "Uncle Gray really should watch his language, Lia," he murmured to the little girl. "I can't imagine your mother would be happy with his choice of words. Perhaps you should repeat it so she'll have to ask where you heard it." He chuckled beneath his breath. The sun felt warm on his face, and Wes clutched his niece closer and kissed the top of her head. "When you come to London, love, I'll take you 'round like this in Hyde Park."

Just as he approached the first of two curves along the path, Wes pulled back slightly on the reins so his bay would take the turn a bit slower. Still they were going fast, and he and Lia slid toward the edge of the bench. Wes loosened his grip on the reins, letting his gelding fly over the flat Kent road.

He glanced over his shoulder, making certain Gray had successfully navigated the curve, and found his brother barreling toward him. It was time to urge his bay even faster.

In his lap, Lia gasped. Wes glanced back at the road and his heart stopped. A milkmaid stood in the middle of the lane, looking just as horrified as Wes felt. He pulled back on the reins for all he was worth, but his phaeton was going too fast to stop. So he directed his horse to the left, making a sharp turn instead. Everything else was a blur.

He and Lia flew through the air when the phaeton flipped. He struggled to keep a grasp on his niece, holding her tightly to his chest and wrapping her protectively in his arms. He took the brunt of the fall on his back, which hurt like the devil.

The air was knocked from Wes' lungs, and he couldn't catch his breath. A harsh cry met his ears from the bundle safely wrapped within his arms. Oh, God. Lia. He loosened his grip on her and looked down. Her pretty blue eyes were filled with tears, and she could barely catch her breath. He lifted her and looked her over, straightening her legs and arms, checking her for bruises. He riffled through her hair, which had escaped its tidy upsweep and hung in wild abandon around her face. She was fine. Scared, but fine. He brushed the tears from her cheeks.

Thank God, Lia was all right. She wouldn't heal the way he could, the way he *would* heal eventually. Damn his back pulsed with pain.

And then Gray appeared, leaning over him and scowling. "You're supposed to keep your bloody eyes on the road, Weston!" His brother scooped Lia up in his arms and began his own search for cuts or scrapes.

"She's all right. I took all the damage," Wes managed to choke out.

Gray's dark gaze focused on him again. "You nearly got yourself killed, you mean."

"Sorry I didn't succeed?" He tried to push up on his elbows, but his back still hurt too badly to move.

His brother handed Lia off to the milkmaid Wes had somehow managed to avoid flattening. "See her to my curricle and watch the pair of them!"

"Of course, sir," the young woman muttered, before disappearing from Wes' view.

"What the devil was she doing standing in the middle of the road?"

"She was *walking*, which you would have known if you were paying attention." Gray loomed over Wes again. "Why are you just lying there?" He glanced up at the sky and then back down at Wes. "Cloud gazing, are you?"

"My back is killing me."

"Such a baby," Gray grumbled as he knelt beside Wes, but then his face momentarily softened. "We can't heal from death, you know. If you'd snapped your neck, you'd be gone right now."

The sincerity in Gray's voice was not something Wes was accustomed to hearing from his twin, which was more than a little disconcerting. So he tried to lighten the mood. "You don't want me to leave you with only Archer for company?"

"Sit up," Gray ordered. "Let's see how bad off you are."

Grunting and wincing, Wes pushed up on his elbows once again. He couldn't hurt any more if he'd been cut into ribbons.

Gray held his shoulder and glanced at Wes' back. "You have quite a bit of dirt and road lodged in there. You won't heal 'til we can get you cleaned up. Can you walk back to my curricle? Or do you need me to carry you?"

Wes scoffed. The day he needed Gray to carry him, he truly would be dead. "I'll be fine." He struggled to his feet, squeezed his eyes shut tightly from the pain, and then he limped across the patch of meadow toward his brother's curricle. His heart sank when he saw the mangled mess of what had been his new phaeton lying a few feet from the road. One of the wheels was actually broken in two.

"Bloody hell, we're in for it now," Gray grumbled.

Wes looked up from the wreckage of his conveyance to see the Eynsford coach headed toward them on the road. "Oh God, it's Cait!" His stomach plummeted to wherever his heart had gone.

"I thought she'd be gone for hours," his brother complained.

Even though Wes' ears had yet to be blistered by his sister-in-law, they began ringing in advance. "Blast it. How does she always seem to know when something's happened?"

"I wish I knew." Gray shook his head. "She'll hang us both out the window by our ankles for this." Then his brother frowned. "I don't suppose you could hurry up? We could race her back to The Park, wash off your back, and pretend none of this ever happened."

That was about as likely as Lady Madeline kissing Weston in front of the entire world. To hell with the world, Wes would take her kissing him in private or even looking at him with a smile instead of the slightly horrified expression she usually donned when she caught sight of him. And blast Gray for even putting the chit's name in his mind earlier. He hadn't thought about her for years, maybe months... all right, days. But he hadn't thought about her *today*, not until his brother had thrown the lady's name out for no good reason.

"Why don't we just stay here and let her pass? We'll wave and act like nothing is wrong. Then we'll head off to the stream and I can wash up there. By the time we return, she won't have a clue as to what transpired."

Gray nodded and motioned for the milkmaid to bring both children to them. He thrust Lia into Wes' arms and took Lucien up in his own. "Just to be safe. She won't kill us if we're each holding one of these little urchins. Maybe."

As though Lia knew she'd been insulted, she glared up at Gray.

If pain hadn't been coursing through Wes, he would have doubled over with laughter just from the look her face. She appeared mortally wounded to be called an urchin. But as it was, he needed all of his strength to stand up tall and keep his niece in his arms.

The Eynsford coach pulled up beside them, and the crested door flew open with a crash. Caitrin bounded onto the road so fast that Wes thought the hounds of hell must have been at her heels. "Doona speak ta me," she ordered as she took Lia from Wes' arms. "Doona even look at me," she commanded as she reached for Lucien. "Doona for one moment," she began, pointing first at Gray and then at Wes, "think I willna tell Dashiel about this. How *dare* ye put my children in harm's way?"

"But, Cait," Gray began, "we were only taking them for a ride."

Her icy eyes speared Gray, and Wes almost felt sorry for his brother. "Doona lie ta me, Grayson Francis Hadley! Ye were doin' more than just ridin'. Ye should ken better than ta even try ta tell me an untruth."

Cait ushered Lucien into her coach and climbed in beside him with Lia in her arms. Then the little girl said quietly, "Uh, oh," as she pointed at her uncles through the open door.

"I'm afraid ye're right, lass." Cait sighed heavily and brushed a lock of hair from her daughter's face. "They are in more trouble than they can even imagine. And I willna bother ta try ta save them this time." Then she glanced out the open doorway and called to them. "Dash will be home this evenin' when he and Archer return from London. I'm certain he'll expect ta see ye both when he finds out what ye've done." She shot them both a pointed glance. "Doona force him ta go out and collect ya."

Yes, yes, he'd be home because of the break from the trial as the Queen's defense team worked on their strategy. So Wes had survived the phaeton accident only to have Dash snap his neck with his hands later this evening. Bloody wonderful.

"Cait," Gray began with the same placating tone he'd used on the nursemaid.

"Doona 'Cait' me, and," she turned her icy gaze on Wes, "doona come home until ye're cleaned up. I willna have ye trackin' blood inta my house." Then she leaned forward and pulled the coach door closed with such force that the carriage rocked a bit.

Three

"I CANNOT BELIEVE THE IDIOCY!" DASHIEL THORPE, the Marquess of Eynsford, roared and pounded his fist on his desk for good measure. His inkwell jumped with the force of the blow, and for a moment Wes thought it might crack in two.

Gray winced in his seat, while their brother Archer Hadley, Viscount Radbourne, lounged against the window casing, wearing an expression of utter boredom. Of course Archer was bored. For once, he wasn't getting chastised along with the twins.

Wes slid forward in his seat, hoping to appease his half brother and pack alpha. "It wasn't that bad, Dash. It was just a little race."

"A little race that left your conveyance nothing more than kindling. You have crossed the line with this antic. My children could have been harmed," Dash growled.

"But they weren't," Wes said. "And we would never let anything happen to either of them. Surely you know that."

"If you're not busting up phaetons, then you're lighting my stables ablaze—"

"That was an accident." Archer pushed away from the window and glared at Wes and Gray as though it was their fault the stable fire had been brought up again.

"You're dangerous and reckless." Dash looked at each Hadley brother in turn. "And I have had all of it that I intend to take."

"What is that supposed to mean?" Gray asked. "Are you resigning as our brother?"

Dash narrowed his eye on Wes' twin. "Is there anything between your ears, aside from air?"

"Well, what *does* it mean?" Wes frowned at the marquess.

Dash shook his head. "I need time to think of the appropriate penance, but rest assured I'll think of something. In the meantime, all of you need to ready yourselves for a sojourn to Castle Hythe."

"Castle Hythe?" Archer grumbled. "I've been traveling all day."

"Her Grace has asked us to attend this little affair, and it will appease Caitrin to some degree if you all attend. So you're all going, even you, Archer."

"But," Archer tried. He wasn't even guilty of the most recent charges and he was still going to be punished. Cait must have been even angrier than Wes had thought.

Dash growled low in his throat, and the hair on Wes' arms stood up. "Fine," Wes muttered at the same time as Gray and Archer murmured, "All right," and "Yes, Dash." One did not put up his fists with the alpha. Not with a warning such as that growl. Certainly Dash slapped them on the wrist often, but none of them wanted to be shaken by the scruff of his neck. And their oldest brother wasn't above doing so.

"I expect you all will look respectable when next I see you," Dash said pointedly. Then he glanced at his watch fob. "That will be in exactly two hours. Do *not* be late." He stalked from the room like some great beast that had graced them all with a reprieve rather than eating them in one bite. Or three, as the case might be.

As soon as Dash was out of the room, Archer smacked Wes in the back of the head with the flat of his palm.

"Ow!" Wes cried as he rubbed at the abused area.

"What is wrong with you?" Archer hissed. "You had to know that he'd get his fur ruffled if you put his children in danger. That was the most idiotic thing I've ever heard of."

Archer crossed over to Gray and lifted his foot to kick him in the shin. But Gray was a little faster than Wes had been. Of course, Gray hadn't been rolled over in a phaeton that day either. So, he was in slightly better form.

Gray yelped and scooted out of Archer's reach. "Because of you," Archer complained, "I have to go to this inane event at Castle Hythe."

Wes snorted. "Oh, did you have something more pressing to attend to? Like spending your newly won fortune?" By now, everyone knew Archer had recently come into some unexpected funds in a card game. No one knew exactly how much. But the rumors were that he'd won more than a fortune from a fellow who'd been so certain of his cards that he'd grown careless. Archer was being curiously circumspect about the whole situation. "Had you planned to buy a whore? Your temperament could be measurably better if you did."

"I agree," Gray chimed in. "You should pay your respects to Dash and Cait and go take care of your temperament problem, Arch. You'll be in much finer form afterward. Perhaps we might even be able to stand your presence."

Wes bit the inside of his cheek to keep from smiling. When Archer glared at him, he threw up his hands in surrender. "I didn't say a thing."

"The two of you are menaces."

"The same could be said about you," Gray remarked.

"Blast you both," Archer growled. "The moonful is quickly approaching. I've been held hostage in the bloody House of Lords forever, and now we're going to be stuck here in godforsaken Kent for the entire week preceding it, since Dash will refuse to let either of you out of his sight."

He cursed beneath his breath. Then he shot them a glare. "The children? How the devil could you race with the *children* in your laps?" He was still shaking his head and mumbling as he strode from the room. Wes heard him grumble something about damn idiot brothers who ruined his week.

Gray whistled softly, a harbinger of doom if Wes had ever heard one. "Now Dash *and* Archer are irritated at us. Way to go, baby brother."

"I vaguely remember not being alone in that race," Wes warned.

"Thanks for reminding me. You owe me fifty quid, by the way."

"I'm good for it," Wes muttered. But he wasn't. He certainly wouldn't admit to only having a few farthings to rub together at the moment. And now he didn't even have a shiny new phaeton to gaze at.

"Sure you are," Gray said as he got to his feet.

Wes sighed. "We probably need to go and make ourselves presentable so we don't embarrass Cait. She'll be angry enough as it is. I think she'll kill us both if either of us looks at her sideways."

"Something tells me she might do it anyway," Gray agreed.

Wes tried to sound completely unconcerned when he asked his next question, as though it didn't matter at all. "Do you think Lady Madeline will be at Castle Hythe tonight?"

Gray's dark eyes twinkled. "I feel certain she will. She's there for the great husband hunt, after all."

Wes' gut clenched. "The *what*?"

His brother shrugged. "That's what Archer's calling it anyway. He overheard His Grace and Dash discussing it in Town. The castle will be overflowing with scheming peers Hythe has brought back with him from London while they're all on break. He figures the castle is the perfect place to display the tremendous dowry attached to his daughter."

"How much?" Wes had never dreamt of asking such a question before. After all, Lady Madeline was well out of his reach.

"Does it matter?" Gray countered. "She's primed for greatness. For a marriage to a cold husband who

will spread her legs, get her with child, and then go off
to his mistress. But he'll be of her same social status. So
that makes all the difference."

Was that bitterness in Gray's tone? It certainly
sounded like it. The very thought of Lady Madeline
being forced into a cold and loveless marriage because
it was her duty to marry well made Wes' head hurt.
And he saw red around the edges of his vision at the
very thought of anyone spreading her legs.

"I assume then that you'll be taking yourself out of
the running for her hand," Wes said with a chuckle.

"I'd never compete with you for the chit's heart," Gray
tossed out. "Not that either of us would ever have a shot
at the duke's daughter." Then he strode from the room.

As he walked out, Dash walked back in, then
rifled through his desk, looking perturbed when he
couldn't find whatever he was searching for.

"Dash?" Wes tried to break him from his reverie.

"What?" his oldest brother barked without even
looking in his direction.

"Loan me fifty quid?" Wes asked. The attention
Dash *did* pay him made Wes turn tail and move toward
the door. "Never mind," he muttered as he left the
room as quickly as he could.

❧

"You'll never believe what Robert just told me."
Sophie burst into Maddie's room without even the
preamble of knocking.

Maddie looked up from the note she was posting
to a dear friend and couldn't help grinning at Sophie.
"Oh? Did he profess his undying love yet again?"

Sophie sighed as she dropped onto the edge of Maddie's four-poster. "He did, but—"

Maddie laid her quill across her desk. "Another proposal?" How many times had her brother asked Sophie to marry him? If Robert wasn't such a derelict, she would love the idea of having Sophie join the family as her sister.

"Yes, but not an honorable proposal. However—"

"I beg your pardon?" Maddie rose from her spot. She must have misheard her friend. Certainly her brother did *not* suggest Sophie become his mistress. "Did you say not of the honorable variety?"

Sophie scoffed and shook her head. "I have no value anymore, not to a man of means. I'm fully aware of how my circumstances have changed. I'm just surprised that it's being presented to me by the same men who thought me respectable a mere few months ago." She sighed heavily. "It certainly isn't the first such offer I've received since I returned to England. I'm sure it won't be the last."

It would be the last time Robert Hayburn would propose anything of the sort. The blasted reprobate. "What did you say to him?" Maddie dropped onto the bed beside her friend.

A smile lit Sophie's face. "That I was so honored by his devotion, but that I had my sights set on Nathaniel. That a girl needed to look out for herself, and why would I choose to be the mistress of a second son when I could be the respectable wife of the heir instead?"

Maddie couldn't help the giggle that escaped her. "Heavens! Robert must have turned purple. What did he say to that?"

Sophie shrugged. "That Nathaniel's offer wouldn't

be for marriage either, and I'd be better off with a fellow who actually cared for me."

"Oh, so caring, indeed!" Maddie forced herself to take a deep breath. If she didn't, she'd have to go search out her brothers and give them both a piece of her mind. How dare they suggest such thing to her friend? "A mistress! How very noble of my brother."

"There are only a few ways for a woman of our gentle breeding to fend for herself when she's all alone."

Maddie's mouth fell open. "You aren't considering…" She couldn't even finish the terrible thought.

"Of course not!" Sophie frowned. "But for some reason it's the first option that pops into the male mind. But, no, I'll manage some other way. I'll find employment as a governess. A lady's companion. Something. If all else fails, I could throw myself at Cousin Freddie's feet and beg for mercy."

The new Earl of Postwick was not terribly generous, and Sophie might very well receive the same sort of despicable offer from her own cousin. "You can stay with me forever," Maddie vowed and squeezed Sophie's hands for good measure. "And if Robert even thinks of suggesting such a thing again—"

Sophie shook her head. "Robert is of no consequence, Maddie. Though I suppose I probably should have accepted either his or Nathaniel's honorable proposals a year or so ago, shouldn't I? I certainly wouldn't be in this predicament if I had."

Maddie scoffed. "You could never love either of my brothers." Honestly, who could? It was all Maddie could do to drum up any charitable feelings for them at times. "You wouldn't want that."

"No, but holding out for a love match is not a luxury I have anymore."

And even though Maddie knew her friend spoke the truth, her heart hurt a bit at hearing the words aloud. "Don't decide anything rash until we speak to Lady Eynsford. With her influence on Radbourne, you might just be able to reclaim your fortune and then tell every reprobate in England to go stick his spoon in the wall."

Sophie smirked. "Well, that's what I really came to tell you. Robert said Lord Eynsford *and* Lord Radbourne will be here this evening with their respective families."

Maddie's mouth fell open. "Grandmamma *never* invites the Hadleys to anything."

"I don't know who did the inviting, but I plan to make Lord Radbourne's scurrilous acquaintance this evening."

What an awful idea. "No." Maddie shook her head. "Trust me, Soph, talking to Lady Eynsford is the way to go."

"You talk to Lady Eynsford then. I have a few things I'd like to say to Lord Radbourne."

A scratch sounded at Maddie's door before she could reply. "Come," she muttered, though she tightened her grasp on Sophie's hands. They weren't finished with this conversation.

Jane, Maddie's lady's maid, pushed open the door and bobbed her head. "Her Grace is requesting your presence in the drawing room, my lady."

"You mean she's *demanding* it," Sophie muttered under her breath.

Jane's eyes grew wide, but she nodded. "Indeed, Lady Sophia."

"Come with me," Maddie suggested. After all, they could finish their discussion on the way to the drawing room.

But Sophie shook her head. "Go on without me. I'm not quite ready for dinner." Then her friend slid from the bed and brushed past Jane into the corridor.

Maddie rose from her spot and took a cursory glance at her reflection in the mirror. She supposed she was as ready for dinner and all of her father's guests as she was ever going to be. Then she started for the corridor and smiled at Jane as she passed her. "Wish me luck."

"I always do."

Maddie made her way from the family's quarters through the gallery and down a set of circular stone steps to the main floor. Raucous male laughter filled the castle, which only made her scowl. What a perfectly dreadful summer this was turning out to be. First, Sophie's insolvency and now the duke's push to see Maddie select some dim-witted fop with whom she would spend the rest of her days.

An escape was most assuredly in order.

Hmm. Her dear friend Mrs. MacQuarrie *had* invited her to Edinburgh. She could borrow one of the ducal coaches and bolt north. What a fanciful notion. Maddie let the idea vanish as quickly as it had arrived. After all, her father would scour the ends of the earth to find her if she ran away. He'd gone to great lengths to parade a battalion of peers from London to Kent so she could look them over. No matter that she knew them all and had no desire to know them any better. Not a single one of them. Turning tail and bolting would only cause her father to pick a fellow of his choice. Besides, she couldn't abandon Sophie, especially not with her degenerate brothers in residence.

She took a steadying breath before she entered the drawing room. It was going to be a very long house party.

                         ∽

Weston didn't think he'd ever seen Castle Hythe's drawing room so filled. One rarely experienced a crush in the country. Of course, usually when Wes was at the castle, it was to play a bit of cards with Rob. And he certainly wasn't greeted in a room as grand as this one. He took a long look around the drawing room and shook his head at the plethora of gentlemen who'd come to vie for Lady Madeline's pretty little hand. They certainly wouldn't be playing cards tonight. Not only were Wes' pockets empty, but he couldn't help but feel a bit beneath the other guests.

He shook the errant thought away. It didn't matter which of these bucks Lady Madeline chose. It wasn't as though Wes was in the running, as Gray had less than eloquently reminded him. Still, as the lady in question entered the drawing room, he couldn't help but stop and stare. He allowed his eyes to sweep from the top of her pretty little head to her dainty slippers.

Damn! She was more radiant every time he saw her. Flaxen curls framed her delicate face, and her green eyes, which always twinkled with intelligence, were an exact match to her simple but elegant gown.

However, the smile that tugged at her lips was the worst farce he'd ever seen, if he read her expression correctly. Was she all right? Had something caused her distress? Wes would love to know. If only he could ask her. But to do that, she'd have to look at him with more than a passing glance.

She assumed a reasonably successful imitation of genteel happiness as she slid past her suitors and offered fellow after fellow a welcome to the castle. When she'd greeted everyone, she stepped up beside Robert and poked him in the shoulder, rather hard if Rob's wince was any indication. Then she leaned closer to her brother, and though Wes strained to hear her words, they were nothing more than hushed whispers that he couldn't hear even with his Lycan ears. Later, he'd get Rob to tell him what the interaction had been about, after he plied his friend with a bit of whisky to loosen his lips.

"Stop staring at the chit," Archer hissed in his ear.

"I wasn't staring." Wes still couldn't pull his gaze from Lady Madeline, so he whispered out the side of his mouth. "She looks sad, doesn't she?"

"Wasn't staring, indeed." Archer nudged him in the shoulder, quite hard, and forced him to look in his direction. Archer's amber eyes twinkled with mirth. "You've got a bit of drool on your chin, pup."

"I do not," Wes insisted, but he swiped a hand across his chin anyway. Blasted Archer was such a liar. "Jackass," he grumbled.

Archer shrugged. "It's your fault I'm here tonight. Don't expect me to thank you for it."

"Don't tell me," boomed Nathaniel Hayburn, the Marquess of Lavendon, as he clapped Archer on the back, "that you've joined the ranks of these Lotharios angling for Maddie's hand."

Archer smirked. "And marry into the *Hayburn* family? We Hadleys do have our standards, you know."

Lavendon chuckled as he looked across the room. "Quite an assortment my father has marched down here, isn't it?"

Archer nodded. "He did seem singularly intent on finding her a match back in Town."

Lavendon shook his head. "Pointless. She's too much like Grandmother. Stubborn and opinionated."

Wes gaped at Lord Lavendon. In all the years since he'd first made Lady Madeline's acquaintance, he would have never compared her with the duchess. Madeline was soft-spoken with a gentle countenance. Perfection personified.

The marquess noted his look and grinned. "Oh, she's less abrasive than Grandmother, but once Maddie's made her mind up about something, it's set. No hope of changing it. Ever." Then a devious smile lit his face. "Speaking of stubborn chits…"

"Beg your pardon?" Archer asked.

Lavendon shook his head, though his eyes remained fixed on the door. "My, how the mighty have fallen. Do excuse me, will you?" Without waiting for a response, the marquess pushed his way through the crowd and bowed before a pretty girl with sable locks.

"Who do you think that is?" Wes asked.

Archer shrugged. "Nathaniel's next conquest, I'd say." He glanced down at his watch fob as though wishing the evening away.

Whoever the chit was, Lavendon was leading her in their direction. Quite a pretty thing, really. Grey eyes. Nice figure. "She seems to be looking at you, Arch."

Archer snapped his eyes back up and smiled at the pair as they approached. "Ah, Lavendon, back so soon, are you? And with such a lovely guest."

"It was the lady's request." The marquess glanced at the pretty girl on his arm. "Lady Sophia Cole, allow me to introduce Viscount Radbourne and his brother Mr. Weston Hadley."

The color drained from Archer's face and his lips thinned. "Pleasure. Do excuse me. I believe Lady Eynsford is signaling me."

But Cait wasn't even in view. Wes watched as his brother pushed his way through the crowd. What the devil was that about? Did Archer know this Lady Sophia? Wes had never even heard the chit's name before. And there hadn't been any recognition in his brother's eyes when he'd first looked at the lady across the room.

Wes smiled at the lady in question. "Please forgive my brother. He can be quite a beast at times."

She cocked her head to one side and frowned a bit. "Oh, I don't think I'll be doing that. But it *is* a pleasure to make your acquaintance, Mr. Hadley."

"And yours as well," Wes remarked absently. What had that remark meant? "Do you know my brother?"

She pursed her lips. "Only by reputation," she said. She seemed quite unable to draw her eyes from Archer's back, which was quite solidly turned in her direction. For some reason, Archer was avoiding her entirely. There was a story there, Wes was certain. But would the lovely lady be willing to share it with him? Did he even want to know?

Wes was too curious not to question the lady, but first he'd have to dispense with the marquess. "I believe your grandmother is now signaling *you*, Lavendon."

The marquess closed his eyes tightly and said, "Duty calls." He looked at Lady Sophia with way too much familiarity. "I will see you later?" he asked casually.

Wes thought it sounded like she mumbled, "Not if I see you first," beneath her breath as Lavendon looked down the bodice of her gown. Then he drew himself to attention and begged Lady Sophia's pardon. He walked toward his grandmother as though he faced the gallows.

"Lady Sophia," Wes began slowly and carefully. "Is something troubling you?"

"Aside from your brother's very existence?" she quipped.

"Beg your pardon?" Certainly he hadn't heard her correctly. "Has he done something to offend you?"

"He's breathing," she said. This time, Wes had to smother a chuckle in his fist. For some reason, he was quite sure laughing at the lady wouldn't help her countenance a bit.

Wes nodded slowly. "Terrible habit he has. That breathing. We've been trying to get him to stop for years."

"I could help you with that. And would do so with a glad heart." Wes looked down at her and finally saw a twinkle in her eye.

"I might take you up on your offer," Wes said. "I'd love to hear more about how you'd plan it. Would you make it terribly painful?" What an absurd conversation to have in the duchess' drawing room. But it was honestly the most sport he'd had all day.

She shrugged her delicate little shoulders. "Slow. Painful. Quick. Pleasant. I don't particularly care." She narrowed her eyes. "Your brother is a lucky fellow, isn't he?"

"With your plot to dismember him, I'd say not," Wes replied. In fact, he'd warn Archer about the lady's animosity at the first opportunity.

She inhaled happily and laid a hand on her chest. A huge smile curved her lips. "Oh, dismemberment!" she cried with a giggle. "I hadn't even thought of that! What a wonderful idea!"

"What's this I hear about dismemberment?" Gray said from beside his shoulder. He looked down at Lady Sophia and bowed slowly.

"Have you met?" Wes asked, his eyes searching for Lady Madeline again. She was thronged by men of means. He hated that the situation bothered him so much.

"I haven't had the pleasure," Gray said as he took the lady's gloved hand.

"Just hope the lady doesn't feel as strongly about you as she does about Archer," Wes mumbled to Gray.

"Yes, I heard a little," Gray confided with a grin at Lady Sophia. "It's the most interesting conversation in the entire room. Do tell what he did to deserve the lady's derision."

"He knows what he did," she said slowly, still shooting daggers at Archer. "Excuse me," she remarked absently as she glided away.

"What was that about?" Gray mumbled.

"No idea," Wes replied. "He's a cad, but it's not every day that a lady vows so vehemently to do him harm. I believe she'd have him drawn and quartered if she was able."

"You don't think he made an improper advance toward her, do you?" Gray looked puzzled. And when Gray was puzzled, he wouldn't stop until he got to the meat of the matter.

"Archer?" Wes shrugged. "I wouldn't put it past him. But, if he did, I'd think he'd be willing to talk to the chit instead of turning tail and running the way he did. He's pretending like she doesn't even exist. There's something odd, there. Who is she? Have you any idea?"

"A good friend of Lady Madeline's," Gray replied.

The mere mention of her name made Wes search for her in the room again. She looked positively miserable sandwiched on the settee between two of the most boring peers he'd ever had the occasion to meet. One of them leaned a little too close to her to talk. And the other touched her. He touched her hand. How *dare* he touch her hand?

"Don't do it," Gray hissed.

"Don't do what?" Wes said from between clenched teeth.

"Don't cause a scene," Gray hissed back. "We're in enough trouble as it is. Cait will never forgive us if we make problems for her here."

"So, I'm supposed to just sit here and let him grope her?"

"For God's sake, he touched her hand."

"First her hand, and then on to other areas," Wes growled back at him "I'll have to kill him."

"Ask Lady Sophia for advice on the most painful method. For some reason, I think she has probably researched it. She might even like practice before she takes on Archer." Gray nudged his side. "See, there." Wes watched as Lady Madeline excused herself and swept gracefully from the room. "She extricated herself from his clutches quite nicely all on her own."

But then Wes saw Lord Chilcombe slink out of the room behind her. Blast and damn. He'd be in trouble before the night was over.

Four

MADDIE STIFLED A SHIVER AS SHE LEFT THE DRAWING room. Over the past three years, she'd dealt with simpering fops who thought much more of her fortune than they did her mind. But now that they'd been invited to formally vie for her hand, some of them seemed like they would stop at nothing to win. In just the short while she'd been in the drawing room, some of them had even forsaken the bounds of propriety and dared to become much too familiar with her person. She shivered again as she thought of the way the Earl of Chilcombe had just pressed his leg against hers and touched her hand. Of course, he'd done it when her family wasn't looking. So, she couldn't even complain.

Rumor had it that Lord Chilcombe had more than one mistress in Town, at least according to Robert. And on the subject of mistresses, Maddie found Robert to be quite the reliable source. If the Earl of Chilcombe thought he could use Maddie's fortune to support his doxies, he was even more addled than she'd originally suspected. Besides, the earl had already lost one fortune at the gaming tables, and if he thought he'd get his hands on hers, he was sorely mistaken. The very thought of his thin little lips pressed against hers made her want to cast up her accounts.

"Lady Madeline," a voice called from behind her. She stopped in her tracks, took in a deep breath, and turned to face the interloper. Of course, he would have followed her. "Are you unwell?" Lord Chilcombe asked and raked a hand through his reddish hair.

"No, I just forgot my shawl," she remarked.

"May I escort you to retrieve it?" he asked, his lips turned in what may have been a nice smile on any other man.

Escort her to the *library* where she'd last seen her shawl? Where they would be utterly alone? Not very likely. "I believe I can find my way," she replied. "I'll only be a moment."

"I'll wait for you here then," he said as he glanced at his pocket fob.

"If you insist," she murmured, moving as quickly down the corridor as she could.

How nice it would be to have a moment's reprieve from this nonsense. However, it could only be a moment, as anything longer didn't seem to be forthcoming. Maddie breezed into the library and sank heavily into an overstuffed leather chair and closed her eyes. However would she manage weeks on end with this lot?

The door creaked as it opened behind her, and Maddie's eyes flew open. The Earl of Chilcombe would need to be dealt with, but in the shadows of the room, it took only a moment for her to realize his lordship hadn't followed her. But the gentleman who *did* approach made her even more uneasy. "Mr. Hadley," she said as she jumped to her feet.

"Lady Madeline," he said in response, his voice tiptoeing across her skin and making her hair stand on end.

It wasn't an altogether unpleasant sensation. She shivered lightly. Heavens, what did Weston Hadley want with her? "Did you follow me?"

He looked a bit chagrined, even with his face enclosed by the shadows the low lighting cast. "I must admit that I did. And I hope you don't mind that I waylaid several of your more ardent suitors along the way."

"Waylaid?" Why did the very thought make her want to smile? Perhaps it was the image of the dangerous Mr. Hadley frightening off the feckless peers with just his scowl.

"Chilcombe was lurking in the corridor," he continued, "And Dewsbury was skulking behind a palm. He was a little more tenacious, so I told him that you were upset about something and looked as though you might cry at any moment. He went very quickly in the other direction." His lips lifted in a slow grin. "I hope you don't mind. But I detest that man." He motioned back toward her chair. "Sit?" he suggested.

She sank slowly into the chair. On one hand, she was increasingly happy for the offer of respite. But on the other, she wasn't quite certain she relished the idea of sharing it with *him*. Her emotions warred within her. One part of her wanted to be afraid of him, just because of who he was, but another part of her wouldn't allow it. She sighed heavily, attempting to take control of her errant breaths.

Mr. Hadley hitched one hip onto the corner of a large table and regarded her quietly. But, whereas the other men at the castle had an agenda, which seemed to involve trapping her in marriage, Mr. Hadley had none. Not that she was aware of, anyway.

"You're wondering why I followed you," he stated.

"I was curious," she replied. She was more than curious. She was intrigued.

"I have nothing but the best of intentions, I assure you." For some reason, she didn't quite believe him, as his eyes swept down her body. He looked a bit chagrined when she sent him a reproving look, but she really didn't want to thwart his hot gazes. What did that say about her?

He continued, "I wanted to speak with you about your friend, Lady Sophia."

Maddie's heart fell. Of course, he wanted to talk about Sophie. To find out how much of a scandalous offer he could make to her very dearest friend in the world. Just like every other man in residence. His agenda wasn't so different after all.

"So you can try to make her your mistress?" Maddie asked, realizing how acerbic her words were the moment they left her lips. They tasted like vinegar and she was immediately remorseful.

Mr. Hadley choked. His face reddened and his breath left him in huge rasping gasps. "Beg your pardon?" he croaked.

Maddie jumped to her feet and crossed to the sideboard, where she poured a glass of whatever her father kept there. She passed it to the gentleman, and he took a healthy swallow of some amber liquid. But that seemed to take his breath away just as much as her words had done. He coughed and sputtered into his open palm. He turned away from her for a moment as his face reddened, and then he composed himself.

"Oh, dear," she cried. She reached out a hand to touch his arm. "Are you all right?"

He coughed once more and then stilled. "Thank you for the whisky," he rasped, with one hand lying on his chest as he turned back to face her.

"Oh, was that what that was?" But what was she to offer him? She didn't have any water within reach.

"It was," he remarked dryly. "And no, I have no ambitions toward your friend. I simply wanted to question you about her animosity toward my brother."

She forced her own reaction to Mr. Hadley to the back of her mind and considered her best friend. So Sophie had made a cake of herself? "She made it obvious, did she?" Of course, her friend would not be subtle the first time she made the acquaintance of the man who'd stolen her father's money and, consequently, his will to live.

"Her distaste for him?" Mr. Hadley asked with a large grin. Her heart skipped a beat. His face was really quite remarkable when he smiled like that. She could barely make out his scar in the dark. He should smile more often, as he didn't seem nearly as frightening as usual. In fact, he was extraordinarily handsome. "It was rather apparent."

"I am sorry." Sorry she hadn't gotten the chance to speak with Lady Eynsford before now. She reached for the man's cup to return it to the sideboard. Could her plan still be salvaged? Or was it a lost cause at this point? "Do you think he noticed?" she asked over her shoulder.

Mr. Hadley wore a curious expression, one Maddie couldn't quite interpret. Was it glee? He took a step closer to her, then another. "Archer was barely introduced to the lady before he bolted in the opposite direction. I don't believe he overheard any of her plans to dismember him, however."

Dismember? Maddie gulped. Where would Sophie get such a gruesomely medieval idea? A small part of her wanted to use the same tactic on some of her most ardent suitors. "His lordship ran off, you say?"

The gentleman nodded. "With his tail tucked between his legs."

"You should seek your brother out then, Mr. Hadley. I'm not one to tell tales. And I'm certain Lord Radbourne will tell you what transpired between himself and the lady's family if he wants you to know."

Something mischievous twinkled in the gentleman's dark eyes, and her belly did that queer little flutter again. "Now you *must* tell me, my lady. For if Archer has no desire for me to know what sort of injustice he has done to the lady's family, that is all the more reason for me *to* know. Don't you agree?"

Maddie blinked at him. She didn't agree at all. And she certainly was not about to divulge the details of Sophie's unfortunate situation to the man. "I am not one to tell tales, Mr. Hadley."

"I'm certain," Mr. Hadley reached for her hand as his voice dropped to a whisper, "if one of your brothers was engaged in some questionable activity, you would want to know the details."

Perhaps that tactic worked with many of the women of his acquaintance. He could probably disarm a lady with his lowered voice and the way his eyes sparkled in the dark. But Maddie forced herself to extricate her hand from the gentleman's grasp, no matter that she didn't want to for some reason, and she spun away from him with a laugh. "On that you are mistaken, sir. You see, I am quite certain that both my brothers are engaged in objectionable activities on a regular basis. However, I find I am much happier not knowing what sorts of depravity they are involved in."

"On second thought, that might be wise."

He knew her brothers better than she thought, if he so readily agreed. That couldn't speak well of him, his acquaintance with those scoundrels. Could it?

"Wes, is that you?" Robert's voice boomed from the threshold. A pang of regret resounded within her. She was enjoying the conversation with Mr. Hadley, enjoying the way he looked at her. "Absconding with my baby sister, are you?"

Mr. Hadley turned to face the door. "Ah, evening, Rob."

Robert stepped into the library. "Or are you regaling the lady with tales of your new high-perch phaeton? Maddie couldn't care less about such things, you know."

Maddie rolled her eyes heavenward. "Mr. Hadley was stepping in for *you*, Robert. Shooing away unwanted suitors and such. Perhaps you could take a lesson from him."

Robert chuckled as he dropped an arm around her shoulders. "And who deemed them unwanted, Maddie? You or Father?"

On second thought, perhaps Sophie was on to something with her whole dismemberment idea.

"What do you want, Robert? I'm certain it isn't my safety or virtue that has sent you in search of me."

Her blasted brother laughed again. "God help whichever of these saps lands you. He'll have my everlasting sympathy."

"Rob!" Mr. Hadley growled.

Maddie glanced up at the gentleman and found him scowling at her brother. The ferocity of his glare made his scar seem even more pronounced. She took a step away from him and closer to her disreputable brother. What she really wanted was to take a step toward Mr. Hadley instead. What a queer notion.

Of course, Robert only laughed harder. "Easy, Wes. She's just my sister." Then he squeezed Maddie's shoulder. "We'll all be going into dinner soon, and Father wants you on Gelligaer's arm."

The Earl of Gelligaer? Maddie somehow managed not to cringe. Of course the Welshman would be at the top of her father's list as he would be a duke himself one day, assuming he lived that long. But, something about the fellow made Maddie wonder if he would survive another year. Whether because of his always red-rimmed eyes, continual cough, or sudden shifts in mood, Gelligaer wasn't *normal*. As far as heirs to dukedoms went, he made Nathaniel look like a prized prince.

She smiled tightly at Mr. Hadley. "Do enjoy your evening, sir."

❧

How exactly was Wes supposed to enjoy his evening when that opium eater Gelligaer would have Lady Madeline on his arm? However, Wes didn't have a say in that matter. Not at all. So he nodded in farewell as Rob escorted his sister from the library, leaving him by his lonesome.

As the slight scent of rosewater drifted away, Wes watched the pair disappear down the corridor. A grin tugged at his lips. He'd just had his first real conversation with Lady Madeline. He would have loved for the interaction to have lasted longer, to have not had their conversation interrupted by Robert, but she hadn't run screaming when her eyes landed on him. He'd actually held her hand, no matter how briefly. She'd even laughed and smiled. And what a radiant smile it was.

After a moment, Wes started back toward the drawing room himself. He should be present when dinner was called, or he'd face Cait's wrath later. However, he hadn't even gotten as far as the drawing room when he saw Lady Sophia slip inside a nearby parlor door. The door didn't close behind her, although she did make an attempt at privacy. Wes stepped closer to the threshold.

"You know who I am." Her clear, proud voice caught Wes' immediate attention.

Curiosity got the better of him, and he leaned even closer to the door Lady Sophia had entered.

"Of course, I do," Archer grumbled from inside the room. "Lavendon introduced us this evening. Or have you forgotten?"

What the devil was *Archer* doing in there? Thankfully, with his Lycan ears, Wes didn't need to lean against the door to hear his brother's conversation. He'd never live it down if he was caught with his ear at a keyhole.

"You knew my name," Lady Sophia accused. "I

saw it in your eyes. Did guilt cause you to slink away? Or were you simply too cowardly to face me?"

"I have nothing to feel guilty about, sweetheart," Archer drawled, arrogance dripping from his words. "Nor am I a coward. And I will forgive your insults because of your most recent loss, for which I offer my condolences. However, you really should turn back around and rejoin the throng of men clamoring for your attention. I'm not one of them and I have nothing for you."

"Those men are clamoring for Madeline, not me, as you are well aware. And *we* have unfinished business, you and I."

Archer snorted.

"And I'm not leaving until I have my say."

"Very well," Archer growled. "I'm listening."

There was a long pause, and Wes thought perhaps his brother's tone had scared the chit into silence. But then she said, "Bindweed Cottage. It's mine and I want it back."

"I'm certain if you ask Lavendon nicely enough, he'll buy you one even nicer. You appear to have quite a few assets with which you may still be able to bargain."

The unmistakable sound of a slap reverberated off the walls. Wes was about to burst into the room when the crowd from the drawing room filtered into the corridor and started in his direction. The worst thing for both Archer and Lady Sophia would be to get caught in each other's company, especially as their tempers ran high at the moment. So Wes casually leaned against the door until he spotted Gray in the crowd.

An instant later, his twin was at his side. "Cait has

been asking for you and Archer," Gray hissed. "What have you been up to?"

"I believe Archer went back to Eynsford Park," Wes called loudly enough for their older brother to hear them inside the parlor. Hopefully, the dolt would get the hint that he should return to The Park while the others were dining, to keep anyone from suspecting he'd escaped the party with Lady Sophia. Having both of them reappear at the same time wouldn't do, not if their absence had already been noticed.

"Why are you yelling?" Gray asked.

"I'm not yelling."

"I'm standing right here and you *are* yelling."

Wes glared at his twin. "I wanted to make sure you could hear me over the crowd," he ground out.

"Uh-huh." Gray furrowed his brow. "With my poor hearing and all, I can see why that would be a concern. Did you addle your brain in the fall today?"

"Let's just head into dinner, shall we?"

Gray shrugged. "As long as you stop yelling, I'll go wherever you want."

How about straight to the devil? Wes pushed his twin back into the crowd and followed the group into the large dining hall, another room in the castle Wes had never entered before.

One could almost imagine a time long ago when feudal lords reigned over their kingdoms from this hall. Lavish dinners, knights, ladies, and lively music. Two long tables sat parallel to each other, and the Duchess of Hythe gestured both Hadley twins to the less grand of the two. Less grand in that the Duke of Hythe sat at the other, along with his daughter, the unhinged Gelligaer, and the higher-ranking peers present. Dash and Cait also sat at the grand table, which was a relief. At least he and Gray wouldn't have their sister-in-law's eyes on them the entire evening.

Just as they were about to take their seats, along with the lesser-titled peers, the duchess approached their table with Lady Sophia in tow. "I hope you gentlemen don't mind if we join you."

"Of course not." Viscount Dewsbury nodded his head. "We'll be honored to have such lovely guests."

The duchess cast a reproachful look in the man's direction. No one thought Her Grace lovely, as she was well aware.

So Lady Sophia belonged at the lesser table as well, did she? Interesting. But why was Her Grace joining their ranks? To keep Lady Sophia from being the only female at the table, most likely. Wes gulped. Having Cait's eyes on them would have been better than the duchess'.

"Mr. Hadley," Her Grace said imperially.

"Yes?" Wes and Gray answered in unison.

The duchess narrowed her eyes on the two of them. "Let's put Lady Sophia between you. Perhaps she can manage to keep the pair of you out of trouble."

Normally, Wes would have had no complaints about sitting beside a lovely young lady, but now he wouldn't be able to tell Gray about the conversation he'd overheard. And with a table full of other guests, he couldn't even question the lady about her connection to Archer or what was so important about this Bindweed Cottage she'd mentioned. To make matters worse, he had a perfect view of Lady Madeline and that blasted Welsh earl at the opposite table.

Five

The rattle of her bedroom door handle startled Maddie awake. She pulled the counterpane tightly beneath her chin. "Who's there?" she hissed.

Immediately, the rattling stopped and she took a steadying breath. Thank heavens she'd been of sound mind enough to turn the key in her lock after she sent Jane away. Did one of her father's guests think to compromise her?

Weston Hadley immediately came to mind, with his dark scowl and even darker scar. She almost wished she could ask him to sleep outside her door to waylay any unwanted late-night guests. He'd been quite effective in the corridor, by his own admission. Maddie smiled to herself at the thought of Mr. Hadley frightening her suitors away with nothing more than his scowl and his scar.

What a wonderful talent to possess! Perhaps the gentleman could be persuaded to spend more time at the castle. At least until her father and all of his guests returned to London for the trial. Fortunately, she didn't have to worry about *him* trying to compromise her.

Until tonight, she'd always been frightened of Weston Hadley, but after their short conversation in the library, she found she *did* like him, strange as that was to realize. He was quite handsome in a dark and dangerous sort of way, too. Funny she'd never noticed that before. Of course, he'd never smiled before, as though he preferred the world to see him as a sinister gentleman on the fringe of society. Why did he do that?

There was something quite charming in the way he seemed concerned about his brother but at the same time fished for information to needle Radbourne. The brothers Hadley possessed a camaraderie Maddie hadn't even realized she envied until now. Too bad her own brothers were such scoundrels. How wonderful it would feel to be part of a family who cared deeply for each other!

A shower of tiny pings hit Maddie's window.

Good heavens! What now? She slid from under her counterpane and crossed the cold, stone floor to her window. A grinning Lord Dewsbury stood beneath her in the courtyard, holding a handful of pebbles. Maddie glared at the man, wishing once again that her scowl was as effective as Mr. Hadley's.

One thing was certain. If she was going to get any sleep, it wouldn't be in her room, which seemed to attract reprobates as honey did bears. Maddie retrieved her wrapper from the edge of her bed. She slid her arms through it and tied the sash around her waist. Then she turned the key in her lock and peeked out into the corridor. Everything was dark. Still, she couldn't make out any male-shaped shadows, which was a relief. So she stepped over her threshold and darted down the hallway and didn't stop until she reached Sophie's room.

Maddie knocked lightly on her friend's door and was relieved when Sophie whispered, "Who is it?"

"It's me, Soph. Open up."

A moment later, Maddie was safely ensconced in her friend's room, having dropped onto the edge of Sophie's bed. "Let me stay with you tonight," she begged.

Sophie rubbed the sleep from her eyes. "Bad dream?"

Maddie shook her head. "Bad houseguests. If one isn't trying to break into my room, another is assaulting my window with pebbles. I think we'll be safer together."

"I have had every sort of proposal known to man within the space of a fortnight," Sophie said. "Who would have thought my value would change so drastically in so short of a time?" She patted Maddie's arm absently.

"How many proposals did you receive tonight? And I'm assuming none of them are of the respectable variety."

"Not a single one," Sophie sighed. "How about you?"

Maddie held up three fingers. "Three offers of marriage." Why did that make her feel so unwanted?

Sophie shot her a look of commiseration. "Honestly, what was His Grace thinking by inviting that lot here all at once like this?"

Maddie sighed. "He was thinking he could finally be free of me."

"Your father adores you. He just didn't think the situation through clearly." Sophie pulled back the counterpane and Maddie climbed into the bed.

Maddie turned on her side so she and Sophie could see each other. "What am I to do, Soph? I'd hop a ship bound for India and find employment training elephants before I'd marry any of those lechers."

"Lord Gelligaer didn't meet your expectations?"

Though it was dark, Maddie could tell her friend wore an impish grin. "When he bothered to talk at all, it was to discuss the color green ad nauseam. You would think there was only so much one could say about a color, but you'd be wrong."

Sophie giggled. "Did it start with him discussing your eyes, by chance?"

It had started that very way. Maddie's response was an unintelligible grumble.

"It couldn't be worse than my dinner companions. Your grandmother barked at everything everyone said the entire night. I almost felt sorry for the fellows assigned to my table. By the end of the evening, Mr. Hadley, the smooth-faced one, just stared into his plate like a scolded puppy."

"Speaking of Mr. Hadley, Soph, I know you said something to Lord Radbourne. What did you say?"

Sophie closed her eyes. "In public or in private?"

In private? Maddie nearly swallowed her tongue. She sat up in bed and stared down at her friend. "You met with him privately?"

"Certain things needed to be said without an audience."

Maddie massaged her temple. "Please tell me nothing untoward happened."

"All right. Nothing untoward happened."

Maddie didn't believe that for a second. "Heavens,

Soph. I told you I would speak to Lady Eynsford. That she'd find a way to straighten all this out."

Sophie shrugged against her pillow. "Well, I'll get a chance to talk to Lady Eynsford myself tomorrow. She wants me to call on her... alone." She let that last word linger on the air. "Very mysterious. I don't know why you think she's capable of sorting out my situation. She seems quite odd to me. Bursting out of parlors in the middle of tea for no reason. Pulling me to the side last night and telling me I must visit Eynsford Park in the morning and to come alone. She is more than a conundrum."

"Lady Eynsford wants you to call on her in the morning?"

Sophie nodded. "Indeed. Though she didn't even give me a hint as to why."

"Hmm." Maddie dropped back on the bed and stared up at the canopy above them. "Perhaps Grandmamma already spoke to the lady and she has a plan to help you."

Sophie yawned and turned on her side. "I'm sure it's something like that." Sarcasm dripped from her words. "Now go to sleep, Maddie. I've apparently got a long day ahead of me tomorrow."

Maddie sighed and settled deeper beneath the counterpane. Thoughts of tomorrow flitted across her mind. From sunup to sundown, she'd be barraged by marriage-minded men who wanted her fortune. All of whom had been hand chosen by her father. Sophie would be going to Eynsford Park in the morning *alone*, while Maddie was left to fend for herself. She wondered absently if the Hadley twins would be there. She couldn't even remember the other twin's name, the one without the scar. But Mr. Weston Hadley was a man she didn't think she'd forget for quite some time.

❧

Wes paced the floor in Dash's study from one direction as Gray walked in the other direction. Occasionally, they crossed paths.

"If the two of you don't stop it, I'm going to tell Dash about that prank you pulled last month in Town," Archer said from where he relaxed in an oversized chair with a newspaper in his lap.

Gray's head snapped up. "You wouldn't dare."

"Try me," Archer gloated from his position. "Sit," he barked.

Gray dropped into a chair with a groan. Wes was still trying to remember which prank Archer might have in mind. Gray must have had a better recollection of recent events, since he seemed more than a little concerned about the threat.

"Sit," Archer growled again. He'd never been a very effective pack alpha. But he did try on occasion when Dash wasn't around.

Wes landed in the chair opposite his twin. Gray nudged Wes in the shin with the tip of his Hessian. "Do you have any idea why we've been summoned?" he asked beneath his breath.

But Wes had no clue and he shrugged his answer. After all, they hadn't done anything since yesterday. They hadn't had any time to get into trouble. For God's sake, the night before they'd been stuck at the lesser table with the Duchess of Hythe. They'd been on their best behavior with her looking down her hawkish nose at them all night. Maybe Archer had done something after he left the castle. But if so, there would be no reason for Wes and Gray to be summoned as well.

Then an unfamiliar floral scent caught Wes' attention. He lifted his nose in the air. "Who's here?" he asked.

Archer made a similar action and grimaced. "Oh, good God," he sighed beneath his breath.

Wes glanced at his twin. "Who do you know who smells like violets?"

"Lady Sophia." Gray smirked. "Which you would know if you could take your eyes or your snout off Lady Madeline for five seconds."

"I can't help it if Lady Madeline's rosewater overpowers everyone else in the room."

"Quiet," Archer growled. His head was cocked to the side, which indicated that he was trying his hardest to overhear a conversation in another part of the manor. "She's here for Cait," he finally said with a sigh, his body relaxing marginally as he lifted his paper and went back to reading.

"I sincerely doubt she's here for *Cait*," Wes said. "But you can delude yourself if you so choose."

"She just asked for Cait, you idiot," Archer growled. "That's a fairly good indication of her intent."

"And what was her intent when she trapped you in the parlor last night?" Wes raised his brow at his brother. Then he sat back and waited for Archer's reaction. He didn't have to wait long.

"And just what do you know of that?" Archer asked, his amber eyes narrowing as he laid his paper to the side.

Wes shrugged. "Not as much as you, apparently. But for some reason, the lady would like to get your bollocks in a vice. I feel certain she has a good reason."

"There are so many to choose from," Archer replied with a wolfish grin.

"She's a good friend of Lady Madeline's," Wes informed him. "You'd do well to leave her alone." He knocked his forehead with the heel of his hand. "I'll wager that's why we've all been summoned this morning. Because *you* somehow offended Lady Sophia, and now Lady Madeline has told the duchess. Who must have told Cait. And now we're all in for it. And it's your fault."

"I sincerely doubt that's why Dash called us all here at this ungodly hour," Gray said beneath his breath as he laid his head back and closed his eyes, as though the very thought of keeping them open for one second longer was much too taxing for him.

Wes kicked him in the shin. "Then why did he call us, if not because of something Archer did? You tell me that. You and I haven't done anything since the race."

"It could be something you did prior to the race," Archer reminded them both. "Sometimes it takes days for the news to get back to Dash."

"Not this time. *You've* offended Lady Sophia. And now we all have to pay," Wes ground out. "You should never have suggested she had nice assets with which she could bargain."

Gray's head bolted upright. He was suddenly

fully awake. "Did you ask Lady Sophia to be your mistress?" he barked with incredulity.

"God, no. Do I look like an idiot?" Archer replied.

"Well, if you must know…" Gray said drolly. Archer scowled at him again. "So, what *did* you do then?"

Wes felt compelled to interject. "I overheard your conversation with the lady when you spoke to her alone in the parlor last night. And I know she slapped you."

He had Gray's complete attention now as he sat forward. "The lady slapped you? I'd have paid good money to see that."

"If only you had any good money," Archer replied.

"Well, now you have enough for all of us, don't you?" Gray tossed back.

"If you think you're going to get your grubby little paws on *my* fortune," Archer growled, "Then you are sadly mistaken, pup."

"So you'd leave us all in poverty while you take Lady Sophia as your mistress?" Gray grumbled.

"I have no plans to do any such thing," Archer barked.

"She would never have you anyway," Wes put in. "Not if her response to being within a few feet of you was any indication. The lady would have scratched your eyes out as quickly as she'd have looked at you."

"I vaguely remember that evisceration was at the top of her list," Gray added.

A grin pulled at Wes' lips. "That wasn't on her list. But I bet if she heard the word, it would be. Perhaps we can plant the seed."

"Thank you both for helping her plan my demise."

Suddenly, the door flew open with such force that

all three men jumped to their feet. Their eldest brother stormed into the room as he raked a hand through his golden hair. For one so fair, he had a commanding presence. Particularly when he looked as though a storm cloud brewed above his head.

Dash stomped across the room and dropped into the chair behind his desk. He sorted through his correspondence for a few minutes without even looking up. Finally, Archer coughed into his closed fist and Dash looked up in a distracted motion.

"You sent for us," Archer stated quietly.

"I did," Dash agreed with a nod.

"We didn't do it," Gray began.

But Dash pursed his lips together and scowled at him. "Just what didn't you do this time?"

Gray's eyes danced toward Wes, as though looking for assistance. "Anything?" He shrugged.

Dash leaned back in his chair and templed his hands in front of his chest. "You expect me to believe that *you* didn't do anything? You've always just done something."

"Not today," Wes mumbled.

"The day just started," Dash reminded them.

"Indeed, it did," Wes muttered back.

"Why don't you get to the meat of the matter, Dash?" Archer finally said with a heavy sigh. "We're here. You requested our presence. We came readily, as any good pup is wont to do. Pray ease our torment by telling us what they did wrong." He gestured toward the twins with his head.

"Very well, if none of you have any misdeeds to confess…" Dash looked at each brother in turn for a

moment before continuing, "I've come to a decision."
He rummaged in his desk drawer.

"Would you care to share it with us?" Archer
asked, his tone flat and annoyed.

"I have decided to hire a governess."

"Aurelia is a tad small for a governess, wouldn't
you think?" Wes reminded him. The little lady was
still a baby.

"Not for her, you idiot," Dash growled. "For the
three of you."

Archer smiled wolfishly. "The last governess I had
was well worth the smack she gave me across my—"

But Gray cut him off. "Oh, God, Archer, I don't
want to hear about how the governess popped your
naked arse again," he cried.

Wes couldn't prevent the grin that tugged at his
lips. "But it's such a good story. It's not often one
meets a female with such…"

"Skills?" Archer suggested.

Wes shrugged. "Call them what you will."

"Will you all shut your mouths?" Dash bellowed as
he rose to his feet. "The whole lot of you has forced
my hand. We could have avoided this if you could
have maintained any sense of propriety. But, no, every
last escapade has gotten back to me or to Cait. And
if hearing about your exploits from her friends wasn't
enough, now you've put our children in danger, too."
Dash took a deep breath. "So my decision is final."

Wes glanced from Archer to Gray to Dash and
back. They all waited patiently.

"The lot of you is more than any one person can
manage. And Cait has her hands full. So, we've hired a

governess." At Archer's smirk, Dash stopped and said, "Not that kind of governess. The kind that has a knot of hair right here that's so tight her eyes are pulled tightly. The kind that has lips that turn down because they don't have any practice at staying upright. The kind that barks orders more powerfully than me." He took a deep breath and shuddered. "And I just met the woman. She makes me worry for all of you. But Cait thinks it's best."

"A *governess*?" Wes scratched his head. What on earth had their brother been doing hitting the whisky so early in the morning?

"A governess. A nanny. A tutor. A social coach. A nurse. A really old woman with a sour disposition. Call her what you will. But you *will* call her your very own until the three of you are fit to be in polite company." He heaved a sigh. "And I do mean very polite company."

Archer looked as confused as Wes and Gray did. That was good. Fortunately, he was the first one to speak. "Dash, I don't think—" he began.

"Precisely," their oldest brother drawled. "You *don't* think. None of you do. You act. You do foolish things. You embarrass us. You put our station in danger. Do you know that Cait wasn't invited to take tea at Lady Jersey's last season? And rumor has it that it's because of Cait's association with the three of you."

That made Wes' heart squeeze a little. He would never do anything to purposefully cause Cait harm. Why hadn't she said something earlier? Sally Jersey was nothing but a pinched-nosed old harridan with the sense of humor of an asp...

"So, from this day forward," Dash continued, "until *she* deems you fit to be released from her care, Miss Wigglesby will be the first person you look for in the morning and the last person you look for at night. She will arrange your social schedule. She will work with you on your manners. She will attend your social events with you. She will be your guiding hand in all things."

Wigglesby? Why did that name sound familiar? Wes scratched his chin. The answer was right on the tip of his tongue.

"I need a new servant like I need a hole in my head," Archer grumbled. That was true. Archer had just staffed several new residences, after all.

"Oh, she's not your servant. She's mine, at least until I return her to the Duchess of Hythe."

Wes' blood ran cold. Now he knew why the name sounded familiar. "Her Grace's companion?" An ancient ape-leader with the worst disposition, if Robert Hayburn was to be believed.

Dash nodded. "Indeed. But before that, she was governess to the duchess' children. And Her Grace guarantees Miss Wigglesby will be able to manage the three of you."

"The full moon is tonight. I hardly think we should bring someone new into the household," Gray protested.

"I disagree." Dash sat forward in his seat. "You need to behave no matter what the lunar cycle, Grayson."

"I'm a bloody peer, Dash!" Archer barked. "I'm not going to have some decrepit nursemaid follow me around Town."

Dash narrowed his eyes at Archer and growled low in his throat. No one in the room doubted which of the two Lycans was their pack alpha, and Archer's eyes dropped to the floor in submission.

"Now then," their oldest brother began, "I would tell you to all be on your best behavior, but I'd rather Miss Wigglesby see exactly what she's dealing with." He gestured to the doorway. "Let's adjourn to the green parlor to meet the woman, shall we?"

Wes and Gray exchanged a look, and they both sighed in unison. Certainly there had to be a way around the situation, but not at the moment. Not with Dash's current posturing, in any event. Wes started for the threshold, followed by his brothers.

He could faintly hear Cait and Lady Sophia engaged in polite conversation a few rooms away, but he was too focused on his own unfortunate future with Miss Wigglesby to pay much attention to his sister-in-law and her curious guest. A governess, for God's sake! The three of them were grown men! They couldn't walk around with a governess, and certainly not the prune-faced Miss Wigglesby.

They entered the green parlor to find the woman exactly as Dash had described. She was dressed in black, and the tight grey chignon at the nape of her neck made the ancient Miss Wigglesby's pointed features more pronounced. Her cloudy eyes raked across each brother before she turned her attention to Dash.

"I believe I can take it from here, Lord Eynsford." Though she was old, her voice had a taskmaster's bite.

Dash nodded in agreement, and then left Wes and the others to their new keeper. What a bloody awful day.

Miss Wigglesby pushed a pair of wire-rimmed spectacles up the bridge of her nose. "You," she looked at Gray. "Your neckcloth is a disgrace. Did your valet dress you in the dark? Or are you always so unkempt?"

Gray looked down at his usual cravat, then at Wes as though hoping for help. "Uh," he finally muttered in response.

"Lack of verbal skills, I see." The old woman harrumphed as she turned her gaze to Wes. "And what did you do to your face? You look as though you were in a dockside brawl."

Wes instinctively lifted his hand to his scarred cheek. He could tell the woman the truth about how he'd acquired his disfigurement, but he doubted she'd believe him. No one would believe such a story, and the telling of it would only land him a spot in Bedlam.

"What does that have to do with anything?" Archer snarled, shaking Wes from his thoughts. "Eynsford said you were to help guide us, not insult us."

"You, Lord Radbourne," the woman rose to her full height, which wasn't all that tall, "will not speak to me in such a tone."

Archer stepped closer to the governess. A menacing growl emanated from his throat. "I am Viscount Radbourne, and I will speak to you or anyone else any way I see fit. You, however, will not address my brothers in such a fashion. Weston can hardly do anything about his appearance, and your discussing such a thing shows your complete lack of breeding. I don't believe there is anything we can learn from you, Miss Wigglesby." He motioned toward the door with a fierce scowl. "You may return to Castle

Hythe and inform the duchess we have no need of your attention."

The governess' eyes did widen a bit and she placed her hand over her heart. "I am not here on your orders, my lord."

Archer laughed. "But you'll be leaving by them." He turned his back on her with the most dismissive move. "Good day, Miss Wigglesby," he tossed over his shoulder.

The old woman gasped. "Well, I never!"

"That's quite obvious," Archer remarked absently. "If you had, your countenance would be much more bendable." The woman needed a moment to realize that he referred to her bedchamber activity, but then she finally understood. Her face flushed scarlet. She frowned so deeply that her eyes pulled back even farther. She sputtered and started for the threshold, only to find Dash blocking her exit.

"Just what do you think you're doing?" Dash looked pointedly at Archer.

"Dismissing Miss Wigglesby."

Their oldest brother shook his head. "Perhaps I didn't make myself clear, Radbourne."

But it was no matter; Miss Wigglesby glared at Dash. "You assured me they would listen to me, my lord. It is clear they have no intention of doing any such thing."

"Oh, they'll listen to you."

She shook her head as she slid past him into the corridor. "I will not remain in an atmosphere of such disrespect, Lord Eynsford. They are hopeless."

Hopeless? She'd made that determination rather

quickly. Wes glanced at his brothers. What had she seen in the trio that would make her come to such a conclusion after just a few moments? Was there something so objectionable about them that she could see it immediately? If so, what was he missing? Was it his scar? There was nothing he could do to remove it. He'd tried. There was something about a vampyre scratch that simply refused to heal, even on one of his kind.

"I am too old," Miss Wigglesby tossed over her shoulder, "to waste my time on lost causes."

Dash stared after the woman, his mouth agape. Then he refocused on Wes and the others. "I'm certain you're proud of yourself, Archer. But this does not change my mind. I'll simply have to find someone with more fortitude. I had thought someone in Hythe's employ would have just that, however—"

"I believe I have the solution." Cait's lilting voice filtered into the room at the exact moment the scent of violets caught Wes' nose again.

Dash turned to find in his wife in the corridor with Lady Sophia at her side. He cleared his throat. "I am terribly sorry if we interrupted your tea, my dear."

"As luck would have it, Lady Sophia finds herself in need of employment." Cait linked her arm with the lady in question, and the two of them brushed past Dash into the parlor. "In fact, we are quite fortunate ta hire her before anyone else can get the chance. She is well traveled and well educated. Best of all, she assures me that Lord Radbourne does no' intimidate her."

Archer intimidated everyone. He'd just chased an old harpy from the room, for God's sake. "That's probably not a good idea, Cait," Wes said quietly.

Dash frowned almost as deeply as Archer and Gray.

"Lass, I—" Dash began, but Cait shook her head, successfully silencing him with just one look.

"I can *see* that this will work, Dashiel," Cait insisted.

Clearly, she'd lost her mind.

Their oldest brother's frown deepened as he searched his wife's face. "You can *see* it?"

"Aye," she agreed. "It's the perfect arrangement. Ye've got ta trust me on this."

It would be a complete disaster. Lady Sophia was their contemporary. Wes wanted to crawl under the nearest rock. The very last thing he needed was for Lady Madeline's friend to know he was being sent back to the schoolroom, for lack of a better term. He'd die of embarrassment.

"I've already asked Price ta send someone ta the castle to retrieve the lady's belongings. I'm sure he'll see ta Miss Wigglesby's safe return as well."

Dash looked at Lady Sophia. *Glared at her* was more like it. The lady simply straightened her spine and glared back at him. "Are you quite certain you know what you're in for, Lady Sophia?" Dash asked her.

Her voice didn't quaver a bit when she replied. "I believe I have a firm grasp of the challenges these young men face. And I also believe I can fulfill my duties."

Cait crossed the room and laid a hand on her husband's arm, then murmured to him, "It'll work out well, Dash. Trust me on this." Then very quietly she added, "I can see that this is the right position for her. For all of them. And she is in need of employment."

"She can do better than employment with these

scapegraces," he grumbled back. But then he rubbed his forehead, took a deep breath, and turned to Lady Sophia. "You're certain you want to take this on?"

"I'm positive," she replied.

Archer cursed beneath his breath from across the room.

"That will be enough of that, my lord," Lady Sophia warned. "While such language might be appropriate for you, it's not appropriate for the ladies present." She raised an eyebrow at Archer when he glared at her. He looked away with another curse when she didn't surrender.

Dash tossed his head back and laughed. He bent and kissed Cait swiftly, then addressed the group of them. "It appears as though it's all settled." Dash bowed to Lady Sophia. "Welcome to Eynsford Park, my lady."

Wes had to get out of the parlor. He had to leave The Park while he could still think, before the dire truth of his situation fully sunk in. "I, um, forgot I promised to go riding with Lord Robert this morning. Do excuse me." Then he bolted before anyone could order him to wait.

Six

My dearest Maddie,

As much as I am surprised to admit it, you were right. Lady Eynsford does have a solution to my problem. You were also correct in that she is quite cunning. I find myself a bit in awe of the lady and think I can learn much from her. I cannot, however, go into the details at the moment. For the foreseeable future, I will be staying here at Eynsford Park as the marchioness' special guest. Please wish me luck in my latest endeavor.

Always your friend,
Sophie

MADDIE READ THE NOTE AT LEAST HALF A DOZEN TIMES, trying to make sense of it. Sophie's things had already been packed by a maid and sent to Eynsford Park, so Maddie now found herself completely alone at Castle Hythe. Well, not *completely* alone. Her feckless suitors were all still ensconced safely within the castle walls. Perhaps it was time to reconsider stowing away to India to work with all of the elephants that were in need of training.

She let Sophie's letter flitter to her desk as she walked across her room to peer into the courtyard below. A number of gentlemen laughed as they tried to best each other at lawn bowling.

But then one of them caught her attention. Weston Hadley's hair shone in the sunlight. She couldn't help but smile. Perhaps he could give her a clue as to what Sophie was up doing at Eynsford Park. And she wouldn't have to fear being accosted by her father's guests. Not with Mr. Hadley among their numbers. One scowl from him would send the others scurrying away like the rats they were.

Maddie grabbed her shawl and ran down to the lower level of the castle. She tugged the muslin about her shoulders as she stepped outdoors. Within seconds, she was thronged by men. But the one she wanted leaned casually against a tree and paid her no mind. And she couldn't get close to him with the others in her way.

"Lady Madeline," Lord Dewsbury called. "Even the sun pales in comparison to your beauty," he pontificated. He pointed upward. "See, it refuses to compete with your radiance and has now ducked behind the clouds."

"Perhaps the sun is hiding from the smell of the onions you had at brunch," Maddie said beneath her breath. Then she looked at Lord Dewsbury and smiled her brightest smile.

"Beg your pardon, my lady?" Dewsbury asked. "I didn't quite hear you."

He'd heard her correctly if the look of devastation on his face and the way he breathed into his closed palm were any indication. But she was much too well trained in decorum to allow him to think he'd done so, even if his own breath did make him cringe. "I said the sun must be hiding from all the masculinity in the garden following brunch."

Mr. Hadley laughed loudly and shook his head. He looked as though he knew a secret no one else knew. She'd love to ask him what it was. If only she could get close enough to him. But he lounged there against the tree and paid her not even the smallest bit of attention. Blast him. She was surrounded by men that didn't matter, while her friend's life and future remained a mystery.

Lord Chilcombe held out a ball to her. "We'll begin a brand-new game for the lady," he informed the rest of the gentlemen.

She'd never get to talk to Mr. Hadley if her suitors didn't amuse themselves without her. She smiled brightly at the assembled men and said, "I would like to offer a boon to the winner. Perhaps a walk in the garden for the one who takes the prize?" She'd regret it later, but it was the only way to occupy them all. It was the only way to find out the truth about Sophie's circumstances.

The men scrambled to set the playing order for a series of new games. Luckily, so many men were assembled that it would take several rounds of play to find a winner. That might give her time to talk with Mr. Hadley. But then he moved to line up with the others. "Might I have a word with you, Mr. Hadley?" she asked. He stepped closer to her and she couldn't refrain from adding, "Certainly, you weren't you planning to line up with the others to compete."

He looked surprised and then uncomfortably resigned. "Certainly not," he said, his voice low and gravely, so quiet that only she could hear it. "With so many vying for your hand, I find myself in an impossible situation," he informed her with a quirk of his brow and a slow grin. "It would be a waste of time for me to line up with the others."

"You're not very good at lawn bowling?" she asked. She felt certain there was some underlying meaning behind his words. But she had no idea what it was.

"I'm an excellent shot," he boasted. "But you'd be wasting your time if you walked with me in the garden. And you don't seem to be the sort who likes to waste her time."

What he said was true, even if it did make her sound like the worst sort of snob. "I'm expected to make a brilliant match," she said.

"Don't sound so happy about it," he teased.

"Is it that obvious?" She tried not to let her distress show but was afraid she failed miserably.

"Almost as obvious as the onions Dewsbury had at brunch," he laughed.

She raised a hand to her mouth to cover her gasp. "You heard me?"

He tapped the shell of his ear. "It's one of my many faults. Excellent hearing." Then he smiled at her.

The man had the most amazing smile, and it made her belly flutter unexpectedly. "I don't believe excellent hearing is a fault," she informed him. "Not unless the one being heard was saying something unkind and assumed no one would be the wiser."

"Don't worry," he soothed. "Your secret is safe with me."

"You promise not to use it against me later?" She threw him her most winning smile.

His gaze moved across her face slowly, as though he could see much more than she wanted him to see. There was heat behind his stare. A heat she didn't fully understand but rather enjoyed. "I promise nothing of the sort."

After she caught her breath, she stammered, "Y-you do plan to use it against me?"

"Only in the most painless manner." He reached up to brush a lock of hair from her face. But instead, he wrapped it around his finger and tugged on the curl gently. "You're not used to being teased, are you?" His voice was silky soft, and he might as well have run his fingertips up her arm with the way the hair on her forearm stood on end at just the sound of his voice.

"Only by my brothers," she confessed. Being the daughter of a duke left her in a position where most were afraid to tease her. But that was obviously not the case with Weston Hadley. She glanced around the lawn, noted that most of the men were occupied with the game, and tugged her hair from his grasp. "I'll take that back now," she said with a grin.

"Pity," he said, his face taking on a wounded expression.

"Are you certain you don't want to play?" She was starting to think she might enjoy taking a walk with him, should he happen to be the winner. She'd enjoy it very much.

"I'm having much more fun talking to you now," he said.

Her heart skipped a beat.

≈

Wes was a fool to have come to Castle Hythe on the afternoon before a full moon. He'd assumed he'd find Rob and entice him into some folly or another. Not that he'd find Lady Madeline in all her glory. Nor that he'd touch her. He'd touched her hair, for God's sake. It felt like silk and he could imagine nothing more pleasurable than letting it trail between his fingers. Aside from having it trail across his naked body.

Her next question ripped him from his thoughts, however. "You wouldn't happen to know the fate of Lady Sophia, would you?"

Aside from the fact that she was his new nursemaid? "I'm not certain to what you're referring," he hedged.

Lady Madeline shook her head and stared off into the distance. "She left this morning to visit with Lady Eynsford, and now she has moved in at The Park. I got one cryptic note from her, but it didn't explain anything. Do you know what's happened?"

How much did they want Lady Madeline to know? He'd prefer that she not know any of it. "I believe she's in residence, yes," he said as enigmatically as possible.

"But why? I was perfectly happy having her here. She could have stayed at the castle forever and a day, and no one would have made her leave. Even with all the indecent proposals…" She let her voice trail off.

"She received a number of indecent proposals? From whom?" For some reason, the thought of anyone disrespecting Lady Sophia raised his hackles.

"My brothers. And probably the majority of those men over there." She glanced up at him from beneath lowered lashes.

Robert Hayburn was an arse, even if he was Wes' friend. And a fool. He had to know that suggesting such a thing to Lady Sophia would get back to his own sister.

Lady Madeline quietly cleared her throat. "You didn't happen to offer for her as well, did you?" Why did his response appear to be important to her?

Wes coughed into his fist to clear the discomfort from his throat. He had nothing to offer anyone of quality, not even the penniless Lady Sophia. "I believe I told you last night I had no intention of making her any sort of offer. I'd never dishonor her or you that way." Not to mention that with Lady Madeline constantly on his mind, there was little room for thoughts of anyone else. "I believe Cait found some sort of employment for her."

A pained expression crossed Lady Madeline's face. "It came to that, did it?" She sighed. "Employment, I mean. I had hoped Lady Eynsford had found a solution that wouldn't ruin Sophia's future."

The lady's future was definitely in peril if anyone learned she would be tutoring three grown men on decorum. Whether she received payment for her work would be inconsequential at that point. All of that was better left unsaid, however, as Lady Madeline looked on the verge of tears.

Wes wished he could make her smile once more, to erase the concern that creased her brow. How sweet she was to worry so about her friend. He wondered if Lady Sophia knew how fortunate she was to have garnered such loyalty and devotion from Lady Madeline. What he wouldn't give to have the lady care for him half as much. A quarter as much, even.

The idea was ludicrous. But it was true. He'd give everything he had, which wasn't all that much, just to experience her gentle touch. Even now, in the safety of her courtyard, with a throng of her suitors within sight, he had the urge to pick her up, toss her over his shoulder, and abscond with her into the forest. But within a few hours, he'd turn into the beast that resided in his soul. And Lady Madeline had no idea of what he was at heart. Nor would she be pleased to find out.

"What are you thinking about?" she asked.

"You," he blurted without thinking.

Her heartbeat sped up at his admission. He could hear it in his head. Then she licked her lips. Good God, he could think of such wonderful things to do with those lips.

"You were thinking of me?" She laid a dainty little hand upon her chest.

Only since the night he'd first met her. Wes shook his head. "I, um, I was wondering which of those fellows would win your boon."

Lady Madeline looked over her shoulder toward the competitors just in time to see Lord Gelligaer's run shot knock all of the other bowls away from the jack, finally stopping in a prime spot. She shivered slightly. "I just hope it's not him."

Wes started to reach his hand out to soothe her but realized at the last moment how inappropriate such an action would be and clasped his hands behind his back. God, he was hopeless. Lady Sophia would certainly have her hands full trying to make a proper gentleman out of him, if such a thing was even possible. He glanced back across the courtyard lawn at the Welsh earl. "I hope not, either," he admitted. "Be careful of the man either way, my lady."

Her green eyes settled on Wes, so sincere, so trusting that she nearly took his breath away. "Do you know something about his lordship, Mr. Hadley?"

Wes was enough of a gentleman to know that repeating tales to the lady of Gelligaer's opium dependency was far from proper. Besides, the Welshman had returned from the Peninsular Wars a different man, and though Wes had been too young to serve in the army he understood that certain horrors could change a person. Perhaps Gelligaer's habit stemmed from his years on the battlefield. Or perhaps he was simply a weak-willed man. Either way, Gelligaer wasn't for Lady Madeline. "I just don't believe he is the sort you would be happy with."

"I'm certain you're correct."

"Ah!" the Marquess of Lavendon exclaimed across the courtyard. "You *are* still here, Hadley. Brilliant."

Of course he was still at the castle. Wes certainly wasn't about to return to Eynsford Park, not now at any rate. This was his last day of freedom, after all. He nodded at Lady Madeline's oldest brother. "I thought I could take you for another hundred quid, Lavendon."

As it was, his wager with the marquess this morning had put a nice bundle in Wes' pocket.

"Wagering so early in the day, Nathaniel?" his sister asked, her brow furrowed in disapproval.

The marquess chuckled. "How is one to pass the time, Maddie, if one doesn't wager? Especially as Lady Sophia has abandoned us for Eynsford Park." He pretended to pout.

"I'm certain any number of things *should* have your attention," Lady Madeline replied primly.

Lavendon ignored her jibe and focused his attention on Wes. "You must stay and give me the opportunity to win back my blunt."

"My blunt now." He couldn't help but grin.

"You are just like Radbourne," the marquess complained without heat.

Wes snorted. "Please tell me I'm not as bad as all that."

"You may be worse." Lavendon laughed again. "Very well, if you won't allow me to win back my own money, help me fleece the others, will you?"

Lady Madeline sucked in a breath.

Wes glanced at her briefly. He'd rather not have her think badly of him, but refusing Lavendon wasn't wise. He couldn't hope to hide out at the castle on this, his last day of freedom, if the marquess was put out with him. "What do you have in mind?"

Lavendon smirked. "Just a little game of whist this evening after dinner. I'd prefer a ruthless partner I can trust over one of those sycophants angling for Maddie's hand."

And Wes would like to fatten his pockets even more, taking what he could from the gentlemen who were deemed worthy by the Duke of Hythe to seek

his daughter's hand. There was something very satisfying about the idea of taking the lot for all they were
worth. "I look forward to it."

"Honestly, Nathaniel, have you no shame?" Lady
Madeline hissed.

The marquess sighed as though he was the most
put-upon fellow in all of Kent. "If I wanted a woman
to flay me whenever she opened her mouth, I'd get
myself a wife. Now run along, love. You've got a
horde of lords on the green about to climb over each
other for your favor."

Without another word, the lady spun on her
heel in a huff and stomped off toward the throng of
gentlemen waiting their turns with their bowls. Wes
almost winced at the loss of her company, but there
was nothing to be done for it. Wishing he was part of
her circle would never make it so.

Maddie found herself furious with Sophie most of
the day. How dare her friend abandon her to a castle
full of men with more hair than wit? She'd had to
suffer a stroll in the garden with the Earl of Steadham
who seemed incapable of answering a question using
more than one syllable. Then she'd once again been
placed beside the strange Earl of Gelligaer at dinner.
And she'd been forced to play the pianoforte for the
gentlemen who were not interested in playing whist
with her brothers and Mr. Hadley. She hadn't even
had Grandmamma's reliable acidic tongue to rely
on, as the duchess had taken to her bed with a fever
that afternoon.

No. Maddie had been completely alone in a castle full of... what had Nathaniel called them? Ah yes, sycophants angling for her hand.

If only Sophie hadn't taken up residence at Eynsford Park, this abysmal excuse for a house party could have been bearable. Well, almost. Some people simply weren't to be tolerated, and Castle Hythe was filled to the brim with them at the moment.

Maddie couldn't have excused herself and escaped to the safety of her room any faster if she'd sprouted wings and flown there. But when she reached her chambers, she found herself doing nothing more than pacing, which did nothing to calm her nerves. After the hundredth pass across her Aubusson rug, she decided a change in scenery was needed. A change of scenery or she'd wear a hole in her floor.

Soon she found herself in the gallery, staring at various portraits of the late Dukes and Duchesses of Hythe. She gazed up at the oldest portrait in the hall, which was of the very first Duke of Hythe. The depiction showed the stoic eleventh-century knight who had crossed the channel along with his good friend William the Conqueror. Tales of the first duke's loyalty and bravery on the battlefield had been passed from one generation to the next. As children, Robert and Nathaniel had brandished wooden swords and taken turns pretending to be their great ancestor. Such simpler times, when they were children.

She left the first duke and made her way down the gallery, finally stopping at her grandfather's portrait. Maddie sighed at the sight of him, strong and virile but relaxed in a chair the color of deep claret. How she missed Grandpapa. Kind and gentle, the exact opposite of Grandmamma in so many ways. "I do wish you were here," she muttered to the painting.

If he was there, she could just imagine the guidance he'd give. *Before you can decide what to do, you need to know where you are.* She'd heard him offer that same advice to Nathaniel countless times.

So where was she? Maddie began to tick her thoughts off on her fingers.

One: She was all alone now that Sophie had taken employment at Eynsford Park. Maddie certainly couldn't trouble Sophie with her problems when her friend had so many of her own.

Two: Her father had her ensconced in a household of men who wanted nothing more than her fortune. Although with the way Lord Chilcombe's gaze raked across her breasts every time he spoke to her, *he* obviously wanted more than just her money. The very thought made her want to cast up her accounts.

Three: Lord Gelligaer made her more uneasy than anyone at the castle. Also, he was clearly not favored well by Mr. Hadley, and Maddie's intuition told her Mr. Hadley knew something fairly disturbing about the Welshman. Whatever the secret was, Maddie needed to learn of it if she was to convince her father to scratch the earl off his list of potential suitors. How could she get Mr. Hadley to divulge such information?

"You would know what to do," she said to her grandfather's image. "Of course, you wouldn't have put me in this situation to begin with."

Maddie crossed to the row of windows lining the

gallery and gazed out at the full moon, which sat low in the sky. Night had barely fallen and shadows hung like heavy veils over the spacious land below. But then she noticed a glowing ember as it moved across a stone path toward the stables. A cheroot, perhaps? It had to be, but the stable hands knew better than to smoke near the stables. Grandmamma had put the fear of God in them about such behavior soon after the stables at Eynsford Park went up in a blaze.

Maddie strained her eyes to see the culprit and gasped as the cheroot-smoking gentleman stepped from the shadows into a spot of moonlight. His hair glimmered like freshly polished brass in the darkness.

Think of the devil!

Mr. Hadley tossed the cheroot to the ground and crushed it with his boot heel. He turned his face up to the moon and spread his arms. His strong jaw and broad shoulders were made even more prominent by the deep shadows. But then Mr. Hadley spun quickly to face the other direction.

Another man approached, drenched in shadows, and Mr. Hadley took a step back, raising his hands to fend off the interloper. There was something odd about the interaction, almost as though Mr. Hadley was trying to appease his companion. If only she could recognize the other fellow!

Her own gasp broke the silence of the gallery when Mr. Hadley ducked to avoid the stranger's fist. Mr. Hadley was quick, however, and the other man simply stumbled forward.

Good heavens! Maddie pressed her face closer to the window, trying to make certain Mr. Hadley hadn't been hurt, but he seemed no worse for wear. In fact, he even smiled at his foe in an obvious attempt to calm him. But then the stranger swung his fist again. This time, Mr. Hadley blocked the blow with his forearm and landed a punch solidly across the man's jaw. The fellow, whoever he was, sank like an anvil dropped from a great height. Mr. Hadley glanced around cautiously, as though making certain no one had seen the altercation.

Then he bent and hoisted the man over his shoulder with what appeared to be no effort at all. Maddie had no idea how strong Mr. Hadley was, but he seemed not to even notice the weight of the other fellow. She strained again, trying to see the unconscious man's face, but he was hidden well by Mr. Hadley's broad form before they disappeared into the shadows once again.

Where on earth was he going?

Perhaps he meant to dispose of his foe and return to the others playing cards. Perhaps this was exactly the kind of leverage she needed to persuade Mr. Hadley to tell her the truth about Lord Gelligaer. She just needed to reach him before he rejoined the others.

Maddie bolted from the gallery and down a flight of stone steps, not stopping until she reached the drawing room where her brothers were entertaining their guests with whist.

As she stood sentry, waiting for Mr. Hadley to make his appearance, Robert stepped out of the room and scowled at her. "You shouldn't be down here."

Why did she have to run into Robert? Nathaniel wouldn't have barked at her as soon as he laid eyes on her. "I live here. Besides, the last time I was addressed

on the matter, this house party was for *me*." She
purposefully raised her nose in the air.

"And *you* were dismissed from your duties as hostess
two hours ago. Since you were, many of these men
are no longer fit company for you. Not tonight." He
turned her by her shoulders and gave her a small push.
"Go to bed."

"But," she began, feeling as ineffectual as a child.

"But, nothing," Robert scolded. "If you go in
there, I'll be forced to defend your honor when one of
them makes a wrong move. You don't want my death
on your head, do you?"

Maddie rolled her eyes. "I could only be so fortunate," she replied, refusing to budge. "Mr. Hadley,"
she started. "I saw him—"

"You would do well to stay clear of *him*." Robert
narrowed his eyes at her. "You don't fancy Hadley,
do you, Maddie?"

How ridiculous. Of course, she didn't. "Is he still
here?"

"You didn't answer my question. Tell me I'm not
going to have call out a good friend, Madeline."

"What question?" Honestly, did Robert ever make
any sense?

"Weston Hadley. Tell me you don't fancy him."

Maddie scoffed. "Don't be a fool, Robert. I only
wished to speak with him." Perhaps blackmail him
into giving her needed information.

"About?" Her brother seemed less than convinced,
which was more than a little maddening.

She certainly wasn't going to tell Robert what
she wanted with Mr. Hadley. "Sophie, if you must

know." Maddie waited until her brother winced to continue. "I simply wanted to make certain she was getting along well at Eynsford Park after being treated so shabbily here."

She hit her target rather well and Robert took a step back toward the drawing room, recoiling from her unspoken accusation.

"Has Mr. Hadley left for the evening?" Maddie pressed.

Robert nodded sullenly. "Yes, and none too soon. He took Chilcombe for all he's worth. Hope he makes it home without being accosted."

Chilcombe. Was that who she'd seen Mr. Hadley haul into the darkness? And all on account of card playing? And Mr. Hadley hadn't returned. What on earth would he do with the earl? And which one should she worry about?

Lord Chilcombe appeared to be unconscious, heaven knew where. But in her heart, she was much more concerned about Mr. Hadley, should anyone discover he'd clocked the earl after fleecing him, to use Nathaniel's words. After all, it was no secret that Mr. Hadley wasn't regarded well by the gentlemen of her father's house party. In fact, all the Hadleys, including Lord Radbourne, were bad *ton.* They were marginally accepted at functions because of Lady Eynsford's devotion to the trio, but something of this nature could destroy what shred of goodwill the Hadleys still maintained in society.

"I suppose I'll have to ask him tomorrow then," Maddie mumbled, then started back in the direction from which she'd come.

As soon as she was certain Robert had returned to their guests in the drawing room, Maddie bolted around a corner toward the garden entrance, thankful her kid slippers made no sound. She rushed outside into the chilly garden and started toward the last place she'd seen Mr. Hadley from the gallery window, the path leading to the stables. Perhaps he was still there.

Maddie lifted the hem of her skirts and dashed across the dew-dampened ground, lit by the full moon above, and didn't stop until she reached the stables, which were mercifully void of any grooms at the moment. Of course, the houseguests were so deep in their cups that not a single one of them would be calling for a mount any time soon.

As soon as Maddie reached the stables, the odor of horses and hay hit her nose like rancid smelling salts. The darkness pressed in around her like a heavy counterpane. Not a single light broke the quiet night, but then a match flared as she heard someone shuffle. Maddie stepped farther into the shadows and pressed her back against the wall.

Seven

Wes cursed loudly as he dropped Chilcombe's inert body to the stable floor and looked around the cavernous room. Over the past few days, he'd daydreamed of ridding England of the obnoxious gentleman, but he hadn't planned to have to haul the earl's body around on the night of the full moon. Already, the power of the moon tugged at his senses. His ears itched to elongate and his snout tingled, anxious to grow long and pointy.

Typically, Wes loved the pain of changing, but tonight, he'd lingered a bit too long beyond nightfall. But he'd figured that arrogant earl and his inept partner couldn't possibly have better cards than his or Lavendon's. The earl certainly hadn't had one all night. Wes hoisted Chilcombe beneath his arms and dragged his body into a stall. The earl would remember Wes hitting him in the morning and then there would be hell to pay, if not from Chilcombe then from Dash when he learned of the altercation.

As Wes straightened and stepped from the stall, the itch of his ears and the tingle of his nose turned to an ache. The moon would take him whether he wanted it to or not. He unbuttoned his jacket and shrugged it from his shoulders. Then he proceeded to disrobe right there in the stables. After all, where else could he go? He'd waited too long to leave as it was. Wes folded his clothes and tucked them into the corner of a stall. He'd come back for them in the morning.

A shaft of moonlight filtered in through the loft and Wes stepped into it, allowing the moonbeams to caress his naked body. The shift from man to beast began, claiming all of his attention. It wasn't until he stood on four feet that he looked up and saw *her* standing there in the shadows. Her face was as pale as the moon, and she'd certainly fall over from the lack of air in her lungs any moment if she didn't run screaming first. It was too bad she chose the latter.

Lady Madeline didn't just scream. She had to scream loudly enough to shake the rafters and wake anyone in Kent who was sleeping. The horses in the stalls began to shuffle and prance, the noise was so deafening. It made his own sensitive ears hurt from the very shrillness of it. He approached her slowly, wishing with all his heart that he could say something to calm her.

She backed toward the door and leaned heavily against it, then cursed beneath her breath when it didn't open at her frantic shove. Who'd have thought such a delicate lady could have such a curse word in the recesses of her mind, waiting for the day she'd have cause to use it? Planted there for the very day she met a Lycan like him. Wes snorted.

She held up one hand out in front of her, as though she could will him away with just that simple gesture. On a normal day, she probably could. But not today. "Don't hurt me," she whispered, her voice cracking as she groped behind her for the door handle.

I won't hurt you, he wanted to say. *I'll explain everything as soon as the moon recedes and the sun comes up. I promise.* Not that the truth would put her any more at ease.

A little squeak left her throat as he took a step closer, and her hand on the handle became more frantic. Thank God that door was too heavy for such a little slip of a lady to push it open. Then he heard the latch click and cringed. Tiny Lady Madeline shoved with all her might and tumbled backward out of the door. She landed in a heap of skirts and immediately jumped to her feet. He wanted to call to her, to tell her not to panic. But he *was* a Lycan, for God's sake. He walked on four feet. He had no voice. He had no way to soothe her. If he was on two feet, he could grab her in his arms. He'd hold her and tell her everything would be all right.

He'd never felt more helpless in his life.

She took two quick steps back and he stepped forward. She cringed and cried out. Then she turned on her heel and ran. Oh, blast and damn. Of course, she'd run. This had to be difficult. He couldn't call out to her. He couldn't do anything. But one thing he absolutely could not do was allow her to go back to the castle. One word of what she'd just witnessed would put his entire family in danger. In fact, just being out in the open the way they were was dangerous enough.

Someone else could see them, come to her rescue. Then he'd be done for.

Wes went after her, hoping to stop her before she could reach the castle.

She tripped on the hem of her dress and tumbled to her bottom. What a stroke of luck for Wes, though he hated to see her in such a state. He stood before her on four legs when a heavy drop of rain landed on the top of his head. Wes glanced up at the moon that had winked at him so playfully only a half hour before to find it was now obscured by dark clouds. Dark clouds that intended to open up and drench them any moment.

Lady Madeline swiped a drop of rain from her cheek. Or was that a tear? Good God, he'd never forgive himself if that was a tear. Wes sat down and tilted his head, watching her quietly. Perhaps if he sat very still, she'd calm and he could… He could what? He could send her mental messages? Pigs would sooner fly. The only mental message she got from him was that he was a dangerous wolf. Wes snorted again.

The sound must have frightened her, because she scrambled back to her feet and bolted for the castle, screaming once more. Wes quickly outpaced her, thank God, and he circled around her like the best little herding dog there ever was. She stopped when he got in front of her. He couldn't allow her to reach the castle. One of two things would happen if he did— either she'd be called the worst sort of idiot or they'd send a watch out to find the rabid wolf that threatened the lady. Neither of those scenarios was acceptable.

"P-please." She took an awkward step toward the castle.

Wes growled low in his throat. What else was he to do? He was a wolf, for Christ's sake. Never had life been more unkind. She stopped where she stood. Keeping a wary eye on him, she tried another hesitant step. He growled again and she halted once more.

Her gaze flashed toward the castle when he heard a rustling by the garden gate. "Did you hear something?" a voice asked. *Gelligaer.*

Oh, damn it to hell! Curse his bad fortune. If Wes wasn't in Lycan form, he'd drop his head in his hands and sob. As it was, all he could do was whimper. Lady Madeline's eyebrows pushed together at the noise. Wonderful. She even sent him curious glares when he was a bloody wolf.

"I didn't hear anything," answered another voice from the garden.

Lady Madeline opened her mouth to call out, but Wes couldn't allow that, could he? He growled low in his throat, advancing upon her until her lovely peach skin turned pale white with fear.

The footsteps from the garden grew closer.

Lady Madeline inhaled deeply, as though she wanted to scream but couldn't find her voice. Another menacing growl escaped Wes, one that caused the lady to pale even further. But at least she closed her mouth.

The voices moved even closer. What the devil was Wes to do now? He couldn't leave her for Gelligaer and his companion to find, not when she knew Wes' secret. She'd put his entire family in jeopardy if she blathered about it.

He could knock her down and drag her into the

safety of the forest. But that would be a most ungentlemanly move. He couldn't imagine getting Lady Madeline dirty, for God's sake. She was always perfect, although she looked a little bedraggled at the moment, with her hair soaked from what was now a pouring rain. He could do it with ease, but the very thought of knocking her off her feet made his heart hurt.

Instead, Wes did what came naturally. He raised his tail, postured, and growled. He slowly walked toward her, forcing himself to make his steps measured and menacing. It was the furthest thing from what he'd ever imagined doing to her. But his desperation from this dreadful situation left him little choice. Wes growled his most menacing growl and raised his lip. She looked like she would swoon any moment. God, he hated this, but even through the rain, Gelligaer was approaching them. Wes snapped his teeth at her, the clatter surprising even him.

Finally, she turned and ran in the direction he herded her, into the forest.

❦

Maddie's blood ran cold when the wolf snapped his teeth at her. Blast it! They were now too far from the castle for her to cry for help. Why had she let him push her into the forest when she'd been so close to home? His sharp teeth did have something to do with that. If only she'd been a hoyden, she could have tried to scale one of the forest trees, but she'd never been a climber and she doubted her sodden kid slippers would be much help with a tree trunk.

Heavens, she was nearly out of breath!

Maddie ran, with the wolf at her feet, his gait long and lupine, his pace slow and methodical, his footfalls soft and quiet. Periodically, he would shift from one side to another, forcing her to change her path. The trees and bushes, heavy with rain, clutched at her clothes and hair. The run was nothing more than play for the wolf. For *Mr. Hadley*? Certainly she'd been mistaken and Mr. Hadley hadn't turned into a wolf in front of her very eyes! But he had, hadn't he? The idea was too ludicrous to believe.

Off in the distance, Maddie saw a light glowing through the trees. A beacon of hope. If she could just reach the light, there had to be some human nearby, didn't there?

Suddenly, the wolf growled, and he darted out in front of her. He didn't want her to reach the light, apparently. Well, Maddie would gladly return home. She turned in that direction and began to run, but then she felt a tug at the back of her gown.

He'd caught her!

The snarling beast had his teeth sunk into her skirts. Still, Maddie fought, struggling to free herself. She would not give up without a fight. But then she felt him touch her shoulders and he shoved, toppling her to the ground with him on top of her. Dear heavens! A *wolf* had her pinned to the forest floor.

"Don't say a word," a low voice growled in her ear.

Mr. Hadley! She recognized his voice, which didn't exactly soothe her fears. She just wasn't mad. At least she didn't think she was.

"Let me go," she managed to squeak out. She squirmed beneath him, the soft forest floor wet beneath her hands.

"That was three words, Lady Madeline," he said.

Maddie glanced over her shoulder and barely made out her attacker's face in the darkened forest. It *was* Mr. Hadley! Scar and all.

"And don't move," he ordered.

But Maddie couldn't move if she wanted to. His body was pressed down the length of hers from shoulder to toes. He was much warmer than the ground she lay on. She groaned her response.

"Dear God." He rested his head on her shoulder. "What am I to do with you?"

"Let me up?" she suggested.

"If you'd stop talking, I could think."

But that seemed the wrong thing to do. If she could keep him from figuring out what to do with her, perhaps she could escape. "I won't tell anyone," she promised. "Just let me go home."

He sighed heavily. "Why did you have to be in the stables?" He sounded truly pained. "Dash will have me drawn and quartered for this."

Lord Eynsford knew that Mr. Hadley was capable of turning into a wolf? Then it was the marquess' fault for allowing the beast to roam around the countryside, but Maddie didn't think voicing such a thing was to her benefit. "I'll never tell him."

"It's too late. You already know." He groaned as though the words were ripped from his soul. "Dear God. You know."

"I–I don't know anything." And, truly she didn't.

What was she to know? That one of Robert's friends was able to transform to a wolf? That was insanity, She wouldn't have to worry about being leg-shackled to Lord Gelligaer or one of the others. She'd find herself in a dark room in Bedlam if she muttered any such thing aloud.

"Stop talking," he grumbled.

Maddie sank deeper into the muddy forest floor. "Please, Mr. Hadley, I'm freezing. Please just let me up."

"You're cold?" he asked, surprise lacing his voice.

Of course *he* was as warm as a stoked fire in winter. Maddie nodded. "I can't run any farther, if that's what you're worried about." She could run all the way to London, if he'd just let her go.

"W-well," he hedged. "The problem... I just..."

Heavens! Why wouldn't he just spit it out and help her up? "Mr. Hadley, please!"

"I-I don't have any clothes with me." The words came rushing out of his mouth.

Of course she knew that part. She'd seen him in the stables, naked as the day he was born, right before he sprouted a tail and snout. Who would think such a creature would be squeamish about nudity? He'd turned into an actual *wolf*, for heaven's sake. There were much bigger issues than the lack of his clothing.

Maddie tried to edge her way out from underneath him, but he was so large, so heavy. "If you let me up, I'll give you my shawl." Not that the drenched muslin would cover him, but while he tied it around his waist, she could make a run for it.

"Very well," he agreed, though he didn't sound pleased.

Maddie wasn't pleased either, not with any part of this terrible night. Not watching a man actually turn into a ferocious animal. Not running for at least a mile in sodden shoes while being growled at by the ferocious animal. And not being crushed into the mud by the very same ferocious animal, though at the moment he *was* a man, wasn't he?

Mr. Hadley slowly rose to his feet. "Can you hand it to me, without… turning around?"

Maddie pushed up on her elbows and pulled the sopping muslin from her shoulders. Then she wadded it up in a ball and tossed it in his direction, though a bit more forcefully than was needed.

As Mr. Hadley turned around to retrieve the shawl, Maddie knew her best chance of escape had come and she couldn't let it pass. Her very life might depend upon it. So she scrambled to her feet and dashed toward the glowing light in the distance. After all, the light, wherever it was, had to be closer than Castle Hythe. "Help!" she called.

"Damn it to hell!" Mr. Hadley yelled somewhere behind her.

But not far enough away for Maddie's comfort. Why hadn't she thrown the shawl even harder?

Maddie pushed through the trees, hoping beyond hope she could reach help before he was on her again. But he was much faster than she was, and within only a moment or two, he caught her about the waist and both of them tumbled once again to the forest floor.

"Get off me!" she demanded, as he rose above her, his head limned by the light of the moon.

"I thought you couldn't run any farther."

"I lied." She squirmed beneath him, managing to slide from beneath him a bit. Mud squished against her back. He reached for her skirts, as though by constraining her legs, he thought to constrain her. Maddie kicked at Mr. Hadley with every ounce of strength she had and heard a very satisfying curse when her foot found his nose.

An inhuman growl escaped him, echoing through the night, terrifying Maddie even more than she had been. Heavens, she'd broken his nose. Would he break her now in return?

Mr. Hadley grabbed her skirts and dragged her back beneath him. "Be still!" he ordered.

She got a good glance at his face in the moonlight. His nose was most assuredly broken, as it looked crooked on his face. Between his nose and the scar on his cheek, he appeared the most fearsome creature of nightmares.

"Please just let me go home. I'll never tell a soul anything I've seen."

He scoffed. "Am I to take the word of a professed liar?"

Maddie winced. That might not have been the smartest thing to confess a moment ago. She wasn't quite certain what to say to convince him otherwise.

He looked pained all of a sudden. "You can't run off. Not until we sort this out."

What was there to sort out? Maddie just wanted to wake up in her bed and forget all about this awful dream. "What do you want me to say?"

"Hush!" he ordered and clamped his hand over her mouth.

A moment later, a man broke through the trees and

stood just a foot away from them. "Oh, dear God," the man breathed.

"Renshaw?" Mr. Hadley winced. "What the devil are you doing here?"

Who in the world was Renshaw? Better yet, would he help Maddie out of this predicament?

The new fellow, Renshaw, cursed under his breath. "Ever since he met her, my life has been turned upside down. But there's no way in hell, I'm getting drawn into *this*."

"Beg your pardon?" Mr. Hadley asked.

Renshaw shook his head in what seemed like frustration. "Her ladyship has lost her fool mind if she thinks I'm getting involved in some madcap scheme."

"Cait sent you?" Mr. Hadley loosened his grip on Maddie. "Why the devil would Cait send you *here*?"

Renshaw swore again. "She said you'd be in need of a driver. She didn't say anything about needing clothes or the defiling of women."

A driver. That's where Maddie knew Renshaw from. He was Lord Eynsford's driver. Why did the marchioness send a driver out to find them? How did she know they were even lost?

"The lady is hardly defiled." Mr. Hadley frowned. "Tell me, did Cait happen to mention a destination?"

"Gretna," the driver complained. "Certainly wouldn't be the first time she's made me dash across Britain as though the devil chased me."

"Gretna?" Mr. Hadley echoed as he scratched his chin. But then a look of resignation overtook his features. He sighed heavily and nodded. "That is a very good plan, actually," he said. Then he rose to his feet, in all his naked splendor, and reached a hand to Maddie. "Come along, my lady."

Maddie could only gape at him, at *all* of him, standing before her. And then his words began to sink in. Gretna? Certainly he didn't think to elope with her! "No, no, no." She shook her head. "I'm going home. I'm not headed to Scotland."

Without another word, Mr. Hadley bent at his waist and plucked Maddie out of the mud. Then he tossed her over his naked shoulder. "Lead on, Renshaw. Time is of the essence."

A beleaguered sigh escaped the driver. He shook his head and then turned back toward the way he'd come through the woods.

He couldn't take her to Scotland against her will. "Take me back to Castle Hythe!" Maddie yelled at the driver. "Do you know who I am?"

"I'm sure he doesn't care," Mr. Hadley remarked.

"My grandmother will have your head!" Maddie threatened. "*The Duchess of Hythe* will have your head!"

"Indeed she will," Mr. Hadley agreed, "*if* she catches us. Therefore, I suggest you drive your team as far and fast as they'll go, Renshaw."

The driver nodded, the cluck of his tongue the only noise as he tromped across the forest floor.

Hanging upside down, Maddie spied the glowing light she'd seen earlier. The farther they walked, the brighter the light shone until she was finally able to see that it was a lantern on the side of the Eynsford traveling coach. If she had managed to escape from Mr. Hadley, she would have run right into the arms of the coachman and still not have been any better off than she was at this moment. What a lowering thought.

The driver opened the coach door as though he was preparing to take them to a formal soiree or ball. "I'll see you hanged for kidnapping," Maddie vowed.

"Fast as you can," Mr. Hadley directed to the driver as he placed Maddie on a coach bench.

"Of course. It's always 'fast as you can,'" the coachman complained. "There's a travel blanket inside, sir. You probably should use it."

Maddie glanced at Mr. Hadley's very naked person. Certainly he didn't think to ride anywhere with her like *that*. "You're naked," she blurted, as heat crept up her face. But she suddenly couldn't take her eyes off his broad shoulders. She was quite intrigued by the light dusting of hair across his chest. And then her gaze traveled lower, to a narrow line of hair that went from his navel down to his...

"Yes, I'm naked. How very observant of you." Mr. Hadley stepped inside the coach and settled on the opposite bench. "And if you don't stop looking at me like that, I'll take you up on the offer your gorgeous little eyes are making." He smirked at her from across the coach.

Maddie covered her eyes with both hands as the coach door closed. Good heavens! How in the world had she gotten herself into this situation?

She heard him moving about on the other side of the carriage as the conveyance lurched forward. What was he up to? Looking for rope to bind her wrists? Or a knife to hold to her throat? Maddie peeked at him through her fingers. The coach lantern swung outside the door, making shadows dance around the interior. Still she couldn't clearly see what was transpiring on the opposite side. "What are you doing?"

His gaze flicked to her across the coach. "Renshaw said there was a travel blanket." Apparently, having found it, he raised it for her inspection. "You may have it, or under the circumstances, I'll make use of it myself, if it would make you more comfortable."

A strangled laugh escaped Maddie's throat. "Under the circumstances?" she echoed, incredulity lacing her words. "What circumstance would that be, Mr. Hadley? The fact that you are a wolf? The fact that you're kidnapping me? Or the fact that we are headed to Scotland and you don't possess a stitch of clothing? Pray tell me which circumstances you are referring to."

Eight

WES SPREAD THE TRAVEL BLANKET ACROSS HIS LAP AND
let the end fall across his bare legs. What a god-awful
evening. Lady Madeline couldn't even look at him.
And what was he doing? Racing for the Scottish
border before her brothers could catch them. And
then what? He couldn't force her to marry him. He
wouldn't want to even if he could.

Of course he'd adored her since the first moment
he saw her, three long years ago. He'd dreamed about
sharing her bed since that very evening. But not like
this. Not kidnapping her and eloping, for God's sake.

But what other choice did he have? Once they
were married, her future would be tied to his. She
couldn't tell anyone what he was. If she did, she'd be
known as the wolf's wife, and that would never do
for a Hayburn. Cait was right, though how she knew
what he needed at the exact moment he needed it was
a complete mystery.

Across the carriage, Lady Madeline swiped a tear
from her cheek. There was no doubt, this time, that
her tears were most assuredly his fault.

"I'm sorry," he offered lamely. But he truly was sorry.

Her eyes widened in surprise, and she sat forward on her bench. "Your nose."

What an odd response to his apology. "My nose?"

"It was crooked." She leaned closer to him. "I-I broke it when I kicked you."

Ah, yes, that he remembered clearly. "I suppose I deserved it."

"Indeed." She nodded. "But it doesn't look crooked anymore. I was certain I broke it."

Wes grinned despite himself. Then he wiggled his nose back and forth with his finger. "All fixed. Not to worry."

"How is that possible?"

"One of my many talents. I heal quickly. So if you're planning on doing me any more bodily harm, you should reconsider. It will only make me angry."

"You heal quickly?" She sat back against the leather squabs. "What *are* you, Mr. Hadley?"

There it was: the question he'd never thought to answer, at least not from her. After all, Lycans lived by a strict code. And one of the covenants was not to reveal the nature of one's beast to any human, with the exception of one's mate. Which, of course, was exactly what Lady Madeline would become. He might as well confess the truth to her. Perhaps it would help her accept their fate more easily. "I'm a Lycan."

"I beg your pardon?" She scrunched up her perfect little nose.

"A Lycan, a werewolf," he explained.

"A werewolf," she echoed under her breath, as if the entire idea was too much to take in, although she'd already seen him in the flesh. Or in the fur, which was even more damning.

"Yes, though we don't like to use the term."

"Why not?"

Honestly, Wes wasn't certain. He shrugged. "It's considered offensive. Used as an insult generally. But it is a bit more descriptive to laymen's ears, and I think it's only offensive if the person it refers to *takes* offense. I don't mind if you call me a werewolf. In private, of course. I'm sure you understand."

She laughed a little hysterically. "I don't understand a thing, sir. And I'm hoping to wake in my bed in the morning and discover this was all a terrible dream."

If she'd lanced his heart with a dagger, it would have been less painful. "I know I'm not the sort of man you were supposed to marry, but that can't be helped, Lady Madeline."

She frowned at him. "It's not too late to return home, Mr. Hadley. Your secret is safe with me. I swear it."

Wes shook his head. "If it was just me, my lady, I'm certain you could talk me into giving up my soul. But there are others I have to protect. And the only way to do that is by either killing you or marrying you. I do hope you prefer the latter as I'm not capable of the former."

"I suppose I should be grateful for that." She regarded him with a serious expression. "You do know my father will never give you my dowry if we elope."

Her fortune was the last thing on Wes' mind. Protecting his brothers, Cait, and the children ranked much higher. "We'll manage without it," he replied.

After all, he'd survived his entire life without a fortune. He couldn't miss what he'd never had.

"And I'll be a social outcast."

"You mean you'll be a Hadley."

"Robert and Nathaniel will kill you."

"They can try," he replied evenly. "I heal quickly, remember?"

"Then why…" Her voice trailed off and she shifted uncomfortably in her seat.

"Then why what?" he prodded.

After a moment she met his eyes, her green orbs tinted with uncertainty. "Never mind."

"No, please continue." Not knowing what she meant to ask was next to torture.

Lady Madeline squared her shoulders. "Then why do you have a scar on your cheek, if you can heal?"

Wes touched the imperfection on the side of his face. "You wouldn't believe me if I told you."

She scoffed. "I just saw you turn from man to wolf before my very eyes. But the story behind your scar would be too much for me?"

No, but the telling wouldn't be enjoyable. He'd never suffered such physical pain as he had the night he'd received his wound. "Have you ever heard of a vampyre?"

Lady Madeline shook her head.

Not that Wes was surprised. She had led a fairly sheltered life thus far, one in which monsters had no place. They still didn't, Wes being the lone exception to that rule. "The telling isn't for a lady's ears."

"Does Lady Eynsford know?"

Wes nodded once. Cait had helped tend his wound,

not that her ministrations had countered the effects of a vampyre attack. "Someday, when we're old and grey, I'll tell you the whole story if you still want to know."

"When we're old and grey. You really do mean to marry me?"

Wes nodded once more. "There's no other way. And come morning, when the castle knows you're missing, it will be far better for you to have eloped than to have simply disappeared with me." Not by much, but it was still true.

"You leave me in an awful predicament, Mr. Hadley."

"I'm aware of that, Lady Madeline. And I'm sorry." At least she wasn't crying anymore. Though she still looked fairly perturbed about their situation. "I can assure you—" he began.

"You can assure me of nothing," Madeline interrupted. "Aside from the fact that I've been abducted and taken to be married against my will."

He had no choice. Didn't she see?

"You cannot assure me that this is the best bargain in my situation."

Bargain? Who'd said anything about a bargain?

"I always knew I'd have a loveless marriage, but this wasn't what I had in mind," she continued as though he wasn't even in the carriage.

"Our marriage doesn't have to be loveless," he said quietly.

"I knew I'd never have love, but I had hoped for a little passion." She continued to talk softly to herself, but he heard every word.

"What do you know of passion?" He had to ask.

"Nothing yet," she spat back at him. "And by

forcing this impromptu marriage, you're removing my only chance for it." She sputtered for a moment. Then she raised her gaze to his and said, "I can read, Mr. Hadley." She sniffed. "I read a lot."

"And this is where you found out about this overwhelming passion you seek?" He bit back his grin. He'd show her passion.

"Don't mock me, Mr. Hadley."

The light from the carriage lantern shifted as Renshaw turned the vehicle and the moonlight danced upon her face. That was when Wes realized that she was filthy. And wet. And she was probably cold. Oh, what a pitiful excuse for a man he was. He'd knocked her to the ground, gotten her dirty, and stolen her one desire in life, to have passion. He couldn't fix the first two. But he could damn well work on the last.

Wes leaned forward and took her hand in his, his thumb brushing caked mud aside as he caressed the top of her hand. "I'm not mocking you, Lady Madeline." Then he stretched out an arm and scooped her into his lap.

"What are you doing?" she protested, swatting at him like he was a pesky fly. Her hands fluttered around as though she had no idea where to put them.

"Be still," he said as he captured those flyaway hands in a gentle grip. When she didn't comply, he followed with, "Please?"

"You don't have any clothes on," she hissed at him.

"I am well aware of that fact." In truth, he was more than aware of it. Her rosewater scent enveloped his senses as she squirmed in his lap. "But I want to show you something."

"If you plan to show me your person, you can just forget it," she said, covering her eyes with her hands.

Wes chuckled as he pulled her hands down and placed them on his chest. "I should like to try something, if you'll allow it." His heart thumped in his chest, and he felt like he'd just run a mile rather than simply hauling a lady across the coach and into his lap. He forced himself to calm for a moment. But the heavy thump of his heart continued. As did the hardening of his member beneath the lap blanket that covered him. He pushed his own desires to the side as much as he was able. "Kiss me, Lady Madeline," he said softly.

She froze in his arms. "Why on earth would I do that?"

"So you can see what this passion is all about?" he prompted. *So, I can show you that loving you is one thing I might do well. It might be to your satisfaction, even if my purse is not.*

"But…" she sputtered.

Before she could utter another syllable, Wes threaded his fingers into the hair at the nape of her neck and pulled her head down to his. His words were no more than a murmur against her lips. "Have you ever been kissed before?"

She shook her head slightly, her face close enough to his that he could feel the whisper of that silky skin as her lips brushed his. Now he could hear her heartbeat in his head along with his own. It beat a runaway rhythm, and Wes doubted that fear was the cause of it this time.

"Never?" Of course, someone had tried to kiss her. She'd had enough suitors.

"Never," she confirmed. Her heartbeat grew louder and louder in his head, thumping as madly as his own pulse. Then she straightened her back and pulled away from him. He could have easily subdued her, but he wanted to kiss her. And for her to want it. "And I'm not going to start with someone like you," she said.

Something inside Wes tripped and he forced himself to steady. "Someone like me? You mean a Lycan?"

"Well, that, too," she said. "But I'm fated for a grand union."

"A grand union with a huge settlement of funds and no passion whatsoever."

"I know very little about passion, so I suspect I'll barely miss it." She jumped up from his lap and landed on the other side. But he couldn't let her go that quickly. He followed and pressed her back in her seat, as he sat on his knees before her. "Must you hover over me so?" she asked. Her lips were open as she inhaled heavily. Her eyes searched his face in the dim light. He hoped she wasn't appalled by what she saw, her eyes lingering on his scar.

"I am not one of your kind, Lady Madeline," he began, forcing himself to stay calm.

"Well, that was obvious, even before tonight."

He forced himself to relax, despite her bruising words. "And now I'm even less a man to you, is that it?"

"It's not that," she started, an appalled expression on her face, as though she'd finally realized the folly of her words.

"You think me beneath you." It wasn't a question. It was a statement. It tore at his pride. The only time he wanted to be beneath her was with her impaled on his shaft, riding him. The beast within him rose and he forced himself to settle.

She seemed to weigh her words. "I think you'd never be an acceptable match in the eyes of my family."

"I don't give a damn about your family. What about you?"

"What about me? I don't even know you."

Wes lowered his head until he hovered a mere breath from her mouth. "You could know me, if you tried."

She opened her mouth to speak, and that was when Wes swooped in and touched his lips to hers. She froze beneath him, but she didn't pull away. Her lips met his hesitantly. Wes tilted his head so he could fit his mouth properly against hers, and he very gently sipped at her lower lip.

The beast within him wanted to growl at her, press her against the squabs, and have his way with her. But he held back and very gently cupped her face in his hands. Her lips were questioning him as surely as any words that could have come from her mouth. Very tentatively, she arched her back and brought herself closer to him, her cold little hands landing on his naked chest.

Wes coaxed her mouth to open and very gently invaded that warm, sweet cavern. She startled for a moment, but then she reached for his shoulders and her tongue rose to meet his. She was a novice at kissing but a most willing student. He didn't pull away until she was soft and pliant in his arms. "Was that what you imagined passion to be like?" he asked, his own voice choppy with desire.

She nodded, her mouth opening as though she

wanted to say something, but no sound came out. He'd obviously affected her with that kiss. Affected her to the point where she couldn't put her words together. A little part of him began to hope. "Is that what you'd hoped for in a marriage?"

"Yes," she finally said. She hadn't removed her hands from his shoulders.

"Yet you still think me beneath you?"

"I never said that," she began. But she avoided his gaze. She still looked a little shocked by the power of that kiss. To tell the truth, so was he. "Are you going to kiss me again?" she finally asked.

"Do you want me to?"

She nodded hesitantly, as though her emotions weighed heavily against her sense of propriety.

Wes moved back to his own seat, and her body rocked forward as though there was an invisible pull between them. It was real. He was certain of it. But she wasn't. "You want me to kiss you, but you don't want to be my wife," he finally said when he was settled on his side of the carriage with the lap blanket hiding the sizeable bulge she'd just provoked. "That doesn't speak of a promising future."

"I didn't say I don't want to be your wife," she said forcefully.

Wes smiled. "Oh, good. Then you'll be much more compliant when we reach Gretna."

"I didn't say I wanted to be, either. I will most definitely *not* be compliant."

Wes scoffed. "You weren't born to be compliant." He *tsked* beneath his breath. "A shame, really, that you have been trained to be so obedient."

"Since when is good breeding a shame?"

He chuckled again. "It's only a shame if you don't get to do any good breeding."

She gasped. "That's what you want to do with me? Breed?"

The very thought made his heart beat faster. "More than anything," he said honestly. "And I really want to kiss you again."

She didn't look up at him as she murmured to herself. "So, what's stopping you?"

"I'll kiss you again when you ask me for it. And not before."

"I beg your pardon?"

"Begging is not necessary, Lady Madeline. You need only ask me nicely."

She pressed her lips together and didn't utter a sound.

Wes had more pressing matters to think about. He glanced down at the blanket covering his lap. What irony: for the first time in a long while he had full pockets. Unfortunately, those pockets were folded neatly with his clothes in the stables at Castle Hythe. He wondered how long it would be before the Hayburn men decided Lady Madeline had run off with him. Hopefully Renshaw could drive like the wind.

Nine

A BRIGHT LIGHT INVADED MADDIE'S DARKNESS, AND she blinked her eyes open. She closed them quickly again and covered her face with her arm. "The drapes," she muttered. Why were the dratted things open? And why did her head throb?

"You snore," a very male voice remarked, from just a few inches away.

She knew that voice. Didn't she? "I do not," she insisted.

"You do." Maddie's pillow moved beneath her head when the man laughed.

Heavens! That wasn't a pillow. And she wasn't even in her bed. Or her room, for that matter. Maddie bolted upright, cracking her head against the fellow's chin in the process. Her eyes flew open once more to find her maddening captor, Weston Hadley, seated beside her. The previous evening's memories washed over her. Blast, it wasn't a bad dream.

"There's no reason to injure me." He rubbed his chin where she'd bumped into him. "I find your snoring delightful."

What a wonderful sentiment to wake up to. "I do *not* snore."

One dark golden brow rose in mild amusement. "Indeed? And do you often listen to yourself sleep?"

Maddie glared at him.

"You may take my word for it that you do. Snore, that is."

Infuriating man or wolf or whatever he was. She couldn't be doomed to spend her days with this cretin, could she? Finally, their surroundings began to sink in to Maddie's awakening mind. Where had he gotten clothes? "You're dressed."

He raised an eyebrow at her. "Very astute for so early in the morning."

That was it? He didn't plan to elaborate? "When did you... Where did you... How?"

Mr. Hadley gestured to the top of the carriage. "Luckily Renshaw is as good at playing cards as he is at driving."

Was that supposed to make some sort of sense to her? "Cards?"

Mr. Hadley shrugged. "Well not on this journey, but his pockets were fairly plump when we left Kent. He bought these off an innkeeper at one of the stops to change horses. I had to give him my vowels in exchange for them."

Now that Maddie took a good look at him, the clothes were rather shabby. Just the sort of home-spun one might expect to be an innkeeper's discards. Still the tattered shirt and slightly too-short trousers were better than no clothes at all. "I slept through all of that?"

He inclined his head once more. "And you slept through breakfast, my lady. But I did save a few apples, currants, and a hunk of cheese for you. Cost me more vowels, I'm afraid, but we'll get all of that sorted out once we return to Eynsford Park."

Whoever heard of borrowing funds from one's coachman? Practically disgraceful. If she wasn't in such an awful predicament, she would have laughed at the ridiculousness of the situation. "Where are we?"

"We're just past Cambridge."

That far? "And you're still alive, I see. So no one has caught up to us."

"With everyone keeping Town hours at the castle? They probably don't even know you're missing yet."

She hated to think he might be right, but his assessment did seem sound. It might be hours from now before her father or brothers finally roused themselves awake. She was a third of the way to the Scottish border, and no one even knew she was missing.

"They'll know soon, however." Mr. Hadley interrupted her thoughts. "I posted a letter to the duke a couple stops back. I didn't want him to worry about you and wanted him to know you're safe."

She must have misheard him. Maddie's blood turned to ice in her veins. "You sent a letter to my *father*?"

"I didn't want him to worry," he repeated. "It seemed a bad way to start off with him, making him worry unnecessarily."

"What did you tell him?" she bit out. Heavens, her father!

Mr. Hadley sighed, and for the first time that morning, he looked distressed. "An enormous lie, of course."

"Well, I would love to know those details."

If she wasn't mistaken, a slight blush stained his neck. "I, um—" He glanced out the window to avoid her gaze. "Well, I told him—"

The suspense was maddening. "Pray tell me, for pity's sake."

He finally looked back at her, frowning a bit. "I wrote him that we were madly in love."

Her father was going to kill her.

"However," Mr. Hadley continued. "I wrote that I knew he would never approve of our match. And since I couldn't stand by and let you marry another, I took matters into my own hands. Then I promised him that we would return from Gretna posthaste and I would accept any punishment he wanted to bestow upon me at that time."

Maddie's mouth fell open. What a thing for him to say! A small part of her wished his words were true, which was silly. She wasn't eloping with Mr. Hadley because they were madly in love. She was eloping with Mr. Hadley because she'd stumbled upon his secret and he didn't trust her to keep it to herself. "No mention of abductions or of your wolfish traits then?"

His frown deepened. "It would be best for you not to mention my peculiarities, Madeline. As soon as you're my wife, your future will be linked to mine. For better or worse."

'Til death would they part. There would be no divorce. If the King couldn't procure one for himself, Maddie didn't have a prayer in that regard. And there would be no annulment. Not after traveling all the way to Scotland and back with the Lycan. Her reputation would be forever tainted. Her father would never seek an annulment. There would be no point. No decent man would have her after this little excursion north with Weston Hadley. No, as soon as she said, "I do," her fate would be sealed. Though in actuality, it had been sealed the moment she saw her husband-to-be transform into a wild animal before her eyes.

"I'll try to keep that in mind," she muttered.

"That would be best for all involved." He retrieved a knapsack from the carriage floor and opened the top. "Apple?"

Maddie's stomach groaned in response. When had she last eaten? Sometime yesterday. She nodded. "Thank you, Mr. Hadley."

"Weston," he replied, polishing a red apple against his sleeve.

"I beg your pardon?"

He handed the fruit to her and grinned. "My name. Weston. If we're to be married, I'd rather you not call me Mr. Hadley anymore, Madeline."

She turned the apple over and over in her hand, a little nervously. Weston. She rolled the name around in her mind. "You said it would be best for *all* involved. Did you simply mean you and me?" He had mentioned protecting other people last night, hadn't he?

Weston released a long sigh.

"There are others like you, aren't there?" she pressed.

He pierced her with his dark gaze. "I'll be happy to answer any question you have on the trip back from Gretna."

Meaning he didn't intend to confide in her until

she was safely his wife with her future linked to his.
Until she had as much to lose as he did, if she told.
"Weston." She said his name slowly and batted her
eyes the way she'd seen Lady Eynsford do with her
husband when she wanted something.

Weston's breathing hitched a bit and Maddie bit
back a smile. How nice to know she affected him in
some way. She thought back to the kiss he'd bestowed
upon her the night before. She wasn't the only one
who'd wanted more, was she? He'd said as much, but
she hadn't quite believed him until this moment.

She nearly shook her head, remembering why she'd
gone in search of him by the stables to begin with.
She'd thought to blackmail him into telling her about
Lord Gelligaer, which meant very little at this point.
But, she wondered, would blackmail have been necessary to begin with? Could she have flirted the answer
out of him?

"Why are you looking at me like that?"

"I have no idea what you're talking about."
Maddie bit into her apple, savoring the tangy juice as
it hit her tongue.

"You looked as though you had some Machiavellian
scheme hatching in your mind."

Maddie laughed. "Heavens! I had no idea you were
such a suspicious man."

"You're not planning on bolting when we stop to
change horses, are you?"

What would be the point in that? She'd already
spent the night with him. He'd already sent that
damning letter to her father. No, her future with
Weston Hadley couldn't be altered, but she would

dearly love to know exactly how she affected him. Maddie leaned forward on the bench and placed her hand on his knee. "I've accepted my fate."

His eyes narrowed, but she heard the noise his throat made when he swallowed hard. "I don't believe you."

"Why not?" She *knew* she affected him. Why wouldn't he believe her? Lord Eynsford never seemed to question his wife's motives.

"Because last night you broke my nose trying to escape me. You threatened to have Renshaw hanged. You swore Lavendon and Robert would see me dead."

Well, there was that. But… "You *had* just chased me across my father's property, snarling and growling at me like a rabid animal," she defended herself. "Anyone would have tried to escape you under those circumstances."

"But *now* you've accepted your fate?" he asked dubiously.

"I am a realist, Weston."

"Indeed?"

Maddie nodded. "Besides, can you blame me for wanting to know more about the man I am to marry? I know very little about you, after all."

"You know more than most," he grumbled. "More than you should."

"Well, that's hardly my fault."

"I suppose you're saying that it's my fault?"

"Well, I'm not the one who turned into a beast and chased a lady into the forest in the middle of the night, now am I?"

"No. You were the one skulking about the stables in the dead of night." He folded his arms across his chest. "What were you doing in the stables anyway?"

Maddie shrugged. "I suppose I'll tell you after we're married." Then she took another bite of apple, relishing the fact that Weston didn't seem able to keep from watching her lips. He wouldn't kiss her until she asked him to? *That* she doubted. He wanted to kiss her right now. She could see it in his eyes. His eyes fastened on the drop of apple juice that slid across her chin. She swiped at it with the back of her hand. A lady didn't do that, did she?

But then Maddie looked down at her clothes and realized that she didn't resemble a lady at all. Her dress was covered with mud. It had dried while she slept, and was now crispy and scratchy. What must she look like? "I suppose I look a fright," she began. Then she reached one hand up to smooth her hair and encountered a feeling she'd never felt before. Gone were her well-placed curls. Gone was the jeweled comb that had held her hair back from her face. Gone was any semblance of beauty whatsoever. What she was left with must look absolutely hideous.

Maddie let the apple drop into her lap and reached both hands up to pat her hair. "Oh, dear," she breathed. She always took such great care with her appearance. Yet here she sat, her gown a mess and her hair sticking out every which way. She felt a lump in her hair and dug her fingertips into the mess, recovering the end of what she assumed must be a leaf. But she tugged and it didn't come free.

"Allow me," Weston said as he leaned forward, his gaze on that object that protruded from her hair. He tugged and tugged and finally gave a jerk, and pulled a twig from the top of her head. "Got it," he said as he held it out to her. Her hand trembled a little as she reached for it. Tears burned at the backs of her eyelids when she saw a few delicate strands wrapped and knotted around the tree branch that had taken root in her hair. What an awful day.

"Oh, dear. You're not going to cry, are you?" he asked, just before she dropped her head into her hands and proceeded to do just that.

Wes had never felt more out of place. Madeline, in all her faded glory, sat across from him and sobbed into her hands. Her shoulders shook with the sheer force of it. He reached out one hand and gently squeezed her shoulder, like he would with one of his brothers if they were worried, but it only made her cry harder. Of course, his brothers would never sob if he'd dragged them from the forest, muddy and bedraggled, and forced them to race for Gretna. They'd simply tell him to go to the devil, kick his arse and be done with it. But she couldn't do that, could she? He wouldn't allow it. He couldn't allow it, not if he wanted his family's secret to remain safe and secure.

Well, she could kick his arse. In fact, he'd prefer it over the sheer torture of seeing her shoulders shake with unhappiness. "Madeline," he said softly. But he quickly realized there was no possible way that she could hear him over the sound of her own sobbing. "Madeline," he said a little more loudly.

"What is it?" she wailed at him.

"Come now, it's not as bad as all that, is it?"

Her head jerked up and her sobbing stopped. Her eyes were rimmed with red and her cheeks were soaked. Her eyes were even puffy. Dear God, what had he done?

"Not as bad as all that?" she cried. She held out her hands and said, "Look at me! I'm a mess! I'm…" She stopped abruptly as though she was looking for the appropriate word.

"Dirty?" he supplied.

She flopped back against the squabs. "Dirty," she sighed. "That's what this has come to. I'm dirty."

"Just a little," he tried. "It's really not that bad."

"Do you have any idea how much I detest being dirty?"

"Quite a bit, if the crying is any indication," he supplied.

"I was raised to be clean, Mr. Hadley," she informed him. He cringed when he realized he'd been reduced to being Mr. Hadley again.

"Weston," he reminded her.

She narrowed her red-rimmed eyes at him. "Do you have any idea how much trouble I got in when I was younger if I even dreamed of getting dirty? It's simply not done."

"You did quite well, in this instance," he couldn't keep from saying.

"*I* did?" she shrieked.

"Well, we did," he corrected.

"We did," she sighed. "*We* got me dirty. Filthy. Completely unattractive."

"I wouldn't go that far," Wes said. "I think you're pretty adorable either way."

"Adorable is a good description for puppies, Mr.

Hadley." She sighed heavily. "I've been reduced to being compared to a *dog*," Her voice broke on the last.

"Then at least you're in good company." He could think of worse things than to be compared to a dog.

"I want a bath." She said it with feeling. Like it was an order.

"Shall I have Renshaw ring for a maid as well? And perhaps someone to dress your hair?"

"That would be lovely." She smiled through her tears. It was the most radiant smile he'd ever seen.

"I'll have him do that right after he climbs off his perch and makes us a dinner of pheasant and lamb." Surely she knew how absurd her request was.

Her stomach growled loudly. A most pretty blush crept up her cheeks. "I love pheasant and lamb," she said softly.

His heart ached a bit of the thought of destroying this fantasy she was living in. But certainly, she had to realize how dire their situation was. He didn't even have a pocket to let. He was wearing borrowed clothing. And hadn't a shilling to his name. And he had Lady Madeline Hayburn imprisoned in his poor state of affairs. He'd brought her along for a very impoverished ride. Certainly, he was accustomed to doing without on occasion. To tying his own cravat and fetching his own drink. But she wasn't. Hell, he didn't think she'd ever been dirty before now. She'd just told him as much.

And it was all his fault. Lady Madeline's fall from grace was on his head. "I don't think you understand how dire our situation is," he began softly as he leaned forward and took her hand in a gentle grip.

She pointed to her hair, which did look more than

a bit bedraggled. "I think I understand quite well how dire my situation is."

She had no idea that to go along with her dirty state and her wild hair, she could also run the risk of being hungry. "There's more at stake here than the state of your hair."

"Can't we stop? Just long enough to have a good meal and a bath?" Her eyes pleaded with him. The tangles in her hair pleaded with him even more loudly.

"If we stop, then anyone they've sent after you could catch up to us," he told her truthfully.

"But they've probably not even risen from their beds yet," she cried. "You said so yourself," she reminded him.

"Let's see how far we get today, and then we can make a decision," he offered, merely to placate her. But then she started to sniffle again. "Oh, all right. Fine. We'll stop at nightfall. Renshaw will need to sleep anyway."

"Thank you," she croaked out as she swiped at the fresh wave of tears.

Ten

THE TEARS DID HIM IN. HE COULD TAKE SOME whining. And he could take some griping. He could even take some grumbling, because his brothers had conditioned him well to that and he'd learned to ignore it through the years. But every time Madeline wrinkled up her pretty little nose to sniffle, it wrenched at a piece of Wes' heart. It was like someone reached inside his chest and squeezed the air from his lungs every last time she spoke with a rasp because she'd been made to cry.

And yes, he'd made her cry. He was well aware that it was all his fault. If he hadn't lingered quite so long over the whist table, he could have been well away from Castle Hythe before his transformation from man to beast took place. Then they could have avoided this trip. He never would have gotten her dirty. And she never would have been forced into this disgrace. For that was what it was, a disgrace. He'd been told enough times throughout the day. It was a total disgrace that Madeline was being treated so shabbily.

Wes cursed beneath his breath and rapped on the roof of the carriage. "We'll stop at the next inn," he told her.

Madeline's head shot up and her eyes met his. "Really? Do you mean it?"

"I do. Renshaw needs to sleep. And I could stand to walk around a bit. We all need some food." The apples and currants from the morning had long since left him empty.

"And a bath," she sighed with a dreamy expression on her face.

"That depends on how much it costs," Wes said beneath his breath. He was wearing borrowed pockets, for God's sake.

"Why does that matter?" she asked, her head tilted at him in question.

"Money matters to us normal folks, Madeline," he reminded her. "We need it in order to survive."

"I'd hardly call you a *normal* man," she remarked absently.

"Don't remind me," he muttered.

"No, I don't mean that," she rushed on. "I mean you're a gentleman. Your brother's a viscount."

"A penniless viscount, until recently," he reminded her.

"Hmm. Until he absconded with Sophie's fortune," she added dryly.

Was *that* what Archer had done? No wonder Lady Sophia would like his head on a platter. How had his brother managed such a nefarious feat? And without Wes or Gray finding out. Wes shook the thoughts away. "That is neither here nor there at the moment. Archer *isn't* here and neither are his funds. It's just you and me on this trip."

"And Renshaw." She folded her arms across her middle. "Let's not forget the fellow who is funding this little excursion."

The way she said that grated a bit. Wes rubbed his brow. "Just so you're forewarned, I'm not certain we can get a bath for you, but we should be able to get some warm water so you can get cleaned up."

"That will never do."

"It'll have to do, Madeline."

She smiled softly at him. "It'll all work out perfectly," she said. "You'll see. Once they find out who I am, they'll jump to bring me anything I want."

He leaned forward and speared her with a glance. "That's just it. They can't know who you are. They can only know that we're Mr. and Mrs. Hadley. And we might not even tell them that much."

"I could be your sister," she offered.

He could never look at her like she was a sister. The ruse would be up in an instant. "You'll be my *wife*. We may as well practice." Thankfully, the coach rumbled to a stop just as he said those words.

A moment later, Renshaw, looking more than a bit exhausted, opened the coach door. Wes bounded out and offered his hand to Madeline.

She stepped from the carriage with his assistance but instead of looking at Wes, her eyes landed on the coachman. "I understand Mr. Hadley has written you quite a number of IOUs during this journey."

"Madeline," Wes growled.

The coachman frowned at the lady, which had little, if any effect on her. She tossed back her filthy hair and stood as regally as a duchess, or at least as regally as any duke's daughter. "I want a bath, Renshaw. I believe I am owed one. And I'll thank you and your funds for seeing that I get one. And when we return to Kent, I will see that you are reimbursed for any monies spent in that regard."

"Is that before or after you see me hanged?" Renshaw asked, a bemused smile lingered on his face.

"Before, naturally. What would be the point in seeing you reimbursed afterward?"

Wes grabbed her arm and began to tow her toward the shabby little coaching inn. "Do not antagonize him, Madeline."

She gasped as the ramshackle establishment came into her view. "Good heavens. I'm not sleeping here!"

"I'm afraid we don't have much of a choice," Wes began.

But she dug in her heels and shook her head vehemently. "Absolutely not. The place looks as though it is crawling with vermin."

She had to be a spoiled duke's daughter, didn't she? His secret couldn't have been discovered by a pious vicar's daughter or a quiet chambermaid, could it? "Madeline, our options are limited. I'll keep any vermin away from you. I swear it." He felt like the worst sort of blackguard for even uttering those words. He was making the lovely and usually pristine Lady Madeline Hayburn spend the night in the most wretched inn he'd ever laid eyes on. Of course she'd balk at the idea. He wasn't all that excited about it himself.

"Weston, no." She clutched his arm. "It looks like the sort of place that caters to highwaymen."

Indeed it did. "Darling, didn't you see the look on Renshaw's face? If we don't stop, he could drive off the road and kill us all. We'll just stay here long enough for him to rest a bit and then we'll leave."

"But—"

"You've seen what I am," he whispered only loud enough for her to hear. "Believe me when I tell you that no harm will come to you. I am stronger than any man inside those walls, and no one will ever hurt you."

She blinked back tears and Wes' heart nearly broke. "I want a *bath*, Weston."

"All right, Madeline." He draped his arm around her shoulders. It was the least he could do. He already owed Renshaw a tidy sum for driving them to the border, for food, for clothes, for shelter. Why not add a bath to the list? He just hoped the coachman's funds didn't dry up before they returned to Kent. "I'll see that you get your bath."

She sniffed back a tear as she nodded.

Wes directed her closer to the taproom doors and squeezed her arm when raucous laughter spilled out into the night air. "You are safe with me," he reminded her. "But do me a favor and let me do all the talking, will you?"

Silently, she nodded once again, a bit of fear flashing in her green eyes.

As soon as they stepped into the taproom, all sounds of jocularity came to an abrupt halt as every gaze seemed to settle on them. The interior was just as Wes had suspected, filled to the brim with swarthy-looking fellows, who might, as Madeline had suggested, actually be highwaymen. He didn't meet anyone's eye except for that of an older man with thinning grey hair who was standing behind the long wooden bar.

"My wife and I are hoping you have a room this evening," Wes said softly, guiding Madeline closer to the bar.

The innkeeper looked them both over, from top to bottom. "Did ya take a tumble from a horse?" he asked, his Yorkshire accent slow and rumbling.

"Fell into a bit of mud earlier," Wes replied. "Have you got a room, sir?"

The man nodded. "Ma-ry!" he called, letting each syllable bleed into the next as the room at large began milling about, once again.

A portly woman in a mobcap emerged from the back room, wiping her hands on a grimy apron. "Ya bellowed?"

The innkeeper gestured toward Wes and Madeline with his head. "Take this couple up to nine, woman."

Mary smiled at the pair of them, her yellowed teeth flashing in the dimmed light. "Well, come on wit' ya." She started for a set of steps in the back of the taproom. "We don't get many overnight visitors."

"You don't say," Madeline mumbled.

Mary turned back to face them, her gaze traveling up and down Madeline's form. "By gum! What happened to ya, dearie?"

"Fell into a bit of mud." Madeline echoed Wes' previous words to the innkeeper. "I was hoping I could have a bath."

The old woman nodded her head. "I should say so. I don't think I've seen a woman in worse shape."

Madeline squeaked in horror, but Mary paid her no heed and began climbing the stairs. "We'll have a tub brought up for ya and some hot water."

"Thank you, ma'am," Wes replied, saving Madeline from having to respond.

A moment later in the tiny corridor, the woman turned a key into a lock and pushed open a bedroom door. She quickly lit a small lamp in the corner of the room, bathing the small quarters in a warm glow.

A mouse ran across the floorboard.

Madeline screamed and hurled herself at Wes. He'd never been fond of mice until that very moment, and he scooped his bride-to-be up in his arms.

She buried her face against his shoulder. "You said you wouldn't let any vermin near me."

"My dear, I will hold you all night if you'd like."

"A bit squeamish, is she?" Mary clucked with disapproval as she slid back into the hallway. "One wouldn't think it with the way she looks." Madeline dug her face deeper into the curve of his neck. As the woman stepped out the door, she said, "I'd worry more about the vermin out there than the vermin in here." She tipped her head toward the taproom.

"Thank you," Wes replied. He shut the door behind the woman with his foot. Then he crossed the floor and sat on the edge of a small bed, careful not to jostle Madeline too much in the process for fear she'd jump right out of his arms. He found that he liked holding her, particularly when she was feeling so compliant. "It's all right, my dear. I've got you."

She pulled back from him, staring into his eyes. "She said she'd never seen a woman look worse than me."

Wes winced. What could he say to that?

"I must look even more frightful than I thought. Did you see her? Have you taken a look around this hovel? And she's never seen anyone look worse than *me*?"

"I'm certain she was exaggerating, Madeline."

"This is the worst day of my entire life. I want you to know that."

He didn't doubt it for a moment. Rolled in mud and abducted, with no choice but to marry him. "I am sorry. I will make it up to you." Someday, somehow. If it took the rest of his life.

She arched one golden eyebrow in disbelief.

Wes couldn't help but laugh. She was adorable, all covered in dirt, leaves, and an occasional twig, yet still as imperious as she'd always been. And she was all his, or she would be very soon. "Do you know how beautiful you are?"

Something flashed in her eyes, but West couldn't quite name the emotion. "If you tell me even the sun pales in comparison to my beauty, I will cast up my accounts right here. I might even do it on your shoes."

"Do that and I might have to go barefoot the whole way to Gretna. I'm not certain we could afford another pair." Then Wes scoffed. "I would wager that I am more skilled at flirtation than Dewsbury. Thank you very much." Her brow rose in disbelief once more, which only made Wes scowl at her. "You needn't look so surprised. A number of females have found me to be quite charming, I'll have you know."

"And did you kiss each of *them*?" she asked tartly before a delightful pink stained her cheeks.

What he wouldn't give to kiss *her* right now. "I don't remember."

"You don't remember?" She blinked at him.

How was he to remember anything, anyone but her, as she sat on his lap, so close that he could feel her heat through his clothing? Wes shook his head, his eyes focused on her delectable, tempting mouth. He swallowed. "Do you want me to kiss you again?"

Her lips parted on a breath. "I—"

A knock sounded on the door. Wes set her down beside him as the door swung open. The innkeeper frowned at the pair of them, sitting on the bed. "Mary said ya wanted a bath."

"Yes, please." Madeline scrambled off the bed.

The innkeeper eyed Wes warily. "Ya want ta help me haul the tub in here, sir?"

"Of course." Wes pushed to his feet and followed the old man into the hallway. Then he hoisted the tin tub over his shoulder, without any assistance, and placed it in the middle of the bedroom floor. Thankfully, the tub appeared clean. It might be the only clean thing in the entire establishment, in fact. Wes nodded to the innkeeper. "Thank you, sir. Now if we might have some hot water."

"The lad's on his way up with a bucket right now."

❧

Maddie kept a keen eye on the floor, watching for any more mice, as the last bucket of water splashed into the tin bathtub. Now if only all the men in the room would disperse, she could finally wash the dirt and grime from her hair and skin. She didn't think she could completely relax in the room, not having seen that first mouse—but she also didn't think anything would bother her once she was submerged in the water.

"Thank you, for everything." Weston gestured the innkeeper and a shabby-looking young man from the room. Then he shut the door after them, locked it, and leaned against it as though he alone could bar them from re-entry.

Certainly he didn't think he was *staying* while she bathed. Maddie waved him toward the door with her hand. "You may go, Weston."

"And leave you to your own devices?" He shook his head. "I think I'll just lie on the bed, if that's all right with you."

"It's not all right with me," she scoffed. Yet all he did was reposition a wobbly screen between the bed and the area where the tub lay.

"There. Now I won't be able to see a thing. More's the pity." Weston sighed.

"That won't be nearly enough," she complained.

"We'll be in Scotland tomorrow, my dear. We'll be married *tomorrow*. There is no need to stand on ceremony. Take your bath, please. I've heard about nothing else the past hour."

That was perfectly fine for him to say. He didn't look as though he should be planted in a garden somewhere. "It wouldn't be proper for you to stay."

He winked at her. "Haven't you heard, Madeline dear, Hadley men are far from proper? Now turn around. I can't imagine you can get yourself out of that dress."

Maddie felt heat creep up her cheeks. "You think to undress me, Mr. Hadley? Did you bump your head when I wasn't looking?" She turned her back on him. "You can send a maid to help me."

Maddie heard the bed creak as he sat down on it. "We can't afford a maid," he informed her as she stepped behind the screen.

"How much does a maid cost?" she called out. Honestly, she had no idea. She'd always had a maid of her own to travel with her.

"More than we have," he said as she saw his stocking feet lift up on the end of the bed.

"I can do it myself." She'd never done it before, but she felt certain she could manage to get herself out of her clothes.

"Sure, you can," he called back to her. Did he chuckle?

Yet, after a few moments, Maddie realized he was right. There was no way she would be able to get herself out of her dress. She sighed heavily and ground her teeth. What was she to do now?

"Are you ready to ask for help yet?" he called from the other side of the screen.

"As soon as you tell me how you became so adept at removing women's clothing," she called back.

"You haven't tried my services yet. I could be terrible at it," he replied. Somehow, she doubted that. With the way that he'd kissed her, she doubted he was bad at anything when it related to women's clothing.

"Just how many women have availed themselves of your services, Mr. Hadley?" she sniped as she glared around the end of the screen at him. He lay on the bed with his feet raised, his hands beneath his head. He looked so handsome that she had to bite the inside of her cheek to keep from smiling at him.

"Call me Weston and I might tell you," he called back without even looking at her.

Maddie reached behind her back until her arms ached from the stretch. There was no way she could unbutton the blasted gown on her own. "Weston," she called sweetly. He was beside her in seconds. He looked down at her, his eyes warm and inviting. "How did you move that quickly?" she gasped.

"Don't you know that all good dogs come when called?" he said with a wolfish grin.

She elbowed him in the side. "Stop teasing me. Really, how did you move so fast?"

He shrugged and took her shoulder in his palm, spinning her slowly to face away from him. "It's a Lycan trait," he said quietly by her ear. He brushed her hair to lie over one shoulder slowly as though he relished the feel of the strands moving between his fingertips. She didn't understand how that could possibly be the case, as dirty as she was, but he didn't seem to care. "There are quite a few traits we have that you should probably know about."

Her voice quivered as he unfastened her dress at the highest point on her back. "Such as?" she breathed.

Hot breath enveloped the skin he uncovered as he worked his way down the row of fastenings. Then as he moved down, he replaced his breath with his lips. Maddie could barely put two words together, but she forced herself to concentrate despite his quiet ministrations and the soft hum that reverberated from his lips, sending chills across her skin. He lifted his lips only briefly. "We can hear really well."

He unfastened another button. His hand swept across the naked skin of her back in a gentle stroke that nearly knocked her knees from beneath her. Yet he almost seemed to sense it and his arm encircled her waist. "What else?" she breathed.

"We heal quickly." His lips trailed from the inside of her neck down to the vee of her back, across the chemise she still wore, his lips whispering across the silk like wind after a rain, drowsy and wet.

"I remember that one," she gasped. "From when I kicked you."

"I do, too," he said, his lips more firmly attached to her shoulder as he shoved her gown down her arm with one hand and held her up with the other. Thank God, he held her up. Otherwise, she'd have dissolved into a puddle on the floor. His arm was anchored around her directly below her breasts, like a band of strength she never wanted to let her go.

"I thought you said you wouldn't kiss me again until I ask for it," she said softly, her eyes closing at the sheer pleasure his lips wrought. Wes very gently scraped at her shoulder with his teeth.

"If I were kissing you," he breathed across the shell of her ear, "it would be because you wanted it. And because you informed me that you wanted it in no uncertain terms. That is correct."

"And you do not consider what you're doing to be kissing me?"

"No," he said, and then he sucked very lightly at the place where her neck met her shoulder.

Maddie's breath caught in her throat.

"Did you want me to kiss you, Madeline?" he asked.

"I'm not certain," she gasped out as his hand rose to stroke the line beneath her breasts. What was he doing to her?

"When do you think you might have a good idea, my dear? Of whether or not I should kiss you?"

A knock pounded fiercely on the door. "More water, sir," a man's voice called out.

Weston let her go as quickly as he'd appeared. She nearly fell to the ground when he turned her loose, her limbs were so weak. There was a thumping everywhere that was unlike anything else she'd ever experienced. He crossed to the door and took the buckets from the man, then poked his head back around the corner of the screen. "Do you still need my help?"

Did she? She needed him to resume his ministrations. To go back to touching her. But she couldn't say that. It wouldn't be proper, not at all. So she squeaked out, "I think I can take it from here."

"You're certain you can get your dress off?"

"Maybe?" she said with a glance down and a frown.

Weston crossed the room in three strides. He shoved her gown down over her hips, tapped the outside of her leg to get her to step out of the gown, and kicked it to the side.

He turned as though he was going to walk away. "Weston," she said hesitantly.

"Yes?" he barked.

She didn't want him to go. She really didn't. "Would you consider helping me wash my hair?"

He very unceremoniously picked her up, set her on her feet in the tub, and then crossed to the nearest bucket. She squealed when he dumped the water over her head. Then he set the bucket to the side, crossed his arms and glared at her. She must have looked like an idiot there in her dripping wet chemise and her hair a stringy mess across her face.

She blew water from her lips as she gasped. Maddie cracked one eye to look at him, but all she saw was his retreating back as he slipped out the door. Then she heard the lock slide into place. He'd dumped water over her head. And then locked her in this awful room.

Eleven

Wes stared at the full tankard of whisky before him, still furious. More at himself than with her. Though he was plenty annoyed with her, too. Touching her made him want her more than ever. To taste her. To claim her. He was only one night past the full moon and struggled for control with the beast inside himself.

But she was in complete control, wasn't she? How lowering to realize he was the only one affected by the other, damned fool that he was. *I think I can take it from here.* Her voice echoed in his ears. If that blasted oaf hadn't come back upstairs with a bucket of water when he had and interrupted Wes' seduction... Now that he thought about it, Wes was beyond furious with that particular fellow, too. Damn his eyes.

When he'd dumped the water over her head, it had poured down her body like a silky ribbon, leaving a trail he wanted to lick from her body. Her chemise had revealed all her secrets with its dampness and the way it clung to her body. He'd wanted to explore her secrets. He *still* wanted to explore them. He should have dumped the bucket of water over his own head. Wes huffed in frustration. He never should have treated her that way. He would kick himself if he were able.

"I suppose I'm paying for that drink." Renshaw's voice from beside Wes brought him out of his murderous reverie.

Wes glared at his brother's coachman. "Shouldn't you be asleep somewhere?"

The driver smiled slowly at him. "Do you know why I agreed to this foolhardy journey, Mr. Hadley?"

"Because you're afraid of Cait?"

Renshaw furrowed his brow as though he considered that possibility. Then he shook his head. "I have wondered about her ladyship a time or two over the years. There's something a bit mystical about her on occasion, but I've never been *afraid* of her. Lord Eynsford, on the other hand…"

Wes nodded in understanding. Only a fool wouldn't be afraid of Dash.

"…I've been in his employ for more than a decade. Long enough to notice certain things, if you know what I mean. And I feel certain you do."

Meaning Renshaw either knew what he was or suspected something equally frightening. "Well, I hardly think Eynsford would sack you for *not* helping me kidnap the lady abovestairs."

The coachman took a swig from his own tankard. "I traveled this same road with the two of them years ago, you know?"

Not really. Wes shrugged.

"At least *your* lady looks at you."

But Madeline wasn't his lady, was she? Just because

he desired her, had longed for her since the day he first met her, didn't mean *she* felt the same way—and she might never do so. He couldn't force her to want him in return. But it mattered little since tomorrow he'd marry her because he didn't have a choice. Neither of them did. Then he'd pine for his own wife 'til the end of time. "Don't you mean she *glares* at me?"

"She hasn't poisoned you, so you've already had a better journey than Lord Eynsford had in his pursuit of the then Miss Macleod."

Poisoned? Wes gave his full attention to the coachman. "I beg your pardon?"

Renshaw chuckled. "Her ladyship led him on a merry chase. Left him unconscious for two days in her attempt to escape him."

How did Wes not know this? Because it made Dash look like a fool, most likely. "Interesting as this is, Renshaw, I hardly see how this has any bearing on my situation."

"It doesn't," the coachman agreed as he took another drink. "I suppose I just thought you might like to know things could be worse."

Things were bad enough as they were. "You mean she could try to poison me?"

The man shrugged. "After you've seen such a thing once, it tends to stick in your mind."

"Something to look forward to then." Though Wes couldn't imagine Madeline poisoning anyone. She might *get her hands dirty*. He shook the uncharitable thought away. It wasn't her fault she'd been raised in the lap of luxury. Her feminine, delicate nature was one of the things that called out to him. He adored that about her. Usually.

"Oh, I think your lady seems more resigned to her fate than Lady Eynsford was." Then he shuddered. "His lordship could barely speak after he woke up two mornings later and found her gone."

Perhaps the coachman really was afraid of Cait, despite his protestations otherwise. Wes might be a little scared of her himself now. Apparently he'd been more than lucky to escape with his tail intact after crashing his phaeton with Lia on his lap. The thought of his adorable niece brought a smile to Wes' face. No one could be happier than Dash with his wife and children. "How did he do it, Renshaw? If her lady-ship went to the lengths of poisoning Eynsford, what did he do to change her mind? She adores him now."

The coachman yawned. "Some of us take a little longer to accept our fate than others. Like I said, your lady seems resigned. That's a good sign."

But Wes didn't want Madeline to be resigned to her fate; he wanted her to be happy. But could she be happy with him? He would have sworn she was on the precipice of asking him to kiss her when that dolt knocked on the door with his damned bucket of water. Wes wasn't foolish enough to believe that if he'd seduced her, she would suddenly fall at his feet in love with him, but it would have been a start. A wonderful start. A start he was dying for.

What was she doing at this moment? Had she climbed in the bed all clean after her bath? Wes rose to his feet, scraping the legs of the wooden chair across the floor in his haste. "I suppose I should go see about her."

Renshaw motioned to Wes' untouched whisky. "As I'm paying for it anyway, sir, I think I'll finish that up for you."

He could drink all the damned whisky he wanted. "Get some rest so we can leave at first light, will you?"

The coachman nodded. "I could drive this road in my sleep I've done it so many times, Mr. Hadley."

᪄

Maddie sat in the middle of the tub, looking around the small room. She had nothing to wear. Not one thing. Her dress was, if not ruined, filthier than the Hythe stables. She couldn't imagine slipping it back over her skin after she'd finally scrubbed the grime from herself. Her chemise had seen better days, too. Somehow one of the ties had even been torn off.

What a miserable night. She couldn't even enjoy her bath after Weston had stormed out and locked her in this hovel. The entire time she tried to figure out what she'd done that had made him so angry. He'd *dumped* an entire bucket of water over her head, blast him. No one had ever done anything like that to her in her life, and she didn't appreciate it. She'd done nothing wrong except want to be *clean*, for heaven's sake. That was hardly a crime. Certainly it didn't warrant him storming off to sulk for some unknown reason.

She shivered a bit as the water began to turn cold. Well she had to wear something, if not tonight, then tomorrow in the carriage for sure. Maddie glanced again at her soiled gown and almost cried. But crying wouldn't get her a clean dress. She peered tentatively over the edge of the tub to the floor, keeping a watch out for any mice in the vicinity. Not seeing one, she stepped out of the tub and picked her dress up off the floor. Then she eyed the tub once more.

If she was feeling generous, she'd save the water for Weston in case he wanted to make use of it himself. But as he'd stormed out of the room like an infant, she wasn't feeling terribly generous at the moment. Maddie knelt beside the tub and dipped her lemon muslin in the bathwater. She cringed as she scrubbed at the muddy stains on her dress. It would never recover but it at least it would be a bit cleaner in the morning. She'd have the thing burnt when she got home…

Dear heavens.

Where *was* home? She certainly couldn't call Castle Hythe home any longer. But where did that leave her? Wherever Weston Hadley took her, that's where. Maddie scrubbed harder at the stains, taking out her frustration with Weston on her ill-treated dress. Where would he take her? Where would they live? What could they *afford*? All day long he'd told her what they couldn't afford. No maids, no baths. What if she was made to live in a hovel like this for the rest of her days?

Certainly being a ruined woman had to be better than living with vermin and dirt and… What had he said to her earlier, something about not bolting when they stopped to change horses? She couldn't bolt this evening as she had nothing to wear. But in the morning when they made their first stop, perhaps she could make a run for it.

A knock sounded at the door. "Madeline," Weston called as the handle jiggled.

She glanced down at her completely naked state and squeaked, "Don't come in here!"

Something, perhaps his thick head, bumped against the door. "I have to come in, darling. I can't sleep in the hallway."

"Just a moment, then." Maddie scrambled to her feet and picked up her dripping wet chemise. It was much too cold to put it on. She glanced around the room and finally yanked the counterpane from the bed and wrapped it around herself.

The door opened just a crack. "Are you decent?" he said through the opening.

"I wouldn't call this decent," she said tentatively.

"Yet, it's the best we can do, I suppose." He entered the room and closed the door behind himself, turning a key in the lock. Wes' eyes settled on her, and Maddie hitched the counterpane up under her arms. "I, um, I suppose I owe you an apology."

As he did appear contrite, Maddie resisted the urge to snort. "For what?" After all, there were so many things he could apologize for. Locking her in the room, dumping a bucket of water over her head, getting her dirty in the first place, abducting her, stealing her future from her, or for being a Lycan. The list was endless.

"For everything." He sat on the edge of the bed and tugged off one secondhand boot. "I know you're accustomed to everything being just so, and I know this journey must seem like a rude awakening." The boot hit the floor with a thud, and he looked at her out of the corner of his eye. "You don't know anything about poisons, do you?"

Poisons? Maddie's mouth fell open a bit. "I beg your pardon."

He shook his head. "I thought not." Then he directed his attention to his other boot.

"Weston," she began, "I do believe that is the strangest question I've ever been asked." When he didn't respond, but let his second boot hit the wooden floor, Maddie stared up at the ceiling. "Do you truly intend to sleep here with me tonight?"

He nodded once. "I thought you wanted me to keep all the vermin away from you." Then he glanced over his shoulder at her. "Besides, we can't really afford two rooms, my dear. I'm sorry for that, too. But things are as they are. We'll have to find a way to make the best of it." Weston stretched out beside her and turned on his side to face her. "Did you enjoy your bath?"

"I feel better now that I'm clean," she replied softly.

He smiled at her, and once again Maddie was struck by how handsome he was when he smiled. "Good. I hate that you didn't have any of your rosewater, but I'll make it up to you once we get home."

There was that word again. "Weston?" She bit her lip.

"Hmm?"

"Where is that exactly? Home, I mean."

His smile vanished, and it seemed as though he hadn't given any more thought to the question than she had. "Well, I was raised in Derbyshire at Hadley Hall." He shook his head. "But these days I'm more often in Kent than anywhere else."

The idea of remaining in Kent put her heart slightly

at ease. "I want to live at *my* home. I'm sure Papa would be amenable to the idea."

Weston tucked a wet lock of hair behind Maddie's ear. "That doesn't sound like the best idea, my dear. I think it would be in our best interests to be away from your family as you get used to your new station in life."

Heavens, he made that sound dreadful, as though she'd be responsible for bedpans or mucking out the stables.

He must have seen the panic on her face because he hastened to add, "I have no claim on Eynsford Park, but I suppose it is home. And it's close enough to your family and the castle, Madeline. I'm sure Cait will welcome you…"

Eynsford Park. Maddie breathed a sigh of relief. He didn't mean to make her live in a dirty hovel. Still, it would be odd living at The Park as there was no official relation between the Hadleys and Eynsford's family. Would tongues wag at the unorthodox arrangement?

"…And, of course, Lady Sophia is in residence now. I think you'll be happy enough there."

How had Maddie forgotten about Sophie? There were so many things to wonder about. Still she shouldn't have lost sight of her friend. "What is Sophie's arrangement at The Park? I would have thought Eynsford's children were a bit young for a governess."

"You think she's there to be the *children's* governess?" A self-deprecating laugh escaped him. "Not quite."

"Well, her note said she was to be Lady Eynsford's

special guest, but I'm not sure what she meant by that. And I know she was in need of employment. Or at least she felt like she was in need of employment. What else could she be doing at The Park, if not caring for the children?" Then an awful idea flashed in Maddie's mind. She gasped. "Tell me she didn't accept an indecent proposal from one of your brothers." Certainly Lady Eynsford would never allow anything untoward to go on under her roof.

"No, she accepted an indecent proposal from Cait," Weston admitted with a wince.

That didn't make any sense at all. "What do you mean by that?"

He lay back on the bed and stared up at the ceiling. "Dash hired her as a governess for us."

"Who's 'us'?"

"The Hadley men. Archer, Gray, and me. To make us respectable." He scrubbed at his forehead as though he could wipe away the very thought of it.

"That's preposterous," Maddie scoffed. Such a thing was completely unheard of. Sophie would be ruined if anyone learned of it.

"The idea of us being respectable?" he asked as he swung his feet off the bed and got up to cross the room. "Yes, I think it's preposterous, too. Imagine, the Hadley men being models of propriety. It'll never happen. But Dash seems to think it will." Weston stepped behind the screen.

"What are you doing?" she asked.

"You're not the only one who was rolling in the mud, darling," he replied.

Maddie could see his form through the screen as

he disrobed. The breadth of his shoulders was in stark contrast to the narrowness of his waist, if the shadows were actually in proportion to reality. She covered her face when he bent to pull his trousers over his feet. Was he naked behind the screen? The very thought made her heart beat faster.

"I feel as though I've been rolling around with swine," he called from behind the screen.

Maddie's mouth fell open. *Swine?* Of all the things to call her. Swine, indeed. She stood up and marched over to the screen, then glared around it. But the sight that met her eyes was unlike any she'd ever imagined.

His hips *were* narrow, his shoulders *were* broad, and his buttocks, they were... well, they were uncommonly attractive. She tilted her head to study him more closely. She'd never imagined a naked man would look so... appealing. When she'd seen him the night before, it had only been by the light of the full moon. She'd missed quite a bit, apparently.

"Do you like what you see?" he drawled slowly, his back still toward her as he glanced over his shoulder at her. A grin lurked on his face.

"Well, I'm not certain *like* is the right word," she murmured, still unable to draw her gaze from his backside.

"Are you lusting for me, Lady Madeline?" he teased as he reached to pick up a length of toweling beside the tub. He wrapped it around those lean hips and then turned to face her. A grin broke across his face that made her want to smile with him. "Would you consider helping me wash my hair, Madeline?" he said with a teasing singsong pitch to his voice.

"I would consider dumping a bucket of water over *your* head," she replied.

Amusement made his dark eyes twinkle. "Make it cold water, would you? Because the sight of you in nothing but that blanket is making me insane." He let his gaze wander down her body. "I'm assuming you are naked under there?" he tossed out casually, as he bent and wet his own hair, then began to soap it while she watched.

She *was* naked and had never been more aware of it. But so was he. Nothing more than a length of toweling covered his most private places. She let her gaze drop.

"Why, Madeline," he teased. "If I didn't know better, I'd think you have designs upon my person." He rinsed his hair, his brown locks darkened even more by the water that sluiced from the ends.

"Y-you're all wet," she stammered. Then she gulped.

"If I had to wager on it, I'd bet you are, too," he drawled slowly. Her heart fluttered within her chest. Then he shook his head like a dog after a bath.

Maddie scurried away as water droplets flew in all directions. She shrieked and ducked behind the screen. "I cannot believe you did that!" she cried. But he barreled around the screen and scooped her up in his arms, then tossed her back onto the bed. She bounced in the middle, clutching the counterpane she'd wrapped around herself to be sure it stayed closed. Even then, a leg slipped out of the opening. She moved to close it, but he got in her way.

"Believe it, Madeline," he growled as he crawled to lean over her and gazed down, a smile gracing his beautiful face. She reached up to touch his cheek. When had he become beautiful to her? She'd always been terrified of him. And his hair stuck out in every direction, and water dripped from his locks onto the naked skin of her chest. "You are stuck for a lifetime with this loyal dog," he growled. Then his face softened as he looked into her eyes, his brimming with something she wanted to delve farther into. "It's regretful that you're getting such a mutt, instead of a purely bred specimen."

"You're purely bred," she corrected him. His parents had been married after all.

"But with pockets to let and no title to recommend me," he tossed out as his lips dropped to touch a water droplet on her chest ever so softly.

"I could think of worse things you could be," she consoled. Why she felt the need to console him, she wasn't certain. "Like bald." She trailed a hand through his damp hair and giggled. She tugged gently at his hair. "I wonder if your hair will turn grey or turn loose when you're older." She couldn't keep from exploding with laughter.

"I may be punting on the River Tick, Madeline," he said regally, "but I do have a full head of hair." He pretended to mull it over. He lowered his lips to the skin of her chest again and very lightly mouthed at the water that shimmered there. "And I have some other assets."

"Do enlighten me," she gasped as his mouth delved down to the edge of the counterpane. The edge of it was just barely tucked beneath her arms.

"Where would be the fun in telling you, darling?" he asked as he rolled from atop her and landed on his back. "You'll just have to figure them out for yourself."

Maddie sat up on her elbow and glanced down his body. "And just where might these secrets be hidden?"

He palmed the side of her face as he grinned roguishly and whispered, "Beneath my towel, Madeline. Where else?"

Maddie rolled to her bottom where she could face him. Heat crept up her cheeks, making her feel like a fireplace that had just been stoked. "You shouldn't say such scandalous things," she whispered. But she was unable to draw her gaze from that blasted towel.

He chuckled as he wiggled his legs with glee, obviously pleased by her discomfort. He laughed until he had to wipe his eyes from the exhaustion caused by his mirth. "Oh, Madeline dear, I'll have so much fun teaching you to be naughty. Though I think you'll be a willing student." His gaze darkened as he let his eyes slide up and down her body. She felt that movement more strongly than any caress he'd bestowed upon her so far. "I think there's a small piece of you that enjoys getting dirty."

"I do not, sir, enjoy getting dirty, and I never, ever will."

"Hmm. We'll see about that." Then he narrowed his eyes at her. "Just to be sure we're on the same page of this book that is now our lives, you do know that everything has changed, don't you?" He reached out as though he wanted to touch her. But then he pulled his hand back. "I'm not wealthy or titled. And to top it all off, I'm a Lycan. You are triply blighted."

She mulled it over for a moment. Things could be worse. He could be Gelligaer or Chilcombe or any number of the other peers her father had brought home to the castle. At least Weston Hadley had had her attention, even before he'd turned into a wolf before her eyes. "I'm not blighted." She shrugged. "So, my circumstances have changed. Sophie's circumstances have changed, and she's making the best of it. I'll do the same."

Weston scoffed. "Sophie took employment, darling. You're taking a husband."

"I knew I'd take a husband one day, and I knew it would be someone I didn't love. This is not very different. As you so graciously mentioned, I was born to be docile."

"God, I hope you're not really docile," he muttered as he rolled to his side and put out the lamp on the bedside table, casting the room in shadows. "I hate docile."

He rolled to face her once again, still wearing nothing more than his towel. She lay down on her pillow, never moving her eyes from his. He looked fairly average with his scar hidden in the pillow. But then he reached out and ran his fingertips slowly up her arm. That wasn't ordinary at all. It made the hair on her arms stand up. It made her nipples press like hard points against the counterpane. "What's wrong with docile?" she whispered to him.

"Docile is fine for other men. And if it's what you *truly* are, I'll be very happy with it. But if it's not, I hope you don't pretend to be obedient or docile just because it's what's expected. I'll expect you to be you."

"And who am I?" She had to ask, wondering if he saw something more inside her than she even knew herself.

"You're Lady Madeline Hayburn, only daughter to the Duke of Hythe. And you're marrying well below your station to become just another Hadley." He cupped the side of her face and kissed her very gently on the lips. "Too late to change any of that, I'm afraid."

What if she didn't want to change any of that? Even if she could? What if, right in that moment, she wanted to throw docility out the window? Was there more to her than that? Maddie had a sneaking suspicion that Weston Hadley had a lot more fun being poor and dirty than she did being rich and clean.

"Go to sleep," he said quietly. "We have to be up early in the morning."

"To get married," she said softly.

"Unless you run off first," he grumbled as he settled deeper into his pillow.

Twelve

WES BARELY SLEPT A WINK THE ENTIRE NIGHT. AT SOME point, Madeline had pressed her lithe body up against his and decided to use his chest as a pillow. She'd burrowed in so tightly that he couldn't tell where he stopped and she started. Not that he'd ever complain about such a thing. If she wanted to sprawl her delight-fully naked body across him all evening, he was more than willing to accommodate her. There was also the matter of her snoring. Though that was an awful word to describe the content, little breathy sounds that emanated from her as she slept. He'd listened to them the whole night and imagined them transforming into sounds of passion. The thought had nearly forced him to get up and sleep in a chair. Parts of him still stood at attention as dawn threatened to break.

She could torture him like no one else had ever done, but that would all end. Today. He'd marry her today and finally relieve the ache he'd felt for her since the moment he'd first laid eyes on her.

The sound of a carriage in the distance caught Wes' attention, and he glanced toward the rented room's small window. A warm orange hue tinted the horizon. Morning was upon them, and they had an important day ahead of them.

"Darling." He caressed her bare back. Dear God, she had the softest skin he'd ever touched. He could touch her all day. Except for today. They had an appointment with a blacksmith, after all. "It's time to wake up, Madeline."

She grumbled something unintelligible and smacked his chest as though he was a pillow she was attempting to fluff.

Wes laughed at his good fortune. "If you want to stay in bed tomorrow, I'll be eager to stay there with you." In fact, he'd stay abed for days if she wanted, making love to her until they were both breathless and sated.

I knew I'd take a husband one day, and I knew it would be someone I didn't love. Her words from the previous evening echoed in his thoughts.

Wes frowned as he stared up at the dingy, water-stained ceiling above them. But what did he expect? Madeline barely knew him. Though he'd met her three years ago, they'd never spoken more than the most cursory of words until recently. However, that didn't mean she couldn't learn to love him. And she hadn't tried to poison him, so that was a positive.

Odds were he'd spend eternity in hell for robbing her of her intended life, and though he would have never chosen this path for her, he couldn't bring himself to feel badly about that at the moment, not with her naked breasts crushed against his chest.

"Hadley!" someone bellowed from the taproom beneath them.

Madeline bolted upright, horror splashed across her face. "Papa," she gasped, clutching the counterpane against her breasts when it would have fallen lower.

Wes was certain his heart had stopped beating all together. *The Duke of Hythe!* Here? Good God. He scrambled off the bed and began to tug his borrowed trousers up over his hips. How the devil had the man caught up to them?

Madeline looked as though she might faint when she glanced down at her unclothed state. "You should never have sent him that note."

Wes snorted. It was certainly too late to rectify that mistake. The one time he'd tried to do the gentlemanly thing and *this* was what happened. "Get dressed, will you?" He crossed the floor to peer down at the innyard below. The Duke of Hythe's sleek traveling coach stood proudly out front, shiny black with gold gilt. A few feet away, Renshaw glanced up and met Wes' eye. The driver gestured toward the Eynsford carriage already hitched with fresh horses. If they could just slip past the duke…

"Hadley! Where are you?" Hythe bellowed again.

Wes couldn't let the duke catch them before they were married. His secret was only safe as long as Madeline needed to keep it, too. He turned back to find lady in question still too stunned to move. He picked up her stained-beyond-repair dress, which was still a little damp from the night before, and tossed it to the bed in front of her. "Get dressed!" he ordered more gruffly than he would have liked. But time was not on their side this morning.

Wes snatched up his own shirt from the floor and slid it over his head.

He heard the innkeeper mutter the number "Nine," and he knew it would only be moments before the duke was upon them. Luckily, Madeline had pulled her yellow dress over her head and was scrambling to put herself to rights.

Wes crossed the floor again and opened the window as wide as it would go. He could easily make the jump, but Madeline couldn't, not unless she was part Lycan and didn't know it. He glanced over his shoulder at her. "Jump and I'll catch you."

Her green eyes grew wide, as though he'd just asked her to sprout wings and fly to the moon.

The stomping of boots pounded up the steps.

"We don't have time to make other plans, Madeline. I need you to jump to me."

She barely nodded, but Wes figured that would be as good as he would get standing there. He looked back over the window, climbed up on the ledge and jumped to the ground below. His legs stung a bit from the landing and he wished he'd thought about his boots before he leapt, but there was no time.

"Madeline," he hissed at the same moment he heard a pounding on the bedroom door.

Then before Wes could say another word, two boots flew out the window, one of them smacking him directly above his left eye. "Madeline!" he growled.

"Sorry." She looked down on him from the window. "You forgot them."

The duke's voice rang out loudly. "Madeline, are you in there? Open up!"

Wes' heart pounded so loudly in his ears, he could barely hear. "Jump!"

She peered over the edge of the window and cringed. "It's too far, Weston."

They didn't have time to plan something else. "I will catch you, my dear. I swear it."

Madeline climbed up on the sill, fear etched across her face. Wes heard the bedroom door break open at the exact moment Madeline leapt from the window. A second later, he enveloped her in his arms, relieved beyond measure that she'd actually jumped. But he didn't have time to revel in the emotion, and he bolted toward the awaiting Eynsford carriage.

"Weston Hadley!" the duke bellowed from the window. "Return my daughter to me at once."

"I can't do that, sir." Wes called back, pushing Madeline toward the open coach door. He glanced up at her father, who was red in the face with fury flashing in his eyes. "I'll be happy to discuss the situation with you tomorrow."

The duke bolted from the window, presumably down the stairs to catch them, which Wes couldn't allow. He motioned for Renshaw to follow, darted back to the sleek Hythe coach, and lifted the rear of it. "Take the wheel," he ordered with a grunt. Before the duke's men could even move, Renshaw had the wheel removed and stood there staring at him like an idiot. Wes released his hold on the carriage, and the conveyance nearly toppled over from the disparity of balance.

There wasn't a second to spare. Wes ran forward, took the wheel, tossed it onto the top of the Eynsford coach, and yelled, "Don't just stand there! Quickly, man," to the still-startled driver. Then, as an afterthought, Wes snatched up the boots Madeline had thrown at him and dashed back to the Eynsford carriage, hurtling himself inside the open door and landing on the floor.

"Go, Renshaw! Go!" he called as the carriage lurched forward.

⤖

Out of breath, Maddie watched Weston scramble to the bench opposite her. He heaved a sigh as he tossed his borrowed boots to the floor. "I didn't think you'd jump."

Maddie wasn't certain why she had. She could have easily turned around, opened the door for her father, and been headed back home to Kent right this moment. Back to the suitors her father wanted her to entertain, assuming he'd been able to keep her flight north a secret from the collection of lords. And Maddie couldn't face that possibility. Weston Hadley wasn't the sort of man she was supposed to marry, nor was he the sort of man she had ever dreamed she would marry. But there was something about him she liked, and that was more than she could say for all the other fellows still in residence at Castle Hythe combined. "I'm not accustomed to leaping out of inn windows."

He smiled as he caught his ragged breath. "Well, allow me to say you did it magnificently for your first time."

Maddie glanced out the coach window, back toward

the little hovel where they'd spent the evening. "It won't take him long to catch us."

"He is now missing one rear wheel," Weston informed her rather smugly, if the truth be known.

Maddie blinked at the Lycan.

"It's on the top of *our* carriage," he said with a chuckle "He won't go far without it."

She wasn't sure she wanted to know how he had accomplished such a feat so quickly. But it was no matter; her father wouldn't give up. Quitting wasn't in his nature. "Papa will simply take a horse and follow us then."

Weston shook his head. "Not from that establishment. The only cattle left are Hythe's coach horses, and who knows how far that group has been driven thus far." He shook his head. "No, we have a lead on your father. But we can't afford to give it up."

His eyes strayed to Maddie's *décolletage*, and she realized her tattered day dress hadn't been buttoned properly. She gasped and smacked a hand to her bodice.

Weston laughed. "Don't know what I was thinking. You couldn't get out of the thing without help last night. Turn around and I'll button you up."

Was he enjoying her state of dishabille? "I woke up to hear my father yelling your name, then had to scramble into this awful dress and jump out an inn window. I didn't even have time to don my chemise. I hardly find my current state amusing."

He motioned for her to turn around, which was easier suggested than done inside a moving carriage. But Maddie did turn her back to him. A moment later, his warm hand stroked across her bare back as he worked at the first button. "If you don't find your dress amusing," he brushed his lips against the side of her neck, "then I won't even mention your hair."

Her hair? Maddie felt the top of her head with both hands. She couldn't see her hair, but she could just imagine it wild and sticking out in all directions. She squeaked in horror. Heavens, every moment she spent in Weston Hadley's company, her appearance became more ghastly. What would she look like after a decade with the wolf?

Weston chuckled again as he finished with her buttons. "You should never go to bed with a wet head of hair, darling."

Maddie glanced at him over her shoulder, hating the mirth she saw reflected in his dark eyes. Of course *he* looked dashing this morning, even with his scar. She hated him in that moment. Why should he look handsome in his borrowed innkeeper clothes when *she* looked worse than a common refugee escaping The Terror a quarter century earlier? Not that she'd ever seen a refugee, but she could well imagine one, and she could well imagine that she looked even worse by half. "I had very little choice as we don't possess a brush. We probably can't even afford one."

A frown settled on his face, which Maddie found strangely satisfying. "I don't want to hear you complain about needing a bath until after we've reached Gretna. Your hair is unruly but it is *clean*."

Did he think she was a dolt? She knew they couldn't stop any longer than it took to change horses along the way. Not with her father fast on their trail.

Still, she couldn't resist goading him by saying, "A novel concept for you, Mr. Hadley?"

Something flashed in his eyes, a hint of wickedness perhaps. "Indeed. Being dirty is so much more appealing. I'm certain you'll grow to enjoy it immensely."

Not if she was made to look like a waif, she wouldn't. She might be marrying into the Hadley family, but she would always be Lady Madeline. No one could ever take that away from her. And ladies, no matter what breed of dog they married, never looked like waifs. Well, except for those refugees who *had* escaped The Terror, but she chose not to give that point any credence.

"Only you," he settled back against the leather squabs, "can look so imperious in a ratty dress and wild hair and," he looked at her feet, "no slippers." Then he tipped back his head and laughed.

Maddie folded her arms across her chest and glared at him.

"My apologies." He actually appeared to be struggling to stop his laughter, but then he started laughing even harder.

How did one strangle the life out of a creature that could heal himself?

Finally his levity came to an end and he coughed into his fist when he saw her glower. "I-I... it's just that," he hastened to explain, "you hit me in the head with *my* boots, but then you managed to leave your own slippers behind."

Maddie tossed her wild hair back regally. "I *had* them when I jumped. They fell off along the way. Be glad you got your smelly boots."

Weston flashed his blasted charming smile and nodded his head in agreement. "I suppose I'll just have to carry you the rest of the journey then."

"I suppose someone will have to," she muttered as she crossed her arms beneath her breasts and flopped back against the squabs. She'd never flopped in her life, but it seemed the appropriate thing to do at the time.

Weston bent and lifted the edge of her dress, then plucked at her naked toe, lifting her foot into his lap. "I'd imagine these pretty little feet have never run bare through the woods or across a pasture?" He arched a brow at her.

She tried to pull her foot back, but he held tightly to it. "Of course not." She was hardly a savage. "May I have my foot back, please?" she asked as sweetly as she could.

"No," he grunted as he examined the arch of her foot, allowing his fingers to slide up the sensitive skin like the gentlest touch of a feather.

Maddie couldn't keep from giggling as she tugged at her foot again.

"Ticklish, are you?" he said, looking like he was thoroughly enchanted by the sole of her foot.

"I suppose I am," she said with a laugh she couldn't withhold. "Let my foot go," she cried.

"But it's cold," he said as he wrapped both his hands around her bare foot.

"I had to abandon my stockings," she reminded him. The warmth of his hands did feel nice. So she stilled her foot, reveling in his ministrations.

He looked up at her with a wicked grin. "Lost your stockings, lost your slippers, lost your underthings," he said as his gaze drifted down her body, almost as though he was looking at her naked. She shivered lightly under his heated look. He'd gone from being winded and worried to being thoroughly entranced by her foot, and now he looked completely taken with the thought of her loss of appropriate clothing. "Lost your dignity yet?"

"Hardly," she replied. She jerked her foot, and he finally released it. He looked slightly bereft without it, like a child who'd lost his plaything.

Before Maddie could even settle her skirts back around her legs, he scooped her up and deposited her on his lap. "Wes," she cried as she pushed weakly against his hold.

"Oh, so I've graduated to Wes, now, have I?" he laughed.

"*Weston*," she corrected herself. "Let me go." Her protests sounded weak even to her own ears. Did she really want him to let her go? Maddie stared into his dark eyes and could imagine losing herself in their depths.

Thirteen

WES HAD ONLY PLANNED TO PLAY WITH HER FEET, since she'd suffered the great indignity of losing her slippers. She'd even gotten the bottom of her foot dirty in her mad dash across the innyard. But he imagined she wouldn't be overjoyed to hear that the bottom of her pretty little foot was less than clean.

But then they'd started talking about her losing her stockings, and all he could think about was the fact that her bare little foot was connected to a bare little leg, and he wanted to run his hand up her bare calf and higher.

Then the thought of her with no chemise made the thoughts even more prominent. So, like the beast he was, the moment she'd said his name, he'd scooped her into his arms and directly onto his lap. Right on top of his rising manhood. "Stop squirming," he warned, adjusting her in his lap as he turned her to face him.

"Put me down," she said weakly. But the flush on her cheeks and the mad thumping of her heart gave him a good idea of her true desires.

"I would if I thought that's what you really wanted." He played with a lock of her hair as she settled comfortably in his lap. Comfortably for her, but not as much for him.

"What makes you such an expert on women's thoughts and feelings, Mr. Hadley?" she asked with an imperious tone.

"A moment ago, I was Wes, and now I'm back to being Mr. Hadley?" The very thought was like a knife to his chest.

"You didn't answer my question," she prodded, and if he wasn't mistaken, there was a teasing sparkle in her eyes.

All Wes could think about was Madeline's lack of underthings and how easy it would be to get her out of that dress and on his lap completely naked. He could toss the dress out the window, and then she'd be completely at his mercy. He could spend the next hours of their trip convincing her that she'd like being naked and poor. "What *was* your question?" he grumbled, trying to concentrate on her words.

"I want to know what makes you so adept at deciphering a woman's thoughts and feelings that you can tell me what I do and do not want." She grinned at him, a playful little grin. He hadn't misinterpreted her expression moments earlier.

"Shall I be honest?" he asked, looking into her enchanting eyes. They were like limpid, green pools he could drown in.

"Please," she said softly. Then she inhaled deeply and held her breath, as though what he had to say would realign the pieces of her world, if the thought was profound enough.

"I don't care about other women, Madeline," he admitted. She looked so serious that he felt like he needed to tell her the truth. She'd just jumped from a window to outrun her father, to stay with him, for God's sake. She at least deserved something in response of her loyalty.

"You need not lie to me, Weston," she said, moving as though to rise from his lap. But he tugged her back down and clamped an arm across her thighs.

"I've been besotted by you since the first time I saw you," he admitted.

"You *have*?" she squeaked. Then she cleared her throat. "You have?" she asked again, watching his face intently.

He nodded. "You were standing in the ballroom of the castle, talking to Sorcha MacQuarrie. You were the most angelic creature I'd ever seen."

Madeline smiled shyly. "You were with your brothers, and Lord Radbourne asked me to dance."

Damned Archer always did have the best of luck, not that Wes had trusted himself to speak to the lady at the time.

"Grandmamma was furious as none of you had been properly introduced."

Fury did seem to be the duchess' natural state. "As I said before, Hadley men are rarely proper."

She frowned, as though mulling over his admission. "You would have run off for Gretna with any lady who saw you turn into a wolf?"

He pretended to ponder her question. "Perhaps,"

he teased. "But I wouldn't have enjoyed it nearly as much with anyone else." He couldn't keep from laughing when she rolled her eyes. Even with all her years of propriety, she could still do something as indecent as roll her eyes. That meant there was a chance she could be persuaded to throw propriety to the wind. There was a chance she'd get on top of him and ride him all through the night. The thought entered his mind, and it wouldn't leave. Damn his thoughts.

"What's wrong?" she asked, her face marred by a worried scowl.

"Nothing," he growled and closed his eyes. But even with his eyes closed, all he could see was her wildly tumbled hair cascading over them both as she climbed atop him. Would she ever do that? Could she ever do that? Or was her damned perfection going to put a damper on any chance he had of getting her wild and wanton in his bed?

"Wes," she said very softly. He cracked an eye open. He was still holding her tightly in his lap, and she didn't struggle against him at all. "Did you really want me, even before you had to have me?" she questioned.

"More than my next breath," he admitted.

"Will you kiss me, Wes?" she asked quietly.

But he didn't even lift his head from where it rested against the squabs. He just said, "You kiss *me*, Madeline."

She looked at him as though he'd grown two heads. "Me?" she asked, indignation high in her voice. "You said all I had to do was ask you if I wanted another kiss."

She was right. He was being an idiot. But she was so damn tempting there in his lap. And if he ever put his lips on her, he wouldn't be able to pull them away. He'd have her naked in the coach and he'd be inside her, and she deserved better than that. "So I did," he grunted.

She huffed. "Well, if you don't want to kiss me, just say so."

He ran a hand through her tumbled hair and cupped the back of her head. "I *want* to kiss you," he breathed, his lips a breath from hers. But just then, the coach rolled to a stop. "Damn him," Wes groaned. What the devil was wrong with the coachman? What on earth could make the man want to stop at this very moment? "Renshaw?" he called loudly.

The driver's voice echoed back at them. "You may want to step outside, sir," Renshaw said.

Wes slid Madeline from his lap. "Stay here."

She nodded and flicked her foot forward as though to remind him that she couldn't go anywhere, at least not very far and not very quickly, without her slippers.

"I'll be right back," he muttered. Then Wes opened the coach door and stepped out into the now bright sunlight. His mouth dropped open at the sight that greeted him. What awful luck! With Madeline's father quick on their heels, they didn't have time to deal with a prostrate gig blocking the road. "Good God!"

"What's wrong?" Madeline's voice called from inside the carriage.

"Nothing, darling. Just an overturned conveyance. I'll take care of it." He followed in Renshaw's wake toward the downed gig. "Do you see anyone?"

The driver shook his head. "Not yet, Mr. Hadley. No horse either."

Well, Wes doubted anyone just abandoned their country carriage in the middle of the road. "Hello!" he called.

But there was no answer.

Perfect. Wes clapped a hand to the coachman's back. "We'd better move it out of the way before Hythe catches up to us."

Renshaw snorted. "*We?* I'm fairly certain you can handle that on your own, sir."

The driver most certainly did know something, but Wes chose not to worry about that problem at the moment. If Renshaw had kept his mouth closed as long as he had thus far, he could probably be trusted to keep his own counsel at least until they returned to Kent. "Just look for anyone who might be thrown or injured, will you?"

As Renshaw pushed his way through the foliage lining the road, Wes grasped the underside of the gig and flipped the small conveyance back upright. It bounced slightly on its wheels, both of which seemed to be in working order. Then the small crest on the side of the gig caught Wes' eye.

He groaned. *Not Dovenby.* He had no desire to see that pompous Lycan for the rest of his days. "See any sign of anyone?" he called to the coachman.

"No, sir."

"Dovenby?" Wes bellowed. "You dying somewhere in the field?" He sniffed the air. He didn't smell the blackguard. Still he waited a moment to see if any reply came.

All he heard was the noise the summer wind made as it moved through the trees. Wes tugged the gig to

the side of the road so there would be enough room
for the Eynsford coach to pass. If the Earl of Dovenby
had gotten himself into some sort of trouble, he could
bloody well take care of himself. "Let's hurry on then.
Hythe is still back there somewhere. I don't want to
lose our lead."

❧

Maddie peered out the carriage window, watching
Weston and the Eynsford driver hurry back to the
carriage. She stared past them to a flashy gig that
leaned forward on its shafts. Hopefully no one had
been hurt.

Just as Weston opened the door, Maddie scrambled
back to her seat to give him room to enter the carriage.
"Is everyone all right?"

He settled on the bench across from her. "Couldn't
see a sign of anyone, but I'm sure Dovenby will be
back for his gig soon enough."

Dovenby? "You know who the gig belongs to?"

A look of annoyance settled on Weston's face. "I
recognized his crest."

"A friend?" she pressed. There was something he
wasn't saying.

"Something like that," he grumbled as the carriage
lurched forward.

What was that supposed to mean? "You're not
worried about your friend?"

"He's not my friend and he can take care of himself."

Maddie frowned. "I just don't understand why
someone would leave a conveyance overturned in the
middle of the road."

"Dovenby is accustomed to leaving his messes for everyone else. Think nothing more of it."

"Do you think he was racing and had an accident?"

Weston narrowed his eyes at her. "I don't know what he was doing, darling. But he's already captured more of your attention than he's worth."

"I never have understood the appeal of racing. Why do men do such foolish things, Weston?"

For some reason he turned a bit red at her question. "I couldn't say," he replied tightly.

Being a man, he most certainly could say, she was sure. "Have *you* ever raced?"

"We are racing your father right now, my dear."

She hadn't really thought of it that way. "I meant for sport, Wes. I don't understand why men do things that could get them injured or killed, all in the name of fun."

"I can't really answer for most men, Madeline."

Because he could heal himself, the risk wasn't as dangerous. She supposed that could be a benefit of marrying a Lycan. Or not. "Does your ability to heal make you more reckless than normal men?"

"Might we change the subject? I don't know how most men think, Madeline," Wes grumbled.

"Neither do I," Maddie said with a long sigh as she sat back and regarded her soon-to-be-husband from across the coach. "But I do know that you'll no longer be allowed to race once we're married."

His head jerked up. She suddenly had his full attention, though she wasn't certain why. "No longer allowed?" he questioned. "Beg your pardon?"

She nodded for emphasis. "You'll have to cease

your reckless behavior. I can't have a husband of mine creating scandal or making a bad name for himself."

Wes sat forward and rested his elbows on his knees. "In case you're unaware, Madeline, the Hadleys already have a name for themselves. You will have to be a pretty good runner if you hope to outdistance it." His gaze raked quickly up and down her body. "Something tells me you're not predisposed to such physical activity."

She huffed and crossed her arms beneath her breasts. He had no idea what she was and was not predisposed to. "All I know is that you'll have to lead a more respectable life, Weston. Between Sophia and me, we can have the Hadley men up to snuff in no time." She began to tick items off on her fingers. "There can be no drinking, no swearing, no racing, no gambling…" She stopped to think.

"Shall I be allowed to breathe, my dear? Or will that tax your delicate sensibilities, too?"

"Breathing will be fine. As long as you don't do it loudly."

He shook his head and chuckled. "I hope I'm able to come up to scratch, darling," he said. Then he whispered dramatically, "If not, you might have to topple from your lofty tower and join me with the plebeians. I promise to catch you when you fall."

Fall? Not in his lifetime. "That will never happen," she informed him. There were certain things she would not give up, and respectability was one of them. "Grandmamma would never allow me to behave irresponsibly."

"Darling, the duchess will no longer be your keeper,"

he said, laughing. "I keep telling you that your station in life has changed. When will you believe it?"

"I have a huge dowry—" she began. But he cut her off.

"Which your family will never put into the hands of a Hadley. You said so yourself."

She had, but that was beside the point. "I don't know how a discussion about your obligations as a husband turned into another discussion about your lack of a fortune."

"I know my obligations as a husband." He narrowed his eyes at her. "Would you like to hear them?"

Would she? Probably not. "If you'd like to share them, I certainly would." Perhaps he would surprise her with his insight.

"I am obligated to keep you fed, clothed, and with a roof over your head."

She opened her mouth to protest, but he held up a finger and shushed her.

"And if you'll give me an opportunity, with little regard to social standing, I might be able to make you happy, Madeline. How would you feel about that?"

Happiness was more than she had hoped for with any of the throng of gentlemen currently ensconced in Castle Hythe, but it wasn't a necessity. "I would feel much better about being respectable."

A wolfish grin settled on his lips. "Respectability never kept anyone warm, Madeline. So if not happiness, then perhaps I'll throw in some passion when you least expect it." His eyes took a leisurely path down her body once again.

Maddie's face warmed and she turned to gaze out

the window. Blast him for affecting her in such a way. Passion, he said? She'd asked him to kiss her and he hadn't done so. Was she only to receive passion when she least expected it? That hardly seemed fair. Somehow she managed not to snort as the Cumberland countryside rolled past the coach window, or the Yorkshire countryside or wherever they were.

Without warning, the coach slowed once again to a stop.

"Bloody hell. What is it this time?" Weston grumbled.

Certainly Papa hadn't caught up to them yet.

"We are in a hurry, Renshaw! Perhaps you've noticed." Weston tossed open the door, with a murderous expression.

"Devil take it!" came a rich baritone voice. "Weston Hadley in the flesh."

Maddie peeked her head out the open door. A handsome man, with hair as black as pitch, stood on the side of the road, his boots coated in mud.

"Dovenby," Weston replied with the warmth gentlemen usually saved for meeting Grandmamma. "You left something of yours in the middle of the road a ways back."

But the gentleman paid Weston's tone little notice and stepped closer to the coach wearing a devil-may-care grin. "Lost more than that. You haven't by chance come across a breathtaking blonde with one of my bays, have you?"

"No," Wes replied curtly.

Then the gentleman's eyes strayed to the coach and landed on Madeline. "No," he agreed. "But you seem to have found a pretty blonde just the same."

Fourteen

"BEST OF LUCK FINDING *YOUR* LOST BLONDE, DOVENBY."
Wes glared at the other Lycan. If he took one step
toward Madeline, Wes would rip the man's head from
his shoulders.

Why had she stuck her head out of the coach to begin
with? What if they'd been stopped by highwaymen
or some other sort of brigands? Had she no regard for
her own safety?

The Earl of Dovenby tipped his hat in Lady
Madeline's direction. "Good morning."

"Not really," Wes muttered, but Dovenby's sensitive ears picked up the comment.

"I say, Hadley, why are you headed north? Doesn't
your pack keep farther south?"

"Just driving through, Dovenby. I'm not
encroaching on your territory."

The damned earl shrugged as though it was no matter
to him whether Wes came or went. "Still, a bit early for
you to be up and about isn't it? Town hours and all."

"As much as I've always enjoyed our conversations,
I really am in a hurry this morning."

"Headed to Penrith?" Dovenby pressed.

"No."

"Past there then? I could use a ride, if you're feeling generous."

No way in hell. "What about your blonde?"

Dovenby shrugged. "There's always another." He glanced back toward the coach again. "Who is your traveling companion, Hadley?"

"My wife." Wes didn't even try to keep the growl from his voice. "And as I said, we are in a hurry. Do visit if you get to Kent."

The irritating Lycan grinned as though he knew Wes was lying. "Allow me to offer my felicitations. I had no idea you'd gotten caught in the parson's noose."

"Well, I suppose it happens to each of us in the end." Wes started back toward the coach. "Do send my regards to your cousins."

Dovenby was at the coach door in a flash, smiling at Madeline as though he'd like to eat her. "Mrs. Hadley, allow me to introduce myself. The Earl of Dovenby at your service."

Before Wes could knock the jackass to the ground, Madeline replied, "My lord, did you say you are in need of a ride to Penrith?"

Wes growled low in his throat. After all, Dovenby could run faster than the carriage if he was of a mind to do so. "We don't have the time to be good Samaritans, darling."

"It is on the way, Weston."

Dovenby flashed a smug grin at Wes before climbing into the coach. Perfect! Not only did Wes have to suffer the infuriating Lycan's presence, but he had the damn wolf's added weight in the carriage. Did she want them to get caught?

More than furious, Wes climbed inside the coach and glared at the Lycan who'd had the audacity to sit right next to Madeline. Wes grasped her hand and tugged her to the other bench, beside him. "As long as we're being generous, we ought to give our guest enough room to be comfortable."

Madeline looked at the interloper as the carriage once again started down the road. "I am curious to hear your opinion, Lord Dovenby."

The earl inclined his head in a way that made Wes want to pummel the life out of him. "I am anxious to give it to you, Mrs. Hadley."

"Lady," she corrected. "Lady Madeline Hadley."

How delightful her name sounded to Wes' ears.

"You may ask me anything you'd like, my lady."

"What is your opinion on reckless male pursuits once a gentleman has taken a wife?"

Wes was certain his mouth dropped open. But he closed it quickly when he saw the Dovenby's expression of true delight. "I hardly think," Wes began, "we should involve the earl in our discussion, darling."

"Discussion?" Dovenby asked. "Or lovers' quarrel?"

Wes glared at the interfering Lycan across the coach from him. "Mind your own matters," he growled.

Dovenby grinned like the blackguard he was. "But the lady *did* ask my opinion, Hadley." Then he turned his wolfish gaze to Madeline. "And I never like to disappoint a lady."

"Of course not. Clearly you're legendary," Wes grumbled. "Women absconding with your bay and all that. Did she dump your coach over trying to get away from you?"

But Dovenby paid him no attention, his gaze lingering on Madeline. "My lady, might I say how stunningly beautiful you are. Such a graceful, slender, *unblemished* neck." Then his eyes shot back to Wes. "How long have you been married, Hadley? Or are you simply not *up* to the challenge of matrimony?"

Meaning the full moon was only two nights ago and Madeline had clearly not been claimed then or ever. Wes bristled at the insult to his masculinity. "True *ladies* are more delicate than others of their sex," he ground out. Even after they were married years, he doubted Madeline would ever welcome him biting her neck under the light of a full moon. She couldn't even tolerate a little dirt. An overly amorous wolf with sharp teeth would be more than frowned upon. "Though I don't suppose you have much experience with the fairer sex. Not the respectable ones, anyway."

The earl's smirk made Wes' fingers itch to open the coach door and toss the jackass from the moving conveyance. "I'd wager I have more experience than you, pup."

"*Pup?*" Madeline squeaked, though she was soundly ignored.

"I do love a wager I'm sure to win," Wes growled. "How much?"

Dovenby tossed back his head and laughed. "Exactly how do you think to quantify such a thing?"

"The wager was your suggestion."

"So it was." Dovenby sighed as though he suddenly found the conversation to be tedious. "Shall I tell you what I think is truly going on here?" He gestured to the two of them.

"What are the odds I could stop you?" Wes narrowed his eyes at his fellow Lycan.

"Well, as you're headed north and you both look as though you've seen better days, you can only be eloping." Then he winked at Madeline. "What are you thinking, my lady? You could do so much better than this unruly mutt."

"Mutt?" Madeline muttered and she slid closer to Wes on the bench.

"Some of us have better pedigrees than others."

"And some of us," Wes bit out, "are guests in someone else's coach."

Dovenby laughed. "The crest on the side belongs to Eynsford, not you. So I'd say we were all guests, Hadley. Or did you win the carriage and driver in a wager of some sort?"

Before Wes could respond, Madeline cleared her throat. "Weston has a very nice high-perch phaeton," she defended with the lofty tone Wes had become accustomed to. "But it wouldn't do to race to Gretna in that, now would it?"

Wes wasn't certain how she knew about his conveyance. Hopefully, she wouldn't learn the thing had been destroyed in a race or he'd never hear the end of that topic.

"I suppose not," Dovenby conceded with smug nod.

"Well, of course not," Madeline finished. "It wouldn't be the thing at all."

"One must live up to certain standards when one is eloping," Dovenby agreed. "So tell me, is anyone hot

on your tail? I cannot believe a loving father would
want to see a daughter of his shackled to a Hadley."

Madeline clamped her lips shut, probably because
she agreed with him wholeheartedly.

"How far behind us is he?" Dovenby asked.

"Not far," Madeline began, "but—"

Wes cut her off with a stern glance that made her
purse her lips even tighter. Thank God. If she would
just keep them shut, the earl might close his own
damned mouth. "Her father is irrelevant."

"About as irrelevant as that carriage wheel atop
your vehicle?" Dovenby laughed. "Brilliant bit of
maneuvering there, Hadley."

How had the blasted earl put all the pieces of the
puzzle together so quickly? Damn him.

Wes leaned forward and reached for the Lycan. "I'll
show you maneuvering," he growled. But Madeline
latched onto his arm and tugged with all her might.

"Didn't I ask you to behave respectably?" she hissed
in his ear.

Dovenby snorted. "I'm afraid you've saddled up the
wrong sort if a respectable ride is what you're after,
my lady."

"Do not talk to my wife about riding," Wes growled.

"Doesn't seem as though she is your wife."

∽∾

Madeline gaped at the two men sharing her space.
What was wrong with the two Lycans? Oh, she had
no doubt the Earl of Dovenby was a werewolf. Sly
mentions of pups and mutts and pedigrees made that
rather obvious if one knew what to look for. Though

she had no idea why they felt such animosity for each
other, there definitely was something going on that
she didn't understand. Any moment, she expected to
have to pull Weston from atop the earl and demand he
sit and stay. She racked her brain trying to remember
where she'd heard Dovenby's name before. It was
attached to some scandal or other, she was certain.
Was that the source of their discord?

Dovenby leaned over to look out the coach
window. "Oh, look," he chimed with gaiety. "There's
my missing bay."

Madeline glanced out the window and was startled
to see a blonde walking down the side of the road,
leading a large bay mare. The girl turned, obviously
startled by the approaching carriage. Then a thankful
look crossed her face, but Renshaw didn't stop. He
drove right past her.

Dovenby even waved and grinned out the window
at the girl. The blonde stomped her foot and dropped
the reins of the great beast she led, and she began to
follow the coach, her skirt up around her knees as
she ran.

"Oh, dear," Maddie breathed. "We have to stop."

"Not if I have anything to say about it," Dovenby
grunted. "She left me without a single look back."

"Must be nice to know that you're that good,
Dove," Wes taunted.

If that man was a dove, it was a soiled one. And so
was the young woman. But they couldn't just leave
her. Maddie tugged Wes' arm. "Tell Renshaw to
stop," she commanded.

Wes narrowed his eyes at her. "You do know that

the good earl wouldn't be caught dead with a respectable lady, do you not?"

That was neither here nor there. They couldn't leave the poor girl alone. She could be eaten by wild animals. Or worse. She could get covered in travel dust. Maddie shivered. "It doesn't matter," she declared. "If you won't stop for *her*, you'll have to stop and let me out so I can walk with her." Which he would never let happen, not if she knew him. Admittedly, she didn't know him all that well, but she *did* know he was in a hurry to make the border. Maddie shot Wes a pointed glance. "And the longer we wait, the more likely my father is to catch up with us."

"Don't tarry," Dovenby teased. "Or Daddy will catch up with us."

With a heavy sigh, Wes tapped on the roof. Renshaw pulled up, causing Dovenby to nearly fall upon Maddie. "Off," Wes barked, as he shoved the earl back into his own seat.

"I'll give you every coin in my pocket if you'll instruct your driver to keep going."

Wes glared at him. "How much do you have?"

Maddie elbowed him in the side, making him grunt. "It doesn't matter how much he has."

"It might. We could use some extra funds on this excursion, darling," he reminded her, as though she needed to be reminded of their near-destitute state. Then Wes smiled wolfishly at the earl. "Of course, we could just take his funds and toss him to the hounds from hell." Wes' dark eyes twinkled with mischievous delight. "Ah, looks like the hound has caught up with us." Then he leaned over Madeline to glance out her window. He paled just a bit and sank against the squabs.

Dovenby snorted. "I told you to keep going."

What in the world was wrong with the two of them? "Are neither of you gentlemanly enough to open the door for me?"

"I'd rather not," Wes admitted. "Why don't we just let Dovenby out, and we can be on our way."

"There's a woman all by herself on the side of the road!"

"She won't be alone if we let Dovenby out."

Of course, the earl didn't move one inch toward the door. Were all Lycans unchivalrous beasts? They certainly were if these two specimens represented the whole. Very well, if neither of them would open the door for her, Maddie was quite capable of opening it for herself.

She pushed open the coach door and dropped to the ground more roughly than she would have liked. Blast her missing slippers! "Ouch!" she muttered when a rock found her heel.

Wes was beside her in an instant. "Are you all right, darling? Are you hurt?"

Maddie glared at him. Had he resembled a gentleman in any way, she wouldn't have had to bound outside on her own. "A little late for your concern."

"Madeline." He tugged on her arm. "We are in a hurry, or have you forgotten?"

But Maddie's eyes were on the pretty girl, adorned in a much-too-daring walking dress for the country, who was coming in their direction. Before Maddie could say a word of welcome, the blonde stomped past her and sailed into the carriage. There she began to pummel the startled Dovenby with her fists. He protested loudly and cursed prolifically as he tried to fend off her blows.

Maddie blinked in bewilderment at the scene. Then she covered her mouth with her hand. "Go help him, Weston," she whispered in horror. Whoever thought a woman could behave in such a way?

But Wes propped himself against the corner of the coach and appeared to be engrossed in examining his fingernails, completely ignoring her and the bizarre kicking and screaming that emanated from the coach. Maddie looked up at Renshaw, who sat in his perch with his head buried in his hands. He was mumbling incoherently.

"Don't use such language around the ladies," Wes called out good-naturedly to the driver.

The coachman lifted his head and replied, "There's only *one* lady present, sir. And she couldn't hear me the way you can." Then he mumbled something about not making nearly enough money to put up with such nonsense.

Dovenby flew out of the coach in a rush, nearly tumbling in the dirt in his haste to get away from the wailing blonde. The earl stood up tall and straightened his coat, then ran a hand through his suddenly unkempt hair. Dovenby circled behind Wes and put Madeline between him and the lady. What a coward.

"Speaking of saddling the wrong ride," Wes started.

"Weston Hadley," the blonde shrieked as she launched herself from the coach as well. "I didn't even recognize you!"

"Of course not. All your ire was directed at Dovenby."

How did this outlandish woman know Weston?

"I think," the blonde replied, tipping back her chin as though she was the queen, "it has more to do with the fact that you look like an unkempt farmer." She gestured to his attire. "Have you fallen on even worse times since we last… met? Never mind. Don't answer that. You are damned lucky you stopped. If you hadn't, I'd have plagued you to the end of your days. Still if you think you'll ever crawl your sorry arse back in my bed—"

Wes stood up straight, suddenly at full attention as he began to speak in an obvious attempt to shut the woman's mouth. He dropped an arm around Maddie's shoulders. "Hardly. I already have a wife to plague me until the end of my days, dear," he said quickly.

Dovenby bent in the middle he laughed so hard.

"Or I soon will," Wes amended, shooting the earl a harsh glance.

The woman looked startled. Obviously startled. Yet she stopped talking.

"Which part are you referring to, Hadley? The 'plague you' part or the 'I'll never let you into my bed again' part?" Dovenby asked.

"Shut up, Dove," Wes growled.

Maddie must look like a complete ninny. She was certain of it. But her brain was racing as she tried to make sense of the scene. If there was one thing Maddie knew how to do, it was be polite. She extended a hand to the lady. "It's very nice to meet you," she said softly, in the voice she'd practiced for years, the one that made people think she was serene and naïve. And at this moment, she'd never felt quite so naïve.

The woman's gaze swept over Maddie's body. Then she sneered, "You usually don't like them skinny, Hadley," she said.

"She's not skinny," Wes started. But he dropped his chin to his chest and inhaled deeply before he continued. "Lady Madeline, this is Lucy Reed."

Lucy Reed? Why did that name sound familiar? Maddie would have let the name roll around in her mind until she had the answer, but she had just been slighted by the girl. So she leaned close to Wes' ear. "Did she really just call me skinny?" Maddie murmured.

But Dovenby answered before Wes could reply. "She did, indeed, dear."

"There are worse things you could be called." Wes winced.

True. Lucy Reed, whoever she was, had said something even more disturbing. "And did she say she has shared your bed?" She still spoke softly to Wes, but Dovenby was bending at the middle again.

"That was a long time ago," Wes tried as he took her shoulders and turned her to face him. Or at least attempted to. "I can explain, darling."

Oh, she had no doubt he would try. But Maddie didn't want to hear one word of it. Not one. "Renshaw!" She called loudly as she stomped to the front of the carriage, ignoring every pebble that found her un-slippered feet. "Are you still in possession of some funds?"

"I have enough, milady," he replied. A grin tugged at his lips, too. Blast them all. None of this was humorous in the least.

"Perfect. Take me somewhere. Anywhere," she said. "I don't care where."

"Yes, ma'am," he said with a quick nod.

"Madeline," Wes began, "we don't have time for theatrics."

But Maddie paid him no heed as she yanked open the coach door and stumbled inside. Blasted bruised feet. She must look completely ridiculous. She scrambled to a seat, trying to maintain whatever dignity she could, smoothing her tattered and worn skirts out with her hands. Before Weston or Dovenby could follow her, the coach lurched to a start, causing the door to flop open. Blast. She hadn't closed it properly.

Maddie stuck her head out the open door and watched, astounded, as Lucy Reed stuck her foot out and tripped Weston. Then Dovenby stumbled across him in his haste to reach the coach. And while it all occurred, the daring blonde hiked up her skirts and jumped in through the open door of the moving carriage. Maddie had to scramble once again to get out of the way.

Lucy Reed fell heavily onto the seat across from Maddie. "Well then, now that it's just us," she panted, "it's nice to meet you."

Fifteen

MADDIE COULD ONLY GAPE AT HER STOWAWAY FOR A moment. "I suppose I can't toss you out." No matter how much she would like to.

The blonde had shared Wes' *bed*. Her Wes. It made no difference that he hadn't been her Wes whenever the interlude or interludes had taken place. He was her Wes now. Though she wasn't certain when that had happened. Perhaps when she'd decided to leap out that inn window and run away with him. And this is how he thanked her? By cavorting with this Lucy Reed person before Maddie even knew she wanted him? She realized how ridiculous her thoughts would sound aloud and was glad she didn't have to mutter them to anyone who would think she had gone mad.

"You could try." Lucy Reed shrugged. "But where would be the fun in that?"

Fun? Maddie somehow managed not to choke on a sob. But she refused to let the blonde see her at her worst. So she straightened her back and glared at the other woman.

"I know who you are, you know?" Lucy shook her skirts out, making dust float in the streaks of sunlight that filtered through the window. "You went to *The Taming of the Shrew* this last Season."

Maddie coughed and swiped at a dust cloud that threatened to envelop her. Everyone had gone to *The Taming of the Shrew* last Season. What did the woman mean by that? "Just how do you think you know me?"

"You're Lord Robbie's little sister. I saw you in Hythe's box with him."

Lord Robbie? Maddie frowned at the blonde. No one had ever called Robert such a ridiculous thing in his life. "And just how do you know my brother?"

Lucy folded her hands in her lap. "He's a very generous patron of the arts."

Patron of the arts? Speaking with Lucy Reed made Maddie's head pound, and she had more pressing things to think about. After all, she had just ridden off without her wolfish fiancé, hadn't she? She probably should have thought that through better, but she'd been so flustered standing in the road in her bare feet, listening to how *her* Wes had shared his bed with the blonde who now sat across from Maddie, that she hadn't been thinking clearly. She still wasn't.

And then it hit her.

Maddie leaned forward in her seat and peered at the woman opposite her. Not Lucy Reed. "You're *Lucinda* Reed." Suddenly the outlandish walking dress made sense.

"So nice to be recognized even in this backwater county. How I let Dove talk me into this excursion is a mystery. I must have been foxed when I agreed to it."

"You played Bianca on the stage."

The blonde actress inclined her head. "I would have done a fabulous job as Kate, but Henry said my *ingénue* presence was better suited for Bianca." She rolled her eyes dismissively.

Maddie held in a snort. If Henry, whoever he was, had seen Lucinda Reed pummel an earl with her fists, trip two grown werewolves, and leap into a moving conveyance, she would have been cast as *the shrew* in an instant. "I'm sure you would have been a marvelous Kate."

Lucinda Reed smiled for the first time since Maddie had laid eyes on her. "That's what Robbie said, too. He's so adorable, your brother. Sent me roses every night of the show."

Patron of the arts. Madeline didn't want to know more. So both her brother *and* her fiancé had a taste for actresses. She could have gone her entire life without that knowledge. Now if only she could forget it. "Oh, yes, adorable. That's what I always say about *Robbie*."

"But your husband is wonderful, too."

"I'd really rather not discuss him at the moment."

"I can see your point." Lucinda agreed with a nod. "If I never lay eyes on Dovenby again, it will be too soon. Black-hearted scoundrel. What did Hadley do to *you*?"

Turned into a wolf before my very eyes. Rolled me in mud. Abducted me. Made me sleep in a hovel crawling with vermin. And kissed me... All things considered, it was best not to think about that kiss. That kiss was what most likely what had propelled her to leap out the inn window that morning. "It's too complicated to explain."

Lucinda Reed laughed. Loudly. "Complicated? Men?" Then she shook her head. "You really are the naïve sort, aren't you? How long have you been married?"

Madeline had no idea how to answer that, so she just stared at the actress.

Not that it mattered. Miss Reed could carry on a conversation with herself. "It can't have been very long or you'd know men are the most uncomplicated creatures on the earth."

"I've always thought them to be perfidious."

"Oh, they're scoundrels, the lot of them." The actress nodded in agreement. "So as long as you know not to trust them, they're easy to understand. They want full bellies and a woman warming their bed. That is it. The whole secret to men's happiness. Quite uncomplicated."

Maddie's mouth dropped open, but she quickly closed it. She couldn't believe the words that fell from Miss Reed's lips. What a thing to say!

"But Weston is a sweet one, for the most part. Radbourne, on the other hand, would scare the devil himself. And Lavendon—"

Maddie held up a hand to stop the woman. "Please." It was bad enough knowing Lucinda Reed knew Robert. If Nathaniel was a patron of the arts, too, Maddie would rather not know. "I have a lot on my mind."

"I should say so. Where are we headed? Somewhere I can catch a mail coach going south, I hope. Dovenby, damn his eyes, can forward my portmanteau on to me in London. I have no intention of spending even one more night in Cumberland." She snarled the last word as though to show her disdain. "The rustics are quaint for about five minutes, and that is all. You can mark my words."

≈

"However did you catch such a marvelous creature, Hadley?" Dovenby asked as the Eynsford coach grew smaller in the distance.

"Perhaps you've noticed I don't have her in my possession at the moment," Wes grumbled as he started after the carriage.

"Bad bit of luck there, Lucy mentioning your bed and all."

Which Wes didn't need to be reminded of. All men had pasts. What a sad excuse of a man he'd be if he didn't have one. But no man wanted his past exploits laid out before the girl of his dreams. And certainly not in front of an audience. "Can you shut your muzzle?"

"What does Eynsford think about this mad dash north? Is he aware you took his coach? Or will you face his wrath when you return to Kent?"

Wes stopped in his tracks and shoved Dovenby with all his might. The Lycan stumbled but didn't fall. "Go back to whatever hole you escaped from, will you? You've got both a bay and a gig needing your attention."

"A simple 'No, Eynsford doesn't know I've absconded with his carriage' will do next time, Hadley."

Wes growled. What he wouldn't give to put his fist though Dovenby's face, but every moment he stood with the Lycan, the farther Madeline got away. But she couldn't outrun him. He'd meet her at the next village, where Renshaw was certain to need a fresh set of horses.

Of course, he could follow along like a good little pup and run behind the coach. But that smacked at his pride harder than any ruler his tutors had ever struck him with. She couldn't get but just so far ahead. He started to walk. Dovenby fell in beside him.

Wes shot him a look. "Don't you have a carriage to retrieve?"

The earl shrugged. "It'll be there when I send someone for it."

"What about the bay?"

"She's lame. That must be why Lucy was walking her."

"So, you plan to accompany me to the next village?" There was no way he could tolerate the arse that long.

Dovenby arched a brow at him. "Do you think I'd miss the look on your lady's face when she steps from the carriage after riding for hours with Lucy Reed?" He shook his head dramatically. "Absolutely not."

He was right. Wes should probably start running, if he wanted to be there to soothe any ruffled feathers. Madeline's. Not Lucy Reed's. He didn't give a damn about Lucy's feathers.

Wes wasn't sure if he was angrier at Dovenby for admitting himself into Eynsford's coach in the first place or Lucy Reed for opening her big mouth. Either way, he'd have some serious explaining to do.

Wes could just imagine the things that Lucy was telling Madeline. He bit back a curse. Surely she wouldn't speak of specific bedroom behavior, would she? She might. He muttered an expletive.

"I'd be worried if I were you," Dovenby sang.

"What were you doing with Lucy, anyway?" The last time he'd seen Dovenby, he'd been engaged to a pretty little heiress with a huge dowry. "What happened to your fiancée?"

"She's with her family." The earl looked none too pleased. "They hate me and the feeling is mutual. I only agreed to the match to please my grandfather." He picked up a stone and sent it skipping along the path. "What about your lady? How on earth did you land Madeline Hayburn? That is who she is, isn't it? Hythe's daughter?"

"It's a long story," Wes murmured.

Dovenby scoffed and made a motion that pointed to all the open space around them. "It's not as though we don't have time."

"It's not important."

"Oh, come now, you can't leave me hanging like this," Dovenby teased. "Or I'll simply make up my own story and be forced to spread it around."

The jackass would do it, too, Wes had no doubt. Still, he doubted the earl could come up with something worse than had actually occurred, at least for a Lycan. "She stumbled upon me on the night of the full moon," Wes admitted.

"All fur and snout?" Dovenby whistled dramatically, the sound long and loud. "Rotten luck, there," he said. But then he got a contemplative look on his face. "So you spent the night of the moonful with her? And now you have to marry her."

"Something like that," Wes prevaricated.

"But you didn't claim her," the earl pressed.

Wes stopped walking and glared at him. "That's none of your concern."

"Pardon me. I'm simply trying to get hold of the events in my mind."

That would be the only time Dovenby had ever arranged his mind. He wasn't exactly known for his acumen.

"Well, you didn't sleep with her. So, I'd imagine your blasted honor is what's pressing you to marry the chit," the earl groused. "What is she thinking, settling for you? She could still do better."

She could, but Dovenby didn't have to be so callous about it. "Go to the devil, Dove," Wes said as he started to walk again. "And she's not a chit."

"Been to the devil already. Her name is Lucy Reed." Dovenby shivered. He poked at his cheek. "How does my eye look? Did she blacken it? She got in one solid punch in the carriage."

"Healed already. You look positively ravishing," Wes said drolly.

"Don't get any ideas. Next thing I know, you'll feel led to marry me."

Wes chuckled. Dovenby might be an arse, but he did make him laugh on occasion. "What did you buy for Lucy to get her to come with you?"

"Necklace," Dovenby said crisply. "A big one."

"I'm surprised she settled for that."

"She didn't. She wants a house."

"You mean to make her your mistress?" Wes gasped.

"*She* means for me to make her my mistress. I mean to ditch the spoiled bit of baggage as soon as I return her to her home." He snorted. "Besides, I'm about to be married, for God's sake." His face looked a bit green at the thought.

Wes doubted a little thing like marriage would change Dovenby's outlook on taking a mistress. But perhaps Lucy had doused his ardor with her temper tantrum in the carriage. "She's a nice chit. A bit dramatic." Lucy had once tossed Wes' clothes out the window when he refused her a bauble. He'd had to ring for a servant bare-arsed and ask for his clothes to be retrieved. "What do you think she's saying to Madeline?"

"I'm sure she's telling her every dirty little secret you have, or at least all the ones she knows about."

Wes' head swiveled so that he faced Dovenby. "She wouldn't be that ruthless."

"You think not?" Dovenby laughed. "You under-estimate her."

Damn it to hell. Lucy Reed would ruin any chance Wes had of winning Madeline's heart. Good God, if she told him even a quarter of the things he'd done, or the women he'd entertained, Madeline would never speak to him again. "I better get to the next village."

Dovenby nodded and fell into step beside him as he began to run. As Lycans, they could both run for hours and might even meet the coach about the same time it arrived at the next coaching inn. Or he hoped so, at least.

Sixteen

MADDIE GLANCED ACROSS THE COACH AND WATCHED as Lucy Reed's mouth fell open and a soft snort erupted. The blonde had finally dozed off, after going on and on about men and their propensity for letting a woman down. Maddie had listened intently until she realized that Miss Reed had no plans to speak of her time spent with Wes. The woman had just smiled and evaded the question, as though she liked having a secret that Maddie would never know.

She should have kicked the tart out of the coach as soon as she'd climbed in.

Maddie took in the tumbled state of Lucy Reed's curly hair and wished for a brief time that her own hair could look so artfully disarranged. She patted the top of her head. Her own hair probably looked as though a rat had settled in it and built a nest.

The dress Miss Reed wore was freshly laundered but showed quite an expanse of flesh. Maddie glanced down at her own tattered neckline. Other than the damage done over the last two days, her gown was respectable and demure. She was everything a lady was supposed to be, while Lucy Reed was not. They both had numerous suitors, but their situations couldn't have been more different. What was it that Wes had seen in the actress? Was it because Miss Reed's gown showed a bit more of her ankles than was proper? Or because she tossed up her skirts freely? Warmth crept up Maddie's cheeks. The very thought of it!

And it wasn't just Wes. Both of her brothers apparently had showered Miss Reed with attention, as well as the Earl of Dovenby until Lucy Reed started thrashing him. What was the allure? She didn't have a fortune or an important family. But Lucy Reed looked like she knew how to have… fun. That was the word. The woman looked like she probably enjoyed her life.

Maddie wished she could say the same, but "enjoy" was too strong a word. Oh, she knew it would be foolish to complain about her life. She was quite fortunate in many ways, but she'd never had the luxury to have fun.

The carriage's pace slowed and then finally stopped. Renshaw probably needed to change horses. After all, they had traveled for hours after leaving Wes and Lord Dovenby along the side of the road. She wasn't even certain where they were headed any longer. This was as good a time as any to find out.

Before she could open the door, it was yanked open from the other side. Wes poked his head inside, anxiety etched across his brow. "Miss me?"

"H-how?" she muttered, but then clamped her mouth shut. How in the world had he reached them? What other abilities did the man possess? She wanted to ask, but she was still too annoyed with him to show any appreciation for his miraculous appearance. "I didn't miss you at all. Please move, Weston. You are blocking me, and I'd like to stretch my legs."

"Without your slippers? The pebbles on the drive will hurt your feet."

Blast her missing slippers. They were the bane of her existence. Still, she thrust her chin upward with every ounce of dignity she still possessed. "I'll manage."

His eyes flashed across the coach to the still sleeping actress. "Look, Madeline, whatever she said, I can explain."

Could he? That Maddie highly doubted. Not that she'd gotten anything of use out of the actress, but had the woman spilled the beans, Maddie couldn't quite believe Wes could explain it all away with just a few words. Still, perhaps she could get him to divulge his own secrets if she went about this the right way. "I wouldn't be so certain if I were you."

Wes' face turned a bit red as his gaze resettled on Maddie. "Why? What did she tell you?"

Of course, Maddie had no answer for that question, so she shrugged instead. "Didn't you tell me as late as last night that I was the only woman you cared for?"

His dark eyes narrowed and a frown settled on his face. His scar made the whole look appear more than a bit menacing. "Perhaps you'll remember, my lady, that for years you were well out of my reach."

Did that justify whatever it was he'd done? "I hardly see how—"

"What would you have me do?" he growled. "You never even gave me a second glance."

"That is hardly true." She'd seen him a number of

times over the years, but until recently he'd simply terrified her.

"Prevarication does not become you, my dear."

"I say, Hadley," Lord Dovenby's voice drifted into the carriage, "I thought we were in a hurry."

Wes took a step backward and Maddie could see the earl standing behind Wes. "*We* are not in a hurry. *I* am in a hurry. Now retrieve Lucy and move out of my way."

"Oh, no, no, no." Dovenby brushed past Wes, and the carriage dipped as the earl climbed inside, settling in a spot beside the still sleeping actress. "Don't think for one moment you're going to leave me behind."

"Get out!" Wes barked.

"I have no intention of missing your blissful union. Besides, you're going to need a couple of witnesses once you reach Gretna anyway." Dovenby stretched his long legs out across the coach as though he was settling in for a long journey.

Maddie wasn't certain what good it would do to have the earl along for the ride. They'd need two witnesses, and Lucy Reed, being female, wouldn't qualify.

"And I'm certain we can find a couple of willing Scots to serve as witnesses." Wes gestured out the door with his hand. "I've got Hythe on my tail and I don't need your added bulk, Dove."

The earl sighed. "Well, then I suppose you shouldn't tarry, Hadley. Every second counts, does it not? Climb on in so we may be off."

Wes did climb inside, though he grumbled as he did so. "If Hythe catches us, I will have your head."

The earl chuckled. "Promises, promises." Then

he tapped on the roof of the carriage for Renshaw to start driving.

❦

Honestly, Wes would like to have Dovenby's head *now* rather than later. If the damned earl had just taken Lucy and stayed at the coaching inn where Renshaw had swiftly changed horses, Wes could have tried to smooth over whatever truths Lucy had let spill from her lips. Madeline's leg was pressed against his, but she was staring out the window beside her as though he didn't exist. How many times over the years had she given him the back of her head in that same way?

But it was different now. He wasn't some penniless gentleman. He wasn't Rob's friend. He wasn't some besotted fool. Well, he *was* all of those things, but most importantly, he was now about to become her husband. And he couldn't even speak openly with her since that damned Dovenby had decided to tag along on their journey.

"Next stop, Gretna Green," Dovenby nearly sang out. "I've never been part of an elopement before."

"You shouldn't be a part of this one," Wes complained.

"Oh, come now. I might actually be of assistance."

"And the King might actually welcome his wife at his coronation."

Dovenby laughed. "You should see the goings-on in that trial. Madness, all of it. I'm embarrassed to have to sit through it."

That was saying something. "I didn't know you ever got embarrassed about anything."

The earl gestured toward Lucy Reed with his head. "I believe we all get embarrassed from time to time, Hadley."

Wes' eyes settled on the sleeping actress. He'd give all his worldly possessions to know what Lucy had revealed to Madeline. How was he to soothe his intended's ruffled feathers if he didn't know what she knew?

"If men would behave with some decorum and common sense, then you wouldn't find yourselves in these predicaments," Madeline murmured from beside him. Then she turned toward him quickly, irritation flashing in her green eyes as she hissed, "For goodness' sake, you're fearful of what she told me. But she wouldn't be able to tell me anything if you hadn't *done* anything, Weston." She crossed her arms beneath her breasts and turned back to glare out the window.

From across the coach, a low voice said, "I didn't tell her anything, Wes, if it eases your mind any." Lucy Reed glared at him for a moment before her eyes drifted shut again. But it was obvious that she had no desire to continue.

Madeline bristled at Lucy's use of Wes' given name. And he couldn't blame her. But, good God, he'd bedded the chit. He couldn't expect her to call out "Oh, Mr. Hadley" in the throes of passion.

Madeline held up a hand to silence him. "I don't want to know."

"Good, because there's nothing to tell," the sleepy actress said quietly.

"I highly doubt that," Madeline sniffed. "There seems to be quite a bit I don't know."

Lucy finally opened her eyes fully and looked at

Madeline. "You and I lead very different lives. Please don't judge my life and I'll refrain from judging yours."

"As though you could cast any negative aspersions on *my* character," Madeline said, her voice full of self-righteous haughtiness.

"I could judge you," Lucy said. "And I'd wager that your servants line up to do your bidding in your castle on the hill. I bet you have nice gowns and people to do your hair. And I'd bet my eyeteeth that you have very rarely had fun. Any kind of fun at all. The kind where your stomach hurts from laughter. The kind where you can't catch your breath because of the sheer enjoyment of it all."

She shot Madeline a nasty look. "I came from your lifestyle, Lady Madeline, and you couldn't pay me enough to go back to it. I choose to be who I am. I don't do what I do because I have to. I do it because I enjoy it. And when you learn to do that, you will indeed be rich and privileged."

Dovenby whistled. "I had no idea you had it in you, dear," he said to Lucy. Then he began to clap. "Bravo."

"Shut up, Dove," she said, before she crossed her arms and made a perfect imitation of Madeline's stance, glaring out the same window.

Madeline's mouth hung open. She closed it tightly and quickly when she caught Wes staring at her. Madeline did lead a privileged lifestyle. She did have all the things Lucy mentioned. And because of that lifestyle, she did have a decided disadvantage in some things. He'd seen Madeline smile. He'd seen her sing and curtsy and be respectful, but he'd never seen her in a fit of side-splitting laughter. He'd never seen her so excited she couldn't sit still. He'd never seen her truly enjoy herself. And that was something he would endeavor to change.

Wes had grown up in a home full of boys. There was constant fighting, constant laughter, and constant pleasurable enjoyment. Not to mention, his gender afforded him some luxuries Madeline didn't have. She had to be a paragon of virtue. He didn't. And couldn't if he tried. But she could learn to enjoy herself. Couldn't she? He could teach her.

"Madeline," he whispered close to her ear. She brushed at his head like he was a pesky fly. "Please don't be angry at me."

"I'm not angry," she murmured back.

"Whisper, dearest, so Dovenby can't hear you."

"I don't care if he hears me," she hissed back. "I have every right to be angry at you."

She did. True. "How long do you think you'll remain angry?"

She shrugged. Then she arched a brow at him. "Until you've learned your lesson?" she asked most pleasantly.

Dovenby laughed into his closed fist from across the coach. Madeline shot him a look, and he instantly pretended to be absorbed in the scenery.

Madeline let her gaze run from the top of Lucy Reed's head to the bottom of her feet. "I can't compete with someone like her," she finally said in a heavy whisper.

"It's not a competition, Madeline," he said, trying to soothe her.

"She's everything I'm not." Maddie sniffed. "And you obviously wanted her at one point."

"I'm not an innocent, darling. Most men aren't. And I feel certain you wouldn't want one who was."

"I don't want you, either," she murmured.

"I highly doubt that's true." He lifted one hand to cup the side of her face. "You want me. You just don't want to want me."

"That's the most ridiculous thing I've ever heard." She finally looked at him. Not toward him or around him. But looked at him. "Do you still want her?"

"The only woman I want is you," he confessed. She was the only woman he'd wanted for quite some time. The others were simply distractions from what he couldn't have.

"You're going to have to ask the driver to stop so I can cast up my accounts if you two don't stop your blathering," Lucy Reed said with more than a bit of censure in her tone. Then she looked at Madeline, her eyes softer than he'd ever seen them. "He's head over heels for you, love. If he wasn't, he wouldn't be trying so damned hard." Madeline's face colored at the actress' curse. "That's something I never got from him. So, take it at face value."

Wes leaned over Madeline and let his lips graze her cheek.

"Is she right, Weston?" Madeline asked.

Good God, the woman needed more assurance than anyone he'd ever met. "I'll show you tonight."

"But tonight we'll be married," she said, her brow furrowing.

"Exactly." Wes settled back to enjoy the scenery with Dovenby. But out of the corner of his eye, he saw the earl reach out and take Lucy Reed's hand in his, and draw it beneath her skirts so no one could see the gesture of affection. And she let him.

Seventeen

MADDIE WATCHED THE QUAINT VILLAGE OF GRETNA Green come into view just as the sun was dipping below the horizon. She had begun to think they might never reach their destination. She still wasn't certain she was making the best decision, but she truly had very little choice in the matter.

She glanced at Wes beside her and noticed the way the shadow in the carriage's waning light hid the scar that had once frightened her. Funny, now that she'd spent days in his presence, she barely noticed the slash unless he was particularly angry.

"I suppose this is it," Lord Dovenby remarked cheerfully. "Your last chance to bolt and pray for an escape."

Wes stiffened at her side, and Maddie glared at the interfering werewolf. "Are you speaking to Weston or to me?"

Dovenby laughed. "Well, you, of course, my lady. Certainly you realize that no matter what you've seen or haven't seen, you can do better."

"What did she see?" Lucy Reed asked, a look of confusion marring her pretty face.

Wes growled deep in his throat. A warning if Maddie had ever heard one.

"I can't imagine why you think I would bolt, my lord." Besides, if the way the two Lycans had caught up to her when she'd left them on the side of the road was any indication, she doubted she could run fast enough for an escape. Not that she was of a mind to do so. "I accepted Weston's proposal and have no intention of changing my mind."

Dovenby's blue eyes twinkled. "As you say, my dear."

"Some witness," Wes grumbled, which only made the earl laugh. Dovenby might as well have been Brutus to Wes' Caesar. "Remind me to return the favor sometime."

"Ah, when I am finally leg-shackled, Hadley, it will be in front of God and all of society in St. George's. I will have my pick of witnesses, all of whom with standings much more exalted than yours."

Comparing Dovenby to Brutus seemed too kind all of a sudden.

"Leave him alone, Dove," Lucy Reed chided. "You really can be an obnoxious arse."

"I can handle my own affairs, Lucy." Wes scowled at the actress.

Lucy sniffed indignantly and folded her arms across her chest. "I know that, Hadley. I've seen you handle fellows worse than Dovenby before. But if you're trying to be on your best behavior to impress your prim and oh-so-proper bride, I can assure you that you're really looking like a dolt."

Maddie sucked in a breath. Why did Lucy Reed find a way to insult her every time she opened her mouth? And she'd insulted Wes, too. "Behaving like a gentleman is to be commended, Miss Reed."

The actress smirked. "Spoken by a lady who doesn't know otherwise. You may take my word for it, Lady Madeline. No woman wants a gentleman in her bedchamber."

Maddie was certain her face was as red as a tomato. The things the woman said!

"Enough, Lucy!" Wes barked just as the coach crawled to a stop. "Wonderful as it's been having the two of you along on this journey, we must part ways now that we've arrived." He nodded in Lucy's direction. "Godspeed on your return to London." Then he glanced at Dovenby, "Best of luck with your own upcoming nuptials."

The earl chuckled. "You keep trying to get rid of me, Hadley. I'm starting to take it personally."

"Perhaps you should," Wes remarked.

Dovenby gestured toward the door with a sweep of his hand. "Do hop out. A Scottish blacksmith awaits."

Wes glared at the other Lycan, but he did open the door. Then he offered his hand to Maddie. "My lady."

His hand enveloped Maddie's smaller one as his dark eyes locked with hers. In that instant, Dovenby and Lucy Reed seemed to fade into the background along with all of Maddie's wits. Wes would let her go if she wanted it. She could see it in his eyes. Despite that beseeching stare that begged her to come with him, he would let her go in an instant if she asked it of him.

But she didn't want to be let go. She'd come this far. She'd left her home and her father behind. She'd jumped out an inn window, for heaven's sake. Maddie smiled at him as a rush of excitement washed over her. Marriage to Weston Hadley would be an adventure. A passionate, fun adventure. With a man who had the potential to love her. It was more than she'd hoped for. More than she'd been schooled for her whole life.

He smiled back. "Are you ready, my lady?"

Maddie's heart pounded in her chest. Was she ready? Really ready? She'd come this far, hadn't she? Not trusting her voice not to crack, Maddie nodded her answer.

Wes helped her alight from the carriage and then scooped her up in his arms. Her bare feet tingled in the cool Scottish breeze as his boots crunched along a path to the entrance of a white stone blacksmith's shop.

A young lass was sweeping the floor and looked up at their approach. "Are ye here for a weddin'?" She swiped at her cheek and left a black smudge across her face.

Wes nodded. "We are indeed, and we're in a bit of a hurry."

"Someone chasin' ye, huh?" The lass shook her head as though she'd seen it all in her short years. "Papa!" she called loudly. "Ye've got more customers."

A moment later, a man dressed in all black, and looking more like a vicar than a blacksmith, appeared in the doorway. "Ye're lookin' ta get married?"

"And they've got someone chasin' them," his daughter informed him.

The blacksmith grinned. "Well, then let's get on with it, shall we?"

"Thank you," Wes replied.

"Ye can put the lass down, sir."

Maddie looked at the dirty ground and tightened her grip around Wes' neck.

"If it's all right with you, I'll hold her."

The blacksmith shrugged. "Suit yerself. Have ye got a ring?"

Wes' body stiffened at the question. He had nothing, she well knew. It wasn't as though this impromptu rush north had been planned with great care. She squeezed his shoulder and then cleared her throat. "I'm already wearing it. Just a moment." Maddie tugged off the emerald ring she'd worn since her mother's passing a decade earlier. The stone glittered in the waning light as she held it out to Wes.

He looked so sad all of a sudden, as though he regretted the fact that he had nothing to give her, but he could give her something more precious than jewelry. He could give her the passion he'd promised, an adventure she would never forget, and the possibility of having a good marriage.

"Ye really should wait until ye're wed ta wear the ring." The blacksmith frowned at her.

But Maddie shook off the censure. The last person she was going to let pass judgment on her was an anvil preacher who knew nothing of her standing. "May we get on with it, sir?"

The blacksmith's frown deepened, but he said to his daughter, "Fetch me a couple of bodies, lass, and be quick about it."

"Only need to fetch one," Lord Dovenby said from behind them. "I'll serve as a witness."

The lass made a quick exit to do her father's bidding, brushing past the earl in her haste.

"Thank you, sir." The blacksmith nodded in Dovenby's direction, then turned his attention back to Wes and Maddie. "All right. Yer names, please?"

Wes puffed out his chest proudly. "Weston Hadley and my bride is Lady Madeline Hayburn."

"About the payment, Mr. Hadley…" the man's voice trailed off.

"I'll be paying," Dovenby replied. "My little wedding gift to the newlyweds."

Wes growled. "I have the funds, Dove."

The earl grinned. "I'm sure you do. But I think I'll enjoy having you owe me, Hadley." He glanced back at the blacksmith. "You may proceed, sir."

"Just as soon as…" The blacksmith looked at someone behind them.

Maddie's heart jumped to her throat. Certainly Papa hadn't caught up to them. She glanced over Wes's shoulder to see who was behind them and breathed a sigh of relief when her eyes landed on a brawny Scot instead of her father. "Fi said ye needed a witness."

"Thank ye, Hamish." The blacksmith gestured Wes and Maddie closer. "We may begin now, Mr. Hadley, Lady Madeline."

Wes stepped closer to the anvil in the middle of the shop.

"Ye really should put her on her feet for the ceremony."

It would only be for a few seconds. She could stand on a dirty floor for a few seconds. Maddie nodded quickly. Wes placed her gently on her feet. Her toes curled from touching the chilled Scottish ground.

Then the blacksmith pulled a golden cord from his pocket and grasped Wes' right hand and Maddie's left.

So that's why he wanted her on her feet. The gesture was quite sweet really, so Maddie pushed the thoughts of dirty, cold floors out of her mind. The blacksmith began to wind the cord around their wrists, binding them together. "Repeat after me, Mr. Hadley. I, Weston Hadley, take ye, Lady Madeline Hayburn, ta be my wife before God and these witnesses."

"I, Weston Hadley, take you, Lady Madeline Hayburn, to be my wife before God and these witnesses." His dark eyes sparkled as he repeated the words, a promise of more to come.

Warmth shot to Maddie's belly.

"All right, Lady Madeline, yer turn. I, Lady Madeline Hayburn, take ye, Weston Hadley, ta be my husband before God and these witnesses."

Maddie tipped back her head proudly. Barring any unforeseen circumstances, she'd only get married once. She was going to do this right. "I, Lady Madeline Hayburn, take you, Weston Hadley, to be my husband before God and these witnesses."

"Ye've got the ring, Mr. Hadley?"

"Yes, of course." Wes fumbled around in his pocket before retrieving Maddie's emerald ring and then he slid it back on her finger. But this time, it slid onto her hand with a promise of the future, rather than a remembrance of the past.

The blacksmith gestured to the two of them. "Ye may kiss yer wife now, sir."

Wes wasted no time drawing Maddie to himself, wrapping his unbound hand around her waist and pulling her flush against him. Then he slowly dipped his head and captured her lips with his. His kiss tasted of desperation. Of comfort. Of something she didn't even understand. It was sweet and kind and hot enough to melt her toes. She stepped up onto her tiptoes to press her lips more firmly to his. But Wes broke the kiss and raised his head.

"Just in time," Dovenby remarked.

Wes took a deep breath and sighed heavily. "Your father has arrived."

The earl grinned as though he had a secret no one else knew. Like he was the happiest man in existence. "You should probably spirit your lovely wife off to the closest inn and climb into bed before he reaches you. I'll stall him as long as I can."

"Are you ready to run again, Madeline?" her husband asked.

Was she? She was. "I'm ready, Wes," she replied.

Once again, he scooped her up in his arms and fled into the darkness of the night, into their unknown future.

❧

Wes let his new wife slide down his front until her toes landed on the clean floor of their tiny rented room. Her hair hung about her shoulders in wild disarray, and he'd never seen her look more lovely. Madeline fell against him like she was meant to be there.

"Do you hate me for doing this to you?" he asked as he nuzzled the side of her neck.

"I'm not very fond of the room," she began with a nervous giggle, "but I can accept my circumstances."

"Someday, Lady Madeline, I will get you the best room at the best inn, and then we'll recreate this night." He could do that, couldn't he? Certainly, he could. But for now, her father was nearby, and if they didn't hurry, he'd have an opportunity to snatch Madeline right out of Wes' grasp. Hurrying was the last thing he wanted to do. He wanted to savor every moment. To taste every part of her. To tempt her with passion like she'd never imagined.

"We should hurry," she said as she turned and presented her back to him. Before she turned, though, he saw the rosy blush that crept up her cheeks. And the way that her hand trembled. Wes worked at the fastenings of her gown with nimble fingers, slowing only momentarily to press his lips to the skin he bared.

"I don't want to hurry," he breathed against her back, just as he reached the last fastening. He held her hips in his hands and squeezed, perhaps a bit too roughly with his frustration, but she didn't complain. "But if we don't seal this, he could take you from me." He stood up and spun her in his arms, then tipped her chin up so that she looked into his face. "You understand, don't you?"

But she was already tugging at the sleeves of her gown, pulling them down. She was naked beneath the gown, having left her chemise at the last inn. He probably looked like a complete dolt staring at her. "Could you turn down the light? Just a little?" she asked hesitantly.

Wes ran a hand through his hair as he crossed the small room, then doused the light. He turned back to face his bride, the only illumination in the room was the light from the waning moon that streamed through the window. The same moon that had started this journey. The same moon that had forced her into his path. God bless the moon.

Madeline was willing to forgo any hint of passion and get this over with quickly. But was he? He wasn't. He wanted her first time to be perfect. He wanted to make love to her, not tumble her like a whore. He wanted to feel her around him, near him, inside his heart.

"Stop," he said. Her head jerked up as she looked at him with curiosity.

"What's wrong?" she asked quietly, clutching the bodice of her gown against her breasts.

Wes groaned. "Everything." He threw up his hands and began to pace. "This isn't how I want this to be."

"How do you want it?" Her voice quavered. "I must admit that I have no idea of what's supposed to happen." She looked as lost as he did, he was sure.

He'd bungled this. Bungled it badly. Wes might have to hurry, but he'd make this wonderful for her if it was the last thing he ever did. He tore his own clothes off with haste and didn't stop until he wore nothing but his smallclothes. And the only reason he didn't remove those was because he didn't want to frighten her.

"Come here," he said quietly. She took one hesitant step toward him, still clutching her gown against her breasts. Wes could only hope that Dovenby could hold off the duke long enough.

Wes dropped to one knee in front of her. Then he tugged at her gown. She covered her breasts with her arm as the gown fell to her hips. As he tugged the gown lower, he couldn't resist pressing a kiss to her belly. It fluttered beneath his lips. "So beautiful," he murmured against her skin.

Madeline's free hand touched the top of his head and then settled in his hair. She touched him. Dear God, she'd touched him. She'd touched him of her own free will. He hadn't asked for it. He hadn't begged or pleaded or forced it. She'd just done it.

Wes pushed her gown down over her hips and stood quickly, then scooped her up in his arms and carried her to the bed. He laid her in the center, shucked his smallclothes, and crawled atop her in one swift move. This might not be the marriage she'd wanted, but he'd make it the marriage that pleased her. At least in this moment.

Her heart was beating like mad. He could hear it in his head. "Are you all right?" he asked as he looked down into her face. She nibbled at her bottom lip and nodded, her green eyes finally rising to meet his.

"I'm ready," she said.

Wes couldn't keep from chuckling. "Not quite," he murmured as he dropped his head to her breast and nuzzled the softest skin he'd ever felt. Her breasts were small and pert and perfect. Perfect for him. They were topped with small puffy crests so desperate for him that they nearly reached his lips. He took one into his mouth, gently tugging as he loved her. Madeline gasped beneath him, her breath catching in the air as he looked up, his mouth still full of her as he looked into her eyes.

She looked at him from beneath heavy-lidded lashes, her mouth open slightly as tiny rushes of air brushed past her lips and across his shoulder. For the rest of his days, he'd never, ever forget the look on her face. There was joy to be had from taking his time. So much joy.

Madeline's hands threaded into his hair as he toyed with her, and guided his head when he switched to her other breast. Her fingernails abraded his scalp when he trailed one lazy hand down her belly and into her curls. Her legs parted of their own volition, just as he touched her center. He found that hidden little pearl he knew would bring her pleasure and circled it, his mouth still full of her breast.

"Wes," she cried.

He raised his head only briefly, just to be certain she was all right. He didn't know why he cared so much. She'd told him to hurry. He just found it impossible to do so. He wanted to savor every moment. "Yes, Madeline," he said, and then he took her nipple back into his mouth.

Her back arched as she tried to get closer to him. "What are you doing to me?"

"It's called passion, darling," he laughed. He dragged his finger harder over that nub of pleasure that so obviously sparked something within her. Her breaths kicked up as he dipped a finger into her heat and brought back some moisture to slicken his way. Wes settled himself between her open thighs and nudged against her heat. Her eyes met his. "I wanted to take more time," he said. But he heard heavy footsteps coming down the corridor. She couldn't hear it, thank God. But with his hearing, he could hear every stomp and every curse.

"Please," Madeline cried from beneath him, her hands frantically fluttering on his shoulders.

Wes pushed at her center, slowing as her heat closed around him like a silken glove. He wanted to shove himself inside her and spill his passion, but she tensed beneath him. He raked his finger across her center again. She cried out his name.

"Maddie, Maddie, mine," he crooned in her ear as he pressed forward. There was a moment of tension from her, a quick indrawn breath, and then Maddie was his. He was fully inside her. He was part of Madeline Hayburn. Madeline Hadley. His wife. He began to move slowly and said quietly in her ear, "Can you put your legs around me, darling?"

She did it without hesitation and he went even deeper. A clatter at the doorway nearly broke him from the moment. But he ignored it, and she appeared not to notice. He rocked inside her, finding a gentle rhythm that pleased her. He'd never felt such purpose. Such perfection. It had never been this way for him.

"I think I love you, Madeline," he murmured against her hair as he sped his fingers, still stoking her passion.

Maddie began to meet his thrusts, small noises leaving her throat. She squeezed his arms, her face pressed into the side of his neck, her sharp little teeth biting his shoulder. Good God, she would destroy him. But then she broke. She shattered beneath him. She squeezed his manhood in an iron grip, and he joined her, spilling himself inside her in one deep thrust. He clutched her in his arms and was afraid to let her go as he settled heavily on top of her.

"Wes," she said softly.

"Are you all right?" He tried to calm himself. But he was still inside her, and she still fluttered around him.

"Someone's at the door," she whispered harshly, her breaths heavy and labored.

He heard Dovenby grunt as a scuffle ensued outside the door. Apparently, the duke was more than angry.

"Shh," he bade Madeline. Perhaps they would go away. Not bloody likely. But perhaps.

"You don't want to go in there, Your Grace," Dovenby said loudly.

"Open the damned door," the duke spat.

The jingle of keys indicated that their moment of peace was about to be shattered. "I'm sorry," Wes whispered to Madeline, and then brushed a lock of hair from her forehead.

The door handle turned, and all Wes could think was *God, I'm still lying between her thighs. And I don't want to move.*

"Don't go in there, gentlemen," a feminine voice called out. Quick, light footsteps heralded Lucy Reed's arrival.

"I will find out if he has defiled my daughter!" the duke bellowed.

"And if they're in the middle of the deed?" Lucy asked. "What then? Do you really want to see that, Your Grace?"

"I have to know," the duke ground out.

"Fine," Lucy said. Wes looked over his shoulder as the door opened slightly. Lucy's head popped around the door, where she very quickly glanced their way and then her head disappeared. "Your Grace," she said solemnly. "I regret to inform you that you were too late."

The duke cursed, a most foul sound coming from such a genteel man.

Lucy Reed continued, "And unless you want to see Hadley's white arse, I wouldn't go in there, if I were you."

"We'll be out in a moment," Wes called to the now closed door.

Then from beneath him, Madeline began to giggle. She giggled so hard that she shook beneath him. Dear God, was she hysterical? "Are you all right?" he asked.

"Kiss me, Wes," she said between giggles. He could deny her nothing, not now, not ever. But as he touched his lips to hers, she laughed loudly. It erupted from her like a fountain spouting.

He couldn't keep from joining her in her enjoyment, however misplaced it might have been. She looked up and down his body as he rolled to land beside her and drop her onto his chest. "I have one question," she said.

She probably wanted to know if it was always that bad. But she surprised him when she said, "Is your arse really that white?" Then she laughed and laid her head on his chest, hugging him tightly.

Eighteen

MADDIE TOOK A DEEP BREATH. EVER SINCE SHE'D re-donned her awful gown, which she couldn't wait to burn, she'd dreaded the interview with her father. But there was no avoiding it. She would have to face him sometime, and now was as good a time as any. Actually now was better than any. Her body still tingled with awareness from her coupling with Wes, and in that very moment she must have resembled the lovesick girl in Wes' foolish letter to her father.

"I'll talk to him, Madeline," Wes promised, tucking one of Maddie's locks behind her ear.

She couldn't help the laugh that escaped her. "Oh, I'm certain he'll want to talk to you, too, but I need to talk to him first."

Fear flashed in his eyes for a moment. "You won't tell him… what you saw that night." His words came out more like a question than a statement.

Wasn't that the point in marrying her? Ensuring her silence on the matter? Maddie shook her head. "Papa has never been my confidant."

He took a steadying breath, one she could only imagine was filled with relief.

"But *you* soon will be, husband. And I'll expect you to finally divulge your secrets. All of them. Who else you're protecting, just for starters."

He nodded quickly. "I did promise I would, Madeline."

"And you shouldn't call me that."

Wes took a step backward. "Beg your pardon?"

He looked so affronted all of a sudden that Maddie giggled. "You called me Maddie when we were…" She let her voice trail off, not able to say *in bed.* Which was silly. They were very small words, after all. But her cheeks warmed at just the thought of uttering them. "My family calls me Maddie." She cleared her throat. "If you want Papa to believe we bolted north because we were so desperately in love, you should call me Maddie."

"Maddie," he echoed, wearing a silly grin. "I could get used to that."

So could she, especially when she thought about him whispering it in her ear while making love to her. Maddie cleared her throat again. "Wish me luck."

Wes frowned. "I think I should talk to him first."

Male pride would be the death of her. "And I think I should calm him down before you do so."

"He can't hurt me, Maddie."

Not physically, no, but… "I can just imagine the male posturing." She sighed. "Wes, Papa may not be my confidant, but I do love him. I'd rather appease him than anger him even more."

Wes scoffed. "Darling, I have absconded with you, married you, and taken your innocence. I don't think he could be angrier."

"Well, you don't know, Papa." Maddie padded across the rug on her bare feet. Then she looked back at her new husband. "How good is your hearing?"

"Very attuned to you. If you call out, I'll be there in less than a second."

She smiled. "Then you'll know when I'm ready for you." Her feet found the wooden planks of the floor and she kept from cringing. When she got home, she would never, ever, as long as she lived, take slippers or boots for granted. She was sure she had more dirt between her toes than she'd ever imagined possible.

Maddie tossed open the door and very carefully negotiated the corridor and steps, making certain to avoid as much filth as possible. She was going to need another bath. Soon.

She met the kindly old innkeeper as soon as she descended the last step. The ancient Scot had been but a blur when Wes had rushed her into the inn immediately after their wedding. Maddie smiled at the old man. "I am looking for the Duke of Hythe."

The innkeeper grimaced. "His Grace is in the private dinin' room at the end of the hall."

Maddie whispered, "Does he seem very angry?"

A look of sympathy crossed the old man's face. "Veins bulgin' in his neck, lass. Are ye sure ye want ta go in there? I would think that big, strappin' lad of yers would be better."

Better if Maddie wanted them to pummel each other until they were both black and blue and gushing blood. "I'll be fine." And she would. She had been raised by her grandmother, after all. And a more

stalwart woman didn't exist. Maddie would just have
to adopt her Grandmamma's steel spine for the interview with her father. "The private dining room at the
end of the hall?"

"Aye, lass." The innkeeper stepped aside, muttering
something about the foolishness of young love.

Love had nothing to do with it. Her relationship
with Weston wasn't based on love, though she vaguely
remembered him murmuring something about it in
her ear when they were in bed. Their relationship was
based on his need for her to keep a secret. And the fact
that she might get some passion in return. Her skin
still tingled from their earlier interlude. Her cheeks
warmed at the memory. Maddie brushed past the old
man and made her way down the corridor, stopping at
the private dining room. Then she took a deep breath
and pushed the door open.

Her father stood rigid as a board beside a roaring hearth.
As he met her eyes, a muscle near his right eye twitched.
"Madeline Louisa Hayburn," he said menacingly.

"Hadley," she corrected.

His eye twitched again. "Was your lover too scared
to come and face me himself?"

"You mean my husband, Papa?"

He snorted as though he still had a hard time
believing the situation. "I didn't even know you were
acquainted with the young man."

"He's been Robert's friend for years."

"And is that how long all of this has been going on?
Years? Is that why you refused every suitable fellow I
paraded before you?"

She'd refused every suitable fellow he paraded

before her because they were awful specimens from which to choose. They may have been rich and privileged, but they were devoid of character. "You would never have accepted Weston if he'd come to you."

"You are right about that." He still made no effort to move from his spot. And Maddie got the impression that if he moved, he might crack. "I would never have let you throw your future away."

"I hope you'll be happy for me, Papa," she said softly.

He could only shake his head, and she wasn't certain if he meant he couldn't be happy for her, or he simply couldn't speak. Then he raked a hand through his greying hair. "You don't honestly think he can make you happy, do you?"

"I hope he can."

"Then you're a bigger fool than I thought."

Maddie gasped. "Papa!"

He took a step toward the dining table a few feet from him and pulled out one of the wooden chairs. He scooped something up in his hands, and Maddie almost sighed when she recognized her damaged-beyond-repair slippers. They would never be worn in society again, but they would feel like heaven right now. "My slippers!"

"Please put them on. You can't be traipsing across the country in bare feet." He held the shoes out to her.

Maddie closed the distance between them and took his offering. It wasn't much. But he cared about her. He'd thought enough of her to bring her shoes. "Thank you."

Her father's frown deepened. "You know you will

never have the life you were born for, don't you?
You mother, God rest her soul, must be turning in
her grave."

"I'm sorry I disappointed you."

"Is your husband a coward?"

"Of course not!"

"Then why hasn't he come to face me like a man?"

"Because I begged him to let me talk to you first."

"Got him wrapped around your finger, do you?
That doesn't speak well for him."

Maddie hadn't really thought of it like that. "I think
he is simply able to listen to reason when it's presented."

"Hmm. We'll see." Then he cupped his hands to
his mouth and bellowed, "Weston Hadley!"

In less than a moment, a knock came from the door
and then Wes stepped over the threshold. "Did you
want to see me, Your Grace?"

"I'd like to see you hanged," her father replied
crisply. "Were you listening at the keyhole?"

Wes shook his head. "I'm just very fast, sir."

"I'll say." Then he glanced at Maddie. "You may
leave. Your *husband* and I have some things to discuss."

"But Papa!" she began.

"Unlike this young man, Madeline, I am not
wrapped around your finger and you *will* do as I say."

"I'd like to stay."

"Maddie," Wes said softly. "Your father is right.
We do have some issues to discuss."

⤫⤫

As soon as Maddie huffed from the room, Wes turned
his attention to her father. The Duke of Hythe had

always been an imposing man. He wore his birthright like a badge. "First, let me say, sir—"

"How much?" the duke grumbled.

"I beg your pardon?" Wes couldn't have heard him correctly.

"I said 'How much.' How much is it going to take for you to walk away from my daughter?"

"Your Grace, Maddie and I are husband and wife."

"That can be remedied."

Wes hardly saw how. Even the King couldn't get his own marriage annulled. "Even if such a thing were possible, I would not walk away. I love your daughter."

"You *love* her?" the duke spat. "If that's true, I can't believe you would subject her to a life as your wife. The blacksmith can be bought. The marriage lines can be lost and you can have a nice settlement if you'll just walk away from Madeline and never look back."

Wes' stomach dropped to the floor. He'd never dared dream that he could have Maddie for his very own, but now that he did have her, he wasn't about to give her up. He'd held her in his arms, for God's sake. He'd smelled her. He'd tasted her. He'd made her his own. He shook his head. "Not for every last farthing in your coffers, Your Grace."

The duke shook his head. "Fools. Both of you."

"I prefer being a fool to being lonely," Wes said. The duke had been alone for ten long years. How awful it must have been to wake alone, to sleep alone, and to dine alone. To be alone even when he was in a throng of people. To know there was no one to comfort him when he was feeling blue. To laugh with him when he was feeling happy. To cry for him when he was sad. Except for Madeline. And now he could imagine Madeline doing all those things for and with him, her husband. Not her father. How utterly bereft the man must have felt.

"You know nothing of loneliness," the duke said. "Try giving your only daughter away to a scoundrel who doesn't deserve her. Then you, too, will know the sting of true loneliness." The duke suddenly looked older. And tired. He rubbed his forehead with harsh fingertips, as though he could rub away the worry Wes and Madeline had caused him. "She's my only daughter. My wife would not have wanted this for her."

She wouldn't have wanted Madeline to find love? "I know you hadn't planned for a love match for her," Wes began tentatively. But the duke was obviously hurting. Hurting more than Wes could probably imagine.

"You have no idea what I wanted for her!" the duke roared. His fist slammed into the sideboard so hard that the man winced.

"Tell me, Your Grace. Tell me what you would have arranged for her that I can't give her." Unless wealth was on the list, Wes couldn't think of anything he couldn't or wouldn't do for Madeline.

"I brought her shoes," the duke croaked. "She can't be without her shoes." The man looked like he would break. But he didn't. He stood up taller. "If I ever find my daughter in a state such as the one I found her in today, I'll… I'll…" He cursed profoundly. "I don't know what I'll do, but I'll make you regret it."

"If I ever harm her in any way, I'll deserve it." Wes

suddenly felt a lump grow in his throat. This man was entrusting him with the care of his only daughter. His most precious commodity. "I'll make a promise to you right now, Your Grace."

"Promises will not get your hands on my daughter's dowry," the duke spat.

Wes didn't give a damn about a dowry. He swallowed hard and forged on. "I promise to love and protect her."

The duke glared at him. "You think you feel strongly for her."

"I know I feel strongly for her. I know exactly where my emotions lie."

"This will be difficult for Maddie," the duke said.

Wes snorted. Falling in love with him? He didn't doubt it at all.

The duke appraised his scar. "You lead a lifestyle she's not accustomed to."

"Yes, I do," Wes admitted. One that involved shifting into a beast under the light of the full moon. And consorting with vampyres. Heaven only knew what he'd come up against next. "I'm not wealthy. I don't have a great fortune. But I have a big heart. And it's completely open to love."

"Love won't keep my daughter in slippers."

Wes dug his hands into his pockets and didn't say a word. What could he say to that? He'd just taken Madeline as his wife. Then taken her innocence. Now he would take her back to his home, not to the castle where she'd grown up.

Maddie stood outside the door and listened. She didn't even care that there were curious patrons about. That people were giving her odd glances. She pressed her ear even harder to the door. Tears welled in her eyes when she heard the pain in her father's voice.

"I do not approve of this marriage," her father said.

"I understand that, Your Grace," Weston said. He didn't sound offended by her father. How could he not be? She was offended for him.

"Maddie's dowry will never fall into your hands."

"I've no need of it, sir," Weston clipped out.

Her father laughed, a sound with no humor at all. "Have the Hadleys suddenly had a change of fortune? Radbourne handles his funds as well as your father ever did."

"With all due respect, Your Grace, I'd prefer it if you didn't speak of my father in such a way. We were very young when he died. Our circumstances would be completely different if he had lived, I'm certain."

Maddie wracked her brain trying to remember the circumstances surrounding the late Viscount Radbourne's death. She could come up with nothing. They'd been known as "those penniless Hadleys" for as long as she could remember. She wasn't sure if their censure was because of their misbehavior or their lack of a fortune. She assumed it was the former.

Her father broke her from her reverie. "Your circumstances are now my daughter's circumstances."

Heavy footsteps moved toward the door. Maddie jumped to the side as the door swung open. "Papa," she said quietly, looking up at him with newfound respect. He looked ten years older.

"You have made your bed, Maddie," he said quietly. "Now you must lie in it." He reached out and pulled her to him by her shoulders, planted a wet kiss on her forehead, and strode from the room.

"Papa!" she called to his retreating back.

He stopped, turned on his heel, and looked back at her, a hopeful smile upon his face. "Yes, Maddie?" he said. He held out one hand to her. But Weston stood on her right. And he looked at her as though she'd hung the moon and the stars in the sky. Like his very future was hinged upon her actions. She'd jumped into this adventure with him with both feet. Now she assumed it was time to grab hold and enjoy the ride. She slid her hand into his and felt Weston grip it tightly. There was strength in his grasp unlike any she'd ever known.

"I love you, Papa," she said softly. Her father lowered his chin quickly, avoided her eyes, and strode from the room. From the inn. From her future. From her life? Maybe.

Tears pricked at the backs of her lashes. A great heaving sob rose within her chest, threatening to steal her very breath. To steal her life. But before she could utter a sound, Wes scooped her up in his arms as though she weighed nothing and carried her back toward the staircase.

She clung to him like a rose clings to a trellis. She needed his support. But she didn't know how to ask for it. When they reached their room, Wes slowly dropped her to her feet. He spun her around and began to remove her clothes. She was numb. She didn't even care. Certainly, he couldn't think they'd be intimate with all the turmoil that was going on within her.

"Shh..." he breathed. It was almost as though he could read her mind. "You'll feel better after you rest."

When he had her fully undressed, he pulled back the counterpane and tucked her beneath it. She felt cold. And empty. And alone. But then he slid in behind her and wrapped his strong arms around her, cocooning her in his warmth. The tears that threatened to fall finally did. The very ones she thought might cleave her into two pieces. They very well might have, had Wes not been there to hold her together.

Nineteen

WES HELD MADDIE CLOSE, LONG AFTER SHE'D FALLEN asleep. Her father's words echoed in his ears. *Love won't keep my daughter in slippers.* Wes hadn't cared one whit about her dowry. All he cared about was her. But life as a penniless Hadley would be difficult for her, more so than it ever had been for him. He couldn't ask that of her. She was his wife. He was responsible for making sure she had slippers and dresses and every luxury she'd ever possessed. He was sorely ill-prepared for such responsibility.

Some evil imp in the back of his mind said it would have been better for Maddie if he'd taken her father's offer. Wes pushed the terrible thought away. For better or worse, Maddie had leapt out of the Yorkshire inn window and into his arms when she could have run to the safety of her father, and she could again have left with the duke this evening. But she'd sought Wes' hand instead. She'd married him, and she was his, and that was all there was to it.

Somehow, some way, he'd find a way to provide anything she desired. It was the *how* that would drive him mad. There was no war being fought, no need for soldiers. And he couldn't ever see himself as a country vicar. So he would have to go into trade of some sort. Actually earn a living. But he knew nothing of shipping or industry. The only things he was truly good at were gentlemanly pursuits. Racing, gambling, whoring…

Gambling. He could never make enough at the tables, and lady luck was fickle. The only true winners at gaming tables were the owners of the establishments. They made money regardless.

Wes pushed the thought away. Going into trade was one thing; being the proprietor of a gaming hell was something else. Still… he *did* know gambling. He *did* know gamblers. But he barely had two farthings to rub together. No one was going to hand him a gaming hall to operate… Maybe Dash would take pity on him. Loan him the necessary funds. If so, Wes would see that every pound was returned to his brother. And certainly Dash could understand providing for a privileged wife.

❧

Maddie woke hours later to find herself lying on her side with her face pressed against a hard wall of… she gently pressed her fingertips against it… a hard wall of *man*. She blinked heavily, trying to remove the sleep from her eyes. The last thing she remembered was Wes taking off her clothes with such care and tucking her between the covers. She'd felt utterly bereft for a moment, and then he'd joined her. He'd wrapped his arms around her and held her close.

Wes had even gone so far as to tell her he'd go and get her father and bring him back to her if she wanted it. He was willing to give her back, he'd said, if she truly wanted it. But she didn't want it. And she'd never been more certain of anything in her life. She wanted Weston Hadley. She wanted to be Lady Madeline Hadley.

The moonlight streamed through the window, casting his face in shadow. His scar was pressed against his pillow, and he looked almost normal in this light. Not that she minded his scar. It was part of him, after all. And she liked him just fine. He was quite handsome lying there with his mouth slightly parted, soft snores erupting from between his lips.

Maddie moved back a couple of inches and smiled as Wes instinctively reached for her, trying to draw her back toward him without even waking. Who would have ever thought that a man who looked so imposing could be so warm? So prone to holding her close?

Maddie took a moment to study him there in the moonlight. His broad shoulders looked perfectly wide enough to shoulder her burdens. She very nearly scoffed. She'd barely met the man. He'd married her and taken her innocence, all in a span of no more than a few days. However, it was no more than she'd have expected from any other marriage her father would have arranged. She'd have had a few outings with the gentleman, been seen in public a few times with her intended, and then marriage would have taken place. And the bedding.

Goodness, the bedding. She couldn't get the thought of that out of her head. He'd said he wanted to take his time, but if he'd taken any more time, she wasn't certain she'd have been able to stand it. She'd have melted into a big puddle of... something. Why had no one ever told her it would be like that? Her mother had died when Maddie was much too young to discuss such things. And proper ladies didn't discuss bedchamber activities. It had come as a complete surprise how much she'd enjoyed it. There should be a book. A book all girls were given so they'd have a clue about what to expect in the bedchamber.

He'd taken her nipple into his mouth, and the fire had shot straight to her belly. The very thought of it now made a pulse beat between her legs. Nice girls didn't think of such things, did they? She'd be like Lucy Reed. And that was deplorable. Maddie inhaled deeply and tried to shove the thoughts away. But all she could think of was the feel of him inside her. The feelings of having him surround her and be *in* her at the same time. She reached out a tentative hand and touched the flat hardness that was his nipple. He groaned, which made her jerk her hand back. But he settled again, and she reached out to touch him. It couldn't hurt to explore his body while he slept, could it?

His nipple responded to her touch, growing hard beneath her fingertip. She wondered if it felt the same to him to have his touched. She'd never know, because she'd never have the courage to ask him. He'd think her disgraceful.

Maddie let her fingers trail through the light dusting of hair on his chest, luxuriating in the scratchy lightness of it. Her fingertips trailed down toward his stomach, and the muscles there tightened almost imperceptibly. "Wes," she whispered. He didn't respond, and his breaths were still even and slow.

His abdomen was soft in sleep, but she'd felt the iron cords that hid beneath the surface. She gently scratched the skin of his stomach with her fingertips. He let out a quick breath. Maddie looked up at him and noted his closed eyes and his relaxed countenance. Her fingertips trailed even lower. She couldn't see it, because it was too dark, but she was supremely curious about that part of him he'd put inside her. The part of him that connected them. What did it look like? If he was sleeping, perhaps she could feel it. Maddie let her fingers trail lower, holding her breath as she explored.

"Maddie," he growled. She nearly jumped from her skin when he spoke. His arms closed tightly around her as he hugged her to him. She raised her hand from where it had been wandering down his body, suddenly overwhelmed by the shame of her exploration.

"Wes," she whispered.

"What?" he whispered back. But his chest rumbled beneath her ear as though he withheld laughter. What on earth did the cad have to laugh about?

"Are you awake?"

"No," he whispered heartily.

"You are too."

"If I go back to sleep, will you go back to what you were doing?"

Heat crept up her face. Thank goodness it was dark. She must be flushed scarlet by now. "I don't know what you're referring to," she clipped out.

Wes very gently took her hand in his and gave it a gentle tug toward the lower half of his body. He grunted as though in pain but he placed her hand very firmly on that part of him she'd been aching to find. He pulled his hand back and left her fingers there. She could have jerked them back up to a respectable place. But she was too curious. Heaven help her, she wanted to touch it.

"I'm referring to the fact you were groping for my manhood while I slept, you naughty lady," he said, his voice rough and gravely. "If you wanted to see it, you only needed to ask."

See it? Goodness, she'd never be able to *look* at it. But her fingertips still rested upon it.

"I dare you," he whispered in her ear, his hot breath stealing across the shell of it just before he sucked her earlobe into his mouth and gave it a gentle, playful bite. Then he moved back and lay there, his body relaxed beside her. But his abdomen was no longer soft. It was hard. Rigid as a board. And so was his manhood, where her fingertips still rested. She gently probed his length. "There's my girl," he rumbled from beside her, encouraging her as she tested the length of him.

All things considered, she couldn't imagine how on earth he'd gotten that inside her. It was much bigger than she'd thought it was. Her fingers slid along his skin. It was like steel encased in warm velvet. How on earth did he walk around with that all the time?

"God, what you do to me," he groaned, as her fingertips traced around the tip. His hand took hers and wrapped it around him. "Like that," he encouraged. Then he went back to lying still as a board.

"Like this?" she whispered as she squeezed him.

"Good God," he groaned as he bent his head and nipped lightly at her shoulder. "I never thought you'd be so courageous."

"This is courageous?" she asked, liking the way he arched into her hand, as though he couldn't get close enough to her.

"Very," he growled as he licked a slow path across her shoulder. He reached down and pulled her hand away from him. "But I'll have to ask you to stop."

"Stop?" she whispered.

"Yes," he whispered back as he rolled her to lie flat and covered her with his body. He looked down at her from where he rested on his hands. "Cease. Desist. Knock it off." He chuckled lightly, just before he lowered his head and touched his lips to hers. "I can't have you because you'll be sore," he growled at her. "Yet you insist on tormenting me."

Sore? She wasn't sore.

"I've been lying here smelling you for hours. Feeling you beside me. But I can't have you." He lifted his body several inches and slid down a bit, until his head hovered above her breasts. "When I close my eyes, I dream about you. When I open my eyes, I see you beside me. When I reach out, I can touch you. It's all I've ever dreamed of."

Maddie's heart thumped like mad within her chest. "Will you do that thing you did before?"

"What thing?" he asked, as he raised his head, drawing his gaze from her exposed breasts to look into her face. "Tell me you want me," he encouraged.

He looked like he needed to hear it. "I want you,"

she admitted. She wanted him with a want unlike any she'd ever experienced. She wanted him to ease her pain. She wanted him to ease the ache within her

Finally, he captured her nipple in his mouth. The feeling of it shot straight to the pit of her stomach. "I don't want to hurt you," he said quietly.

"You won't." For some reason, she believed with all she was that he wouldn't hurt her on purpose.

"I want to take my time and make love to my wife."

His wife. Goodness, she was his wife. In every sense of the word. Wes wiggled his hips until he was settled firmly between her thighs. Then he slipped lower, licking a fiery trail down her stomach, his hands skimming down her sides as he went.

"What are you doing?" she asked, as he went lower and lower. Then his head dipped down between her thighs. She tried to close her legs and push him away. But then his tongue touched her. It touched her in a way she'd never expected. She couldn't contain her gasp as he found that pulse point that had been pounding ever since she'd touched his manhood. Ever since she'd woken to find him beside her. She reached down, threading her hands into his hair, ready to push him away. What he was doing was scandalous, wasn't it? It certainly wasn't normal. But then she stopped caring about propriety when he slid a finger inside her and worked at that pounding pulse-point with his tongue.

"Does that hurt?" he asked, quickly raising his head as he began to move his finger within her.

He chuckled when she didn't respond and just

thrashed her head on the pillow as she shoved him back down where she wanted him. "Guess not," he laughed as he went back to his ministrations. He took her higher than he'd taken her earlier in the day. That coupling had been sweet and soft. And she'd shattered at the end of it all. But this… this was different. He was moving something inside her, like pieces of a puzzle that needed to be lined up before one could win. And winning was close. So close. It built within her, slowly, then more quickly. Then she toppled over that precipice. He stayed with her, wringing every last bit of pleasure from her, before he wiped his face on the counterpane and climbed up her, then smiled down into her eyes.

"Oh, my goodness," was all she could breathe as she swiped an arm across her forehead. Goodness, she was sweating. Ladies didn't sweat. Ever. But she was too tired to care.

Wes settled his hips between her thighs once again and pressed at her center. She felt like a limp doll, just waiting to be rearranged for his pleasure. Her muscles were weak and placid, but when he surged inside her with such great care, she somehow found the strength to wrap her legs around his hips. And within moments, he was stoking that fire once again. He was warming her more and more and more. And she was rising to meet him. Then he tensed above her and grunted. "Come with me, Maddie," he urged.

His hand stole back down to her heat and stroked across that pleasure point he'd worked so masterfully before. When he shuddered above her, she joined him. He spilled himself inside her as her walls convulsed around him. They finished together. So close. He held her close to him as he rolled to the side, pulling her atop him. "Dear God," he groaned.

Maddie could barely catch her breath. But she knew she was sticking to him. His sweat or hers, it was still sweat. And she didn't care. Goodness, she didn't care. She giggled.

"What's amusing?" he asked, his voice rich and strong, even though his breaths were still ragged.

"Nothing," she replied, settling her head against his chest, her body nestled snugly beneath his arm.

"Hmm," he grunted as his body relaxed beneath her. "I can't believe you woke me from a sound sleep just to have your way with me."

"Surely you're not complaining."

He hugged her tightly and kissed the top of her head. "Never, but you need your rest, darling, and so do I. We have a long day ahead of us tomorr…" His words faded off as he fell asleep. Maddie followed him as easily into sleep as she had followed him into pleasure only moments before.

⚜

Maddie blinked her eyes open and shivered. Scotland was freezing even in the summer, apparently. She pulled the counterpane up under her chin and tried to rub some warmth into her arms. "Wes?" she croaked out. She instantly missed the warmth of the man she could now call her husband. She shook her head in bemusement.

She called for him again, but there was no response.

Groggy, Maddie rolled to her side, but she couldn't

see her husband. "Weston," she said louder, lifting her head to peer around the room, though there was no sign of him. Where was he?

She shivered again. Why would he leave their room? She touched the side of the bed where he had slept the previous night, only to find it just as cold as she was. He must have been gone quite a while. An uneasiness seeped into her bones. Was he angry that she'd woken him the night before? She probably shouldn't have done so. She'd groped him, for heaven's sake.

What sort of lady does such a thing? The sort who jumps out of inn windows, runs from her loving father, and throws away the promising future that would have been hers. The sort who wanted the all-encompassing passion her husband had shown her. Maddie wasn't even certain who she was anymore. None of those things sounded like something she'd do, and yet she had done every one of them. Something in the way Weston looked at her made her want to trust him, made her want to revel in his strong arms around her, made her do reckless things.

Well, she'd have to do one more reckless thing— order her own bath. Just the thought of sliding down into a tub of hot water made her smile. She could get warm and clean all at once. But first she'd have to don her tattered dress one more time. Maddie scowled at the thought. But there was nothing else to do.

She slid out of the bed, wincing as the cold wooden floor struck her feet. As quickly as she could, Maddie tossed her dress over her head and reached for her ruined slippers. A stab of regret pierced her heart as she thought about her father carrying her shoes all the way from Yorkshire to Scotland for her. His look of utter devastation was one she doubted she would ever forget.

Even so, Maddie tried to push the image from her mind as she opened the door and started down the hallway. She padded down the staircase, steadying her shaky legs by holding on to the well-worn rail. Who would have thought an evening spent with Weston would make walking difficult?

In search of the elderly innkeeper, Maddie entered the taproom and froze in her tracks. She spotted her husband sitting at one of the tables, with Lucy Reed sprawled across his lap. The actress giggled and pressed a kiss to Wes' jaw. Maddie's heart sank at the sight. She clamped her lips closed. Maddie refused to give Lucy Reed the satisfaction of seeing her upset.

She turned on her heels and scampered back up the steps to the safety of her room, barely managing to keep tears from spilling down her cheeks. She was the biggest fool ever born. Wes had promised her passion. He'd never promised fidelity. And she had no idea how much infidelity could hurt.

"Whoa," came a male voice as Maddie slammed into what felt like a brick wall.

She glanced up to find the Earl of Dovenby frowning at her as he caught her by the shoulders to steady her.

"Are you all right, my lady?"

Maddie couldn't hold back the tears or the sobs that had been threatening to erupt ever since she spotted Lucy Reed draped across her husband's lap. Maddie couldn't find her voice but shook her head as tears began to fall.

"Good God," the earl mumbled. "Come with me." With his warm hand on her back, Dovenby ushered her into a sleeping room that must have been his own. He handed her a handkerchief and soothed, "Don't cry, my lady. Tell me what's wrong."

Maddie choked on a sob. How could she tell him what was wrong? Everything was wrong. She'd made a mess out of her life, thrown her entire future away because Wes had made her feel something. And now she felt something else entirely.

What a fool she was. She'd always known men were the most perfidious of creatures, but even that knowledge hadn't helped her in the end. Numbness settled in her stomach and she thought she might be sick. "C-can you take me home?"

"Home?" he echoed.

"T-to my father," she clarified. Papa had said she'd made her bed and she'd have to lie in it, but maybe he would forgive her and take her back.

"I think you better tell me what's wrong, Lady Madeline."

How could she tell him? Just the thought made her tears fall faster.

"There, there, my dear, it can't be that bad. Do you want me to find Hadley for you?"

Maddie squeaked in horror. "I never want to see him again." Not as long as she lived. He could take his fraudulent looks of devotion and go hang.

"Well, you probably should have decided that yesterday before you married the man."

The earl was right. If only she'd never agreed to marry Weston. If only she'd never leapt out that window to him. If only she'd never seen that blasted wolf on the night of the full moon. "Perhaps something can still be done about that."

Dovenby shook his head. "You married Hadley, and your father is well aware your marriage was consummated. Nothing can be done about that situation, my lady."

And even though she knew he was correct, Maddie was determined to find a way to remedy her mess. So she was married to Weston Hadley. He couldn't make her stay with him. She could go home, and now that she was a married woman, all of her father's fortune hunters would have no reason to pursue her anymore. She only needed to make her father forgive her.

"Please, Lord Dovenby, I just want to return to Castle Hythe. I want my father and my grandmother."

"Hadley has clearly upset you. Whatever it is, let him make it up to you. I've never seen a pup so besotted."

Besotted. Maddie snorted as the image of the actress in her husband's lap flashed again in her mind. "I'd hardly call him that."

The earl raised his brow in question. "He really has done something dreadful, hasn't he?"

Maddie nodded and more tears trailed down her cheek. "I saw Weston." She dabbed at her cheeks with his handkerchief. "And Miss Reed. H-he held her in his lap and she kissed him, and I just want to go home."

"*She* kissed him?" A dark look settled on the earl's face, the intensity of which made Maddie shiver.

"I thought he cared about me."

"We've all been deceived a time or two," Dovenby muttered with a slight growl to his voice.

Was he talking about Lucy Reed? The first glimmer of hope sparked in Maddie. If the earl was upset about the situation, too, he might be persuaded to return her to her father. "Please, will you help me?"

Dovenby's expression grew even darker. "It would be my greatest pleasure, Lady Madeline." He led her over to his bed. "Wait for me here. I won't be long."

"Th-thank you," she muttered. Now if only she could persuade Papa to take her back as easily. She had a few days to figure out how to convince him to do so.

Twenty

WES SWIPED LUCY'S KISS FROM THE SIDE OF HIS FACE and shoved the actress unceremoniously from his lap. She stumbled and came to her feet, then regarded him with a ferocious glare. "I was just getting comfortable," she said.

"Go get comfortable with someone else," he suggested. The very idea of Lucy Reed parking her obnoxious little arse in his lap was preposterous, particularly since he'd left his wife, the only woman he wanted anywhere near his lap, upstairs all warm in their bed. He was dying to get back to her. "Why aren't you with Dovenby?" he asked as the actress flopped into a chair across from him.

"He hasn't apologized properly." She shrugged.

Properly probably meant with the offer of a house and a monthly stipend to fulfill all her needs. From what Wes had heard, Lucy was an expensive piece to keep.

"I can continue on with you and Lady Madeline, can't I?" Lucy asked, drawing a circle with the tip of her finger on the back of his hand. He jerked it out of her reach and scratched at the itch she'd just provoked. Like fleas. Like vermin crawling across his flesh. He'd known she had a reason for perching herself in his lap. There was always an agenda with Lucy Reed. Her own.

"Absolutely not. Dove will put you on a mail coach, if you've need of transportation."

"What did I ever do to you?" she sniped.

Nothing. And she wouldn't do anything to him or for him in the future.

Wes glanced at his pocket fob. He'd been waiting for the damned innkeeper to return for more than twenty minutes. One would think one could get some service, since Dovenby had paid all his debts. Wes looked toward the staircase. Those steps were all that stood between him and his wife. Between sliding back between the sheets and drawing her into his arms. But he really wanted to order a bath for her. She enjoyed bathing. She liked being clean. And he felt a grin tug at his lips at the very thought of helping her wash her hair. And everywhere else.

She'd woken him the night before with her gentle exploration, and now he couldn't get her questing little hands off his mind. Or the rest of her.

Dovenby strolled into the room and stopped short when he saw the two of them sitting at a table in the quiet room. "Don't you two look cozy?" he drawled.

Cozy? Irritated was more like it. Wes would much rather be with his wife. Damn that innkeeper for being gone so long. "Morning," Wes said as he drummed his fingertips on the table. "Have you seen the innkeeper about?"

"Haven't seen the man," Dovenby said with a

shake of his head. The earl sat down beside Lucy and grinned at her when she straightened her back and looked at everything in the room but him. "What have you two been up to, I wonder?"

"Nothing," Wes muttered.

Dovenby sniffed at Lucy, like a dog checking for a scent. It was almost as though the earl was looking for the scent of a man. Certainly Lucy hadn't found another man during the night to make Dovenby jealous. She wasn't that foolish, was she?

After a moment, Dovenby reached into his pocket and retrieved a satchel of coins. He held it out to her. She grabbed it like a hungry bird. "That's not for you," he said.

Lucy pouted up. "Who's it for?" she said, with more than a bit of whine in her voice.

Wes had forgotten how annoying she could be.

"Why don't you take Hadley shopping so he can buy his wife a new dress?" he suggested. "Last night I heard about a small shop in the village. Apparently, the woman there has quite the steady business from all of elopers who left with nothing but the clothes on their back."

Wes sat forward. What on earth was Dovenby up to? He'd never been the generous sort without wanting something in return.

The earl looked over at him with a mock look of compassion. "She can't keep parading around in that excuse she's calling a gown. Poor thing is looking more than a little bedraggled."

He was right. Maddie looked more like a fishwife than a duke's daughter. "Why do you care what she looks like?"

Dovenby shrugged. "*You* should care what she looks like." He held his hands up as though in surrender. "But by all means, neglect her, for all I care. She'll love you all the more for it, I'm sure."

Wes plucked the leather satchel from Lucy's greedy fingers. She jumped for it and very nearly ended up in his lap again. He fended her off and pushed her gently back to her own chair. "I don't need Lucy to accompany me," he said as he shoved out of his seat. "I'm capable of picking out a dress on my own." He looked down at the funds in his hand. "And I'll pay you back, Dove, as soon as I get home."

"You'll pay," the man muttered. "You'll certainly pay." But then he straightened and scoffed. "You don't know anything about women's clothing, Hadley. Take Lucy with you."

Wes arched a brow at him. He'd removed more women's clothing than Maddie would want to know about. "I believe I can handle it."

"I'd suggest a woman's opinion," Dovenby said. "You may have held your wife's hips in your hands, among other parts of her anatomy." He grinned and shot Wes a look. One that made Wes want to punch him in the nose. But the blasted Lycan would heal within seconds. It probably wasn't worth the scuffle. The earl continued, "But you don't know actual measurements. And to go and ask her would ruin your surprise." He took a deep breath. "Do something nice for the lady, for God's sake. She sent her father packing for you."

That was true. And she would feel better when she looked more like herself. He could get her some new underthings, too. The kind with lace. She might even want to walk around the room in them. God, he did love the idea of her in nothing more than her unmentionables and firelight. A grin tugged at his lips.

Dovenby elbowed Lucy in the side. "Go help him," he encouraged. "The poor sop is clueless." The earl didn't look like he was joking when he said that. Had Wes somehow offended the man?

"Everything all right with you, Dove?"

The Lycan just smirked at him. "Fine," he said crisply. Dovenby looked at Lucy and said, "Go with him, love. Get something for yourself. You deserve everything that's coming to you."

"I do, don't I?" she preened.

"I'm certain you do."

Wes glanced around the room. "I wanted to order a bath for Madeline." But the damned innkeeper still hadn't returned, blast his hide.

"I'll take care of it for you," Dovenby said with a breezy wave. "You'll be surprised by how much I can accomplish while you're gone."

Wes looked down at the satchel of coins in his hand. Maddie would like a new dress, wouldn't she?

"Let's go pick out something beautiful for that wife of yours, shall we?" Lucy chirped, eyeing the purse as though it was ripe for the picking.

"Something modest," Wes reminded her. Lucy would dress Madeline up as a whore, given any opportunity. "Maybe something pink." It would match the flush on her cheeks when she smiled at him. Pink would do nicely.

"Take your time," Dovenby called to his retreating back.

Wes waved over his shoulder without looking back. "Thanks, Dove."

"Don't mention it."

⤜⤞

Maddie was certain a millennium had transpired since Lord Dovenby had left her; however, in truth, it must have only been ten minutes or so. Still, it seemed as though her entire life had been turned upside down during his absence. She would have paced away her nervous energy, but she didn't trust her legs well enough to stand.

Finally, the earl stepped back into his room and offered her his hand. "We should be off, Lady Madeline, before they return."

Return? Maddie didn't know her heart could sink any further than it already had. Weston had left with that actress? "They're gone?"

He smiled sadly. "I sent them on an errand so we could depart without any unfortunate scenes."

That was clever of him, she supposed. Maddie accepted his proffered hand and allowed him to pull her to her uneasy feet. "Thank you."

Lord Dovenby directed her over the threshold into the corridor. "Hadley is a fool."

No, her husband was a cad, and Lucy Reed was a trollop of the worst sort. But Maddie didn't voice her feelings. There was no point in doing so.

They quickly descended the steps, and the earl ushered her through the taproom where he stopped.

He retrieved a bottle from his jacket and offered it to Maddie. "If you would be so kind as to douse yourself in this, my lady."

"What is it?" She unstopped the bottle and winced when the scent of oranges met her nose. "Oh, that's potent," she said, pushing the bottle back toward him. "No, thank you."

"It's imperative that we mask your scent, Lady Madeline. Otherwise, Hadley will catch up to us within moments." He narrowed his eyes. "You don't want him to retrieve you, do you?" He looked offended for a moment, but Maddie couldn't tell if that was a ruse or not. "You asked me to help you. I'm trying to do so." He again offered her the bottle, which she reluctantly took. She applied the offensive oil to her neck and wrists. Dovenby leaned over and smelled her. "Not quite enough," he said as though to himself. Then he upended the bottle and dripped the contents onto her skirts.

Maddie groaned loudly. This day was not going at all as she had planned.

"It's not as though we can make the dress much less appealing, is it?" Before she could even gasp at his outrageous words, he took her arm and led her into the coaching yard where the Eynsford carriage awaited. Maddie dug in her heels when she saw an unknown driver holding the door of the coach.

Dovenby looked down at her in surprise. "What is it, my lady?"

"Where is Eynsford's driver?" she muttered so low that only the earl could hear her.

His lordship raised a brow. "Do you really want to know?"

"You didn't harm him, did you?"

"Of course not. There's not a malevolent bone in my body." Then he tapped his hat toward the hired driver and said loudly, "Let's be off, shall we?"

The driver nodded in agreement. "Of course, my lord." And he opened the coach door wider.

They were going to take Weston's traveling carriage? That might slow her husband down some.

"But first," Lord Dovenby scowled at the coach, "we need to do one last thing." He dropped Maddie's arm and hefted the large carriage wheel that still remained on the top of the conveyance, the very one Weston had stolen from her father, and dropped it unceremoniously to the ground. Then he dusted his hands on his trousers. "Now we may depart."

Wes would return to find a carriage wheel, an empty room, and that his coach had gone on without him, with his wife inside. How fitting.

Maddie climbed inside the carriage and settled against the squabs. Lord Dovenby was right behind her and sat on the opposite bench.

"You seemed a bit chilly, my lady. So I acquired a hot brick for your feet and a traveling blanket, if you would like it." He retrieved a folded blanket from the bench beside him and handed it to her.

"Thank you, my lord." Maddie took his offering gladly and tried not to think that in the few short minutes she'd spent with Lord Dovenby, he'd taken better care of her than her own husband had ever done. She choked down a sob, refusing to shed even one more tear over Weston Hadley.

"You might as well call me Dove, Madeline. I'm

certain we will get to know each other remarkably well along this journey."

As if on cue, the coach lurched forward and they were off, leaving Weston Hadley, Lucy Reed, and the quaint village of Gretna Green behind them.

"Thank you, sir, for everything."

He sighed as though he was suddenly tired. Of course, he had been quite busy preparing for their departure. Then he closed his eyes as though he meant to go to sleep.

Well, that was fine with Maddie. She wasn't exactly in the mood to be terribly social.

After several miles down the road, Dovenby broke the silence when he yawned, stretched his arms over his head, and sat up, looking much more rested. "How are you feeling?"

Still a little numb, not that she wanted to admit it. Maddie shrugged. "Better the farther we get from the border."

He smirked as though he felt the same way. "Tell me something, how did you even get tangled up with Hadley in the first place, if you don't mind my asking?"

She'd rather not think about her husband at the moment. And she'd rather not recount that awful night in the stables. But the earl had helped her. She could at least give him some answer to his question. "He's a friend of my brother's and…"

"Ah, yes, Robert Hayburn. I nearly forgot."

Maddie nodded. "Yes, and well, Mr. Hadley and his brothers do spend an inordinate amount of time at Eynsford Park in Kent."

"Of course, Eynsford. You are neighbors, are you not?"

"Yes." She nodded again. "Though I didn't know much about the marquess until the last few years. Before his father died, the pair was estranged and he never spent any time at The Park."

"I was so furious that I hadn't thought about actually having to deal with Eynsford on this," Dovenby mumbled. "Though I suppose that can't be helped now. What's done is done."

That didn't make any sense at all. The marquess had nothing to do with this situation, other than the fact that he owned the carriage they were riding in. And she did intend to return it as soon as the earl took her home. "I don't understand why Lord Eynsford needs to be brought into any of this."

Dovenby shrugged. "You know what Hadley is."

A werewolf. And so was Dovenby; she was certain of the fact. Maddie nodded.

"Well, we have certain orders that are to be maintained, rules that must be followed. You are essentially part of Eynsford's pack, my dear. And he will see me as having absconded with his property."

"I beg your pardon!" Maddie nearly sputtered. Property! Of all the ridiculous things to say. "I'm not anyone's property!"

"I meant no offense, Madeline. It's simply the way of things. You do belong to Weston Hadley and he belongs to Eynsford. It's as simple as that."

Weston belonged to Lord Eynsford? Maddie gaped at the man across from her. He might as well have grown two heads with all the nonsensical remarks he was making. "It doesn't sound simple at all. I simply want to return to Castle Hythe and my family and forget I ever met any of you." She immediately wanted to bite those words back when he looked offended. "I'm happy to have met you, of course. But you understand, my lord."

"Dove," the earl reminded her. "And I'm afraid taking you home will be out of the question, Madeline. Eynsford will be none too happy with me. And I aim to put off that confrontation for as long as I can."

So Eynsford's realm extended to more places than just Maddie's existence within it? She glared at the beast. "Well, then you can put me on a mail coach and I'll be out of your hair and find my own way to Kent. You can return the carriage at your convenience."

He shook his head. "No, I don't think that sounds like a very well-thought-out plan either. Perhaps it would be best to take you home with me instead."

Maddie could only gape at the wolfish earl. Take her home with him? She wasn't quite certain what he meant by that, but it didn't sound good. She had a sinking feeling in her stomach that whatever he had planned for her wouldn't be in her best interest. And she suddenly felt like a pawn very much like Helen of Troy. Only instead of legions of Greek and Spartan warriors, she had the bad fortune to be dealing with English werewolves. And Lord Dovenby didn't remind her of Prince Paris in the least. Helen had been a willing prisoner, after all. "You can't possibly mean that," she choked out. "You're going to take me to my father."

Dovenby scratched his chin. "I've given that a great deal of thought. And I don't think it's what's best."

"And you think abducting me is the right choice?"

He *tsked* at her. "'Abducting' is such a harsh word. Borrowing is more appropriate, don't you think? You did come with me of your own free will."

Maddie sat forward. "Unless you plan to take me to my father, you can let me out right this instant." Weston would do the right thing and take her home, even after the spectacle he'd made of his relationship with Miss Reed that very morning. Wouldn't he? Oh, dear, this wasn't a good plan at all.

"I have a bit of a score to settle with Hadley, Lady Madeline. I'm very sorry to say it, but I believe I'll use you to get to him, just as he used Lucy to get to me." He shrugged and settled deeper into his seat.

"I don't have any idea what you're talking about." And she didn't. Not at all. Was he mad? She hadn't thought so until now.

"Lucy Reed was mine," he drawled slowly, as though he was mulling over what he wanted to say. "And I don't take kindly to people who interfere with what's mine."

Maddie had informed Dovenby herself about Lucy and Weston's kiss that very morning. Now he wanted revenge? Oh, dear, she'd thrust herself right into the line of fire.

"Lucy doesn't seem like the sort of lady who wants to marry," Maddie began.

But Dovenby cut her off. "I've no intention of marrying her," he scoffed. "I would never make her any such proposal."

Then what was he talking about? A man didn't usually go around saying a woman was his unless he intended to give the woman his name. "But you said…"

He silenced her with a wave of his hand. "Let's just say that Hadley and I have a history of competition. We've been competing with each other over one thing or another since we were boys in school. The Lycanian Society seeks to match Lycan boys with other Lycan boys when we go off to school, so we have someone to bond with when the moon is full. So, Hadley and I got thrust together more often than either of us ever enjoyed." His face took on a wistful expression. "That's how we met. It's also why Hadley hates the very ground that I walk on."

"I don't understand," she began again.

"And you very likely won't," he said quickly.

Maddie folded her arms across her breasts and tried to think of a way out of this mess. "Wes will find me," she finally tossed out, using her most haughty duke's daughter voice. She'd been raised to look down her nose at people. She just didn't like doing it. Not until now.

"He will find a trail of oranges. Oranges that match the scent of a patron we both smelled last night." He pointed to the top of his head. "Did you see the woman with the ostrich plumes on her hat?"

Maddie shook her head. She didn't recall much from the previous evening. She recalled Weston taking her innocence. She recalled the look of utter devastation on her father's face. And she recalled a much more intimate interlude with her husband in the middle of the night. But she didn't remember any woman with ostrich feathers.

"Well, you can rest assured that Hadley did." He touched his own nose. "She was hard to miss. Absolutely reeked of oranges. Like a Spanish orchard in the summertime." Dovenby appraised his finger-nails. "By the time Weston realizes that you're the oranges, we'll be too far ahead for him to catch up." He sat up straight and fanned the coach air toward her. "That citrus is perfectly hideous, by the way. When this is over, I hope you stick with your rosewater. It's much more becoming."

Thunder boomed in the distance, and Dovenby smiled broadly. "Brilliant. Rain will help to mask the scent even more. Not to worry, Madeline. You are perfectly safe from Weston Hadley catching up to us."

Fabulous. So, now she stank, she was once again being abducted, and her new husband had already been unfaithful less than one day after marrying her. Or she didn't have him. At this point, she didn't know if having him was better or worse than not having him. She buried her head in her hands and groaned loudly. It was a horrible sound, and nothing like any sound she'd ever made before. In fact, she'd been raised not to make noise. Or get dirty. And now look at her. She was sullied in more ways than one.

Dovenby kept talking, chattering like a magpie as though they were having tea instead of being jostled around inside a racing carriage as they fled from her soon-to-be angry husband. "It could have been mud. Mud is a great masker of scents. But I thought you'd enjoy the oranges so much more."

Fantastic. So nice of him to think of her comfort as he planned to abscond with her. "Oranges are better than mud," she grumbled.

"I knew you'd think so." He reached over and patted her knee, grinning at her like the idiot he was.

Oranges were not better than mud. What would have been better than mud would have been for her to have forgone her curiosity and stayed inside on that full moon night, rather than having to stick her nose in where it didn't belong. If she hadn't let her curiosity overrule her common sense, she'd be tucked snugly in her bed with a maid to bring her hot tea in the morning. And her father would still love her. And she'd never have had to disgrace herself by marrying Weston Hadley. And he'd never have had an opportunity to break her heart.

Maddie had always known that any husband she married would probably be unfaithful. Most men were, weren't they? But she hadn't thought it of Weston. Why did it have to hurt so much? Tears pricked at the backs of her eyelids. However, she refused to cry. Absolutely refused to cry. No. She would not do it. If she did, they would win. So, instead, she settled back against the squabs and began to plot her escape.

Twenty-One

"HOW MUCH DID HE GIVE YOU?" LUCY ASKED AS SHE nearly skipped beside Wes on their way to the dress shop a stableboy had pointed out.

"I haven't counted it."

"Give it to me and I'll count it."

If he gave the satchel, he'd never see it again. "I think I'll just hold on to it."

Her lower lip thrust outward. "You don't trust me."

He never really had. "We are to get *Madeline* something to wear."

"I don't have a traveling valise with me either, you know. Besides, I can't see your high and mighty wife wearing something ready-made. She must have her own personal modiste whose entire life revolves around the lady's wants and needs."

Wes rolled his eyes. "There is no modiste locked away in the Hythe dungeon and only let out to cater to Madeline's whims."

Lucy snorted. "I'm certain nothing less than the finest Indian silk has ever touched her skin. She won't wear anything less. You should just let me pick out something for myself."

"You can work your wiles on Dovenby, Luce. You'll find I'm immune to your charms." Wes opened the door to the small dress shop, and a bell tinkled overhead. "Or have you turned your attention to someone else since we arrived in Scotland? Dove seemed annoyed with you this morning, almost jealous."

Lucy scowled. "If either of us has a right to be jealous, it's me. He's the one marrying some feather-brained twit with more hair than sense. All I want is a little security."

All she wanted was to be set up like a queen, but Wes held his tongue. He gestured to the interior of the shop. "After you, my dear."

Lucy stepped over the threshold and graced the shopkeeper with her most winning smile, the one she'd wear on stage to convince the audience of her sweetness and sincerity. "Good morning," she chirped.

"Good mornin'," a plump woman replied, dropping a clump of tangled ribbons on the counter. "Can I help ye?"

Wes cleared his throat. "I need to purchase a few things for my wife."

The shopkeeper grinned. "Just eloped, did ye?"

"How did you know?" Wes asked.

"Most of my business is from couples who left England with little more than the clothes on their backs." She glanced to Lucy and grinned. "What are ye lookin' for, lass?"

"Well, I'd like a new dress that isn't travel worn.

And new gloves. And do ye have any bonnets? My hair has been a mess ever since…" Lucy began.

Wes coughed. Loudly. "She is *not* my wife. She has come to help me pick out something for my wife as a surprise."

The shopkeeper frowned. "I see."

What was the frown for? Wes shook his head. "My wife is a tiny thing, but I need to get her a dress to travel in, some drawers, a chemise…"

"A tiara," Lucy put in with a feigned smile.

Wes glared at the actress. "I don't even know why Dove insisted you come along. I can handle this all on my own."

"Oh, you're doing fine. Don't mind me." Lucy stepped away from him to run her fingers along a rack of dresses a few feet from her.

Wes turned his attention back to the shopkeeper. "And a night rail, if you have any." Though he preferred Maddie with nothing on, she'd probably like something soft against her skin. And he might enjoy removing it.

The woman frowned in Lucy's direction, then turned her old eyes on Wes. "Let me see what I can find, sir." She gestured to the rack of ready-made gowns Lucy was perusing. "The only dresses I have are over there. See if ye think somethin' will work for yer wife, and I'll retrieve some unmentionables from the back."

"Thank you." Wes crossed the small room to rifle through the selection of dresses as the shopkeeper disappeared into a room off the back of the store.

"She won't wear any of these," Lucy said matter-of-factly, peering around his arm. "I just looked."

Somehow Wes managed not to grind his teeth. "Mind if I take a glance?"

The actress grandly gestured to the dresses before them. "By all means. I'll save my 'I told you so' until you've finished."

Wes ignored her and began to look at the dresses one by one. Truthfully, none of them looked like Madeline. The dresses were mostly serviceable and the material was far from the finest quality, but anything had to be better than what she had been wearing for days on end. He selected a light-blue muslin and held it up for better inspection. The bodice was delicate and the dress felt soft enough. Not as soft as Maddie, but it was better than the others.

"That will swallow her up," Lucy declared. "Look how long it is."

It could be long enough for an Amazon warrior for all Wes cared. It wasn't as though Maddie would be walking anywhere. She would be *riding* and if she needed him to carry her over more than one threshold, he was happy to do the honors. "Thank you for your opinion."

She turned her nose regally in the air. "That is why Dove sent me. He said you were clueless."

Wes had thought that about Dovenby a time or two in the past, so he brushed off the insult. "Did you find something *you* wanted, Luce?" Perhaps if he got her something, she'd leave him in peace.

The actress shrugged. "I might be interested in a ribbon or two, but even I wouldn't wear any of this, and I don't have a modiste locked in my dungeon, waiting to tend to my every need."

Wes growled low in his throat. "Go look at the ribbons, by all means. Just keep your opinions to yourself, will you?"

She rolled her eyes, but she did cross the shop floor to peruse the pile of ribbons the shopkeeper had been sorting when they walked in.

Wes lifted the blue muslin higher. There was nothing wrong with the dress. True, it wasn't as ornate as the gowns Maddie normally wore, but he could still imagine her in it. And he could imagine taking her out of it. The dress would suit their purposes until they reached Kent.

A moment later, the shopkeeper returned from the back room, carrying a small package wrapped in paper. "The smallest chemise I've got. A night rail. Drawers. And I tossed in a pair of gloves."

"Thank you." Wes smiled at the woman and offered her the blue muslin. "And I'll take this as well."

After paying for his purchases and a couple of ribbons Lucy couldn't seem to live without, Wes started back for the inn, Lucy at his side. For once in his life, Wes wished he didn't have perfect hearing. If he could just block out Lucy's whining and chattering, he'd be a happy man. And if he could get back to the inn and to his wife, he'd be a very happy man.

"Can I ask your opinion, Hadley?" Lucy asked.

Wes groaned. "What is it, Luce?"

She batted her eyes coquettishly at him. "Don't you think a man should want to buy me a nice little cottage and take care of me?"

Wes shook his head. "I am not getting dragged

into your situation with Dove. Work it out between yourselves."

Her expression turned mutinous. "I should have known you'd take his side."

"Oh, for the love of God. The only person whose side I'm on is my own… and Maddie's. I have no desire to entangle myself in your mess. But…" An image of Dovenby sniffing Lucy that morning flashed in his mind. "If some Scotsman kept you warm last night, you'd better reconsider any attempt at making Dove jealous. He's not one to mess with."

"A Scotsman?" Lucy turned up her nose. "I highly doubt there's a man in all of Scotland who could afford me."

That might be the truest thing she'd ever said. Just as they entered the inn's taproom, a blast of oranges assaulted Wes' senses. He coughed and his eyes began to water. That ostrich-feather woman must have already come down for breakfast. He coughed again. Citrus scents should be used sparingly. Did the woman not have the sense of smell?

"You all right?" Lucy asked and smacked his back in a feeble attempt to help.

"Fine," he bit out. Then he noticed the innkeeper in the far corner of the room. "Morning," Wes called to the elderly man.

The innkeeper smiled and nodded in Wes' direction. "Mornin' ta ye, too, sir."

"Did Lord Dovenby order a bath for my wife?"

The man shook his head. "Nay. I havena seen his lordship this mornin'."

Wes heaved an irritated sigh. How nice of Dovenby

to follow through on his promise. "Well, then will you send one up? I'm certain she'd like to refresh herself before we start home this morning."

"Of course, sir."

Wes bounded up the steps with Maddie's packages in his arms. He could hardly wait to see her. It had only been a few hours, but he found himself quite impatient to draw her back into his arms and shower her with kisses and caresses and…

He tossed open their door to find the room completely empty. "Maddie!" he called.

But there was no sign of her anywhere. Wes stormed out of the room and down the corridor. Where on earth could she be? Certainly, she wouldn't venture out on her own. He stopped and sniffed for her, but the only scent he could smell was that of the oranges the plumed lady had decided to douse herself in. He rubbed at his nose as he reentered the taproom. The innkeeper was still nowhere to be seen.

Wes nearly jumped sky high when a voice from the other end of the room boomed at him. "Well, what a surprise to find you here of all places."

Wes spun to face the voice so very much like his own. His twin brother, Grayson, sat in a chair that leaned precariously on two legs as he wiggled his booted feet on the surface of the table. "What are you doing here?" Wes took a step toward his brother.

"Saving your mangy hide," his twin replied as he slowly lowered his feet and sat up. He shook his head slowly at Wes. "Dash is beyond furious. How could you do it?"

"I don't have time for you right now," Wes said

absently. He had to find Maddie. She couldn't have wandered far. But for some reason, the hair on the back of his neck was standing at attention. Something was wrong.

Grayson shot to his feet. "What's the matter?" He was beside Wes in the blink of an eye.

They'd always shared a bond, despite the fact that they argued like children, even as adults. Of course, Grayson would know something was amiss. Lucy Reed chose that moment to walk back into the taproom. "You haven't seen Dove anywhere, have you?" she asked. She pointed toward the stairs. "I went to go and thank him for my ribbons, but his room is empty and all his things are gone."

All his things were gone? "What things?"

"He bought a few essentials last night after you and Her Highness went off to fornicate," Lucy said. "But they're all gone." She looked a little bewildered.

"You went off to fornicate?" Gray muttered beneath his breath.

"Shut up, Gray," Wes growled. This was certainly not the time.

"Hi, Lucy," his brother said. Gray's gaze swept appreciatively down her form. "Nice to see you again." His brother's eyes twinkled with mirth. Or was it appreciation? Wes couldn't tell and he honestly didn't have time to worry about it.

"So nice to see *you*, Mr. Hadley," Lucy chirped, instantly enthralled by his brother's appraisal. It didn't take much to light Lucy Reed's fire.

Wes glanced at them both and rolled his eyes. "Why don't you two get a room?"

"Fine by me," Grayson stated as he stepped toward Lucy.

But Wes caught his shoulder. "How long have you been here?"

"Just arrived a moment ago," his brother said. "Why?"

"Maddie's gone." Where on earth could she be?

"And Dovenby's gone, too." Lucy pouted.

Wes didn't give a damn about Dovenby. The man could go hang for all Wes cared.

"How did you end up traveling with Dovenby, Lucy, and Madeline Hayburn, for Christ's sake?" Gray asked.

"Hadley," Lucy broke in.

"Yes, love?" Gray responded.

Wes chucked him on the shoulder. "She wasn't calling your name, idiot."

Lucy looked supremely smug as she said, "Lady Madeline Hayburn is now Lady Madeline Hadley."

Gray choked out, "Since when?"

"Since yesterday," Lucy informed him.

Wes stepped to the door to look outside. A few coaches were milling about as the coachmen readied themselves for impending journeys. In fact, Renshaw should be out there doing the same. Something was wrong. Something was terribly wrong.

Gray jerked Wes from his reverie. "You married Lady Madeline?"

"He did," Lucy continued, as though Wes wasn't even in the room. "Then he had his wicked way with her and now she appears to have vanished. And so has Dovenby."

"Sweetheart, you can do so much better than

Dovenby," Grayson said slowly as he stepped toward Lucy again.

"Put it back in your pants, Gray. Something is wrong."

Grayson sighed heavily. Then he gave Wes his full attention. Finally. "Very well. Start at the beginning," he said.

With Lucy Reed around, he couldn't very well tell Gray about how Maddie had caught him shifting into wolf form. "Excuse us, will you, Lucy?" he asked. Then he led his brother up the stairs and into his and Maddie's room.

Gray whistled as soon as he crossed the threshold. "Someone's marriage was consummated," he said as he sniffed the air. "More than once."

Wes shot him a look.

Gray held up his hands as though in surrender. "Sorry, do tell."

"You remember I went to Castle Hythe the night of the full moon?" Wes started. Hopefully, he could make this short.

"I remember you bolting from Eynsford Park after Dash made his decree that Lady Sophia should tutor us." He smirked. "I think she may have bitten off more than she can chew with Archer, by the way."

That was the last thing that concerned Wes at the moment. "Anyway, Lavendon partnered with me in whist. And I ended up staying longer than I should have."

"Lavendon?" Grayson scoffed. "I'd wager he's just the start of your troubles."

"Finally, a bet you'd win," Wes said sarcastically. Then he inhaled deeply to calm himself. "Our cards were great and we kept winning. I couldn't just abandon him."

Gray's brow raised in surprise. "Heaven forbid you abandon Lavendon."

"I should have," Wes agreed. "Chilcombe didn't take the fleecing well."

"What a surprise," Gray remarked drolly. "What did he do?"

"Well, I was on my way to the forest, and Chilcombe came after me." Thinking back on it, Wes could have done so many things differently. With a better outcome. Although Maddie was the best bit of luck he'd ever stumbled across.

"Man never did know how to lose graciously."

"I'd waited much too long," Wes began hesitantly.

"We've already established that." Gray picked at a loose string on his trousers.

"And I ended up knocking Chilcombe in the nose. He went down like a stone."

"Soft chin, that man," Gray said with a whimsical sigh.

"I had to hide the body."

"Of course, you did. Where'd you put him?"

"Hythe's stables."

Gray nodded as though he would have done the same thing.

"There was a storm brewing," Wes continued, "and no one was about, or so I thought. I didn't smell her rosewater until it was too late."

"Lady Madeline caught you hiding Chilcombe's inert body?"

Wes winced as he continued. "Then she saw me change under the full moon. I couldn't stop it. She was in the wrong place at the wrong time. And so was I."

Gray shot to his feet. "You let Lady Madeline see your wolf?" he cried.

"Would you shut up?" Wes hissed at him.

"I can't believe you did something so stupid." Gray shook his head. "Dash is going to rip your tail off when we get home." He thought it over a minute. "So that's why you took off for Gretna? How on earth did you convince Lady Madeline to marry you?"

"I didn't give her a choice," Wes grumbled.

"Oh, dear God," Gray said, his eyes open wide as he listened for the rest of the story.

"I left a note for her father that said we were madly in love. And that I was taking her away to marry her."

"So, she had no choice but to marry you." Gray rubbed his brow as though to stave off a headache. "But that still doesn't explain why Lucy and Dovenby were with you."

Wes waved him away. "They're inconsequential. We found them on the road. Dovenby worked his way into the carriage. And here we are."

"But now two of you are missing."

"Dovenby?" Wes asked. Surely the earl wouldn't be so stupid as to take Wes' wife. What purpose would that serve? "He wouldn't."

"Dovenby has more than one score to settle with you. Starting back with that very first cricket match at Eton."

"If he has taken her, I'll kill him."

"What if she went willingly? Perhaps her night in your arms wasn't as good for her as it was for you."

"It was good for her," Wes said with pride.

"How do you know?"

"Shut up, Gray," Wes growled. He rubbed at his forehead the same way his brother had done. His wife and Dovenby were both missing. But Dovenby had no coach. "The coach," Wes croaked.

"You mean Dash's coach? He's more than a bit miffed about that. He's like a pup with a thorn in its paw."

But Wes was already on his way down the corridor, headed for the stables. "Go find the innkeeper and make some inquiries," he called over his shoulder. He didn't even wait to hear his brother's response. Gray might irritate him to no end, but he'd do what Wes asked.

Wes sprinted for the stables. He inquired politely about Renshaw, but no one had any idea of where the driver was. Suddenly, a shriek came from the privy. Wes ran in that direction. He stopped short when he found Renshaw trussed up better than a Christmas goose, bound with rope and stuffed in the corner of the small closet. "Oh, dear God," Wes breathed, as he bent to loosen the man's bindings.

One curse after another flew from the driver's mouth as Wes took the rag from between his teeth. For the first time in his life, Wes feared bodily harm from the man. He ducked as Renshaw threw a punch at him. "You and your kind," the driver growled. "You're nothing but trouble."

"What happened?" Wes asked, trying to maintain a semblance of patience.

As the driver began to relay the events of that morning, Gray strode into his line of sight. "Renshaw, nice to see you," he said in greeting.

"Not another one of you," the man grumbled. Then more curses flew from his lips. Even Wes winced at the ferocity of them.

"The innkeeper hadn't seen Dovenby, but his

wife did. Said he was in quite a hurry to leave this morning," Gray informed him. "She said he was traveling with a blond lass."

Maddie. Wes' heart constricted. Why would she leave with the blackguard? "Did he have her bound and gagged?" That might make sense.

Gray shrugged. "She didn't mention anything like that. I feel certain she would have, had it been the case."

"I hate all of you," Renshaw grumbled.

"I did catch a scent out by the road."

"All I can smell is orange," Wes said, rubbing his nose and willing the scent away to no avail.

"Unnatural is all I can say," Renshaw continued beneath his breath.

Gray and Wes both looked at him and said in unison, "Would you shut up?"

The man kicked at a stone in anger, but he didn't say another word.

"The orange scent goes south. But it goes north as well, along with a very slight rosewater scent like Lady Madeline normally wears," Gray said.

Wes growled beneath his breath.

"You can't blame a man for noticing," Gray rushed to explain. "The orange and rosewater scent goes north."

"Why on earth would he take her north?"

Gray shrugged.

Wes had no idea either, but he planned to find out. And when he caught Dovenby on his northward dash to wherever, he'd kill him.

Off in the distance, thunder rumbled overhead. Wes ground his teeth together. "We need to hurry before her scent is washed away."

Twenty-Two

MADDIE SHIVERED AND PULLED THE TRAVEL BLANKET tighter around her shoulders. She curled against the side of the coach as rain pelted the conveyance from all sides. Lord Dovenby lightly snored on the opposite bench, and Maddie wished she could open the door and leap from the conveyance to freedom. But that would be foolish. She could hardly escape a full-grown werewolf in the rain with a broken leg, which she'd most assuredly receive from such a fall. Besides, she was certain he would awake as soon as she threw open the door, making the attempt a poorly chosen one.

No, she'd just have to patiently wait for the coach to stop to change horses. Of course, stopping wouldn't secure her freedom. She could bolt, but he'd catch her in just a step or two. She could quietly make an escape, but she already smelled like a sack of rotten oranges. A normal man would be able to track her scent. For a man like Dovenby, it wouldn't even be a challenge.

Maddie glanced around the carriage, wishing she

had something to cosh him over the head with. But nothing caught her eye. Then she considered her blanket. She could smother him with the travel blanket… but he'd wake before she finished the job and he was much stronger than she was. Then she'd be in even worse trouble.

She sighed out of frustration. There had to be something she could do.

"Did you know," Dovenby began, nearly making Maddie leap out of her skin, "you sigh more often than most women. Quite distracting."

Had he only been pretending to sleep? Maddie glared at the Lycan. "I am certain *most* abducted women sigh just as often as I do."

He chuckled. "It wasn't meant as an insult, Madeline. Just an observation." Dovenby blinked open his eyes, sat up straight, and glanced out the window. "Ah, there we are."

What exactly did that mean? Maddie scrambled to look out her rain-splattered window and saw a small inn in the distance. "Time to change horses?" she asked hopefully.

The earl smirked. "Don't get any ideas, my dear. Running off would just make me angry. And I promise you don't want to do that."

How did he know what she had planned? Had she given something away with all of her sighing? Maddie feigned what she hoped was her most innocent look. "I'd just like to use the necessary, my lord. Or is that not allowed?"

"I'm not certain why you perceive me to be such a beast, Madeline."

"Perhaps because you're holding me against my will. Or perhaps because you *are* a beast."

"You asked me to remove you from Hadley. I did so."

"I asked you to take me to my father."

"You'll be safer with me." He dismissed her comment with the wave of his hand. "Do you really need to use the necessary? It's coming down pretty steady out there."

No. She really didn't need to, but Maddie nodded her head. "Most women do need to do so at some point, my lord."

"Very well," he said as the coach slowed to a stop. "I'll wait outside the door then."

Maddie kept from groaning. How would she ever escape him if he stood sentry outside the door? "Thank you," she mumbled. "And I should like something to eat if possible."

He smiled, reminding her of how handsome she'd thought him when they first met. She shook the thought away. Appearances were often deceiving. "Whatever you wish, my lady."

"Whatever I wish?" she couldn't help from asking.

"Well, mostly," he clarified as he opened the carriage door, stepped into the downpour, and offered her his hand. "We won't be heading to Kent, if that's what you were going to ask me."

Of course not. Maddie accepted his hand and allowed him to help her alight from the coach, wincing as the muddy ground threatened to swallow up her slippers. Dovenby had mentioned that mud disguised scents, hadn't he? If she could escape him, she could roll herself in mud once more. It might be her only opportunity to free herself. Besides, her dress couldn't possibly become any worse for wear than it already was.

Maddie glanced around the coaching yard, hoping to find someone who looked like a good Samaritan, but to no avail. Not with the rain pouring as it was. Even imbeciles knew to come in out of the rain.

Dovenby quickly guided her around the stables to a small privy, using his jacket above their heads to keep what little rain off them he could. "Here you are, my lady. Do be quick, will you?"

Just as Maddie had feared, there was no way to escape with him standing guard. So she stepped inside the small closet and made certain to rustle her skirts to keep him from being suspicious. After a moment, she knocked on the door and he let her out, shielding her once more with his jacket from the storm.

"Feeling better?" he asked.

"Much," she lied.

"Good. Let's see about some lunch, shall we?"

Maddie agreed with the nod of her head. Then the two of them bolted around the stables and finally into the safety of the taproom, which was fairly dark and devoid of anyone other than a tavern maid.

"My wife and I are drenched and quite famished," Dovenby said to the woman behind the bar, and Maddie had to work to swallow her gasp at his audacity. How dare he? "Do you have something hearty, lass?"

"Meat pies baked this mornin'," she replied.

"Wonderful. We'll take two along with some ale."

Dovenby held out a chair for Maddie, and after she sat, he took a seat beside her.

"Wife?" Maddie hissed under her breath.

"I wouldn't want to damage your reputation, my dear. Now smile and behave yourself."

Behave yourself? Maddie was tired of behaving. She'd been behaving all of her life—well, except for when she jumped out that Yorkshire inn window and when she'd actually married Weston Hadley. And though that situation hadn't ended like she'd hoped, she wasn't ready to go back to behaving herself to appease the men around her. The Earl of Dovenby's handsome looks would be most improved with meat pie dripping from his hair and eyelashes. What a pity she didn't have her pie yet.

※

"We are not taking you with us," Wes said for what seemed like the hundredth time that morning in the taproom.

Lucy Reed thrust out her lower lip in a very practiced pout. "But I have every right to go. There are a few things I'd like to say to the esteemed Earl of Dovenby."

Gray dropped his hand on Lucy's shoulder, a mischievous twinkle in his dark eyes. "I don't see the harm, Wes."

So much for brotherly loyalty. Wes managed not to snort. His twin only wanted to secure Lucy's affections. "It is about to storm, Grayson. I cannot be slowed down. So if you are too busy to travel with me, perhaps you should say here with Lucy."

Gray frowned. "Very well," he grumbled and squeezed Lucy's shoulder. "Wes is right, love. It could be dangerous, and I wouldn't want to see you hurt or get rained on. Do you want to wait for me here? Or do you want me to put you on a mail coach back to London?"

"It's so nice to be around a true gentleman, Mr. Hadley."

"Tell that to his tutor," Wes mumbled under his breath only loud enough for Gray to hear.

Gray spun Lucy toward him and pressed a kiss to her forehead. "Wait for me here, Luce?"

She shook her head and her blond curls back and forth. "I really must be getting back to London. Visit me there?"

"It will be my honor."

She grinned at Gray. "Promise me something."

"Anything," Gray vowed.

"Will you break his nose for me?"

Gray laughed. "What a bloodthirsty wench you are. I'll be happy to break the fiend's nose and blacken his eye all in your name, Miss Reed."

She batted her eyelashes at him. "I always knew you were my favorite Hadley."

Wes somehow managed not to roll his eyes. "We really should be off, Grayson."

"Of course, of course." His brother gestured to the exit. "After you, brother."

As soon as Wes stepped outside, lightning flashed in the ominous grey sky. Damn it to hell, they had to hurry.

Thankfully, a sour-faced Renshaw held two mounts

steady for the brothers Hadley. "If you don't tell Lord Eynsford his coach was stolen from me, I'll forgive your debt."

Wes shook his head. Poor Renshaw really had endured an awful morning. "My lips are sealed, old man. But I'm still good for my debts. I don't hold you responsible for Dovenby's scheme." Then he mounted a sturdy bay at the same moment Gray swung up onto a chestnut.

"Northward!" Gray declared and kicked his horse's belly before bolting for the main road.

Wes followed suit, trusting his brother's nose more than his own at the moment. Hugging his bay close, Wes barreled north as the grey sky darkened overhead. Dear God! They needed to find her before her scent disappeared completely.

Gray rode like the wind, as fast as his chestnut would carry him. The one thing they had on their side was speed. The coach was heavier and couldn't travel nearly as fast as they could on horseback. But Dovenby did have quite a large head start.

But after a few miles, the sky opened up and a deluge of rain nearly washed the road out from beneath them. Gray headed for the closest tree line and Wes pulled up beside him.

Gray shook his head. "I can't catch her scent. Can you?"

Wes' heart sank. All he could smell were horses and the scent of a Scottish rainstorm. "When the rain lets up, we'll keep heading north." There wasn't anything else they could do.

Gray sighed and looked sincerely sorry. "You

know as well as I that the storm will wash away all trace of her."

"She's my wife, Grayson!" Wes growled, wanting to knock his brother from his horse to the sodden ground. "I can't give up. I *love* her."

"I know," his twin replied as though the weight of the world rested on his shoulders. "You always have. I didn't mean we should give up. Just that it's going to be difficult."

Wes scoffed. "We're Hadleys. When have things not been difficult for us?"

"True enough," Gray agreed. "True enough."

&c⌀

Maddie shoveled the warm meat pie into her mouth. She was so ravenous that it nearly melted on her tongue. She probably looked like an uncivilized heathen who hadn't eaten in weeks, but she couldn't help herself.

"Would you like me to get you another?" Dovenby asked, amusement lacing his voice.

"Only if you'd like to wear it," she returned haughtily and stiffened her back the way her grandmother always did when she was affronted.

The earl laughed. "You've truly become a Hadley, haven't you?"

A pain squeezed Maddie's heart. *Weston.* She shouldn't have run off. She should have demanded that Wes return her to her father instead of trying to escape him. She was in a much worse situation than she would have been if she'd done things the right way. Now she was at the mercy of an unscrupulous werewolf. "Just what do you plan to do with me, my lord?"

He dabbed his mouth with his napkin and sat back in his chair. "I suppose I haven't quite decided yet."

Hardly helpful. "Well, where are we headed? Or is that a mystery to you as well? Shall we just travel the length of Scotland until an idea strikes you?"

"You do have a saucy tongue, Madeline." He smiled wolfishly. "I like that."

Maddie glared at him.

"But so conflicted," he continued. "I can see it in your countenance. You've been raised to be a proper lady, genteel, subservient, obedient. A very interesting mix, my dear."

"Where are you taking me, my lord?" she asked again.

Dovenby shrugged. "I've got a set of stables a few hours north of here."

"Stables?"

"I dabble in breeding," he explained. "There's something about the Scottish air that makes the cattle stronger. I do quite well on the racing circuit with my horseflesh."

"How wonderful for you," she muttered.

"And for you. I'm certain there's something you can change into at Strathwell. Something my sister left behind. Something belonging to one of the maids." He grinned. "Or perhaps you'd just prefer to take a nice warm bath and then slide into bed instead." The way he said the words made her certain he meant *his* bed.

The idea churned Maddie's stomach, and bile rose up in her throat. What an awful thought. She couldn't imagine any man touching her the way Weston had. She didn't want any man to ever touch her the way Weston had. Blast him! When had she fallen in love with her perfidious, unfaithful husband? "I'm a married woman," she reminded the earl.

"Who has left her husband."

"That doesn't change my circumstances, as you reminded me in Gretna."

He agreed with a nod. "Do you know how many married women I've entertained?"

Maddie's mouth fell open.

"A world of opportunities has opened up for you, Madeline."

Opportunities? Most certainly a euphemism for whatever he had planned for her. "I am not a whore."

"No, indeed. A lady born and bred." His wolfish grin returned. "A true lady whose beauty can't be disguised by mud, ruined dresses, or the harshness of travel. I bet you'll be stunning in the morning. The sun transforming your locks to golden silk fanned against my pillow. Your soft skin bared for my touch. I think we'll rub along quite well, Madeline."

She picked up her tankard of ale and splashed it in his face. The meat pie truly would have looked better on him. "Take me back to my husband."

Dovenby chuckled as he wiped the ale from his face with his napkin. "Hadley doesn't deserve you."

"Neither do you."

He nodded in agreement. "And yet we find ourselves thrust together anyway. Fate, perhaps?"

Fate would never be so unkind to her. "Nefarious scheme," she countered.

"Word play is so much more interesting with you than it ever was with Lucy."

"I'm certain my instructors would be so proud," she grumbled.

Dovenby rose from his spot, and the legs of his chair scraped the wooden floor. "Have you finished?"

Maddie glanced back at her plate. She only had a few bites left but still no solid plan for escape. Drat! Where had the time gone? "I thought you were going to order me another," she replied, hedging for more time.

"And I believe you threatened to dump it on my head. Under the circumstances, I'd rather forgo that, if you don't mind."

She probably shouldn't have said that, on second thought.

"Besides, you'll eat well at Strathwell tonight, Madeline. Cook will see to it."

Maddie froze in her spot. If he took her from this inn, she might never get another chance for escape. She'd already *used* the necessary. She'd already eaten lunch. What else could she do to delay their departure? "I'm not at all well, all of a sudden."

He narrowed his eyes on her. "I am not a dolt."

"You're not?" she asked and then bit the inside of her cheek. She probably shouldn't have said that either.

Dovenby sighed warily and pulled her chair out from the table. Then without warning, he yanked her from her seat, bent at the waist, and tossed her over his shoulder.

Maddie gasped. "Put me down, you beast!" She beat at his back with her fists. "Put me down this instant!" She lifted her head to find the tavern maid gaping at her from behind the bar. "Help me!" she begged. "This man is abducting me!"

Dovenby smacked her bottom, making Maddie gasp even louder. "My wife is a little put out with me at the moment," he said to the woman smoothly.

"I am *not* his wife!" Maddie squealed as they strode outside and rain pelted her backside.

A moment later she was unceremoniously tossed inside the carriage, landing on her bottom. An irritated Earl of Dovenby climbed in after her, shaking the water from his head like a dog. "What was that?" he snarled, dropping onto the bench across from her.

Maddie folded her arms across her chest. "You smacked my bottom!"

"Try something like that again and I'll smack it harder next time."

The coach lurched forward and Maddie lunged for the door handle. She had to escape or she'd never get another chance. But Dovenby caught her around the waist and plopped her on the bench.

"Sit," he ordered. "Stay."

Maddie blew her hair from her eyes. "I am *not* a dog."

Twenty-Three

WES SNIFFED THE AIR. THEY'D BEEN TRAVELING THE same road for hours but the rain had washed away all trace of Maddie. Thankfully, the storm had subsided, but it had left both Hadley brothers drenched and exhausted. Defeat swamped Wes, but he refused to give up. He pushed his bay farther down the road, Gray at his side.

"We're going to have to stop," his brother said. "If for no other reason than to get new horses."

Wes nodded once. "Just to change horses. We have to keep going."

Gray sighed. "You look like you've aged a decade, little brother. We're going to have to stop eventually for sleep, you know?"

But Wes couldn't think that way. Last night, he'd held Maddie in his arms. Last night he'd made love to his wife, and his heart ached to think what was happening to her in his absence. It was much easier to rail at his twin. "I'm not your little brother," he groused automatically. "We're the same bloody age." Of course, they'd been having that argument for the past quarter century.

Gray chuckled. "Beat you into this world, and I beat you at everything else."

"You are lucky I am tired, Grayson, or I'd knock you on your arse."

"You could try," his brother goaded good-naturedly.

Somewhere in the back of Wes' mind he realized Gray was trying to keep him occupied so worry wouldn't seep in. He looked over at his twin and sighed. The bond they shared was closer than with either Archer or Dash. "You don't have to be a jackass to distract me."

"That obvious, was it?"

Wes snorted. "No one is ever more obvious than you. Think, would you? What do we know about Dove? Where would he take her? Why north, farther into Scotland?"

"Because you wouldn't expect it?" Gray suggested.

Perhaps. But Dovenby's pack was in England. If he was going to abscond with Maddie, it would make sense to surround himself with his cousins and the others for their support and strength. Going it alone didn't make any sense.

"Up there," Gray pointed to a small inn in the distance. "We'll change horses there."

Wes urged his bay faster toward the inn, ready to stretch his legs if only for a moment.

From behind him, Gray sped past him, chortling. "Beat you at riding too, little brother."

Wes kicked his horse's belly and chased his twin all the way to the inn.

Gray dismounted first, handing his reins to a stable lad before ruffling the boy's hair. "You haven't seen a crested coach come through here today, have you? It would have had a team of four carrying it."

The boy shook his head. "Nay. Ye're the first travelers we've seen today, sir."

Wes' heart sank once again. It had been that way at every inn they'd stopped at. No one had seen the Eynsford coach. He would have worried that the carriage had slid off the road in the rain, but he and Gray hadn't wavered from their path and they hadn't seen any evidence of any sort of accident. He dismounted his own horse and stepped toward the lad. "We'll need some fresh horses."

"Of course." The boy grinned and started for the stables, leading Gray's chestnut.

Gray slapped a hand to Wes' back. "We'll find her."

Wes nodded, wishing he felt as certain has his brother sounded. "We have to."

⸎

Maddie stared out the coach window as a manor house grew closer and closer. She sighed, more in hope of annoying the earl than because she felt the need to do so. He'd said he had a few stables. He had several from what she could see. The estate was more than sizable.

"Isn't it lovely?" Dovenby asked. "Won it off a fellow on the turn of a card."

That made Maddie think about Sophie and the ill-fated late Earl of Postwick. "Hardly commendable," she muttered. "Far from honorable."

He chuckled. "I'm sure you'll feel differently after you've bathed and changed into something dry. You'll be more comfortable." He shot her a glance. "And perhaps of a better temperament."

But Maddie was sure he had never been more wrong in his life. "I won't feel differently." She sniffed and raised her nose in the air. It was a move her grandmother had taught her years before. The duchess had a way of making people feel small with a simple tilt of her nose. Perhaps Maddie would be able to do the same someday. "I'll still hate you just as much after I'm clean."

"Then perhaps I shall allow you to stay dirty," he taunted.

He wouldn't dare. Would he? He would. She looked down her nose at him even more, and he chuckled at her. "Just what do you find to be so amusing?" she asked.

"If a heavy rain began, I swear to the heavens, you would drown, Madeline."

"Then perhaps you should leave me outside so we can test your theory," she countered.

He took her elbow in his hand and led her toward the main house. "And let you get away? Absolutely not. I won't make it that easy on you."

And she wouldn't make it easy for Dovenby. Not for a single moment.

As they stepped over the threshold, an aged servant approached on quiet feet and Maddie opened her mouth to call to him. Before she got the words out, Dovenby had her tossed over his shoulder once more and was carrying her up the stairs. The butler just nodded in her general direction. Could this be common behavior for the earl?

"I'm here against my will," she called loudly as she pounded on Dovenby's back.

"Of course you are, darling," Dovenby said smoothly. Then he said in a conspiratorial tone aimed at the butler, "They all like to pretend it's against their will, don't they? Makes it easier on their pride when they take that tumble."

"Tumble!" Maddie cried. "If you think you're going to tumble me, you have lost your mind."

"Bound for Bedlam, I am," he agreed as they slipped beyond the butler's hearing and up the steps. The man obviously wasn't going to save her, no matter how much she protested. "You can save your voice," Dovenby informed her. "My servants are loyal."

"And as dishonorable as you are, obviously."

"I'm not dishonorable, my lady. I saved you from Hadley, just as you asked."

"Do you always twist everything for your own benefit, my lord?" she taunted.

"Only every chance I get," he replied with a grin as he finally deposited her on the floor of a large bedchamber. It boasted heavy drapes and a huge, four-poster bed.

Maddie folded her arms across her chest. "Take me to my father now!" she demanded, her toe anxiously tapping on the hardwood floor.

The earl shook his head. "Are you accustomed to ordering all the men in your life about? Is that what you did to Hadley?"

Maddie's heart clenched again at the sound of her husband's name.

"Well, that won't work with me, Madeline. I'm used to giving orders, not receiving them. So sit down and behave."

She wouldn't sit and behave. Not on his life.

"Just where exactly are we?" She looked around the opulent room.

"Master's chambers," he said absently as he sat down on the edge of the bed and began to tug off his boots.

How dare he do such a thing in her presence? Maddie managed to keep from gasping at his audacity. "And where will I sleep?" she asked.

He patted a spot on the mattress beside him. "Right where I can keep my eyes on you," he said with a big grin. Then he yawned widely. "Don't want you running away while I'm asleep."

"Oh? Do you sleep with your eyes open, my lord?"

"I suppose you'll find out, won't you?"

If only she had a knife to thrust into his back as soon as he closed his eyes. Maddie frowned as she walked over to the window. She rested her head against the beveled glass and wished Weston would find her. But he probably wasn't even looking for her. He probably thought she'd left of her own free will. Which she had, of course. The whole debacle was no more than she deserved. "If you think I'll share your bed, you are sorely mistaken." She glanced at him over her shoulder.

"You already said as much," he replied with a nonchalant grin. Then he sobered a bit and rolled his eyes. "Don't worry. I don't particularly like the idea of taking Hadley's leftovers. So you are perfectly safe with me."

Leftovers! How dare he!

"I have a score to settle with Hadley. But you can relax. You're not my prize. You're my bait." He yawned widely. Then he crossed to the door and opened it. He looked back over his shoulder at her. "I'm more than parched. Would you care for something to drink?"

"I don't want anything you have to offer," she said. Her stomach grumbled in response, which made him smile.

"Suit yourself," he tossed at her. Then he slipped out the door and closed it behind him. She very nearly clapped her hands with glee at being left alone. But then she heard a key turn in the lock. The blackguard had locked her in. Now she had no chance of getting free. She dropped onto the edge of the bed. There was a time when she would have flung herself across it and cried herself to sleep. But that didn't seem quite as effective if no one was around who cared. Dovenby wouldn't be scared of her tears the way her father or brothers were. He wouldn't care at all. In fact, he'd probably laugh.

Maddie once again crossed to the window and looked out at the cloud-filled sky. Rain still pounded the windows like the hooves of a runaway team. She remembered another time and another window, not all that long ago. She'd seen Weston Hadley carrying a body across the lawn at Castle Hythe, and that was what started all this mess. She shoved at the window and winced when it creaked loudly but opened a tiny bit. Rain washed over the sill.

Freedom was within her grasp!

She pushed at the window with all of her might and it moved again, just enough for her to climb through. Though Maddie could barely see two feet in front of her, she was fairly certain she could make out the stables in the distance. If she could get to a horse, her problems would be solved. She threw one leg over the now-drenched sill, sat on the edge and dangled by her waist for a moment, and then she threw caution to the wind and shoved off.

Twenty-Four

"WE HAVE TO STOP FOR THE NIGHT." GRAY GESTURED with his head toward an inn up ahead.

"We have to find her," Wes insisted.

His twin growled. "You'll be no help to her this evening, Weston. You can barely keep your seat on the horse. We'll start our search first thing in the morning."

Wes knew his brother was correct, but he couldn't stomach leaving Maddie to Dovenby's whims. "How about if we eat supper?" he suggested, hoping to appease Gray.

His brother pushed his mare through the rain, and headed the last few yards to the inn with Wes right on his tail. As soon as they handed their reins to a stableboy, Gray asked the question he'd asked all day. "Have you seen any crested carriages today?"

"With the rain?" the lad asked. Well, it was worth a try. Wes started for the taproom entrance, but the lad's next question stopped him short. "Whose crest is it? We get some fribbles comin' through here every once in a while."

"The coach belongs to the Marquess of Eynsford,"

Gray remarked. "I doubt you've seen it this direction before."

An idea occurred to Wes. Other fribbles frequented this area of Scotland? "What about the Earl of Dovenby?" he asked. "Have you seen the earl's coach in the past?"

The boy's eyes lit up. "Oh, aye. Are ye lookin' for Lord Dovenby?"

For the first time that day, Wes' heart filled with hope. "We are."

The stableboy shrugged. "I havena seen him for a while, and certainly no' today with the storm. But ye might want ta try lookin' at Strathwell."

"Strathwell?" Wes repeated.

"Aye." The lad nodded. "Won the stables from Mr. Ross in a card game from what I hear."

"Gregor Ross?" Gray asked.

"The very one. Do ye ken Mr. Ross?"

They did, indeed. Gregor Ross had the best stables in all of Scotland. "I heard Dove had started breeding horses and running the circuits," Gray said. "I didn't know he'd taken Ross' stables."

"Can you tell us how to get to Strathwell?" Wes asked the stable lad.

"Of course, sir. Ye're nearly there as it is. Ye follow the main road until ye come ta a small church. There's a fork in the road right after. Ye want ta veer ta the left. After about a mile ye'll see Strathwell Manor."

"You're not even going to let me eat supper, are you?" Gray asked, exhaustion laced in his voice.

"We're so close, Grayson."

"Yes, yes." His brother sighed. Then he climbed

back atop his mare and looked at the stable lad. "Main road. Church. Left at the fork in the road. Then we can't miss the manor. Is that correct?"

The lad nodded. "Aye, sir. Ye got it."

Wes quickly mounted his gelding. Together they barreled down the main road, following the stable lad's instructions at every turn. Finally, a manor house loomed in the distance and Wes took a deep breath. Maddie was nearby; he could feel it.

"Just for the record," Gray began with passion as he blew a torrent of water from his lips, "I'm fully prepared to help you bury Dove's body."

"There won't be enough left of him to bury," Wes drawled. Then he kicked his mount closer to the entry gates. He'd kill Dovenby when he saw him. He'd eviscerate him. He'd demolish him with his bare hands.

Wes didn't stop to knock as he burst through the front door. He growled low beneath his breath when an aged butler called out to him, but the sound of his growl must have been more than the man could bear. The servant turned himself toward the corner and faced it like a good little beta. "Where is my wife?" Wes barked.

The butler pointed toward the stairs, his hand shaking in fear.

"Find Dovenby," Wes said to his brother.

But just then, the earl sauntered around the corner. "Ah, Hadley, what a surprise," Dove said casually. He held out a glass. "Whisky?"

Wes smacked the glass out of his hand. "Where is she?" he growled, grasping the earl's jacket with his hands. If he didn't know better, Wes would think he could shift into wolf form at any moment because the beast inside him was so strong.

Dovenby looked down at the broken glass and spilled whisky. "Has no one ever taught you any manners?" he asked.

"Where is my wife?" Wes snarled.

"Calm yourself, Hadley," the earl said, his tone flippant, but less so than normal. Still there was a quiver beneath his words. Dovenby must have finally realized the consequences of his actions. "She's safe."

"She'd better be." One hair out of place, and so help him God, Wes would knock every tooth from Dovenby's head and then he'd start removing appendages.

The earl sighed. "She asked me to help her escape you."

Wes didn't believe that for a moment. Not after all they'd been through together. Not after the night Maddie had married him. Not after he'd made love to her. "Where is she?"

"In my chambers. Top of the stairs to the left."

In his chambers? Wes growled low in this throat.

Gray clapped a hand onto Wes' shoulder as though to calm him. "Go get your lady," he said. "I'll take care of him."

Wes pushed the earl away from with such force that he heard the wall Dovenby fell into actually crack.

"Lucy Reed asked me to give you something," Gray remarked conversationally.

But Wes didn't look back as he ran up the stairs three at a time, not even when he heard Dovenby howl in pain after Gray's fist met his nose. A startled housemaid slunk back against the wall with a gasp as Wes ran past her. He turned the key in the keyhole and flew through the first door on the left as Dovenby had instructed. However, no one was inside and the window was open. One of Maddie's ruined slippers lay on the rug. He picked it up and looked at it. *Love won't keep my daughter in slippers* came back to taunt him once again.

He rushed to the window and looked out at the grounds below, but he couldn't see a thing for all the rain. However, he could smell her. The faint scent of rosewater and the rather strong scent of citrus lingered in the air. Wes dashed back down the stairs and ran toward the front door and out into the night, into the pouring rain. Maddie was out there, somewhere in the pouring rain. She was probably drenched. And cold. And miserable. And alone. And it was all his fault.

Wes saw a shadow moving in the distance. But he couldn't tell if it was male, female, or equine, and Maddie's scent had been washed out completely. He hugged her slipper to his chest. He cupped his hands around his mouth and called out, "Maddie! Madeline!"

Her faint voice reached his ears. "Weston?"

Dear God, she sounded like she was winded. What had Dovenby put her through? She wasn't made for rigorous activity. Through the pounding rain, he didn't even see her or hear her when she barreled into him. "Maddie?" he said, catching her by the shoulders. But she was climbing all over him. Kisses rained down on his face.

"I knew you'd find me," she cried, her voice choked with emotion.

"Of course, darling." Wes scooped her up in his arms and carried her back toward the house.

As he entered through the front door, he heard his brother and Dovenby say, "Oh, dear God," in unison.

Wes didn't have time to stop for them. Maddie was cold. And wet. And dirty. And she smelled god-awful. He strode up the steps and down the corridor, and burst into the chamber where he'd found her slipper. Slowly, he lowered her to her feet. "I found your slipper," he said lamely, and held it out to her. But she threw herself against him again instead of taking it.

వచ్

Wes brushed her heavy locks back from her face and drew Maddie into his arms. "I've never been so happy to see anyone in my life," he said, his voice gravelly with an emotion Maddie couldn't name. She swiped at the mud that had begun to crust beneath her eyes. Wes grumbled and set her away from him. "What the devil is that smell?" he asked. Then he leaned close and sniffed at her hair. He grimaced. "I think it's you, darling."

"It's just mud. It doesn't smell that bad," Maddie said, sniffing her forearm. There was a slight scent reminiscent of a horse farm she'd once visited. But that was all.

Wes grimaced. "That's *not* mud, Maddie." He crossed to the corridor and bellowed loudly for a servant. Low voices she couldn't understand reached her ears, mumbling. Then Wes closed the door and turned back to face her. "Not to worry. They're bringing a bath."

"Thank you," she said. She couldn't think of anything more than "thank you" to say to her husband? This was a sad state of affairs, indeed.

"Oh, Maddie, you're so dirty," he said slowly.

Maddie looked down at herself. She was. Filthy. And she didn't care. She'd gotten away from Dovenby with her own cunning and her own intellect, and Wes had found her. She'd put forth commendable effort to escape her captor. And all her husband could think about was the fact that she was dirty? Maddie shrugged. "A little dirt never hurt anyone, did it?"

Wes scratched at his nose and avoided her gaze. "We'll get that off you in just a moment. Please don't get upset."

It really wasn't that bad. She'd made a genius move when she'd painted herself with the mud near Dovenby's stables. "I've been abducted, not once, but twice. All in a very short span of time."

Wes raised a brow at her.

"Once by you and once by Dovenby," she clarified.

"Of course," he said quietly and motioned for her to continue.

"And now you're worried I'll be bound for Bedlam over some dirt."

Wes coughed into his closed fist. "It's not dirt, Maddie," she thought she heard him mutter.

"Beg your pardon?" Perhaps the rain and cold had done things to her sense of hearing. "Of course, it's dirt."

Just then a scratch came on the door and Wes said something that sounded like, "Thank God," as he turned to open it.

Several servants entered with a large tub and buckets of steaming hot water. A slight maid followed with towels and soap. "Would ye like some help with yer bath, my lady?" the maid asked with a small curtsy.

Actually, she would. Maddie would love for someone to wash her hair. To pamper her. To take care of her for a few minutes.

"I'll help her," Weston said, breaking into her musing as the other servants filled the tub with water.

"My lady?" the maid asked, eyeing Wes as though he was the last man on earth Maddie should choose. In truth, he looked just as bad as she did. His clothes were plastered to his body, just as hers were.

"I'll be fine," Maddie said, waving the maid away. As the lass slipped out of the room, Maddie watched Wes closely. "I feel like I've missed something," she said, running through events in her mind.

"Why are you covered in that… stuff, Maddie?" Wes asked as he hitched a hip onto the end of the footboard.

Maddie grinned. "Well, Dovenby let it slip that mud masks scents. So, I thought I'd have a better chance of getting back to you if I used it. Did I do all right?"

❦

She looked like a child waiting for approval as she stood there watching him. He was amazed that his mild little Maddie had had the fortitude to escape Dovenby by painting herself in mud. But it wasn't mud. It was worse. Much worse. Should he tell her, or should he just wash it off her body and be done with it?

"I am missing something, aren't I?" Maddie mused, her head tilted to the side as she looked at him. She didn't even look like herself. She was painted brown, and her hair hung in a muddy mess around her face.

She brushed a lock back, but it flopped back against her cheek with a wet plop. It trailed down to her lips. Her little pink tongue came out to lick her lips.

"No, Maddie, you don't want to do that!" he cried.

"Do what?" she asked, looking a bit bewildered. "What is wrong with you, Weston? You haven't even tried to kiss me since you found me? Aren't you happy to see me?"

"Ecstatic." God, he'd never been happier to see anyone in his life. "But let's get you cleaned up, shall we?"

Maddie nodded, and he pushed her shoulder gently to turn her away from him and began to work the fastenings of her gown. "You don't know how happy I am you found me. I wasn't certain how I'd manage to walk all the way back to the border and I lost one of my slippers, I'm not even sure where."

Wes chuckled; he was so happy she was safe and that this nightmare was over. "I found it in here, darling. But we are going to have to find you a pair of slippers that won't go missing every time you turn around." He peeled the gown from her skin and let it drop in a heap at her feet. The dress would have to be burned at this point. "Don't step into the tub, Maddie, just stand here until I can get this off you."

She looked longingly at the tub. "Can I at least put one toe in the water?"

Wes laughed again. He couldn't help it. "Darling, I plan to let you take a nice luxurious bath, but you won't want your water contaminated."

"It's just mud, Wes."

There was nothing else to do. He had to tell her.

"It's not mud, Madeline. It's dung. You have painted yourself with wet horse dung. I can't believe you can't smell it."

"I don't have a nose like yours…" she said hesitantly.

"You don't have to have a nose like mine to smell dung, Madeline."

She held her hands out to the side, and tears welled in her pretty eyes. "I thought that's how mud smells."

"That's not how mud smells, darling," he said with a chuckle. "Now let me clean you off. I'll take care of all of it."

"I have dung in my hair?"

"Not for much longer," he said, trying to placate her.

"I have animal dung on my face?" she asked, her voice hitching a little. A piece of Wes' heart broke along with her voice. Dear God, what he done to her?

"Lean over the basin," he directed, hating himself for ever having put her in this situation.

Maddie followed his orders, and Wes slowly dumped one of the buckets of water over her head. Wes soaped a cloth and gently began to wash the brown mess from her face. The skin beneath was slightly abraded from the harshness of the dung. "I'm sorry, Maddie," he said softly. "Just let me take care of everything."

A lone tear ran down her cheek. He lathered soap in her hair and rinsed it away with some more water from the bucket. As Wes washed the mud from her neck, he sluiced her with water again and appraised the sensitive skin where her neck met her shoulder. Good God, simply by claiming her, he'd have to mar her once again.

"Is it coming off?" she asked, forsaking all her dignity in the pursuit of cleanliness.

"Yes," he said quietly.

She breathed a sigh of relief, and Wes wished he felt the same relief.

"All right," he began, "you can step into the tub now." She wasn't pristine, but she was mostly clean. The bathwater and soap would take care of the rest.

"Thank you," she said quietly.

Wes guided her back to the tub and held her hand as she stepped inside. She sank into the water and stared at him with pitiful green eyes. His heart could barely take any more. He'd done this to her, to his perfect Lady Madeline. He was so far beneath her that he may as well have been horse dung himself. He wasn't worthy of her. Wasn't worthy at all. He hadn't taken care of her. Not well enough. Not nearly well enough.

"I have done a poor job of caring for you so far," Wes admitted.

"It has been a rough few days," she agreed.

That was generous of her. She hadn't eaten well in days. He'd had to borrow money from Dash's coachman, for crying out loud, simply to feed her. He'd even taken money from Dovenby to clothe her. He wasn't deserving. Not at all. He had no right to even consider claiming her.

"It might be a rough few years," Wes muttered to himself, but after all she'd been through, she deserved the entire truth. Then he inhaled deeply and said, "Do you know that a Lycan marks his mate?"

Her eyes grew wide at hearing this. "What does that mean?"

"When a Lycan claims a mate, he takes her into the woods with him on the night of the full moon. And when he's inside her, and their pleasure is at its greatest, he bites her shoulder. He marks her as his very own."

Maddie raised a hand to her shoulder, as though protecting the area. "That seems a little barbaric," she said, her mouth hanging open wide.

Was it? To Wes it seemed the most natural instinct in the world. He didn't want to know the answer to his next question, but he had to ask it. He drew in a deep breath. "Would you be proud to wear my mark? For people to see my mark on your skin and know you're mine? Or would you detest it?"

"You would scar me?"

"In a sense," he said. He couldn't explain. He'd never done it. He had no idea what it was like, but he'd like nothing more in the world than to claim Madeline, to claim all of her heart, body, and soul.

"I suppose I could cover it up when we go out in public. With some powder. Or a high-necked dress."

Wes' heart nearly stopped. "You'd be ashamed of it."

"Well, I don't have any scars," she began to explain.

Of course, she didn't. She'd been coddled and protected her whole life. She'd never even been dirty. Not until he'd forced her to run off with him. They were from two completely different worlds. "Your skin is perfect," he agreed.

"If it's something you have to do, I suppose I could tolerate it." Her voice was small and unsure.

She could *tolerate* it. Wes' heart hurt a bit at the

admission. He supposed he didn't have to claim her. She could be his wife in every other sense. Not every Lycan marriage was sealed with the bond. He could be happy in knowing that she chose to marry him when she didn't have to. That could be enough. It would have to be. He wouldn't hurt her any more than he already had.

"Wes," she said softly. "Are you all right? You look upset."

He *was* upset, but it wasn't her fault. Not really. She wasn't from his world. She couldn't understand. Wes shook his head and tried to smile through his pain. "Just relieved to have found you."

She smiled at that. "I promise not to run off again. I should never have done so in the first place."

"Run off?" he echoed, staggering a bit toward the four-poster to catch his balance. "Are you saying you really did run off of your own accord?"

Maddie must have seen the surprise in his eyes because she sat up straight in the tub. "I just wanted to go to my father."

If her bathwater had turned to pudding, Wes would have been less surprised. "Your father?" He raked a hand through his still damp hair. "Why?"

"Well, there was Lucy…" Tears slid down Maddie's cheeks. "And, well, I thought it was the thing to do at the time, and I thought Lord Dovenby was honorable enough to take me."

She really had tried to escape him. Wes' vision began to blur just a bit. He hadn't believed Dovenby's account, but apparently the jackass been telling the truth. She wanted to go back to her father. Wes shouldn't be surprised. Look at what he'd put her through in the past sennight.

He made a split-second decision. One that would break his heart, but he truly had no choice. Besides, his heart was already broken and she wasn't meant for him. She wasn't meant to be his Lycan mate. Or even his friend. They were too different. It would never work.

"I'll take you back to your father, Madeline," he said. She wasn't even Maddie to him anymore. She was Lady Madeline.

"I don't know that I want that anymore." Water sloshed over the side of the tub as she started to stand.

"Are you all clean now?" He recognized the emotion in his own voice and strove to harden his heart. But it was impossible.

She looked down at her pink skin. "I think I am."

"I plan to keep you that way."

"Weston!" Her voice raised an octave. "What are you saying?"

"You're not made for a life like mine." He shook his head and couldn't figure out how on earth he'd ever thought this would work out. "You're clean, pure, and rich. And I'm dirty, scarred, and poor. I can never be what you need."

"How do you know what I n-need?" she asked, tripping over her words.

"No one knows about our marriage, Madeline," Wes said, hearing the resignation in his own voice. "The blacksmith who married us can be bought." He shook his head. "And I'll return you to your father. I'm certain he'll be delighted to take care of the details. Tell him to send me a bill for any fees he incurs. I'll pay them."

"Wes, stop," she said, stepping out of the tub and walking toward him. Her eyes flashed with anger. Of course, she was angry; he'd abducted her, rolled her in mud, nearly starved her, made her sleep in vermin-infested hovels, and he'd just finished washing dung from her body. Any lady would be angry. "Is this because of the biting thing? You can do it if you need to."

No, that was only a very small part of it. Wes leaned over and pressed a lingering kiss to her forehead. "Gray and I will escort you home. Back to your father. And you can go on with your life." He turned and crossed the floor in only a few strides. Then he stepped into the corridor and closed the door behind him. He leaned against it and inhaled deeply, needing a full breath almost as much as he needed her.

"You are my husband!" she cried.

But he heard her through the closed door. He also heard her curse. God, how he'd lowered her. Now she was cursing, for Christ's sake.

"I don't have any clothes to follow you, Weston Hadley," she called through the door. Wes closed his eyes tightly. He inhaled, then breathed out slowly. Of course she didn't. This was what she'd been reduced to. *Love won't keep my daughter in slippers.* A truer statement had never been said.

Wes descended the stairs and found his way to one of Dovenby's parlors, where his brother was keeping a close eye on the jackass.

"Is she all right?" Gray asked, rising from his seat on the settee.

"She will be," Wes muttered, "just as soon as she reaches Castle Hythe."

"Castle Hythe?" Gray frowned at him. "All day long you've pushed me through this godforsaken country because you love the lady. And now you're going to take her to the castle?"

Wes gestured toward Dovenby with his chin. "He was right. It's what she wants. It's what I should have done from the beginning."

"Oh, I'm certain she would have been quite happy to keep your wolfish secret in the beginning." Gray scoffed. "You didn't have a choice."

"But I did." Wes strode over to Dovenby's sideboard and poured himself a glass of whisky from a beveled decanter. "I'm sure you don't mind," he said to their unintentional host.

"By all means, help yourself," Dovenby grumbled.

"Wes," Gray began, crossing the floor to stand before his brother, "you have loved Madeline Hayburn since the day you first laid eyes on her."

Wes agreed with a nod. "And I should have loved her enough not to thrust myself into her life." He swallowed half the whisky in his glass and wished the burn in his throat could wipe away his memory of Madeline.

"You should have loved her enough not to dally with Lucy Reed then," Dovenby muttered sourly.

Wes' head shot up and he stared at the earl. "I didn't dally with Lucy Reed."

Dovenby glared at Wes. "Try telling that to a fellow who doesn't have excellent smell, Hadley. Your scent was all over Lucy this morning."

Wes snorted at the ridiculousness of that statement. Clearly Dovenby had somehow lost whatever sense he'd once possessed. "Were you always this big of an idiot?"

"Denying it?" Dovenby taunted. "Don't bother. Your wife saw you with her own eyes."

Either the man was mad or an awful liar. Wes turned his attention back to his brother. "Hythe told me he could pay the blacksmith to lose the marriage lines. With her dowry, she could still find a decent man even without her innocence."

"I cannot believe you're talking this way." Gray gaped at him. "For years I have heard you sing her praises, wax poetic about her perfect beauty and graceful countenance. I'll be the first to admit I never thought you had a chance with the chit, but she *is* your wife."

"I can't ruin what's left of her life, Grayson!" Wes bellowed. "She deserves better than this, and I'll see she gets it."

Dovenby snorted from his spot on the settee. "You almost convinced me of your sincerity. Almost."

"Shut your muzzle," Gray growled. "No one asked you."

Wes looked back at the earl, who was scowling at him. They had never been friends. They'd never even liked each other. But there was more hatred than normal in his old foe's light eyes. "Do you have something for Madeline to wear? Something one of your paramours might have left behind?"

Dovenby leaned back in his seat and kicked his long legs out in front of him. "I'm sure Whyte can find you something suitable."

Twenty-Five

MADDIE'S THOUGHTS WERE ALL JUMBLED. SHE WASN'T certain what she wanted anymore. When Weston had come for her, she'd never been happier. Well, she would have been happy not to be drenched and covered in what she thought was mud and missing a slipper, but her heart had expanded in her chest when she had heard him call out for her. In that moment, she'd thought for certain he truly did care about her. He'd searched for her all day, followed her across Scotland, and by some miracle he'd actually *found* her. But now it had been days and he still wouldn't even look at her.

She wanted to bite her own tongue off. She'd just been so shocked when he said he wanted to bite her that she hadn't known how to respond. Somehow she must have said the worst possible thing because he hadn't made eye contact with her since.

He'd made certain a tray was sent up to her the night they spent at Strathwell. And he'd made certain clean clothes and a maid were waiting for her when she woke the next morning. And at each stop along their journey south, he'd made certain she had a soft bed, a warm bath, and enough food to feed an army. But he'd avoided her at every turn, choosing to ride alongside the carriage instead of in it with her, arranging for separate rooms at night, and taking his meals alone. She tried to pry information out of Grayson Hadley whenever she had the opportunity to speak to her brother-in-law, but he just frowned at her and promised they'd see her safely to her father.

But she wasn't sure she wanted to be returned to her father. On the other hand, she wasn't sure she wanted to stay with Weston, either. Not if he couldn't look at her anymore. And that realization nearly broke her heart. She thought about all the times she'd spied him watching from afar, how he'd seemed frightening and dangerous and made her uneasy with his attention. Now she'd sell every slipper she possessed if he'd just look at her once more. If she could just look into his eyes, perhaps she'd find the answer to the questions plaguing her.

The Kent countryside passed outside the coach window, and Maddie pulled the curtain back to watch the landscape. Weston, proud and regal atop a black mare riding a few feet away, caught her attention, and she willed him to look in her direction, but to no avail. If he would just *look* at her...

In the distance, Castle Hythe loomed on the horizon, and a pit formed in Maddie's stomach. It wouldn't be much longer before she was home, if the castle was still her home; and she still didn't have a clue what she would do when she got there or what she even wanted. Maddie sat back against the squabs and closed her eyes, hoping the answers that had evaded her thus far would finally become clear.

❧

Wes watched Castle Hythe grow larger with each step his mare took. He couldn't get there fast enough. If he could return Madeline to her father, he could start trying to forget her, he could try to get on with his life. The life he was meant to lead without her.

"Last chance," Gray said as he rode up beside Wes. "We can ride on to Eynsford Park instead."

But that wouldn't be best for Madeline. Wes shook his head. "We've been over this."

"And I still think you're making a mistake."

"You always think I'm making a mistake."

Gray agreed with a nod. "But I think this one is bigger than most. She doesn't know why you're doing this, you know. Every night she asks me about you. She asks what she did to make you stop loving her."

"I'll never stop loving her and that will be my cross to bear, but that doesn't mean she should have to bear it, too."

"What if she wants to bear it? What if she loves you?" Gray asked.

"She doesn't. She got caught up in my foolishness the night of the moonful, and I can't ruin her life because of that."

"Weston," his brother dropped his voice, "the girl cares about you. I can see it in her eyes when she talks about you."

"She's confused," Wes replied. "It's not the same thing. Once she's with her father, she'll be able to forget this adventure ever happened, and she'll be better off than she would be with me."

"As long as you're certain." Gray frowned, but he said nothing else as they crossed onto Hythe property.

After riding in silence the rest of the way to the castle, Wes was relieved when he was finally able to pull back on his reins and dismount. Just a few more minutes and this would all be over. The coach stopped a few feet away and Wes allowed Renshaw to open the door for Madeline. Out of the corner of his eye, he watched her gaze up at her father's home. Worry marred her brow, but she needn't be concerned. Hythe would forgive her and welcome her back into his fold. "Gray," he motioned to Madeline with his head. "Will you escort her please?"

His brother agreed with a slight nod and Wes strode to the castle's main entrance. Hythe's butler opened the door and stared at Wes with wide eyes.

"Please tell His Grace that Weston Hadley begs an audience."

The butler frowned as he looked past Wes to where Gray and Madeline stood behind him on the path. "Of course, sir. Right this way." The old man led Wes to the first parlor they came to, then turned his attention to Madeline. "Might I inform Her Grace that you've come for a visit, my lady? She has missed you terribly, if you don't mind me saying so."

"Thank you, Bailey. Is she in her private parlor?"

"Yes, my lady."

"Then I'll find Grandmamma myself." As the butler left them, Madeline cleared her throat. "Weston, don't you think we should talk before you do this?"

Hearing his name on her lips tore at Wes' heart. "Go visit with the duchess, Madeline," was all he trusted himself to say without letting emotion crack his voice.

She stood on the threshold for what felt like an eternity, just staring at him; but Wes couldn't return the look. He'd lose all his resolve if he gazed into the pretty green depths of her eyes, and for the first time in his life, he needed to put someone else first. Madeline wasn't from his world. She didn't fit in his world. She would be better off with one of her kind.

"Very well," she muttered before disappearing down the corridor.

Gray clapped a hand to Wes' back. "You're sure you're doing the right thing?"

"If you ask me that again, I'll drive my fist into your jaw."

Gray sighed. "A simple 'I'm sure' will suffice, Wes."

"Weston Hadley!" Robert Hayburn's angry voice preceded him into the parlor. "I will see you dead!" His old friend appeared on the threshold, his face red and his jaw clenched. "How dare you show your face here?"

"Rob," Wes said in greeting. "I am here to see your father, not you."

"Oh, you'll see me, right before I put a ball in your chest."

"That's enough," the duke said from behind his son, making everyone look in his direction. "Robert, why don't you go visit with your sister?"

Rob scowled at Wes. "This isn't over."

But it was. It was over between Wes and Madeline. And it was over between Wes and Rob. Wes nodded at his one-time friend. "Until next time, then." As Rob stalked from the room, Wes turned his complete attention to the Duke of Hythe. "Thank you for seeing me, sir."

"I told you not to expect Madeline's dowry, Hadley. I can't imagine what you're doing here."

That damned money Wes had never wanted. How could the duke think that was all he cared about? Wes sighed and his heart clenched as he knew what he had to do. "I haven't come to see you about money, Your Grace. I'm returning your daughter to you."

Hythe scoffed. "A little late for that, isn't it?"

Wes hoped, not for Madeline's sake. "I have given our last conversation great thought, sir, and I believe you were right on all accounts. Madeline will be better off without me."

"I suppose you should have thought of that before you married her then."

"You said the blacksmith could be bought, and I'm certain with your power and connections, you can do whatever you set your mind to, sir."

Hythe stared at Wes, a muscle twitching in his jaw. "I'm not sure if that is possible at this point, Mr. Hadley. The man must have registered the marriage by now. If we'd done something that evening, perhaps. But now…"

"You must try," Wes pressed. "Madeline deserves a chance at reclaiming her life. Whatever it costs, I'll see you reimbursed."

Hythe shook his head. "I would give my entire fortune to see my daughter free of you. I won't take one farthing from you to see it done."

Wes most certainly deserved the duke's derision. He'd absconded with the man's daughter, married her without his consent, and taken her innocence. "As you wish."

❧

Once Maddie entered her grandmother's private parlor, she could no longer keep the tears from spilling down her cheeks.

"Madeline!" the duchess exclaimed, struggling from the settee to her feet.

Maddie nearly toppled her grandmother as she threw her arms around the old matron. "I've missed you." She'd missed her grandmother's strength and fortitude just as much as her love.

"So I can tell." Then duchess pulled out of the embrace to look at Maddie, who felt very small under her grandmother's scrutiny. "What have you done, my dear?"

"I'm not sure." Maddie swiped at the tears streaming down her face. "But somehow I made a mess of everything and I'm not certain what I did."

The duchess directed Maddie back to the settee, sat, and patted the spot beside her. "Your father is very hurt, you know?"

She did know. Maddie nodded, then she sat beside her grandmother and brushed away her tears. "And my husband is hurt and I'm hurt and I don't know what to do, Grandmamma."

The duchess snorted. "What does your husband have to be hurt about, Madeline? Seems to me the young man has gotten everything he's ever wanted, or so he professed to your father."

"H-he's returning me to Papa." Sobs wracked Maddie and she couldn't say anything else. The truth nearly tore her soul in two. That admission was one of the hardest she'd ever had to make.

"Returning you?" Her grandmother puffed out her chest indignantly and handed Maddie a handkerchief. "What nonsense. Men don't return their wives. That just isn't done."

But Weston was returning her. He'd made that very clear. "I-I wanted to come home," she tried to explain. "A-and I ran off."

The duchess shook her head as though nothing Maddie said made sense. "You eloped, you mean?"

Maddie dabbed at her eyes. "Well, yes," she hastened to explain. "We did elope, but after that there was this actress and Weston… and then I wanted to come home. And I thought there was a fellow I could trust to help me, but he wasn't trustworthy. And I ended up somewhere in the middle of nowhere and I couldn't escape him. But Wes found me anyway and then… and then he said he was returning me to Papa. And he won't even look at me, Grandmamma. He hasn't looked at me for days." Maddie chanced a glance at her grandmother to find the duchess' mouth had dropped open.

"I'm not quite certain what to say, Madeline. I'm not even certain I understood half of your ramblings."

But she couldn't explain it any better. She didn't know how. And she couldn't tell her grandmother about the biting conversation. That was entirely too intimate a topic to discuss. "I'm not certain I understand it all myself, Grandmamma."

The duchess frowned. "I never would have dreamed you would elope to the border, for heaven's sakes. For you to have thrown caution to the wind, there must be something redeemable about the young man. But I'm having a very difficult time finding it."

"It's not Wes' fault, Grandmamma. It's mine. I said or did something that made him angry."

"Men get angry with their wives," her grandmother agreed. "And wives get angry with their husbands. And it's been that way since the beginning of time. But neither men nor women can simply decide to return their spouses. It just isn't done. I can't imagine the chaos if such a thing were allowed."

Tears formed in Maddie's eyes again. "If he would just look at me…"

"He sounds like an impressive fool," her grand-mother declared. "Not at all the sort I would ever have imagined you would pick."

And she wouldn't have. Maddie would never have picked Weston Hadley of her own accord. And she would have never known what she was missing. "I love him."

"Then he's not the only fool."

Maddie gasped at her grandmother's curtness.

"Close your mouth," the duchess ordered. "Let me explain something to you, Madeline. If your mother was still here, I'm sure she'd tell you the same thing. You can't allow men to make decisions for you. We'd be in a sad state of affairs if they did so."

"But…"

"Oh, I know they think they're in charge. And it's to our benefit to let them think that. There are always

ways to get what you want. There are always ways to manage even the most difficult man. Your poor mother certainly had her hands full in that regard—"

"Maddie," Robert said from the threshold.

She glanced up at her brother but couldn't even manage to feign a smile for his benefit.

"You're not needed at the moment," the duchess informed Robert. "We'll send for you if that time ever comes."

Robert scowled. "Father sent me up here to visit, Grandmother."

"And I'm sending you away. See how that works, Robert? This was all your fault to begin with. So be gone while I try to fix it."

"*My* fault?" her brother echoed in outrage.

"Of course it's your fault. If you hadn't brought that fellow into the castle, Madeline never would have met him. You should choose your associates more wisely, Robert. You'd find that you wouldn't end up in nearly the number of scrapes that you currently do." She gestured toward the corridor. "Now, Madeline and I are in the middle of a discussion that does not concern you."

Robert's face turned a bit purple. "Well, do excuse my interruption. I suppose I'll just call the villain out and be done with it then."

Maddie leapt to her feet. "Don't you dare touch one hair on his head, Robert Hayburn."

"Maddie," he complained.

But she shook her head to stop him from saying more. "He *is* my husband, even if he doesn't want me, and I won't have you speak ill of him."

"Good-bye, Robert," the duchess replied crisply.

After another scowl, her brother vanished from the
threshold without another word.

Maddie looked back at her grandmother to find the
duchess frowning at her. "I can't imagine why you
would want to be with such a man, Madeline, but if
you truly want him, I'll see if I can help."

Grandmamma was formidable and generally got her
way in any situation, but Maddie couldn't see how
she could possibly remedy this problem. "How?" she
asked anyway, hoping against hope that her grandmother could do something.

"Well, I'll just have put my head together with
Caitrin Eynsford. I'm sure between the two of us, we
can come up with something."

❦

Wes slunk through the doors of Eynsford Park, Gray
right behind him. Misery had him so captured in its
clutches that he didn't even notice Price until he
had almost bowled the old butler over. "Apologies,"
he muttered.

But his voice was loud enough that Dash apparently
heard it all the way in his study. "Weston!" his oldest
brother bellowed.

"Now you've done it," Gray mumbled under his
breath. "Could you have at least waited five minutes
before catching his attention?"

Then Wes heard stomping and stalking from the
direction of the study, and within mere seconds, the
Marquess of Eynsford stood before them, glowering
like the pack alpha he was. "What exactly have you to
say for yourself?"

"Take it easy on him, Dash," Gray said softly. "He's had a rough time of it."

Dash turned his intimidating golden glare on Gray. "You have explaining to do as well, Grayson. I didn't hire Lady Sophia so you could run out on your lessons without a moment's notice."

"Twins know when the other is in trouble," Gray replied, though is voice was softer, more subservient. "I knew Wes needed me."

"Next time," Dash growled, "tell someone before you bolt. The two of you took ten years off my life making me worry about you." Then he returned his gaze to Wes. "My study. Now." He stalked off and didn't even look back to see if Wes followed him.

Wes *did* follow, however. He'd been given an order from his pack leader, and he had no choice but to comply. Besides, he needed to tell his brother all that had transpired, and now was as good a time as any.

Dash barreled through his study door, rounded his desk, and sank into his large leather chair. He gestured to one of the high-backed seats before him. "Sit."

A woman cleared her throat from the threshold, and Wes looked over his shoulder to find his sister-in-law holding Lia in her arms. "Dashiel." Her Scottish lilt drifted across the room. "We discussed this."

Dash stared at his wife. "I don't tell you how to run things with your… friends."

Cait rolled her eyes. "Because ye wouldna ken the first thing about it. I *do* ken somethin' of this."

Lia squealed and wiggled in her mother's arms as she reached for Wes. At least someone was happy to see him.

"Caitrin," Dash growled, which made Wes wince. His brother rarely called his wife Caitrin. Cait or Caitie often, but Caitrin only if he was thoroughly angry. If she was smart, she'd turn tail and never look back.

"Doona 'Caitrin' me." Cait bent down, placing the squirming Lia on the ground at her feet. "And doona pretend that ye werena just as foolish as Weston when ye were younger. I am well aware of yer early exploits, as ye well ken. Do ye no' remember what it was like ta fall in love with me?"

Lia toddled over to Wes' seat and tried to climb up his trousers with her pudgy hands. Wes snatched her up and placed her in his lap and couldn't help but smile at his niece. "I missed you, Lia."

Dash speared Wes with a withering look. "Don't think for one moment that just because you have my daughter in your arms I'll show you any mercy."

Cait walked farther into the study, a blue fire flashing in her eyes. "Ye are the most stubborn lout in existence, Dashiel Thorpe. How many times do I have ta tell ye that Wes dinna have a choice?"

He hadn't had a choice, but how on earth did Cait know that? Wes stared at his sister-in-law. Was there something he was missing with her? Something he should have realized years ago? She always *did* seem to know everything that happened. He'd always assumed she could interpret his expressions, that something in his face gave him away. But Cait hadn't seen him since the day Dash hired Lady Sophia and he'd escaped to Castle Hythe. And Renshaw said Cait had sent the carriage to him that night. How had she known to do so?

"We don't go around abducting our neighbors' daughters and eloping with them in Gretna," Dash replied calmly, a little too calmly for Wes' peace of mind. And how did Dash already know the particulars?

"His heart is broken." Cait swiped at a tear. "Keep that in mind as ye eviscerate him. He's already been punished more thoroughly than ye can ever do." She held out a hand in Wes' direction. "Come along, Lia. Yer father has business ta attend ta."

Lia clutched Wes' jacket with her hands. He smiled again at his niece, kissed her forehead, and then placed her back on the floor. "Go with Mama, Lia. I'll see you soon, sweetheart."

After Lia toddled over to her mother, Cait settled the child in her arms. She sent one last look at her husband, then she disappeared down the corridor.

Wes glanced at his brother who was now frowning. "Just get on with it. Whatever you intend to do with me."

"I don't know what I'm going to do with you yet." Dash heaved a sigh. "But while I decide about the proper way to handle this situation, I do know that you will not leave Lady Sophia's side except to go sleep at night. I don't know if it's even possible to salvage your reputation, Weston, but attending lessons with her is at least a start."

Twenty-Six

WES STOOD ON THE THRESHOLD OF THE NURSERY, watching Lia stack some blocks and Lucien topple them to the ground with one swipe of his hand. Wes smiled to himself, remembering simpler times.

A dainty hand touched his back, but Wes didn't need to turn around to know Cait stood behind him. Her honeysuckle scent caught his nose. "Thank you for trying to help me."

Cait sighed and stepped to his side, peering up at him. "If Dash finds out ye're no' at Sophie's side, there willna be anythin' I can do ta help ye."

Wes looked back at the children once again. "I promised Lia I'd come see her."

"I am sorry ye're hurtin', Weston. If there is anythin' I can do ta help, ye ken I would do it."

Wes glanced down at his sister-in-law and studied her pretty face, so angelic and sweet. "How did you know I was in trouble that night? How did you know to send Renshaw to me? To tell him to take us to Gretna?"

She smiled softly and shrugged. "Intuition, I suppose."

In a pig's eye. No one could have possibly known what had transpired that night. No one could have known the details Dash mentioned in his study. "Can you see the future, Cait?"

Her tinkling laugh reached his ears, but it sounded forced. "What a silly question, Wes."

But she hadn't answered it, had she? Wes took her hand in his and squeezed firmly. "Tell me Madeline will be all right, Cait. Can you see that?"

She shook her head. "I wish I could tell ye want ye want ta ken, Wes. But I canna do so."

"Does that mean she won't be all right? Does that mean I've truly ruined her life?"

"It means," she squeezed back, "that I canna tell ye what I see or what I doona see. Yer future is in yer hands alone."

But he was almost certain she could see the future, as a torrent of memories flooded his mind. Every time Cait seemed to know something she couldn't possibly have discovered on her own. He wasn't sure how she could see the future, but he knew without a doubt that she could do so. "Please, Cait. Tell me what you see."

"No one should ken what the future has in store for them, Wes. It would disrupt the natural order of things. My best advice for ye is ta listen ta yer heart and follow it."

"I did that already. And look where it got me." He scrubbed a hand down his face in frustration.

Cait stepped in front of him, capturing his complete attention. Her blue eyes seemed almost intense enough that she could look into his soul. It was a little disconcerting. "Where did it get ye?" she asked softly.

Wes didn't want to have this conversation. He'd already returned Madeline to her father. Hythe would undo the mess Wes had created with his ridiculously naïve actions.

But Cait pressed on. "Where *did* it get ye, Wes?"

Wes jumped to his feet and began to pace. "Nowhere," he groaned. "Alone." He took a deep breath as he watched his niece and nephew play. He wanted that. He wanted a family of his own. Sure, he was tightly aligned with his brothers. But the way Madeline made him feel, there was nothing like it. And now she was gone.

"I feel badly for forcin' yer hand in this," Cait said softly. "I should have left it alone."

"What do you mean?" He glanced back down at her, and she looked a little more than chagrined by her admission.

"That night, would ye have thought about goin' ta Gretna if I hadna sent Renshaw ta ye?" She tilted her head as she regarded him, studying him much too closely for comfort.

"It was a very logical conclusion," he said. "She'd just learned something that only our mates know. So, making her my wife was the only way to keep our secret."

"And is that the only reason why ye wanted ta marry her? Or does it go a little deeper than that?" She put her hands together as though in prayer. Or as though she wanted to beg him. "Please search deep inside yerself. How long could ye love her from afar?"

"Forever." And that was the truth. He could have. "But I'm not good enough for her," he growled. Then he realized that he was raising his voice at one of his only allies. "I'm sorry, Cait," he said. "It's better this way." He nodded his head quickly, as though he could convince himself if he tried hard enough, instead of just her. But that was impossible. "She's too good for me."

A voice broke the sudden silence that descended upon the room. "Don't worry, Mr. Hadley," Lady Sophia said from behind him in the threshold. "Maddie's been taught that very thing since the day she could walk. So, please take note of what a leap of faith it must have been for her to get in that carriage with you…"

Not that he'd given her a choice that fateful evening.

Lady Sophia continued, "…What a leap of faith it must have been for her to marry you. To leave her father, her home, her fortune. And when you look at all that, ask yourself how she's feeling now that you've put her back on this pedestal that she's been trying to jump down from her whole life." The lady sighed heavily. "Imagine that you've been groomed for greatness. For respectability. Imagine what it's like to be locked up in that little box your whole life. And imagine what it might feel like when you find someone who'll let you out. Who'll love you for the kindness in your heart. For the future you can have together. You're more than she ever hoped she'd find."

"You have no idea what you're talking about," Wes interrupted. And she didn't. The lady knew nothing of the past sennight.

"I know what it's like for your life to change in an instant."

"It's not the same thing."

"Certainly it's not," she scoffed. "But I've known Maddie most of my life. And I can see that you're so busy wallowing in your own self-pity that you don't see the truth that's staring you in the face. Maddie gave up her fortune. She gave up her family. She gave it all up. For you. You'd be a fool to give up on her now. I thought you Hadley men were made of sterner stuff." She sniffed, raising her nose in the air. "And although you and your brothers are quite disrespectable, I have no doubt about your intellect. You're smart, the lot of you. I think you like wreaking havoc. I think you like being scandalous."

"It's not your place to make a determination about this," Wes scolded. But what if she was right?

"Would you like to make something of yourself? To be worthy of her?"

Wes snorted. He'd like nothing more.

"Then let me do what I was hired for. Let me teach you to be respectable."

"Do you have any idea how difficult a task you have, my lady? The Hadleys have more to overcome than the average family."

She waved a breezy hand in the air. "Posh," she scoffed. "You know how to dance. How to respect the social niceties. You know how to be respectable. You're just not." She narrowed her eyes at Wes. "Do you have a way to support her?"

Wes avoided her gaze. He'd spent hours of their wedding night asking himself that same question. "I have some ideas," he mumbled.

"Ideas aren't worth anything until you put them into motion," Lady Sophia said. "This is the question, Mr.

Hadley—can you pull yourself together soon enough? Before her father finds some way to dissolve your union? Can you come up with a plan so you can afford her? Can you make yourself into someone she and her father can respect? That, Mr. Hadley, is up to you."

"Well said," Cait added softly.

Lady Sophia smiled at her, then turned her attention back to Wes. "I'm here if you need my guidance, Mr. Hadley. Now I believe there is an unruly viscount awaiting me in the music room." She nodded quickly at Wes, then disappeared from the nursery as quickly as she'd arrived.

"Cait," Wes started.

But she didn't listen. She laid a hand on his forearm and squeezed. "I kent I liked her. She'll give yer brother a run for his money." She laughed lightly. "I canna wait ta watch it all."

Wes almost swallowed his tongue. Lady Sophia and one of his brothers? Certainly not Gray. *Archer?* Wes laughed out loud. Cait was right: that would be something to watch. But his mind went right back to the problem at hand. Could he make himself worthy of Madeline? And if by some miracle he was able to, would she have him? "I had a business idea occur to me in Scotland. I suppose I should go talk it over with Archer and Gray."

Cait grinned. "I have a feelin' that idea will be a great success." She waved him toward the door. "Go on," she urged. "Hurry, though, before Madeline gives up on ye."

Wes descended the steps in search of his brothers. Lady Sophia had mentioned the music room, hadn't she?

He started in that direction and heard the lady

singing, "*Oh, once I had thyme of my own. And in my own garden it grew. I used to know the place…*"

Before he could reach the music-room doors, Gray came up from behind Wes and clapped a hand to his back. "Archer's in hell in there. Let's go the other way," he whispered.

"*…where my thyme it did grow. But now it's covered with rue, with rue. But now it's covered with rue…*"

"What is she doing?" Wes kept his voice low as well.

"Expecting him to sit through a musical performance and feign interest and keep his temper." Gray rolled his eyes.

"*…The rue it is a flourishing thing. It flourishes by day and night…*"

Wes bit back a smile. "Problem is, I need to speak with Archer. And you, too."

"Should we save him then?"

"*…So beware a young man's flattering tongue. He will steal your thyme away, away…*"

Wes could certainly use his older brother's good-will. "We'd better."

He stepped into the music room to find Lady Sophia standing beside the piano, her hands clasped in front of her as she continued singing. "*…He will steal your thyme away…*"

Wes cleared his through. "I beg your forgiveness, my lady. But I seek an audience with my brother."

Archer leapt to his feet like a dog who had just been saved from taking a bath. "I really must speak with my brother, Lady Sophia. I'm sure you understand."

The lady pursed her lips. "You do realize that this sort of behavior is exactly why I'm here."

Wes smiled at Lady Sophia. "You asked if I could afford my wife. I am hoping to answer yes to your question, my lady. But I will need an audience with Radbourne in order to do so."

"You are using my affection for Maddie against me, Mr. Hadley, aren't you?"

He nodded in agreement. "I suppose I am."

"Very well, you may have his lordship for half an hour. Then I will expect all three of you to meet me back in this room."

Wes didn't even have time to thank Lady Sophia for her indulgence because Archer grabbed his arm and dragged him into the corridor. "I owe you," he hissed.

"I'm glad you think so," Wes replied. "Because I truly do need to speak with both of you." He made his way to Cait's pristine white parlor, and after his brothers joined him, Wes firmly closed the door behind them. They'd have to whisper to keep Dash from overhearing their conversation, but no one else would be able to hear them from this spot.

"I must say," Archer began drolly, "you certainly do know how to make a mess of things. Lady Madeline?" He shook his head in awe. "I didn't think you had it in you, pup."

"We only have half an hour, Archer. Will you shut up and listen?"

His brother bristled at the comment, but he gestured for Wes to continue with a wave of his arm. "By all means."

Now that he had both Gray and Archer's attention, Wes wasn't quite sure how to tell them about his idea. He knew Dash would be opposed, but he didn't know anything about any other business. "What do you think about opening a gambling establishment?"

Gray's eyes widened and he dropped onto the settee behind him.

Archer smirked. "I think that between your elopement and opening a gaming hell, Dash will be too busy with you to pay any attention to me."

Gray coughed into his fist.

Wes glared at his older brother. "Just consider my proposal, will you?"

Archer sighed. "All right. Tell me, why do you want to operate a gaming hell?"

"I don't know how to do anything else," Wes admitted. "In my mind I know Madeline is better off without me, and I know Hythe will do everything in his power to dissolve our marriage. But he might not be successful. And in my heart…" Wes shrugged and felt like a green lad, so open, vulnerable, exposed. "I'll always love her. But I can't provide for her. My income is quite pitiful, as you well know. So what options are open to me? Can you see me as a country vicar?"

Gray chortled.

Wes scowled at him. "Neither can I."

"There are a million options between being a vicar and running a gaming hell."

"Something in trade." Wes agreed with a nod of his head. "But I know nothing of shipping or of being a merchant. I do know gambling and I know gamblers. And you know as well as I, luck comes and goes, but the fellow who owns the tables always makes money."

Archer's brow creased as though he was seriously considering the possibility for the first time. "And you think this is the way to go about winning her? I can't see Hythe happy with his daughter married to the proprietor of a gaming hell."

"I wish you wouldn't call it that. I don't want the place to be smarmy. More…"

"Upscale?" Gray provided.

"Exactly." Wes smiled at his twin. "Upscale. Something the three of us can do together. Increase each of our fortunes."

"And if Hythe is successful at dissolving your union?" Archer asked.

"Then I'll have something to focus on and throw myself into."

"I'm tired of being one of the penniless Hadleys," Gray said from his spot on the settee. "I would never have thought of this, Wes. But I do like the sound of it."

Archer smirked. "And I can just imagine Lady Sophia's reaction. How on earth will she make gentlemen out of gambling proprietors? She'll be so disgusted by the idea that she'll wash her hands of us, and I'll never have to sit through another faux musicale."

"Cait said it would be successful," Wes tossed in.

"You told Cait?" Gray's voice rose an octave. "Are you mad?"

Well, he hadn't really told her, and he wasn't certain how to explain his bizarre conversation with their sister-in-law. "She went toe to toe with Dash for me."

"She always does." Archer rubbed his chin. "I still wouldn't have told her."

"Cait can be trusted."

"You'd better hope so," Archer replied. "Because

I don't intend to say one word to Dash about any of this, not until things are set in motion in any event."

That meant he was in. Wes smiled at his brother. With Archer's new fortune, he didn't have to participate in this venture, but it warmed Wes' heart that his brother was willing to do so anyway.

"In fact," Archer continued, "I have the perfect plot of land in mind."

"You do?" Gray asked.

Archer nodded. "I own a nice spot in Sunbury along the Thames. We could ferry fellows in from London. Charge for rooms. Provide entertainment."

A plot of land Wes was certain Archer had obtained from the late Lord Postwick. "I'm guessing Lady Sophia won't be happy about the location, among other things."

A flash of something crossed Archer's face but it was gone just as fast. "I can't imagine that she would."

"What would she care about that?" Gray asked, completely bewildered.

Archer growled low in his throat. "We haven't been gone half an hour yet. What could she possibly want now?"

And then Wes noticed the soft essence of violets. How interesting that Archer was so attuned to Lady Sophia's scent. A soft knock at the door heralded her formal arrival.

"Go away," Archer groused.

But Wes strode to the door and opened it, revealing their tutor in the flesh. "My lady," he said.

Lady Sophia swept into the room, holding a ledger in her hands. "We have work to do."

"You gave us half an hour reprieve from your presence, or have you forgotten?" Archer grumbled.

"No." She shook her head. "I said you needed to be back in the music room in half an hour. It's not the same thing." She tapped her ledger with her fingers.

"What the devil is that?" Gray asked, his eyebrows drawing together.

Wes was almost afraid to ask himself.

"A listing I put together of all the exhibits at the British Museum." She perched on the edge of the settee. "I'd like for you all to be familiar with each and every piece."

"Why on earth would we want to do that?" Archer asked, cursing beneath his breath.

"Because it will show Lord Eynsford and others how cultured you've become, my lord."

Archer snorted. "Cultured? You are destined for failure, Lady Sophia. We are Hadleys. Culture is not a word in our vocabularies."

"Then you'd better learn it," she said primly. "I'm to make gentlemen out of you, and *gentlemen* know a thing or two about art and culture."

"They know more about gambling," Gray muttered under his breath, only loud enough for his brothers to hear.

Archer laughed.

"Something amusing, Lord Radbourne?" Lady Sophia lifted one imperious brow in his direction.

"I find a great number of things amusing, my lady."

She smiled at him, though there was an icy chill behind her eyes. "I am so relieved to hear it. When conversing with a lady, you should always strive to engage her with witty conversation."

"I've never had a problem engaging a woman, sweetheart. And I've never heard any complaints." Archer let his gaze roam down Lady Sophia's body, and for the first time ever, that made Wes more than uncomfortable. He felt a sudden urge to protect the lady.

"She's trying to help us," Wes said placatingly.

Archer smirked. "But we're just fine the way we are."

No. No, they weren't. Their unruly and unconventional upbringing had left Wes less than worthy of the woman he loved. By quite a long shot. "I want her help," he said softly.

Lady Sophia smiled at him, and he could see the sweetness in her gaze. "You'll make a fine husband for her."

Wes wished he could be as certain as Lady Sophia was. If he learned everything there was about every object inside the British Museum, if he read *The Times* every morning to be knowledgeable of current events, if he was a master waltzer or fencer, would that really make the difference to Madeline? To Hythe? To himself? He would always be Weston Hadley.

Archer *tsked* at him. "Which will it be, Wes? Business ventures or artifacts in museums?"

"Business ventures?" Lady Sophia asked.

"I'm afraid our new business venture will take us far from Kent for a while, my lady," Archer said with a superior gleam in his eye. "So perhaps you can instruct Lord Eynsford on the intimate goings-on at the British Museum in our absence."

"This is the first I've heard of a business venture." Lady Sophia frowned. "I'm certain I don't have to tell you that gentlemen don't dabble in business, my lord."

"What do you think I've been trying to explain to you, my lady?" Archer winked at her. "We're *not* gentlemen. We're Hadleys."

But that didn't mean they couldn't be better. Wes offered a conciliatory smile to the lady. "When we return from our trip, I'll look forward to your instruction." He'd look forward to doing anything that might make Madeline see him in a better light. But the Hadley brothers' gambling business wouldn't grow itself, and *if* Madeline was stuck with him, he needed to ensure that he could take care of her. That had to be more important than learning all the details about the Elgin Marbles, didn't it?

Twenty-Seven

IF MADDIE WASN'T WEARING GLOVES, SHE'D BE biting her fingernails, which wasn't like her at all. But she was such a bundle of nerves that she could barely sit still.

"Appear serene," her grandmother ordered as their coach stopped on the circular drive before Eynsford Park. "You want him crawling back to you, Madeline. You don't want him to have the upper hand."

Maddie would be happy to have any hand at all. As it was, she had nothing. But if only she could catch Wes' eye, she might see something in his depths that would confirm her deepest desire. He'd professed to her father that he was in love with her. She'd heard him with her very ears. He'd told her himself that he'd wanted her for years. Could all of that have disappeared because she hadn't wanted him to scar her? To appease the duchess, Maddie nodded her head as serenely as she was able. "Of course, Grandmamma."

"And keep your distance from Sophia. That gel is a bad influence on you."

Somehow Maddie managed to keep from snorting.

Her life had been turned inside out and upside down. How could Sophie's influence possibly make things any worse?

The driver opened the coach door, helped the duchess alight from the conveyance, and then offered his hand to Maddie. She linked her arm with her grandmother's, and together they strode down the white stone path to the grand front door that opened before either of them could knock.

Eynsford's stoic butler bowed. "Your Grace, Lady Madeline."

"Lady Eynsford should be expecting us," the duchess replied regally.

"Of course, madam. Her ladyship is awaiting you in the white parlor. This way." He led them just a short distance, then cleared his throat before a doorway. "The Duchess of Hythe and Lady Madeline have arrived, my lady."

"Wonderful," the marchioness gushed from inside the room. "Thank you, Price."

The butler gestured Maddie and the duchess over the threshold, and at once, Maddie's eyes flew around the room in hopes of finding her husband there. But he was not. Sophie, however, was. Her old friend smiled and gestured to the spot beside her on a white damask settee. Ignoring her grandmother's directive, Maddie quickly crossed the floor and took the seat beside Sophie.

The duchess harrumphed but took a spot in a high-backed chair a few feet away.

Immediately, Sophie grasped Maddie's hand and squeezed. "Are you all right? I've been so worried."

Only some miracle kept tears from forming in Maddie's eyes, but she refused to let them fall. When she *did* see Wes, she would not have tear-stained cheeks. "I am fine, all things considered."

"I am so glad ye've come ta call," Lady Eynsford said warmly. "I've already ordered some tea and biscuits, but in the meanwhile, I'd like ta ken how ye're gettin' along."

Maddie cleared her throat. "Castle Hythe is calm." It was almost like a graveyard, but Maddie wouldn't dare say such a thing. "If it isn't too much to ask, Lady Eynsford, I should like very much to see my husband."

Sophie hand tightened on Maddie's, and the smile vanished from Lady Eynsford's face. "I am sorry," the marchioness replied. "Weston is no' in residence at the moment."

Maddie hadn't known her heart could plummet even further, but it did. "Where is he?" she breathed, terrified of the answer. Had she made him so angry that he'd fled Kent to avoid her?

"Working on some secretive business venture." Sophie frowned.

"Business venture?" the duchess barked.

Lady Eynsford shrugged. "Alas, I really canna say any more than Sophia has. Weston has no' confided his plans ta me."

Maddie closed her eyes, hoping for strength. She'd spent the entire previous evening planning what to say to her husband. She'd imagined his every response and her every counter. She hadn't planned on him not being in residence. "Wh-when will he be back?" she asked, her voice small to her own ears.

"I'm certain he'll be back as soon as the time is right, Lady Madeline."

The duchess cleared her throat. Loudly. "Do you suppose, Caitrin, he could be compelled to return to attend my birthday ball a fortnight from now?"

Maddie opened her eyes and stared at her grandmother. Birthday ball? What was she talking about?

"I'm certain Eynsford could be compelled ta ask him ta return, Eugenia."

"Splendid." The duchess' cane tapped the floor in mild agitation. "As I'm finally inviting him into my home, I'll expect him to be on time."

Lady Eynsford's blue eyes twinkled. "I doona foresee any problems with punctuality."

The duchess harrumphed again.

At that moment, the butler returned with a tea tray and Lady Eynsford directed him to place it on a table near the window. Then she turned her gaze on Maddie. "Will ye help me pour?"

Maddie rose from her spot and crossed the parlor to the table where the tea service awaited. As the duchess began to question Sophie on her living arrangement at The Park, Maddie poured the first cup. But then Lady Eynsford stilled Maddie's hand with her own. "Doona fret, my dear."

Maddie blinked back tears that were threatening to spill down her cheeks. "I'm sure I'll be fine."

"I ken ye are aware of what Weston is," the marchioness whispered. Then she tugged at the collar of her gown to reveal a crescent-shaped scar, the size of a man's mouth, where her neck met her shoulder. If Maddie hadn't been staring at the blemish, she wouldn't have even noticed it. "There is nothin' ta fear. Ye may trust me on that."

Maddie nearly dropped the silver teapot to the floor. With shaky hands, she somehow managed to return it to the tray without spilling a drop. "Lord Eynsford?" she asked quietly.

Lady Eynsford nodded. "Aye. And it is wonderful, Madeline."

And from the dreamy expression on the marchioness' face, Maddie believed her instantly. "I didn't mean to hurt him," she confessed.

"Ye've both hurt each other, though I ken neither of ye meant ta do so. Neither of ye were placed in the best situation, but that's all in the past. It's the future we need ta look toward."

Maddie nodded. The future. But could she have a future with Wes? He'd fled Kent, for heaven's sake.

"I want ye ta ken, Madeline, ye can come ta me with anythin'. I ken a thing or two about these creatures and how ta best manage them."

Maddie swallowed nervously. "What if he won't forgive me? What if he won't have me?"

"Ye are in charge of yer own destiny. I'm certain ye can think of somethin' ye can do ta make him see reason."

But she'd tried all the way from Scotland. Maddie stared out the window before her, as though the answer would appear in the sky. What could she do to make Wes see reason? What could she do to make him see that she loved him? That she accepted him the way he was?

❧

Wes stared blankly at the invitation in his hand. The Duchess of Hythe was requesting *his* presence at her birthday ball? That could only mean one thing. The duke had been successful in his quest to annul the marriage. Dread washed over Wes and a pit formed in his stomach. He doubted he'd ever feel right for the rest of his days. He tried to shake off the feeling. This was what he'd asked for, after all. An opportunity for Madeline to get a fresh start, to pretend that their union had not occurred.

"What are you doing?" Archer's voice interrupted Wes' thoughts.

"Nothing."

His older brother scoffed as his fork scooped up a helping of baked eggs. "Nothing? You're crumpling that invitation so much it won't be recognizable. Who is it from, anyway?"

Wes dropped into a seat at the breakfast table across from his brothers and tried to remember how to speak.

"Wes?" Gray prodded. "I know it's rare for us to receive invitations." He grinned. "But we have received some a time or two."

Wes heaved a sigh, then looked across the table at his brothers. "It's from the Duchess of Hythe."

Archer's brow lifted and Gray sat a little straighter. "Well, we've never received one of those before," his twin replied. "What does it say?"

"That I'm to attend her birthday ball at the castle next week."

"If I was you, I wouldn't step over that threshold. Robert's likely to have a dueling pistol aimed at your heart." Archer placed his fork back on the table.

"He has to go," Gray said. "I imagine Hythe wants to tell you in person…"

"That he's had my marriage annulled," Wes added. "Yes, I know." He tossed the invitation to the table and raked a hand through his hair. "What bad timing, since we're so busy with architects and hiring laborers."

Gray snorted. "Don't be a coward now. You're the one who asked for this."

He *had* asked for it. But that didn't mean the idea didn't turn his stomach. "She'll be better off now."

"And what about you?" Gray asked quietly. "Will you be better off now?"

His brother knew the answer without asking, Wes well knew. Being twins, Gray could sense Wes' heartache and suffering more than anyone in the world. "I want what's best for her."

"You didn't answer my question."

"I don't really need to, do I?"

Archer chuckled to himself. "I suppose you could always talk her into eloping again. I doubt even Hythe could have two marriages annulled."

Wes glared at his older brother. "You are a jackass."

Archer agreed with a nod. "Family trait."

Gray leaned forward and rested his elbows on the breakfast table. "He has a point, Wes. Not the eloping part, but she does care for you. All might not be lost."

Wes' chair legs scraped against the floor as he quickly stood. "We've been over this, Grayson. Madeline doesn't belong in our world. She's…"

"Too perfect?" Gray supplied with the roll of his eyes.

"Unblemished," Wes corrected. "Everything about

who we are would destroy her. I won't be a party to that." Doing so would hurt just as badly as he was hurting now.

Archer sighed. Loudly. Then he dropped his napkin to the table. "If we are through with this maudlin conversation, we have work to do today, gentlemen."

"Arch!" Gray complained.

But their older brother rose from his seat. "Leave it alone, Grayson. He's made his decision. He has to live with it."

Twenty-Eight

WES WATCHED MADELINE FROM ACROSS THE ROOM. One gentleman after another drew her into his arms for a dance, touching her waist where *his* hand should have been. Looking into her eyes, where he only wanted his own gaze to land. Smelling her rosewater scent, which should have been his alone to devour. He swore beneath his breath.

"Go ask her to dance," Grayson grumbled beside him.

"I'm going home," Wes informed him.

"You can't. You haven't spoken to Hythe yet."

"Hythe can go hang." Wes raised a nasty-tasting orgeat to his lips and took a deep swallow. Being forced to watch Madeline was sheer torture. And he'd been doing it for what seemed like hours. "Wish I had some bloody whisky."

Archer stepped up beside them. "Did someone say 'whisky'?" he asked beneath his breath.

Gray gestured to Wes with his head.

"How can you drink that?" Archer asked. "The punch is foul."

The orgeat was the least of Wes' problems. At that

moment, Lord Chilcombe led Madeline from the dance floor toward the refreshment table. "I can't stay here anymore. Hythe can find me in the morning. I'm going home."

"Don't even think about it," Archer growled. "Dash says I can't leave until Lady Sophia says it's time. So if I have to stay here, you have to accept the torture as well." He grimaced as the orchestra began a new set. "I believe I'm partnered with the lady of my brother's affection, myself, on the very next set."

Wes' eyes shot back to his brother's. "You're dancing with Lady Madeline?" he croaked.

Archer sighed. "The esteemed Lady Sophia arranged the dance cards herself, from what I hear. Apparently she asked all of her acquaintances from before her fall from grace to put the Hadleys on their dance cards. I'm not certain what hold she has over them, but they agreed."

"He's right. I'm partnered with Miss Pritchard." Gray shivered lightly.

"Watch your toes. Her feet are a little unwieldy," Archer warned.

"If you had feet that big, they'd be a little unwieldy, too," Gray laughed.

"I haven't been assigned any dances." Wes looked across the room to where Lady Sophia was watching them beside Cait.

"She must like you best then," Archer complained.

Wes was certain that had nothing to do with it. Archer had been assigned partners and so had Gray. But neither of them would frighten Lady Sophia's delicate friends. Automatically, he touched a hand to his scar. Madeline, too, had been afraid of him once. "What's the next dance?" he asked.

"A quadrille, Lady Sophia says. Why?" Archer gazed at him with a curious glance.

Gray smirked. "He doesn't want you waltzing with Lady Madeline."

Damn his twin to hell. He always knew what Wes was feeling, which was bloody inconvenient sometimes. "Go to hell, Gray," Wes snarled.

"Already there, brother," his twin replied, his voice droll and unconcerned as he gestured to the ballroom at large.

Dash appeared at Archer's side. "Are the three of you behaving yourselves?"

"Yes, Dash," they said in unison.

"Good. Continue on then," he said, shooting them each a heated glance before he crossed the room to claim Cait for a dance of his own.

"How long do you think he'll torture us with this training?" Gray asked with a heavy sigh.

"Until you're respectable," Archer said as he punched Gray's shoulder hard enough to make him stumble. "So, get respectable quickly, gentlemen. I can only take so much." Then he placed his glass on a tray as a servant walked by and tugged at his jacket. "My turn with Lady Madeline," he said with a smirk.

"If you touch her…" Wes began, stepping in front of him.

"You gave her away, Wes," Archer said playfully. "She's fair pickings." His brother let his gaze roam up and down Madeline's body from across the room. "Quite fair, if I do say so myself." He looked into

Wes' eyes. Wes was startled by the intensity he found there. "I think she'd like wearing my mark. More than she liked the idea of wearing yours."

"Arch," Gray warned softly.

"Don't make me kill you," Wes growled as he laid a hand on Archer's chest to keep him from advancing toward Madeline, who was now looking around, as though waiting for her next dance partner. Then she looked down at the card dangling from her wrist and scowled.

"What's the matter? Too close to the full moon for you, Weston? Perhaps you should retreat with your tail between your legs." He pushed Wes, who stumbled on the dance floor from the force of the shove.

Wes righted himself and started toward Archer, fully ready to rip his brother's head from his shoulders. But Gray's arms wrapped around him and he hissed in his brother's ear. "Don't do it. You're causing a stir."

Wes glanced around, and indeed, many gazes had swung in their direction. But, he didn't particularly care. The thought of Archer touching Madeline had the hair on the back of his neck standing up. He could barely see his older brother standing before him through the rage-red haze that clouded his vision.

"What's the matter, Wes?" Archer taunted. "You gave her away. You were content to let every other man here dance with her tonight. Am I not good enough for her, either?" He straightened his jacket again and looked over at Madeline, who was even now on her way across the ballroom toward the lot of them.

Good God, Wes had done it again. He'd disgraced himself and hadn't even planned to.

"Do you still want her, Weston? Or do you want to let someone else have her? Because if you don't want her, I'll give her a go myself. Maybe I can take her back to the duke afterward and he'll accept her back into the family fold." Once again, Archer's lascivious gaze dragged up and down Madeline's body. "It would probably be worth it." Then he looked into Wes' eyes. "Was it worth it, Wes? Having her and then giving her away?"

"You're going too far, Archer." Wes heard Gray on the periphery, once again warning their brother.

But the eldest Hadley paid him no heed. "Oh, but I plan to go farther still," Archer said with a smirk. Then he started toward Madeline.

"Archer!" Wes yelled to his retreating back. The orchestra stopped and all the movement in the room came to a quick halt. Hundreds of pairs of eyes were suddenly focused in their direction.

Archer looked over his shoulder at Wes, still smirking. Wes would take great pride in wiping that look off his brother's face with his fist.

Archer turned around to face him, his voice rising. "What's the matter, Weston? If it's not me, it'll be someone else."

It wouldn't. It wouldn't be anyone else. Not while Wes lived, breathed, and loved that lady. No one else would have her. No matter what he'd said to Hythe. He couldn't bear it if she chose another.

The crowed twittered, nervous women whispering behind their fans and men making crass remarks under their breath. Wes heard it all. He scrubbed a hand down his face in frustration, wishing it was possible to tamp down the beast inside him.

"Gentlemen," a quiet voice came from beside Wes' shoulder. He looked down to find Lady Sophia scowling at them all. "What's going on?" she hissed.

"It appears as though you have failed, my lady," Archer taunted. "Once again, the Hadley brothers breach the bounds of propriety." He bowed sarcastically in her direction. "You have outdone yourself in our training, sweetheart."

Dash stormed across the room, looking like a great avenging beast bent on destruction. He outpaced Lady Madeline, who was still walking slowly in their direction. Only the fools headed toward them. The rest pulled back so that they had a wide circle of open space around them. Madeline stood on the outside of the circle and watched them with a curious stare.

Dash stormed into the circle, looking like he was ready to shake the whole lot of them by the scruffs of their necks. "Out," he snarled, nodding toward the door.

"Can't," Archer said with a quick shake of his head. "I have a lovely lady waiting for my attention." He turned toward Madeline and bowed lower than Wes had ever seen. His nose would hit the floor if he dropped any lower.

"This is not amusing," Dash snarled.

"No, it's not amusing at all," a quiet voice said from the edge of the crowd. Madeline. Madeline had spoken. He hadn't heard her voice in almost three weeks. And there she was, her dulcet tones stroking across his skin. He squeezed his eyes shut tightly.

"I'm sorry, Lady Madeline," Wes said. "We were just leaving."

"The devil we were," Archer chuckled. "I plan to dance with the lady." He tilted his head at Madeline. "If she'll have me."

She smiled softly at Archer. "Why not? Your brother doesn't want me."

Wes choked. That couldn't be further from the truth. He wanted her more than he wanted air. More than he wanted sunshine. More than he wanted anything. More than his own life.

Dash wrapped a strong arm around Wes' shoulders. "Let's go," he said quietly.

With more strength than Wes knew he possessed, he disentangled himself from Dash's grasp. He bowed at Lady Madeline. "I'm sorry to have disgraced myself once again." Then he turned to leave. He would walk out under his own power, if it was the last thing he ever did.

But as he slipped into the throng of people, he heard her call out. "Weston Hadley," she said crisply. He stopped and squeezed his eyes shut again because he couldn't look at her. "Wes, please don't walk away from me," she said, her voice cracking on the last word. His eyes flew open and he spun to face her. Tears brimmed over her beautiful lashes, threatening to fall.

"Lady Madeline," Wes began.

"Is that who I am to you now? That's not what you called me when you held me in your arms," she said, her voice ringing out in the quiet of the room like the bells at St. George's. "That's not what you called me when you were inside my..." Her voice trailed off as she laid a hand over her chest, smiled, and said, "heart."

The ladies in the room began whispering behind their fans. Wes didn't know what to do. She'd ruin herself. She'd ruin her future. She'd ruin her life. Wes looked at the Duke of Hythe who suddenly stood beside his daughter, his hand on her elbow. Thank God. His Grace would keep her from doing irreparable damage to herself.

"What are you doing, Madeline?" the duke asked, his voice low to keep other guests from hearing.

But she didn't answer him. She just gazed at Wes. And the pause between her words became pregnant with expectation. He waited. Then he said to her father, "Perhaps you should take her to bed. She might be feverish."

"The only person I want taking me to bed is you, Weston Hadley," Madeline's voice echoed through the room.

Nervous laughter from those assembled followed. The duke leaned down and asked, "Are you certain this is what you want?"

But she ignored him again. "Take me to bed, Wes," Maddie asked softly, but loudly enough that everyone could still hear her. More laughter ensued. But it wasn't humorous to Wes. Not at all.

"Well, when a lady asks for someone to take her to bed, and the object of her affection refuses to step up..." Archer said as he started toward Madeline.

Damn his jackass brother! Wes would kill him for sticking his snout in where it didn't belong.

Wes turned and started toward Madeline. Then he stopped. His head warred with his heart.

But Madeline started to talk. She said her words

loudly and crisply so they could be heard by one and all. "You see, everyone. What you don't know is that Weston Hadley is my husband." She took a dramatic breath. "But then he decided he didn't want me after all, and he returned me to my father." She reached for her father's hand and squeezed it tightly. "And my father has done his best to end the marriage. And I have tried to end the way I feel about Mr. Hadley, but it seems to be an impossible task."

"What are you saying, Madeline?" Wes asked from where he stood several feet from her. The two of them were the only ones in the center of the ballroom, as everyone else moved back.

"I'm saying I want to be your wife, Weston Hadley." She raised her nose in the air. "And I want you to bite me, too." She took another fortifying breath. "And I want you to hold me in your arms. I want you to tell me you love me again. I want you to keep me." She smiled broadly. "I want you to do that thing you did, when you made me feel..." Her voice trailed off. "You were there. You remember."

He remembered. He'd never forget the smell or taste of her.

"I want you beside me day and night. I want you to hold me while I sleep. I want to have your children."

Was that what this was about? Was she forced to make this declaration because she was with child? Wes hadn't even considered the ramifications. "Are you?" he breathed out.

"Not yet." She shook her head. "But I want to be," she softly.

"You don't know what you're saying..." Wes began.

She held up one finger. "On the contrary, I know exactly what I'm saying."

"But you can't," he hedged. She couldn't. Could she? Dare she? Would she?

"I do," she said succinctly. Then she dropped to her knees in the middle of the ballroom. She held her hands up as though pleading. "Do you want me to beg you?"

"Get up, Madeline!" her father hissed. But she didn't. She stayed there on her knees, probably getting her gown all dirty in her quest to... do what?

"You said if I wanted you to kiss me, all I had to do was ask."

<hr />

If he didn't accept her soon, Maddie would be forced to rip her clothes off and stand there in the middle of the ballroom naked. She hadn't realized until she'd gotten her monthly courses how disappointed she was not to be with child. It had come as a complete shock, the utter loss she felt when she'd realized she lost her only tie to Wes. He'd cut all the rest of the strings. What else was she to do?

She inhaled deeply, wondering if he would abandon her again. If he truly didn't want her after all. "Wes?" she asked softly. "Will you kiss me?"

Wes sank down on his knees before her and took her face in his strong hands. He caressed her jaw with his thumb as he gazed at her, his eyes brimming with... tears? Certainly not. He coughed gently to clear his throat. "You've always been too good for me, Madeline," he said.

Her heart fell. "Only because you've put me on

a pedestal that I don't deserve, Wes." She held her hands out to the side, indicating her current state of subjugation. "I'm already on my knees begging. I can't go much lower."

"Stand up, Maddie." He stood up and pulled her to her feet.

Had called her Maddie? A smile tugged at her lips. Dare she hope?

"I love him," she said more to the crowd than she said to him, as she needed for everyone to know. She rose up on her tiptoes, captured his face in her hands, and pressed her lips to his.

He gaped at her for a moment. But then she pursed her lips in a kiss and waited for him to come to her. How could he refuse? He clutched her tightly to himself. He pressed her body against his, his hands pulling her closer than she could have ever imagined being. And he did it in front of everyone. Maddie's heart soared. He finally pulled back and rested his forehead against hers.

"We should go somewhere and talk," she whispered.

He scooped her up in his arms without even a word and spun around so quickly that she squealed with the joy of it. The crowd parted like the Red Sea, making a path for them. Maddie reached out and touched Sophie's fingertips as they passed her, and her friend smiled. At least she had one friend who was happy for her. And, if she wasn't mistaken, her father looked happy. Relieved, even. The rest could all go hang. Wes carried her out into the garden and didn't stop until he'd kicked the door shut behind him. He set her on the garden wall and pushed her hair back from her face. "What have you done?" he asked softly.

"I've fallen in love," she said with a quick shrug. There was no other explanation. "With you," she said for clarification.

"It had damn well better be with me," he chuckled. "Why did you do that in there?"

"Because I didn't know how else to get your attention."

"You have all my attention." He sipped at her lips with tiny touches to her mouth. "I'll ruin your life, Maddie."

"Kiss me? Hold me? Love me? Be mine forever?" she said with a laugh. She leaned forward and pressed her lips to his. It was too late to take any of it back.

"You made them all think I didn't want you. But that couldn't be further from the truth."

"You could have fooled me," she said as she dragged her skirts up and wrapped her legs around him. He pressed against her warmth, as though he was meant to be there. He was. God, he was. She pointed to the place where her neck met her shoulder. "I want you to mark me."

"I can't," he said, but he did press his lips to the spot and suckled her skin lightly. It made her belly drop to her toes.

"I want to be yours in every way. I'll be proud to be a Hadley. To be your Lycan mate. To be the mother of your mutts."

He cocked his head at her and grinned. "Mutts?"

"Lycans," she clarified as she rolled her eyes. "Mutts. Whatever they are, they'll be mine and yours, and they'll be perfect."

"Yes, they will," he agreed. He looked into her eyes. "Do you really love me?"

She smacked at his shoulder. "Would I have done

all this if I didn't? I just dropped to my knees in a crowded ballroom and begged you to make love to me, for heaven's sake."

"You needn't do me bodily harm, Maddie," he growled. His lips danced across her collarbone. Maddie tugged her skirts higher and reached for the fastenings of his trousers. "What are you doing?" he growled, already growing hot and hard for her.

She leaned her forehead against his as she exposed him to the night air and took his manhood in her hand.

He glanced around the empty garden. "You're going to kill me," he growled.

"Tell me I'm the only one," she urged. "Tell me I'm the one you love. Tell me I always will be. Please."

"The only one. Ever," he declared. Then he wrapped her legs around his waist, cupped her bottom in his hands, and lifted her, then sat down on a nearby bench, draping her so that she straddled his lap.

He lifted her skirts until his hands found her bottom and pulled her forward to ride the ridge of his manhood. She slid across his taut skin like satin, wet and ready for him.

"Can we do it like this?" she whispered against his mouth.

He nodded, his lips brushing hers as he did so. "Ride me," he said softly. Then he rocked her bottom forward and slid his length into her. He groaned loudly as he did so. "It's like coming home," he whispered, his voice broken by emotion. "God, I love you," he said.

But he'd taken any rational thought from her head

when he slid inside her. Her cry was her only response. She couldn't put two words together in her mind for all the pleasure that occupied it.

His hand slid into her curls as she rocked against him, taking her higher and higher and higher until her cries filled the night air. "Shhh…" he whispered against her lips. But she couldn't. Not with the way he made her feel. She rose and fell on him, controlling the movements of their bodies with her quickening movements. But then she toppled over that precipice, fluttering in ecstasy around him as he groaned and spilled himself inside her. He held on to her hips, holding her above him, buried deep inside her as he finished. She dropped her head onto his chest and drew in great heaving breaths.

"Do you think anyone heard me?" she asked quietly.

He pushed her hair back and looked into her eyes. "I'm afraid everyone probably heard you, Maddie. You've been completely ruined."

"Oh, thank God," she sighed. It was difficult being perfect. Everyone needed a little ruination if it meant finding love, didn't they?

"Why is this a good thing?"

"You can't possibly give me back to my father now," she informed him. She needed to be clear that he was stuck with her. By her own choice. He was hers and she was his forever and always. "I'm yours. I'll ask you to kiss me every day."

"You won't have to ask, Maddie." Then he leaned forward and did just that.

Epilogue

"I DO NOT LIKE SURPRISES, WESTON," MADDIE complained, tugging at the dark cloth covering her eyes.

"Behave," he growled and swatted at her hands. "We're almost there."

"Almost where?" she asked, though she knew he'd never tell her. He'd been more than secretive ever since they boarded the ferry in London.

"You are worse than a child," he replied, then he kissed her cheek to soften his words.

"Can't I get at least a hint?"

"Hmm." He draped his arm around her shoulders and leaned his head against hers. "I made a promise to your father some time ago—"

"Weston Hadley, if you think you can be rid of me again—"

He laughed. "Spoiled and impatient, Maddie. May I please finish my sentence?"

She huffed indignantly and folded her arms across her chest, pursing her lips in the process.

"He didn't like the state in which he found you in Gretna and told me if he ever saw you in a disheveled state again, he'd have my head on a platter, or something like that."

"I did look awful."

"You're beautiful. Even in muddy clothes and wild hair, you're the most beautiful creature in the world."

She couldn't help but smile at that. "You're just partial since I'm your wife."

"Anyway." He cleared his throat. "I took him at his word. My income was never very much—"

"I don't care about that." Besides Papa *had* relented and given Wes her dowry when he saw how much she truly did love her husband.

"Well, I did. I do," he clarified. "I want to support you and care for you and…" Wes untied her blindfold. He gestured to a large structure near the edge of the water that was in the process of being built, if she wasn't mistaken.

"What is that?"

"That is my legacy. Mine, Gray's, and Archer's. It's a gambling establishment, or it will be once the construction is complete."

Maddie couldn't help the giggle that escaped her. "You are so fortunate that Papa has already given you my dowry. He will faint dead away when he finds out."

Wes grinned at her. "I don't care about your father. I only care about you. Can you stand being married to man who runs a gaming hall?"

Maddie gently touched the mark on the side of her neck. "I'm not sure," she teased. "It is so very Hadley of you." Then she looked down at her belly and touched it with her hand. "What do you think? Shall you be embarrassed to have a father who owns a gaming hell?"

Wes' smile vanished and his mouth fell open a bit.

"Hmm." Maddie bit back a smile. "Wolf got your tongue, Wes?"

"Are you saying I'm going to be a father?"

She nodded and softly touched the scar on his cheek. "I love you, Weston Hadley. I will love you if you run a gaming hell. I will love you all the days of my life."

Wes lifted her to his lap, wrapped his arms around her, and pressed a kiss to her lips.

About the Author

Lydia Dare is a pseudonym for the writing team of Tammy Falkner and Jodie Pearson. Both are active members of the Heart of Carolina Romance Writers and Romance Writers of America. Their writing process involves passing a manuscript back and forth, each one writing 1,500 words after editing the other's previous installment. Jodie specializes in writing the history and Tammy in writing the paranormal. They live near Raleigh, North Carolina.

If you enjoyed *The Wolf Who Loved Me*,
you'll love the rest of Lydia Dare's
sexy Regency paranormal romances:

A Certain Wolfish Charm

Tall, Dark and Wolfish

The Wolf Next Door

The Taming of the Wolf

It Happened One Bite

In the Heat of the Bite

Never Been Bit

And watch for the next book
in the Hadley brothers trilogy,
coming *November 2012*
from Sourcebooks Casablanca.

Never Been Bit

by Lydia Dare

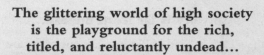

**The glittering world of high society
is the playground for the rich,
titled, and reluctantly undead...**

Alec MacQuarrie's after-life has become an endless search
for pleasure in an effort to overcome his heartbreak and
despair. Wandering through the seedy world of London's
demimonde, he's changed into a dark and fearsome
creature even he doesn't recognize until he stumbles into
a magical lass he knew once upon a time and sees a glimpse
of the life he could have had.

**But the ton is no match for one
incorrigible young lady...**

After watching each of her coven sisters happily marry,
Sorcha Ferguson is determined to capture a Lycan husband
of her very own. When she encounters Alec, she decides
to save her old friend from what he's become, all while
searching for her own happily-ever-after.

Over his dead body is Alec going to allow this enchanting
innocent to throw herself away on an unworthy werewolf,
but that leaves him responsible for her, and he's the worst
monster of them all...

For more Lydia Dare, visit:

www.sourcebooks.com

In the

b

Chivalry

Matthew Halkett, E   en
in the *ton* who can   —
because that's precisely what he was before being turned
into a vampyre. When he spies a damsel in distress in the
midst of a storm in Hyde Park, his natural instinct is to
rush to her aid…

But not every woman needs to be rescued…

Weather-controlling witch Rhiannon Sinclair isn't caught in
a storm—she's the cause of it. She's mortified to have been
caught making trouble by the imposing earl, but she doesn't
need any man—never has, and is sure she never will…

But when Rhiannon encounters Matthew again, her powers
go awry and his supernatural abilities run amok. Between
the two of them, the *ton* is thrown into an uproar. There's
never been a more tempestuous scandal…

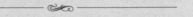

*"Heartwarming romance, engaging characters, and
engrossing plot twists…fast becoming 'must buy'
books. I recommend them all."*—Star-Crossed Romance

For more Lydia Dare, visit:

www.sourcebooks.com